SEA RAPTOR

JOHN J RUST

Darryl,
Have fun with
this Sea tale.

John J. Rust

SEA RAPTOR

ONE

Glenn Flynn wanted her, right the hell now!

Play it cool, man. Wait for your opening.

He wondered if he could wait much longer as the bikini-clad redhead bent over the cooler. Glenn ran his eyes up her smooth legs, stopping at her nice tight ass.

My God, she was hot!

"Yo, Glenn. Catch."

Sara Monaghan tossed him a beer. Despite the gentle bobbing of the speedboat, he caught it.

"Woo-hoo! You got good hands," Sara cheered.

"You don't know just how good these hands are." He waggled his eyebrows.

"Glenn." Sara giggled and blushed. She took a swig of beer and turned on the MP3 player. A deep, thumping beat blared from the speakers. Sara lifted her arms and swung her hips.

Glenn didn't think he could get any harder.

"Don't just stand there," she said. "We're here to party. C'mon."

Glenn recognized the look in Sara's eyes. He'd seen it before in many of his other conquests. That inviting look.

His opening.

Sara cheered as they grinded against each other. Glenn ran a hand up and down her side. She gave him a seductive smile.

High school girls are so easy. It didn't take much to impress them. He played football for Temple University. He came from a well-to-do family. His father had a sweet boat which he let him borrow whenever he wanted.

To a 17-year-old hottie, he was god-like.

When they finished dancing, Glenn drained the rest of his beer. The cool liquid felt good going down his throat, what with the blazing July sun beating down on him.

"How about some more?" Sara shook her empty can in front of him.

"Sure." Glenn would have rather had her than another beer, but this next one would be Sara's fourth. In his experience, the more booze a chick had in her, the harder it was for them to say no.

One more and I'm in like Flynn. He smiled at the catch phrase the Temple broadcasters used whenever he caught a touchdown.

1

Sara chucked her empty can over the side. So did Glenn. He stared at Sara's fine ass as she grabbed two more beers. When she straightened up, she looked at the water and tilted her head.

"What's that?" She leaned closer to the side.

"What's what?"

"That." Sara pointed to a spot of water a few feet away.

Glenn stared hard, then shrugged. "I don't see anything."

"There was, like, a shadow. A big one." She turned to him with a distressed look. "Do you think it's a shark?"

"So what if it is. It's not like they jump into boats. Besides, I'm here to protect you." He put and arm around her waist.

"Glenn." She giggled and pressed her body against his.

Yup, it was almost time.

He leaned in, ready to plant a kiss on Sara's neck.

That's when she squirmed out of his grasp.

"What the hell?" he blurted.

"Oh, keep your pants on. At least for another minute." She flashed him a big smile.

Glenn looked down at the bulge in his swim trunks. He doubted he'd be able to keep them on another second, never mind an entire minute.

Sara reached into her handbag and pulled out her cell phone. "I wanna record this and send it to my friend Maddy. She's gonna be so jealous that I hooked up with a stud like you."

She leaned against him, one arm around his waist, the other holding out her cell phone. Glenn wondered if he could convince her to record them doing it. Some of the other girls he'd nailed had been willing, and his sex vids were always a hit with his friends at parties.

"Hey, Maddy. Just wanted you to see the really, *really* hot guy I'm with at The Shore. Think about me and think about him while you're on your lame family trip to New Hampshire, because we're gonna—"

A splash of water erupted behind them. Glenn turned.

Something heavy slammed down on the boat. The bow rose out of the water. Sara screamed as she and Glenn fell. He hit the deck hard. His head throbbed. He closed his eyes and grimaced.

Sara screamed louder.

Glenn's eyes cracked open, then went wide.

A maw of razor-sharp teeth hovered over him.

He tried to move, to get the hell away. Fear paralyzed his muscles.

The teeth clamped down on his head. Glenn Flynn felt a moment of intense, piercing pain.

Then nothing.

TWO

"For God's sake, Jack, relax. I'm your father, not a general."

Jack Rastun groaned under his breath as he loosened his muscles. Being out of the Army for nearly a year had done nothing to lessen the military bearing drilled into him since his ROTC days. Standing at attention before a superior officer was instinct for him. As Director of the Philadelphia Zoo, his father was, for all intents and purposes, his superior officer.

Dad leaned his portly frame back in his seat, the overhead light shining off his balding dome. His eyes shifted from Rastun to a cushioned chair in front of his desk, then back to Rastun.

"Are you waiting for an invitation?"

"Sorry, sir." He sat down.

"Jack, how many times do I have to tell you? This isn't the Army. You can call me Dad when we're in here."

"Right." Rastun didn't know the exact number of times Dad told him, "This isn't the Army." He just knew it aggravated him every time he heard it.

Dad clasped his hands together. "So, here it is. Your six month evaluation."

"Mm-hmm."

Dad stared at him, as though expecting him to say more. When Rastun didn't, he tapped on the keyboard of his laptop.

Rastun passed the time by looking at the photos of various animals on the walls. His gaze shifted to the desk, cluttered with paperwork and flanked by framed photos. One in particular caught his eye. Him in his Class A Uniform with his tan Ranger beret.

He looked down at his blue slacks and white shirt with a SECURITY patch over his left breast.

How the mighty have fallen.

"I have to say," Dad said. "Most of the comments that Dick had about you were positive."

"Most?" Rastun wondered what Dick Camilli, the head of zoo security, didn't like about the way he did his job.

"Well, he says you're punctual and follow instructions. You haven't been written up for any discipline issues or received any complaints from zoo guests."

"I sense a 'but' coming."

The corners of Dad's mouth curled. "Dick expressed concerns that, at times, you overstep your bounds."

"How so?"

"During our last emergency drill, you and two other guards were assigned to check Independence Schoolhouse. You started yelling at them when they couldn't keep up."

"It's a big building," said Rastun. "We need more than one guard to do a thorough search. Every second counts during an emergency. I can't afford to wait for them and neither can anyone who needs help."

"Both those guards are in their fifties," Dad explained.

"Then maybe they should be doing something else if they can't keep up. Who knows what we could be facing in that building? I need to know the people assigned to me are going to be with me when I make entry. Quite frankly, that should be a four-man job, so we can go in two-by-two and make sure one guard is always watching the other's back."

"Yes, you explained that to Dick, along with your recommendations for security upgrades to the zoo."

"Not that he listened to any of them." The result of all his meetings with the zoo security director did not sit well with him. He'd known Dick Camilli since his senior year in high school. He'd always gotten along with the retired cop and felt he'd be receptive to his ideas.

Instead, Camilli said he was being more than a little paranoid.

"He did listen to them, Jack. It's just that some of your suggestions, many, in fact, don't fit the public image we want to present."

"What about our responsibility to keep our guests safe?" Rastun countered.

"We do that. We have adequate personnel, security cameras, first aid stations, audible alarms, clearly marked exits."

"There's plenty more we can do and should do."

"Doing it your way would make this place look like a prison. Metal detectors, barbed wire on the fences, motion sensors. I'm surprised you didn't ask for guard towers with machine guns."

"That, actually, would be going overboard," said Rastun. "Those other recommendations are practical for a place like this."

"Uh-huh." Dad leaned forward. "What about your recommendation for armed guards?"

"Not with pistols. I'm talking about less lethals like tasers and pepper spray."

"Do you have any idea how much our liability insurance will go up if we give those things to our guards? All it takes is one person to complain about excessive force and we're looking at a multi-million dollar lawsuit."

"What if something major goes down here? I don't mean a fire or an escaped animal. I'm talking worst-case scenario."

"I assume you mean a terrorist attack."

"They do prefer soft targets, and this place is as soft as the cotton candy at our food court."

Dad's shoulders sagged. "Jack, I can only imagine what kind of hell you went through over in Iraq and Afghanistan. But this is a zoo, not Baghdad."

"That doesn't make us immune to something like a lone nut with a gun."

"We have procedures in place in the event that happens."

Rastun scoffed. "Yeah, I got drilled on those procedures. If we can't get our guests out of the zoo, we hole up somewhere and wait for the cops. What if a hostile ambushes people we're trying to evacuate? What if he breaks into a supposedly secure area? We need the guards to carry something more than just keys to give them a fighting chance. A guard without a weapon isn't a guard. He's a victim waiting to happen."

"Jack, I know what you went through when you were in the Army probably colored your view of the world."

"Oh for God's sake."

"Jack, please. I'm just trying to tell you that you're not in a war zone any more. Sending guards who aren't trained to deal with those kinds of situations will likely result in more people getting hurt or killed."

"Or wind up saving more lives. You don't stop a threat by sitting around waiting for help. You stop it with direct action."

"That may be what you did in the Army, but what works best in the Army isn't necessarily what works best at a zoo."

Dad let out a heavy sigh. "Look, I gave you this job so you could do something productive while you figure out what you want to do with your life. Well, you've been out of the Army for a year. I doubt you want to be a zoo security guard for the rest of your life."

You got that right. Rastun almost said it out loud, but figured it would not be a wise thing to say during an evaluation, especially with his father the one doing the evaluating.

"It's time to consider going back to college. You qualify for the GI Bill. You can get a degree in business or zoology or biology. You already know more about animals and zoo operations than a lot of the staff here. With your Army experience, you'd be perfect as a zoo administrator."

"I'll think about it."

"You say that every time I bring this up. I think the time's come to do it instead of thinking about it."

"I said I'd think about it. Is that all?"

Dad leaned back in his chair, his disappointment clear. "Yes. You passed your evaluation. You can expect a raise in your next paycheck."

"Thank you." Rastun stood and headed for the door.

"Jack. One more thing before you go."

He stopped with his hand inches from the doorknob. "Yes?"

"Smile more when you're out there. We're trying to maintain a welcoming atmosphere for our guests."

"It's kind of hard to take a security guard serious when he's grinning like an idiot."

He left the office before Robert Rastun, Director of the Philadelphia Zoo, had a chance to respond.

The rest of the afternoon passed uneventfully, save for helping an elderly woman who had become dehydrated. That happened at least a couple of times a week during the summer. It baffled him how some people could forget to do something as simple as keep a bottle of water handy. In Iraq, he and his fellow Rangers drank constantly.

Once his shift ended, Rastun headed to the parking lot and got in his car. He flowed along with the rush hour traffic down City Avenue and onto the West Chester Pike before entering the suburbs of Havertown. He pulled up to the curb in front of a two-story white house with a blue roof and trim. His parents' home.

Twenty-nine years old, a former Army Ranger, a combat veteran, and he was living with his parents.

How pathetic am I?

Rastun didn't see his parents' cars. They'd probably be home in a few minutes. He went inside and headed into his bedroom to strip off his security guard uniform in favor of shorts and a t-shirt for Marshall University, his alma mater. He then rattled off 100 push-ups. More than a few friends let themselves go once they left the Army. Rastun was determined not to let that happen.

When he finished, he sprang to his feet and checked himself in the mirror attached to the door. A slight smile formed on his round, youthful face. His five-ten, 170-pound frame was still as lean and firm as it had been during his Ranger days. He kept his brown hair cut very short, per Army regs.

Rastun looked every bit the soldier, even if he no longer was one.

He went downstairs and paused by a nest table with a cluster of framed photos. His eyes immediately fell on a black and white picture of a man in Army fatigues clutching a Thompson submachine gun. Roger Rastun, his uncle. His inspiration for joining the Rangers.

Memories flooded back to him. Uncle Roger telling him stories of climbing the cliffs at Point Du Hoc during D-Day and charging up Hill 400 in Bergstein. Taking him to the local VFW to meet other veterans.

Crying when Mom told him Uncle Roger had died.

Rastun looked at other photos of himself. One showed the day he received his black belt in Tae Kwon Do. Another was of him in the red and gold uniform of his high school cross country team. His gaze finally settled on the image of him receiving his Ranger tab upon graduation from Ranger School. Two months of running, combat drills, survival courses and hiking through swamps and mountains. The sadistic bastards who ran the school pushed him beyond the point of exhaustion. Still, he overcame it and became a member of one of the world's elite fighting forces.

And therein lay the problem.

Rastun had run cross country to increase his stamina. He visited Uncle Roger's friends at the VFW to find out what military life was really like. He took Tae Kwon Do to learn self-defense and discipline. Everything he had done since the age of 15 had been geared toward helping him become a Ranger. He hadn't thought of a fallback plan in case he didn't make it. That hadn't been an option.

Now he had to think about it.

The trouble was, he couldn't find a single job anywhere near as challenging as being a Ranger. After six months of no prospects, he decided to take Dad up on his offer to be a zoo security guard just to give him something to do.

Dad had been right about one thing. He didn't plan on being a zoo security guard forever. But what else was there? He'd mulled over Dad's suggestion about going back to college. However, the thought of working behind a desk didn't appeal to him.

Being in the Rangers appealed to him, but one moment of anger fucked that up.

The front door opened. He turned to find Mom coming in.

"Hi, Jack."

"Mom."

She gave him a quick peck on the cheek. "So, how did your evaluation go?"

"I still have a job, so I guess it went well."

Mom frowned, probably wishing for a more enthusiastic response.

Probably wishing he'd figure out what to do with his life.

"Good." She forced a smile. "I'm going to go change and get dinner started."

Rastun just nodded as Mom walked past him and went upstairs. A minute later he went up too, returning to his bedroom. He opened the closet where he kept his DVD holders. Maybe what he needed was a good movie to forget about his problems, at least for a couple of hours.

The Devil's Brigade. Back to Bataan. Tears of the Sun. Patton. Band of Brothers. He passed on all of them. Right now all they'd do is remind him of everything he'd lost. He'd be better off with a sports movie, or a comedy, or both.

Rastun searched for his copy of *Slapshot* when his cell phone rang. He checked the screen.

S. LIPELI.

His eyes widened in surprise as he answered it. "Colonel?"

"Captain Rastun," replied Lt. Colonel Salvatore Lipeli, his former commanding officer with the 1st Ranger Battalion. "It's been a while. How are you?"

"Fine, sir. And you?"

"Doing well. Actually, I'm heading into Philadelphia as we speak."

"You're in Philly? What for?"

"To see you, of course."

"That's a hell of a long trip just to come up and say, 'Hi.'" Lipeli had stuck around Savannah, Georgia, where 1st Battalion was based, after retiring from the Army last year.

"I'm not just coming here for a reunion. I've got something I want to talk to you about. Something you might be interested in."

"What is it?"

Lipeli paused. "I'd rather talk to you about it in person. Trust me, this'll be worth your while. Is there anywhere near your place where we can meet?"

"Loaded Bases. It's a sports bar and grill about three miles from my house."

A few seconds of silence passed. "Okay. I programmed the name into the GPS. I should be there in about a half-hour."

After Rastun said good-bye, he stared at the cell phone, his curiosity piqued. *"Something worth his while."* Did Colonel Lipeli mean a job? Something to give him a new sense of purpose?

You can but hope.

He changed into slacks and a casual polo shirt before heading downstairs. He apologized to Mom and Dad, who'd gotten home a few minutes ago, for missing dinner. Neither seemed to mind when he told them about the phone call from Colonel Lipeli. In fact, both looked very happy and wished him luck.

When Rastun got to Loaded Bases, he waited near the front doors for Colonel Lipeli. At one point, two women around his age walked toward the entrance. He held the door open for them.

"Thank you," they both said, the redhead smiling much wider at him than her dark-haired friend.

Rastun smiled back, admiring the woman's slender figure and pretty face. She wore her hair straight and shoulder-length.

Just like his ex-fiancée Marie had.

He felt a sting in his chest as he let the door close. Marie. Being forced to leave the Rangers had been bad enough, but for her to do what she did to him . . .

Rastun grunted and shook his head. He hadn't been with another woman since Marie.

Twenty minutes later, a burly, tan-skinned man with dark hair strode up to him, carrying a mini laptop.

"Captain." Colonel Lipeli stuck out his free hand. "Good to see you again."

Rastun resisted the urge to salute. "The Lip" was now just like him. A civilian.

"Likewise, sir." He shook Lipeli's hand. "It's been a while."

"That it has."

The pair went inside, where a hostess in shorts, sneakers and a white and red baseball jersey led them to a booth. Most of the tables were filled, with dozens of different conversations going on. Everywhere he turned he saw TVs tuned to one baseball game or another.

After giving their orders to the waitress, Lipeli looked across the table at Rastun. "So, how's life at the zoo?"

"I'd say it's okay, but then you'd know I was lying."

Lipeli nodded. "I can't imagine being a rent-a-cop suits someone like you."

"No it does not." Rastun turned away for a second, letting out a slow breath. "Making the transition to civilian life hasn't been easy. I've been out a year and I still don't know what to do. I can't see myself wearing a suit and tie, sitting at a desk and doing the same thing day after day."

"A lot of ex-military go into law enforcement. Did you ever think about that?"

"I have. But remember how we used to complain about how the panty wastes in Washington kept handcuffing us in Iraq and Afghanistan? It's probably a hundred times worse if you're a cop."

The waitress returned with their drinks, a Diet Coke for Lipeli and water for Rastun. When she left, he continued. "To be honest, sir, after all the stuff we did, I can't find anything in the civilian world that's as remotely challenging as being a Ranger." He emitted a sardonic laugh. "Maybe I should have given more thought to life after the Army. Here's to hindsight."

Lipeli said nothing, just gave him a hard stare.

Rastun leaned back in his seat. "I guess this is where you tell me to quit feeling sorry for myself, get my head out of my ass and get on with my life."

"Quit feeling sorry for yourself and get your head out of your ass."

"Noted."

"Good." Lipeli opened the mini laptop and tapped a few keys. "Now, as for the getting on with your life part, I can help with that."

He turned the laptop toward Rastun. The screen showed a logo featuring the silhouettes of an ape-like creature and a large serpent.

"The Foundation for Undocumented Biological Investigation? You work for them?"

"Started two weeks ago. I would have let everyone know, but I've been busy as hell moving from Georgia to Virginia and getting settled in."

Rastun stared at his former CO, impressed. The FUBI had been formed less than a year ago, following the discovery of a living Sasquatch in California's Klamath National Forest. "So what do you do for them?"

"I'm Director of Field Security Operations."

"What, you keep the field researchers from getting eaten by Bigfoot and the Lake Champlain Monster?"

Lipeli grinned. "No. For the most part the cryptids haven't been a problem. Hell, the Sasquatch are actually pretty shy. Our researchers usually can't get more than thirty feet from them before they turn tail. Our main problem is poachers."

Rastun felt anger lines form on his face. For someone who'd been around rare animals all his life, poachers ranked very high on his scum list.

"Ever since that hunter stumbled on that injured Sasquatch," Lipeli said, "our field expeditions have found five Sasquatch colonies in California and Oregon. We also have leads on other colonies in Missouri, Ohio and Florida. Now that we know more about their habitat and behavior, it's easier to find them. Because of that, poachers have shadowed some of our teams. A few have been threatened at gunpoint. We also had one woman raped and another researcher shot, not fatally, thank God. But these expeditions are unarmed and in a lot of cases, the nearest cop is fifty to a hundred miles away. I need someone to safeguard them, someone who's experienced operating in all kinds of terrain and environments. Someone who can keep their head when everything goes to hell. Someone who can neutralize a threat when it pops up."

"Someone like me."

Lipeli nodded. "Captain, you were one of the best Rangers I had in my battalion. That, and your knowledge of animals, makes you perfect for this job."

"I take it I'll have something better to protect people than a set of keys and a whistle."

"Standard issue for field security specialists are a Glock pistol and a Steyr AUG rifle."

The choice for rifle surprised Rastun. The Austrian-made Steyr AUG was well over 30 years old. Still it was compact, lightweight and accurate. An all-around good rifle, despite its age.

"They seriously only gave you keys and a whistle at the zoo?" asked Lipeli.

Rastun snorted in disgust. "Yeah, we were really well-equipped if any serious shit ever went down. But I made up for it."

"How?"

"You know that Black Ops tactical knife I had. The one my former platoon sergeant in the Eighty-Second gave me before I went to Ranger School?"

"Yeah."

"I kept it hidden in an ankle holder. I wanted to have something I could use if anything serious ever happened."

Lipeli smiled wide. "You always were prepared for anything. That's why you'll make a perfect field security specialist. So, are you interested?"

"What about Western Sahara? Is that going to cause any problems?"

"As far as anyone is concerned, you were honorably discharged from the Army. I don't think we need to bring up some of the unpleasant details surrounding it."

Rastun mulled it over. He had a chance to work far beyond the four walls of an office, to help with the discovery of creatures previously thought to be myths and to protect people. It may not be the Rangers, but it was probably the closest he'd ever get to it.

"Count me in, Colonel."

"Terrific." The two shook hands. "So when can you get started?"

"Yesterday."

"I thought you'd say that."

Their food arrived, a chicken teriyaki sandwich for Rastun and a cheeseburger for Lipeli.

"So," Rastun picked up his sandwich. "Where do I need to be to crack some poacher skulls?"

"Actually, this time it's the cryptid giving us problems, not the poachers, and you won't have far to travel."

Lipeli leaned forward. "Better stock up on sunscreen, Captain. You're going to the Jersey Shore."

THREE

After six months of war, Piet was ready for a change of pace.

He downed the last of his Jack Daniels and gazed at the enormous, three-story ranch house before him. Hundreds of acres of rolling fields stretched in all directions. Here and there herds of cattle grazed.

Piet viewed it all from the comfort of a chauffeured town car, complete with a mini-bar in the backseat. A pleasant change from the tents, battered Land Rovers and government soldiers he put up with in the Central African Republic. He knew with this client he probably wouldn't have to deal with people shooting at him. Not that he was skittish about bullets flying around him. That came with the territory. But long ago Piet decided he couldn't keep jumping from conflict to conflict. The more wars you fought in, the more the odds increased that the bullet with your name on it would find you.

The town car pulled up to the house. The chauffeur opened the door for Piet. As soon as he got out, two men in dark suits and sunglasses approached. Both looked about Piet's size, 6'1 and 210 pounds, all of it muscle. They also wore their hair in crew cuts, like him, except theirs was darker while his had grayed. Everything about them screamed ex-military, probably with special ops experience. His client only hired the best for his security detail.

"Arms out," one of them ordered.

Piet complied. He'd gone through this routine on previous visits.

One guard ran a metal detector wand over him while the other patted him down. They found no weapons. Despite his best efforts, that nervous feeling scratched the back of his mind, the one he got when he wasn't packing. He didn't like going anywhere without a weapon. But a lot of these rich clients didn't trust anyone, save for their bodyguards, to carry a gun or knife so close to them.

"You're clean," said one guard. "Follow me."

The man led him into the foyer and ordered him to wait before heading back into the blazing Texas heat. Piet looked around the large living room, his eyes resting on the animal heads mounted on the wall, deer and elk mainly. Animals that were legal to hunt.

What his client really craved were the ones you couldn't hunt legally. Tigers, mountain gorillas, Komodo dragons, rhinoceroses and many others. The client had contracted Piet on numerous occasions to bring in these endangered species, sometimes alive, sometimes dead, depending on his mood. A much easier task than ambushing soldiers, mainly because animals couldn't shoot back. Sometimes, though, he'd run into environmentalists conducting research on his target. They were usually unarmed and abhorred violence.

Their noble beliefs hadn't saved them.

The armed security patrols at the African wildlife preserves could present a challenge. But many of them didn't have his level of training and experience, and certainly nowhere near his bank account. A bribe or a bullet usually took care of them.

Low risk, high reward. That's what Piet liked about this client.

"Mister Piet?"

A petite blonde in a short skirt approached him. She looked to be in her mid-twenties and wore blood red lipstick and too much make-up on her heart-shaped face. It made her look like an expensive whore.

Not that he considered that a bad thing.

"I'm Piet."

She gave him an alluring smile. "Mister Gunderson will see you now. Follow me, please."

The woman, probably Gunderson's personal assistant, turned and walked toward a long hallway. Piet followed, running his eyes over the woman's hips and ass. He wondered if Gunderson was buggering her. He must be. Any boss who didn't fuck a piece of ass like that had to be a fruit.

"You're new here," said Piet. "What's your name?"

"Allison."

"Allison. That's a pretty name."

"Thank you." She flashed him a grin.

She led him up to the second floor and to a thick wooden door flanked by two bodyguards who could have been clones of the ones outside.

"Mister Piet for Mister Gunderson," she told one of the bodyguards.

The man nodded and tapped a keypad on the door, making sure his back was to Piet so he couldn't see what numbers he hit. He opened the door. Allison went inside, followed by Piet.

The office had brown wall-to-wall carpeting, with a polar bear pelt lying in front of a large mahogany desk. An aquarium sat in the left corner, with piranha swimming around. Glass cases throughout the room displayed many animals, including a bald eagle, a Bengal tiger and a clouded leopard, all stuffed and mounted.

This was the office where Norman Gunderson conducted his illegitimate business.

The man himself rose from behind the desk. Gunderson was just under six feet, with a compact, unsmiling face, a sizeable paunch and receding dark gray hair.

"Mister Gunderson. Mister Piet to see you."

"Thank you, Allison."

Piet noticed the lecherous smile on Gunderson's face and the way his eyes fixed on Allison as she left the office.

Oh yeah. He's fucking her.

When the door closed, Gunderson waved him to one of the leather chairs in front of his desk. "Good to see you again, Mister Piet," he said without a trace of that cowboy accent that made Texans sound ridiculous.

"You too, Mister Gunderson."

"Care for a bourbon?" Gunderson walked over to his wet bar.

"I would, thank you."

Gunderson poured two fingers of the dark orange liquor into a pair of tumblers. He handed one to Piet and sipped from the other as he returned to his desk.

"So how was the Central African Republic?"

Piet took a gulp from his tumbler before answering. "Typical Third World shithole. But you have to go where the fighting is."

"They're still fighting there, last time I looked."

"I fulfilled my contract. Showed the *kaffirs* how to ambush soldiers and police, kidnap VIPs and do interrogations. Now they can straighten out their own mess."

Gunderson nodded. "I suppose one man can't win a war by himself. Well, the task I have in mind for you shouldn't be as unpleasant as your last one. It will probably be more profitable, too."

Piet looked around at the endangered animals that decorated the office. "Let me guess. You want me to bring you a Bigfoot. Your country seems obsessed with that ugly bugger."

"Sorry, but it's not Bigfoot. One day, most definitely, but not today."

"So what is it this time?"

Gunderson picked up his iPad. "Have you heard of Glenn Flynn?"

"Should I have?"

"He's a wide receiver for Temple University's football team in Philadelphia. That's our kind of football, not yours."

Piet grunted. Pussies played football. Real men, like him, played rugby.

Gunderson continued. "He was sailing along the Jersey Shore with some girl a couple of days ago. They both went missing."

"I take it there's a reason you're so interested in a missing athlete and his whore."

"There's a very good reason I'm interested." Gunderson tapped on his iPad. "Look at this."

Piet's brow furrowed when he saw an image of a serpentine neck ending in a long snout filled with razor sharp teeth. "This a clip from a horror movie?"

"That image came from the girl's cell phone. The Coast Guard recovered it when they found the boat, which was covered in blood."

"This thing ate them?"

"It appears so."

Piet looked at the image again. "So what is it?"

"Your next job. I want that creature."

Piet rested the iPad on his right leg and stared at Gunderson. "This isn't like the other hunts you've sent me on, you know? It's a lot harder to track an animal in the ocean than on land. Do you have a submarine I can use?"

Gunderson gave him a slight smile. "You don't have to worry about catching this creature, Mister Piet."

"Come again?"

"The Foundation for Unidentified Biological Investigation is putting together an expedition to find it. All you have to do is shadow their activities. When they catch it, you hijack their boat and secure the creature for me."

"Then what do I do with it?"

"I have a secret research facility on the East Coast. It will be brought there."

"That could be a problem." Piet took another gulp of his bourbon. "What if they get out an SOS? Even if they don't, they're certain to check in with their headquarters regularly. When they don't hear from them, they're going to send out search parties. There's a good chance I'll be spotted."

"I've already planned for that contingency. I'm sending one of my research vessels, the *Sea Sprite,* to the area, ostensibly to determine if methane pockets under the Eastern Seaboard can be converted into an alternative energy source. When you've secured the FUBI vessel, you'll rendezvous with the *Sea Sprite* and hand the creature over to them."

"And the FUBI vessel?"

"Lost with all hands. I have no doubt you can arrange that. The Coast Guard will search for days with nothing to show for it, while the *Sea Sprite* slips away with no one the wiser."

Piet stared out the thick, bulletproof window behind Gunderson, thinking. The plan was doable, but riskier than his previous hunts. Only one thing would convince him whether or not the job was worth taking.

"How much?"

"Four million."

Piet's eyes widened. That was triple the price Gunderson usually offered to bring back exotic animals. "You must really want this thing."

"I do."

Piet finished his bourbon. "What about the FUBI vessel? How many are on board?"

"Nine." Gunderson motioned for Piet to give him back the iPad. "One of my contacts in the FUBI provided me with the files of all the expedition members."

It didn't surprise Piet that Gunderson had spies inside the FUBI. The man loved collecting rare animals, and the Foundation dealt with some of the rarest, most intriguing animals in the world.

Gunderson handed Piet back the iPad. He checked the files. The expedition consisted of three scientists, a tech specialist, a ship's crew of three, a photographer and a security specialist. Only three had prior military experience. Two were former U.S. Navy, one a boatswain's mate, the other an engineer. Neither had probably fired a weapon since basic training. The third, Jack Rastun, could prove a problem. The man had been a U.S. Army Ranger with tours in Iraq and Afghanistan.

His attention turned to the two women in the expedition. One looked to be in her forties, but still fairly attractive. The other . . .

Piet grinned as he studied the woman's smooth, round face framed by shoulder-length brown hair. Very beautiful. He ran a thumb over her picture, imagining all the things he could do to her.

He took a deep breath, trying to push aside his fantasy and focus on business.

"I'm going to need at least three more men."

"That's not a problem."

"We'll need weapons that are compact and easily concealable. SIG Sauer pistols and MP5 submachine guns will do nicely. I also want suppressors for them, along with body armor, tactical radios, burn phones, fake IDs and credit cards and one hundred-fifty thousand dollars cash for expenses."

"Done."

Piet suppressed a smile. This was what he liked about working for wealthy clients. They all had some peculiar hobby or interest and didn't mind committing vast amounts of money and resources to satisfy them.

"You said the price is four million. What's our bonus upon delivery?"

"It depends," said Gunderson. "Should you deliver the creature alive, you will receive another four million dollars."

"And if it's not alive?" asked Piet.

"Then the bonus drops to five hundred thousand. A dead specimen is still valuable, but nowhere near as much compared to a live one."

"What if the FUBI doesn't find this beastie?"

"You'll obviously receive no bonus, but you can keep the original four million for your troubles."

Piet tapped a finger against the side of the iPad, considering the offer. A few seconds passed before he stretched out his hand. "You have yourself a deal, Mister Gunderson."

They shook on it, then spent the next hour working out the details of the job. Piet felt good as he left the office. Even if the FUBI didn't catch this sea monster and he lost out on the bonus, he'd still walk away with a shitload of money. How could he turn down a job like that?

Piet thought of the brown-haired beauty on the expedition. Whether the FUBI caught the monster or not, he would still get his bonus.

FOUR

Rastun gazed around the Point Pleasant Marina, taking in the rows of boats and jet skis and the blue ocean beyond them. He inhaled the cool salt air, memories resurfacing of trips with family and friends to the Jersey Shore. Relaxing on the beach, diving into the water, going on whale-watching tours, enjoying all the boardwalk had to offer.

You're here on business, not pleasure.

Putting thoughts of warm sand and cheesesteak stands out of his head, Rastun closed his car door, picked up his duffle bag and made his way through the parking lot. The docks and shops were more crowded than he expected. Two boats left their slips and headed out to sea. More prepared to cast off. The deaths of Glenn Flynn and Sara Monaghan hadn't hurt the tourist trade. It may have even caused an increase, with people hoping to catch a glimpse of the Point Pleasant Monster.

He passed a bait and tackle shop and noticed a pink flyer with a drawing of a fierce-looking plesiosaur. It read, "$500 cash and $500 worth of fishing supplies to anyone who photographs the Point Pleasant Monster. Image must be clear."

Yeah, encourage people to go looking for this thing, why don't you?

Rastun recalled the photos the Coast Guard took of the young couple's boat after they found it. He hoped none of those curiosity seekers laid eyes on this monster. It could be the last thing they ever see.

He continued on, glancing at his reflection in the window. He was grateful to be out of the drab rent-a-cop outfit he'd worn at the zoo. Colonel Lipeli didn't mention anything about a standard uniform for field security specialists, so Rastun improvised. He wore Woodland BDU pants, a navy blue t-shirt with the FUBI logo and Corcoran paratrooper boots. Topping off his unofficial uniform were a pair of BTB-230 sunglasses and a ball cap with the emblem of the 75th Ranger Regiment.

It almost made him feel like a soldier again.

He walked past another store when a paunchy young man with curly black hair stepped out the door and into his path. Rastun skidded to a halt before they collided.

"Whoa!" blurted the young man. "Sorry, dude."

Rastun nodded and waved for him to continue.

"Thanks." The young man carried a cooler chest out the door, helped by a thin man with a scruffy beard. He nodded to Rastun, then focused on his t-shirt.

"Hey, you're with the FUBI?"

"Yeah."

"Dude, cool. Yo, Darrell, hold up. This guy's with the FUBI."

"No way." Darrell set down the cooler and extended his hand. "Awesome to meet you, man. I'm Darrell Wasser and that's my bud, Jerry Edler."

17

"Jack Rastun." He shook Wasser's hand first, then Edler's. He guessed them to be early-to-mid twenties.

"So what do you do?" asked Wasser.

"I'm a field security specialist."

"Uh-huh." Wasser looked at Rastun's ball cap. "So, like, were you a soldier?"

"Army Ranger."

"Did you fight in Iraq and Afghanistan?"

"Yeah."

Wasser's face lit up. "Cool."

"No, it wasn't cool. Trust me."

"Oh. Uh . . ." Wasser looked away, rubbing the back of his neck.

"Um, me and Darrell wanna work for the FUBI," Edler chimed in. "We're gonna get some video of the Point Pleasant Monster and put it up on YouTube. You think the FUBI'll hire us if we do that?"

"That's not a good idea, guys. That thing's dangerous. It's already killed two people. Best leave it to the professionals."

"Aw, we'll be careful," said Edler. "No way can it outrun our boat."

Rastun stared at the younger man in irritation. He couldn't do anything to stop them from going out there. All he could do was give them sound advice, which apparently, they chose to ignore.

"It was cool meeting you, Mister Rastun." Wasser gave him a small wave. "Maybe we'll be working with you one day."

I seriously doubt that.

The two amateur monster hunters grabbed the cooler and walked away.

"You guys be careful," Rastun told them.

"Yeah, we will," Edler answered in a tone that indicated the warning went in one ear and out the other.

Rastun continued along the docks and spotted an 80-foot Hatteras yacht with a curved bridge. The pennant fluttering in the breeze bore the logo of the FUBI. The name on the hull read *Bold Fortune.*

He strode up the gangplank, noticing three people standing near the bow. One was a bearded middle-aged man with sandals and a blindingly bright Hawaiian shirt. An overweight man with uncombed gray hair and a lean, dour woman with short auburn hair stood on either side of him.

"Excuse me." Rastun walked over to them.

"Well." The bearded man stepped forward. "Camouflage pants, stiff posture, no nonsense expression. You must be our photographer."

Rastun couldn't help but crack a smile. "No. I carry a gun, not a camera." He set down his duffle bag and extended his hand. "Jack Rastun, field security specialist."

"Randy Ehrenberg." He gave Rastun a hearty handshake. "Pleasure to meet you."

"The pleasure's mine, sir. I've seen you on some Bigfoot documentaries."

"Was that before or after Bigfoot was discovered?"

"Both."

Ehrenberg beamed. "Ah! So you were one of the few who took me seriously before someone finally found it."

Rastun chuckled. Ehrenberg certainly appeared the type who didn't take himself too seriously.

He hoped that trait didn't affect his ability to lead this expedition.

"Let me introduce you to the rest of our intrepid band." Ehrenberg slapped him on the shoulder. Rastun already knew everyone on the expedition from the files provided to him by Colonel Lipeli. Still he let Ehrenberg do the introductions.

"This is Doctor Raleigh Pilka, our marine biologist."

"Mister Rastun." Pilka gave him a perfunctory shake of the hand.

"Doctor." Rastun took note of Pilka's ruddy complexion and veins on his nose, signs of years of hard drinking.

Is he still doing it or has he sobered up?

From the file Colonel Lipeli provided him, Pilka had been a big deal at a marine institute in Palm Beach until ten years ago. After that, he taught at a couple of community colleges in Virginia before coming to the FUBI. It sounded to Rastun like Pilka had lost his dream job and his life just fell apart.

Perhaps this expedition was Pilka's second chance to get his career back on track.

When it appeared Pilka wouldn't say another word, Ehrenberg steered him toward the woman. "And here we have my good friend Doctor Lauren Malakov, our animal behaviorist."

"Ma'am." Rastun stuck out his hand.

Malakov did not shake it. Instead she glared at him. "Don't call me ma'am. My title is doctor."

Rastun stifled a groan. "Fine. Doctor." Again he stuck out his hand.

Again Malakov did not shake it.

"Oh, Lauren, come on," Ehrenberg urged her. "We're all on the same team here."

"I don't want him on this team, period." Malakov turned back to Rastun, a harsh look on her face. "This is a scientific expedition. We are here to capture and study the Point Pleasant Monster, not kill it. Do you understand?"

"Yes, ma'am ...I mean, doctor."

Malakov's face twisted in anger. "You better."

"But just so you understand, as field security specialist, it's my duty to ensure the safety of every member of this expedition. If that creature endangers anyone's life, I will kill it."

Malakov sucked in a sharp, angry breath. "Did you not hear what I said? You are not to kill this creature."

"I understand our priority is to capture it alive, but it will not be done at the cost of someone's life."

"Get this through your thick, Neanderthal head!"

"Lauren, come on."

She ignored Ehrenberg, thrusting a finger at Rastun's face. "The Point Pleasant Monster is one of the most unique animals on the planet. If you kill it, if you so much as bruise it, I swear I will do everything in my power to make your life a living hell."

"How? By sending me back to Afghanistan?"

Malakov glowered at Rastun and stalked off.

"By the way, doctor?"

"What?" she yelled.

"About your Neanderthal comment."

"Yes?"

"Just so you know, I graduated cum laude from Marshall University, and no, I didn't cheat on my tests." Rastun grinned. "Not bad for a Neanderthal, huh?"

Malakov bared her teeth, then stomped across the deck.

"I guess we're not going to be best friends," Rastun muttered.

"Sorry about that, Jack," said Ehrenberg. "Lauren's never been a fan of the military. But she really is a good person. I'm sure eventually she'll warm up to you."

"With all due respect, sir, I'm not going to hold my breath."

"Well, we'll see. C'mon, I'll show you to your cabin."

"Thank you, sir." Rastun picked up his duffle bag.

Ehrenberg barked out a laugh. "Jack, I'll tell you right now, I like being called 'sir' about as much as Lauren likes being called 'ma'am.'"

"Sorry. Doctor, then?"

"How about Randy? That's the name my parents gave me. Be a shame to see it go to waste."

The request caused Rastun to slow his pace. Ever since his ROTC days, it had been drilled into him to call his superiors "sir." As expedition head, Dr. Ehrenberg was, in effect, his superior officer. Calling him 'Randy' went against nearly ten years of indoctrination.

But if that's what he wants . . .

"Okay. Randy it is."

"Ah. There's hope for you yet."

Rastun grinned as Ehrenberg led him below deck. He scanned the bright white and gold ceiling, the teak cabinets, the leather sofas and the plush carpeting.

"Pretty luxurious for a research ship."

"The FUBI actually got this at a government auction," Ehrenberg explained. "It used to belong to some drug dealer until he got busted. The FUBI converted it into a research ship and left some of the amenities in. The galley and the master bathroom are the same as the day they got her. They did reduce the size of the master salon and the fly bridge social area to put in more equipment, storage space and sleeping quarters. Oh, and speaking of sleeping quarters, I hope you weren't expecting a king-sized bed and a mini-bar. What we have here makes a college dorm room look like a studio apartment."

"You know how many times I've slept in a tent or under a tree or against a rock? If I have a bed and a roof over it, I'm not going to complain."

Ehrenberg led him to the aft compartment. He grabbed a door handle and slid it open. "Here you go."

Rastun looked inside. "You weren't kidding about the size, or lack thereof."

The cabin had a bed and a trunk. That was it. Just past the bed was the door to a shared head with the cabin next door.

"I'll let you get unpacked. As soon as everyone's onboard and squared away, we'll get together in the main salon and talk about our little cryptid hunt."

With a parting smile, Ehrenberg turned and left.

Definitely the most unique boss I've ever had.

Rastun carried his duffle bag into the cabin. He'd put half of his clothing in the trunk when he heard a thump from the corridor. He stuck his head out the door.

A woman stood outside the cabin across from his, burdened by two travel bags and a wheeled travel case. She wore a t-shirt and shorts that showed off a slender frame and well-toned legs. Her face was smooth and round. Rastun guessed she was around his age. A black-green-brown tiger stripe boonie hat covered her light brown hair.

"Need any help, ma'am?" He straightened up and stepped into the corridor.

The woman swung around and gasped in surprise.

"Sorry." Rastun raised both hands. "I didn't mean to startle you."

"That's okay. I didn't realize anyone else was down here." The woman adjusted the strap on her bag, a camera bag.

"You must be our photographer. Karen Thatcher, right?"

"That's right." She gave him a quick scan. "I take it from that outfit you're our bodyguard."

"Field security specialist. Jack Rastun."

Karen adjusted the strap on her bag and shook his hand. "Nice to meet you." She smiled, a very beautiful smile, Rastun noted.

"You need any help with your stuff?"

"Um …yeah, sure. Thank you."

Rastun took the travel case and one of Karen's bags and followed her into the cabin.

"I think you may have to leave some of your stuff outside," he said. "It's not like they gave us a lot of room here."

"Yeah, it is kind of a tight fit."

The point was emphasized when their shoulders lightly brushed together. It made Rastun tense for just a moment.

He put Karen's luggage in the far corner of the room. She then handed him her camera bag.

"Careful with that."

"What, you think I'm going to swing this around like Thor's hammer?"

Karen frowned. "Sorry. It's just that my livelihood's in that bag. I'm almost as protective of my camera equipment as I am of my daughter."

Daughter? Rastun wondered if she was married. He found himself hoping that wasn't the case. "How old is she?"

"Ten. She's staying with my aunt and uncle in Tampa while I'm on this monster hunt."

Rastun nodded. Aunt and uncle, not her father. Is he out of the picture?

He gently set the camera bag next to the travel case, then pointed his hand at it. "Careful enough for you?" He tacked on a grin.

Karen quietly chuckled. "Yes, it was. Thank you, General."

"I actually retired as a captain. I did my work in the field, not from behind a desk."

"Oh. Gotcha. Well, Captain, I assume your job is to keep that monster from eating all of us."

"That's what they're paying me for."

"In that case, can I make just one teensy request?"

"Sure."

Karen slid a couple of inches closer to him, which put them nearly face-to-face. Rastun caught the sweet scent of suntan lotion coming from her. He felt a hitch in his breath.

"Before you blow this monster up, please let me snap a few pictures of it. I mean good ones, not those out-of-focus pieces of crap where all you see is some dark hump. When I shoot it, everyone's gonna know it's a sea monster and not a piece of driftwood."

"Noted. If you want, I can get it in a headlock, then you can get some real good close-ups."

Karen chuckled again. "Thank you. I appreciate it."

"Well, it was nice meeting you, ma'am."

"Karen, please."

"Karen. I'll let you get stowed away."

"Thanks. It was nice meeting you, too... General." She gave him a wry grin.

Rastun responded with a short laugh. He took a quick, admiring glance at Karen's legs before exiting her cabin.

This definitely beats being a security guard at a zoo.

FIVE

Whatever lavish furnishings the main salon of *Bold Fortune* once featured had been replaced by an oak conference table and a dozen black swivel chairs, all bolted to the deck. A plasma screen TV hung from the overhead. Rastun noticed someone had the foresight to set out water bottles in front of each seat.

Malakov sat at the far end of the table, taking a sip of water. The moment she saw him, she glared at him.

Rastun ignored her and looked at the others already seated. Three were men he hadn't met yet, two middle-aged with beards and paunches, the third young and thin. *Bold Fortune's* crew.

He also saw Karen, the chairs on either side of her unoccupied. He took the one on her right.

"Hey." Karen flashed him a grin.

"Hi." Rastun nodded. Before he could say anything else, someone called out, "Hey, Army!"

He looked down the table at the bigger of the bearded men. "The name's Rastun, actually. Sam Keller, right?"

"*Captain* Sam Keller. So what's the FUBI doing bringing a grunt to sea?"

"I'm here to make sure the Point Pleasant Monster doesn't get you. With all that meat on you, you'd make one hell of a meal for it."

Keller barked out a laugh. So did the other bearded man, who sported tattoos up and down his arms. Rastun recognized Nick Tamburro, the boat's engineer, from the photo in his personnel file.

"I'm touched by your concern." Keller put a hand over his heart. "Let me return the favor. There's a whole bunch of sea sickness pills in the medical locker. Why don't I grab you a bottle? I know you grunts aren't used to being on boats."

"I've been bounced around on C-130s that are older than me. If I didn't lose my lunch there, I'll be fine here."

Keller reached into his pants pocket and got his wallet. He pulled out a bill. "Twenty bucks says first sign of rough seas, you're upchucking over the railing."

Rastun tapped a finger on the table, thinking it over. "Well, I do need a new Phillies ball cap. You're on."

"Easy money, Sam." Tamburro smiled and nudged Keller.

"Macho bullshit," Malakov grumbled.

Rastun smiled at her. Malakov's face turned crimson.

"What's up with them calling you grunt?" Karen asked, keeping her voice low so Keller and Tamburro couldn't hear. "That sounds kinda nasty."

"It's just slang for a foot soldier. Trust me, I've been called worse."

"Oh." Karen paused for a few moments. "So how long were you in the Army?"

"Six years. One with the Eighty-Second Airborne, five with the Rangers."

"So you were over there?" She nodded to the east.

"Yup."

"Uh-huh. Um, it looks like you made it out of there okay."

"Yeah, I did." He stopped himself from saying, "A lot of people I knew didn't."

"So, how long have you been with the FUBI?" Rastun tried to change the subject.

"I just started. I've pretty much done freelance work the past few years. *National Geographic, Smithsonian, National Wildlife.* I made a decent living, but I figured it was time for something more stable. And let's face it. What photographer would turn down the chance to shoot the sort of creatures the FUBI looks for?"

Rastun had to admit, the prospect of finding previously undocumented creatures was exciting. Animals like lions, gorillas and tigers had been studied in great detail. What could they learn if they discovered sea monsters, dinosaurs and more sci-fi type creatures such as the Chupacabra or the Beast of Bray Road?

"Okay, people!"

Rastun turned around to see Ehrenberg entering the salon, followed by Pilka and a chubby, bespectacled man. Charlie Montebello, their underwater systems tech.

"Let's get through the gabfest and go find ourselves a cryptid."

Rastun was a bit surprised by Ehrenberg's cavalier manner. He'd never been part of a briefing that started off in such a way. Again it made him wonder about the cryptozoologist's leadership abilities.

Montebello sat in the chair to Rastun's right. Pilka stood at the far right corner of the table, staring intently at something. Rastun followed the man's gaze . . .

To Karen. Her expression hardened. She took a deep breath, regaining her composure.

Pilka briefly scowled and settled into a chair.

I wonder what that's about.

Before Rastun could dwell on it, Ehrenberg clasped his hands together. "Well, since we're all going to be working very closely for a while, I think we should start off by introducing ourselves."

The group went around the table, stating their names and their assignments.

"Okay, now we'll see how long it takes to forget everyone's names."

A few people chuckled at Ehrenberg's joke. Rastun, himself, grinned.

"All right, first we're going to give some theories on what this cryptid might be, then go over our strategy for finding it. If anyone has any questions, suggestions or anything else to offer, don't be shy. And if you have to go to the bathroom, well, we're all adults here. Just get up and go."

Another smattering of laughs.

"I think most of you have seen this video already." Ehrenberg tapped on his laptop. "But in case you haven't, this is the reason we're all here."

The plasma TV switched on. It showed the video from Sara Monaghan's phone, which caught a glimpse of the cryptid before falling to the deck and blacking out. Rastun gritted his teeth, imagining what followed. He prayed it had been quick.

He glanced around the table to see how the others reacted. Pilka, Malakov, Keller and Tamburro looked impassive. Karen and Ehrenberg closed their eyes, sympathy on their faces. Montebello and *Bold Fortune's* first mate, Manny Hernandez, grimaced and turned away from the screen.

"This is how we start out this expedition," Ehrenberg said in the most serious tone Rastun had heard from him. "With two dead kids. This isn't going to be like looking for more Sasquatch or some lake monster, trying to find it for the sake of finding it. We need to locate this creature before it kills again."

He turned to Pilka. "Raleigh, your thoughts."

"The creature was only visible for a few frames, but judging by the head and the snout, it has to be reptilian in nature, maybe closely related to the Crocodilia order. The only thing is, animals like that prefer warmer waters. So why would it be this far north?"

"Its original habitat could have been overfished, limiting its food supply," suggested Malakov. "Or it could have been driven out by pollution. It might even be on a migration pattern. In this part of the Atlantic, the average water temperature during the summer is between sixty-five and seventy-five degrees. It could stay here for a few months, then head south when the water cools. But all this is guesswork. It's hard to figure out the behavior of an animal no one's ever seen."

"We can't say no one has ever seen it with absolute certainty, Lauren. There have been sea serpent sightings up and down the East Coast for centuries."

"But how many of them are really monsters?" asked Karen. "And how many are eels or seals or other animals that have been misidentified?"

Ehrenberg nodded. "That's always one of the problems in cryptozoology. Some people see a dark shape under the water or a hump on the surface and immediately think sea monster when it could be something as common as a seal. But there's always that small percentage of sightings that can't be explained away so easily. We should look into past sea monster sightings along the East Coast and see if there are any descriptions that match the Point Pleasant Monster."

"Sounds like Google is gonna get a workout," said Karen.

"And then comes the hard part," Rastun chimed in. "Separating legitimate reports from the BS, and more BS comes out of the internet than out of Washington."

Several people around the table chuckled. Malakov was not one of them.

"Can't argue with you on that, Jack." Ehrenberg grinned. "Thankfully, I have a pretty good database on sea monster sightings, and I know a few other cryptozoologists who deal exclusively with aquatic cryptids. Between all that, we should be able to find something, hopefully."

"What about checking with the Coast Guard on missing boaters?" Rastun recommended. "This may not be the monster's first attack. This thing might have associated boats with food long before it came to The Shore."

"Good idea," said Ehrenberg. "Give 'em a ring when we're done and see what they have."

"Yes, sir... I mean, Doc... Randy."

"Don't worry. Sooner or later you'll learn what to call me."

Rastun grinned. Malakov scowled and folded her arms.

"Speaking of the Coast Guard," Karen spoke up, "are they searching for the Point Pleasant Monster, too?"

"They are," Ehrenberg answered. "They have cutters and helicopters patrolling up and down the coast. They're also urging people in small boats to stay as close to shore as possible."

A look of disbelief formed on Karen's face. "You'd think after two people got killed by a sea monster they'd want to keep people from going out into the ocean."

"The attack occurred roughly seven miles from shore. The Coast Guard is sensitive to the fact this is the height of tourist season. Closing beaches and restricting watercraft would hurt the local economy. They felt urging boaters to stay within a mile of the shoreline was a reasonable precaution."

"Until a tourist gets attacked by this thing," said Pilka. "During the Jersey Shore shark attacks of 1916, one man was killed swimming just 130 yards from the beach. Later, another man and a young boy were killed in Matawan Creek, sixteen miles inland. Staying close to shore may not be as safe as the Coast Guard thinks."

Rastun stared at Pilka, mulling over what the man had said. "You know, what Doctor Pilka just said gave me another theory."

Ehrenberg spread out his arms. "Well, share with the rest of the class."

"This thing does have some crocodilian features. What if it also behaves like a crocodile or alligator? What if it can live on land just as well as in the water? It could have a nest somewhere along the shore."

"You honestly think you can come up with a valid theory from looking at a few frames of a previously undiscovered creature?" There was no mistaking the condescending tone in Malakov's voice.

"Isn't that what we're all doing?"

"Do you have advanced degrees in biology or zoology?"

"No, ma'am. My degree is in Communication Studies."

Malakov snorted. "So, somehow, learning how to have a conversation with another person makes you an expert on animal behavior?"

"Obviously not. But having a father who's director of the oldest zoo in the country, and having a mother who's the head vet at that same zoo, and having worked plenty of summers there myself . . ." Rastun shrugged. "Well, I wouldn't call myself an expert, but I learned a few things about animals."

"And I have been studying animals for nearly thirty years. So perhaps you should leave the theories to actual experts and concentrate on the only thing you know how to do. Shooting your damn guns."

"Lauren, come on," said Ehrenberg. "Everyone's opinion is welcome here."

"Even from Neanderthals who enjoy killing—"

"Lauren, enough."

Rastun was surprised by the sharpness of Ehrenberg's tone. It seemed out of place from a guy who looked like a beach bum in Key West.

"I think Mister Rastun's theory is plausible," said Pilka. "Alligators can survive in water as cold as forty-five degrees Fahrenheit. The same could be true for the Point Pleasant Monster, which would explain how it came to be this far north."

Ehrenberg looked to Pilka, then Rastun, then nodded. "Good points, guys. We may want to consider doing some searches on land as well."

Captain Keller ran down the equipment *Bold Fortune* had to track and capture the monster, which included one of the most advanced sonar systems available for civilian use. Once they located the creature, a lift net would be used to capture it.

"The FUBI and the Coast Guard have also set up hotlines for people to call, text or e-mail if they see the Point Pleasant Monster," Ehrenberg told them.

"No offense, Randy," said Malakov, "but that's going to be a waste of time. Most of the calls and messages we get will come from cranks."

"I know. We just have to do our best to separate the fakes from the legit ones."

Ehrenberg looked around the table. "So, I think that covers everything. Any questions?"

There were none.

"All righty. Captain, are you ready to shove off?"

"Just say the word, Doc," answered Keller. "Ship and crew are good to go."

"Then let's go."

Everyone rose from their chairs. Rastun headed out of the main salon when Karen appeared next to him. "Hey. What's the deal with you and Doctor Malakov?"

"She hates the military and I'm ex-military. It's a match made in Heaven."

Karen glanced at Malakov, then back to him. "I can tell you two are going to have fun together."

"I worked with plenty of unpleasant people in the Army. You learn to deal with it."

"Yeah." Karen looked over at Pilka. Her lips pressed together in a tight line.

Pilka stiffened as he met her gaze.

Rastun's eyes flickered between the two before settling on Karen. "You okay?"

"I'm fine."

Karen strode out of the main salon, keeping her eyes straight ahead, as though determined not to look at Pilka.

Well that's bullshit.

SIX

Two days passed without a sign of the Point Pleasant Monster. The few large sonar hits *Bold Fortune* got turned out to be schools of fish, seals or dolphins. Much as it pained Rastun to admit, Malakov had been right. Most of the calls and messages to the FUBI and Coast Guard hotlines turned out to be bogus. The wildest one had to be the person who e-mailed that he witnessed UFOs seeding the Atlantic with sea monsters as a prelude to an alien invasion.

Rastun's inquiry to the Coast Guard regarding dead and missing boaters produced three incidents where empty vessels had been found adrift with significant amounts of blood. One had been off the coast of North Carolina, the other two a few miles outside Delaware Bay, just over a hundred miles south.

Maybe it is working its way north.

Right now, however, they had no proof the Point Pleasant Monster had anything to do with those incidents.

Rastun walked around the port side of *Bold Fortune*, pausing to sweep the ocean with his binoculars. Just like every other time, he spotted nothing unusual.

At least if the monster did show itself, he'd be ready. In addition to his Steyr AUG and Glock pistol, Rastun carried a Model 389 rifle for firing tranquilizer darts, a Night Stalker combat knife and his trusty tactical knife. He also had a few other items commonly carried by members of elite units. A Swiss Army knife, a cigarette lighter and a roll of duct tape. Some people might wonder what he'd need the last item for in the middle of the ocean, but if he got into a close quarters situation with the Point Pleasant Monster, he could wrap a couple lengths around its snout. If it was like an alligator, the muscles it used to open its jaws would be very weak and unable to break the tape.

Rastun hoped he wouldn't have to put that theory to the test.

"Hey."

He turned around to find Karen coming through the aft sliding doors.

"Hi." He gave her a little wave. A smile spread across his face. He noticed himself doing that a lot whenever Karen was around.

"So, have you seen anything yet?" she asked.

Rastun stared out at the ocean, then back to her. "Water. Lots of it."

Karen gave him a cross look. "Ha-ha. I didn't know they let comedians be soldiers."

Rastun chuckled. He had to give it to Karen. She had a quick wit.

"So what have you been up to with no sea monster to shoot?" he asked.

"Watching YouTube."

"I don't think the FUBI brass will appreciate you watching videos of the latest dance craze."

"If you must know, Randy wanted me to check out some videos posted of the Point Pleasant Monster, or supposedly of the Point Pleasant Monster."

"I take it all of them were fake?" asked Rastun.

"Some were just dark shapes in the water that could be anything from a shadow to a whale. The others . . ." Karen rolled her eyes. "My God, they were so bad. A first year photography student could tell they were fake."

"And by tomorrow there'll be twice as many on YouTube."

"And I'm looking forward to watching every single one of them ...not."

Karen walked over to the railing. The wind played with loose strands of brown hair that spilled out from under her boonie hat. Rastun gave her a subtle, admiring glance. Not only was she blessed with gorgeous looks and a great sense of humor, she was passionate about her work and very friendly.

Except when she happened to be around Dr. Pilka.

Rastun thought back to the files he'd reviewed on both Karen and Pilka. Nothing in them indicated that they had ever crossed paths. Then again, personnel files never told the whole story.

Still, it was obvious something happened between the two in the past. Exactly what, he had no clue. Whatever it was, they had been professional enough to not let it interfere with their duties. As long as they confined their hostility to glaring at one another, Rastun could live with it.

"So I take it, being in the Army, they didn't have you do much on the water," Karen said.

"Part of my Ranger training did include riverine insertion, not that there was much need for it in Iraq or Afghanistan. What about you? Have you ever done a shoot in the water?"

"Quite a few, actually. I dove on the *Oriskany* reef in Florida, the one they made from the old aircraft carrier, to document the marine life around it. But the best was doing a shoot at the Great Barrier Reef."

"That must have been awesome," said Rastun. "That's a place I'd love to go one day."

"You should. It's beyond beautiful."

An image formed in Rastun's mind of him swimming around the Great Barrier Reef with Karen by his side.

"Hey." She raised her camera. "Give me some kind of macho soldier pose."

"What?"

"For the FUBI website. Since there's no sea monster to shoot, I gotta fill up the photo gallery with something."

"Well, since you asked so nicely." Rastun slipped the Steyr AUG from his shoulder, made sure the safety was on and held it diagonally across his torso.

"Perfect." Karen snapped a few pictures of him.

"Sorry if I'm not as interesting as a sea monster."

"You'll do, until we find it. Then things should get exciting."

"In my experience, exciting doesn't always equal fun. Hopefully when we do find the Point Pleasant Monster, I tranq it, we reel it in, oh, and you get your money shot."

Karen smiled, a very beautiful smile at that.

"Then," Rastun continued, "we drop it off at the Camden Aquarium. Mission accomplished."

"Simple as that?"

"Yeah, right. I have a feeling capturing something like this thing will be anything but simple."

***

"Shit, this stuff stinks."

Jerry Edler grimaced as he tossed more chum over the side of the boat.

"Not only that," said Darrell Wasser, who sat on the deck by the engine, arms resting on his knees. "You know how expensive that stuff is? Between that and renting this boat, we're pretty much tapped out."

"It'll all be worth it once we get a video of the Point Pleasant Monster."

"You mean *if*. Shit, Jer, we've been this for, like, two days, and we haven't seen anything."

"We will, man." Edler's face twisted in disgust as he flung more chum into the water.

"How do you know?"

"We will, okay?" Edler groaned and shook his head. Sometimes Wasser could be the biggest fucking whiner on the planet. Well, if he wanted to go home, whatever. Edler was determined to stay here until he had one good picture of the monster. It beat the hell out of sitting at home with his mom bitching at him to get a job. Like he hadn't tried. Who the hell could find work in this suck-ass economy? It took him five years to earn his art degree from Montclair State, and what did he get for it? A job as a bus boy for a restaurant that closed six months ago.

Getting this monster on video would be his big break. The FUBI would definitely hire him. He'd watched shows like *Destination Truth, Finding Bigfoot* and *Ghost Hunters* for years. He knew what it took to be a field researcher. Maybe he'd even work with that Rastun guy he met a couple of days ago. The dude was an Army Ranger. He could teach him all sorts of special ops/ninja shit. No one would ever fuck with him again.

"Dude, look!" Wasser shot to his feet and pointed.

Edler scanned the water. His mouth opened wide in surprise when he saw a gray shape snap at the chum.

"Oh man. Ohmanohmanohmanohman!" He whipped his head left to right. Where did he put the damn camera?

Edler spotted it laying on the deck a couple of feet away. He grabbed it and turned back to the gray shape.

It was gone.

"Fuck!" He kicked the side of the boat, then clenched his teeth in pain.

"It's back, man!"Wasser hollered. "It's back!"

Edler held the camera up to his face and hit record. He zoomed in, a thrill running through his body. This was it, he could feel it. This was the Point Pleasant Monster. He'd record it for a while, race back to shore and contact the FUBI. Then he wouldn't be Jerry Edler, loser, any more. He'd be Jerry Edler, monster hunter.

That would definitely land him a girlfriend.

Wait a minute.

The thrill evaporated when he recognized the blunt nose, the razor-sharp teeth and the dorsal fin.

It was just a fucking shark.

"Dammit!" Edler kicked the bucket. It toppled over, spilling chum all over the deck.

"Dammit!" he cursed louder.

"Aw, dude." Wasser frowned as he stared at the chum. "We're gonna have to clean that up before we bring the boat back."

Edler scowled. He shut off the camera, put it down and picked up a handful of chum.

"Here! Here's some more for you." He threw it into the water. "Fucking shark fucking up everything."

He tried to spot the shark, wanting to curse at it some more.

It had vanished.

"Fuck." He turned away from the water, grinding his teeth in anger. Who was he kidding? He'd never find the Point Pleasant Monster. He'd never get his dream job with the FUBI. He'd just be a fucking loser with a worthless degree who'd spend the rest of his life working in convenience stores or fast food joints.

Edler threw his hands up to the sky. "I hate my fucking life!"

"Dude." Wasser started over to him. "C'mon, man. Don't be like—"

Something bumped the bottom of the boat. Wasser stumbled into the gunwales, nearly falling overboard. Edler grabbed the driver's seat to keep his balance.

"You okay?" he called to Wasser.

"Yeah, man. Shit, what was that?" Wasser leaned over the side, trying for a better look.

A fountain of water exploded in front of him.

"Darrell!" Edler screamed.

Wasser went into spasms. Water cascaded onto the deck.

Some of that water was red.

Edler's skin turned ice cold as Wasser slumped and fell to the deck. Small, frightened gasps came from Edler's gaping mouth as he stared at his friend.

His friend who no longer had a head.

"D-Darrell?" he stammered, his legs shaking.

This isn't happening. This isn't happening.

Edler looked around, heart slamming against his chest. *What do I do?*

His eyes settled on Wasser's body. Blood streamed from his severed neck. So much blood. More than he'd ever seen in any movie or video game. And it was coming from his best friend.

Another huge fountain of water exploded toward aft.

Edler screamed. He fell to the deck, scrambling on all fours toward the driver's seat. Beside it lay his backpack. He unzipped it, reached inside and pulled out his mom's Smith and Wesson .38.

Something heavy dropped onto the boat. The bow rose. Edler slid down the deck.

"No! No!" He rolled on his back. His eyes bulged when he saw the beast in front of him.

Edler screamed and brought up the revolver. He pulled the trigger once, twice.

He never got off a third shot.

SEVEN

Rastun stood near the *Bold Fortune's* bow as USCG Station Manasquan Inlet came into view. The unpleasant feeling of failure crept through him. He tried to convince himself it was foolish to feel this way. The FUBI hadn't been sitting around yanking their cranks. They'd spent three days going up and down the Jersey Shore doing their best to find the Point Pleasant Monster.

Their best, however, hadn't been good enough.

The Coast Guard had notified them around 0800 this morning that they located a speedboat drifting four miles from shore, abandoned and covered in blood. While a USCG vessel towed the speedboat to Manasquan, *Bold Fortune* patrolled the area where it had been found. Four hours of plowing through the water turned up squat.

All their searches had turned up squat.

Rastun closed his eyes, inhaling the tangy salt air. Getting upset wouldn't change anything. They just had to keep at it until they found the damned monster.

Not that it would help whoever had been in that speedboat.

Bold Fortune slowed as it entered the inlet. He saw the speedboat sitting on a trailer on the boat ramp, with two people in dark blue uniforms examining it. Beyond them was the colonial-style administration building.

After *Bold Fortune* docked, Rastun followed Ehrenberg, Pilka, Malakov and Karen down the gangplank and toward the boat ramp. As they neared the speedboat, one of the Coasties, a squat woman with brown skin and her hair in a bun, came over to them.

"You must be the FUBI people."

"That's right." Dr. Ehrenberg shook the woman's hand, introducing himself and the rest of the team.

"Chief Warrant Officer Prashad. That's my partner, Petty Officer Tolleson." She pointed to the gangly man with thick glasses by the boat. "Coast Guard Investigative Service. They brought us in to do the forensics on the boat."

"Did you find anything?" asked Ehrenberg.

"We did. Come on, I'll show you."

They followed Prashad over to the speedboat. Rastun looked over the gunwales. Patches of blood stained the deck. The stench of copper and what smelled like raw meat surrounded the speedboat

"My God," Ehrenberg muttered. The cryptozoologist clenched his jaw, as though trying not to throw up. Karen and Malakov both grimaced, while Pilka began to look a little green.

Ehrenberg squared his shoulders, trying to regain his composure. "So was this the Point Pleasant Monster?"

"It appears so." Prashad went over to a table containing several items, many in plastic evidence bags. She picked up a white bucket and motioned for them to come over.

"Whoever was in this boat, they had this bucket filled with chum. We found small chunks of it scattered about the deck." Prashad turned the bucket around. Ehrenberg's eyes widened. Karen took pictures of it.

Lines of jagged puncture marks ran along the length of the bucket, as though something had bitten it.

Something big.

"This could be a shark," suggested Pilka.

"Not unless it jumped into the boat, said Prashad. "We also found a video camera onboard."

"What was on it?" Pilka stepped forward, his curiosity evident.

"No monster, if that's what you're hoping for. The last thing on there was one of the boaters filming a shark eating the chum. It sounded like he was upset it wasn't the Point Pleasant Monster, because he threw a fit and kicked over the chum bucket. After that, he shut off the camera. But we know one of the boaters didn't go down without a fight."

"What do you mean?" asked Ehrenberg.

Prashad placed the bucket back on the table and picked up a plastic bag.

"Is that a gun?" asked Karen.

"Yes it is. Smith & Wesson Model 638. Thirty-eight caliber, five-round chamber."

"Did he get off any shots?" asked Rastun.

"Two. I have no idea if he hit the monster or not. We won't know until we've examined all the blood on the boat."

Ehrenberg nodded. "Do we know who the boat belonged to?"

"Yes." Prashad set down the gun and picked up an iPad. "The boat was rented from the Point Pleasant Marina by Jerry Edler, age twenty-four, from Lakewood. He also had a friend with him, Darrell Wasser, same age, also from Lakewood."

Rastun's brow furrowed. The two names echoed in his head. Jerry Edler. Darrell Wasser.

Aw shit, are you kidding me?

"So what were they doing out there?" Malakov spoke in a sharp tone. "Trying to attract the Point Pleasant Monster so they could kill it?"

"No," said Rastun.

Malakov turned to him. "And how the hell would you know?"

"Because I actually ran into those two."

The group stared at him in surprise. So did Prashad, at least for a few moments before her professionalism returned. "When was this?"

"Three days ago at the Point Pleasant Marina. I nearly bumped into them when they were coming out of a shop. They told me they were going to go out and find the monster. I warned them against it, said it's too dangerous." He looked at the speedboat. "Needless to say, they didn't listen."

"Find it?" Malakov scoffed. "Yeah, so they could kill it."

"They didn't want to kill it. They just wanted a picture of it."

"Then why did they bring a gun?"

"Probably for self-defense, though I doubt a dinky thirty-eight would do much against something the size of the Point Pleasant Monster."

"Bullshit. If all they wanted to do was take a picture of this cryptid, they wouldn't have needed a damn gun. They wanted to kill it. To hell with the fact this is an extremely rare creature." Malakov barked out a humorless laugh. "Well look what happened to those idiots. The Point Pleasant Monster got them before they got it. How karmic."

Rastun stared at her, statue still. He barely noticed the disapproving and shocked expressions from the others.

Eyes narrowed, he stomped toward Malakov.

"Doctor Malakov."

"What?"

"Do you have children?"

"What business is it of—?"

"Do you have children?" Rastun cut her off.

Malakov glared at him. "Yes. I have two daughters."

"And Jerry Edler and Darrell Wasser also had mothers, mothers who are mourning their deaths as we speak. So maybe, as a mother yourself, you should think about how you'd feel if, God forbid, anything ever happened to your daughters and have some damn compassion!"

Malakov's face went red. She started to bare her teeth. Rastun prepared himself for the coming eruption.

Malakov glanced over at Ehrenberg. The cryptozoologist stood with his arms folded, a stern look on his face. He shook his head.

With a parting glare at Rastun, Malakov stalked off. He hoped the animal behaviorist would take a few minutes to cool off, realize how insensitive her comments had been and apologize.

She didn't. Their entire time at Coast Guard Station Manasquan Inlet, Malakov never said one thing about her remarks regarding the deaths of Edler and Wasser. That pissed off Rastun even more.

Once they finished examining the evidence collected from the speedboat, they headed to a nearby Wendy's. After Rastun got his food, he sat at a small booth on the other side of the restaurant away from the rest of the FUBI group. Particularly, away from Malakov. He still fumed every time he looked at her.

Get a grip, Jack. He stared at the tabletop, chewing his chicken sandwich. Most times he was successful at clamping down on his emotions. In his line of work – *former* line of work – it was essential. Soldiers who got too scared, too grief-stricken or too angry in combat usually got themselves and others killed.

He'd just sit here, eat his meal in peace and try to rid himself of his anger. Forget try. He *had* to stop being angry at Malakov.

Rastun found it tough to do every time he recalled her words.

"You mind some company?"

He looked up to find Karen standing beside the table. He waved her to the seat across from him.

"You okay?" she asked as she sat.

"I'm fine."

"You sure as heck don't look it."

Rastun grunted and popped some french fries in his mouth.

Karen lifted the lid on her salad and picked up a pack of dressing. Instead of opening it, she stared at Rastun. "Um, you mind if I ask you something?"

"Shoot."

"I know what Doctor Malakov said about those two guys was uncalled for, but you seem to be taking it a bit personally. I mean, you only talked to them for a couple of minutes."

Rastun leaned back in his seat. "I see what happened to Edler and Wasser, I start thinking about all the men their age, even younger, that we, that I, lost in Iraq and Afghanistan. Just walking around one minute, like everything's normal. Next minute, they're dead, and in the most violent ways you can imagine. I've been to my share of memorials for the men we lost, saw their families, looked into their eyes. You can just see this pain, pain you know is never going to go away. Sometimes I wonder if I'm responsible for that pain."

"But how? You didn't kill those men."

"It can be tough to convince yourself of that. When you're back at base, when it's just you and your thoughts, you start wondering would that soldier be alive if I'd given a different order or found a better place for cover or given them better advice on staying alive in a war zone? Then I think of their families, the hell they must be going through. Just a few years before, their kid was playing football, bugging them for a car and taking some girl to prom. Now they're burying him, if there's even anything left to bury."

Karen said nothing. She just stared at him with a sympathetic look.

Rastun continued. "Were Edler and Wasser dumbasses? Yeah. They had no business going out there playing monster hunter. But even dumbasses have people who love them." He shook his head. "Why didn't they just listen to me?"

"Jack." Karen reached across the table and lightly touched his hand. He held his breath as she spoke. "They'd just met you. They had no reason to listen to you."

"Yeah, you're right." He looked down at Karen's hand on his, relishing the warmth and softness. "That's four now."

"Four?" Karen gave him a quizzical look. Realization dawned on her when she understood four was the death toll in the Point Pleasant Monster attacks. "Well, let's hope we find this thing before we go up to five."

"Yeah, let's hope."

EIGHT

"Happy anniversary, Gabrielle."

The champagne spilled over the flute, splashing on Scott Horn's trousers. He stared at the stain, shrugged and put the bottle back in the ice bucket. The speedboat bobbed in the open water as Horn gazed into the hazy horizon.

He lifted the flute and drained it.

Horn reached into his pocket and pulled out his phone. He called up a photo of him in a tuxedo next to a medium-built brunette in a wedding dress. Five years ago today that picture had been taken. How many of their friends got divorced during that time? Yet his and Gabrielle's marriage grew stronger each day.

Then the leukemia hit. Horn had to watch the woman he loved weaken and waste away, until her body gave out four months ago.

He choked off a sob. Horn never believed in soulmates until he met Gabrielle. Now she was gone and he had no idea how to continue.

He refilled his flute, looking around the boat before he drank. Horn had proposed to Gabrielle in this very boat, around this very spot, six-and-a-half years ago. They always returned here every year to celebrate their anniversary.

This year, it was just him and his memories of Gabrielle.

Horn gulped down the champagne and poured more into the flute. It wasn't long before he drained the entire bottle. A heavy feeling surrounded his body. His mind dulled. He slumped in his chair, letting the flute fall to the deck. The boat kept drifting further away from shore. He didn't care. What the hell was the point of going home anyway?

A stubby white shape appeared in the distance. Horn leaned forward for a better look. Dizziness swept through his head. He groaned and fell back against his seat. The sun was in his eyes. He struggled to bring up his hand, which felt like lead. When it didn't come up fast enough, Horn turned away...

And fell out of his seat. His face slammed against the deck. His nose and lip throbbed in pain.

Horn lay there for a while before pushing himself up. He crawled to the gunwales and leaned over the side. Droplets of red fell into the water.

He wiped a hand across his face and stared at his palm. It was stained with blood.

He slumped against the gunwales, staring at his red-streaked hand until it became too heavy to hold up. Horn let his arm drop to his side.

That's when he heard the growl of a boat engine.

"What the hell?"

A white boat with an orange stripe pulled next to his speed boat. His drunken mind managed to register the words on the side.

U.S. Coast Guard.

A lean young man in a blue uniform and ball cap stepped out of the pilothouse.

"Afternoon, sir." He paused and scrunched up his face. "Are you okay? Did you hurt yourself?"

"Huhwha?" Horn slurred his words together.

"Hang on, sir. I'll be right back."

The Coastie went back inside the pilothouse. When he returned, he carried a first aid kit. He jumped into the speedboat and knelt in front of Horn.

"What's your name?" asked the Coastie.

"S-S-Scott Horn."

"Where are you from, Scott?" The Coastie took out a gauze pad and sprayed some water on it.

"Uh, Point Pleasant."

"How did you hurt yourself?"

"F-Fell."

"Uh-huh." The Coastie wiped Horn's face. "Yeah, looks like you got a cut just above your nose. You in any pain?"

"Umfine." Horn tried to pull away from the Coastie, but his body felt too heavy to move.

"You know you're not supposed to be out here. The Coast Guard issued a restriction on all civilian vessels. You can't sail more than a mile from shore. Didn't you hear that on the news?"

"Uhh . . ." Horn racked his muddled brain. Hadn't there been something on the radio about that this morning? Damned if he could remember.

The Coastie put a bandage over the wound. "That'll do for now, but you're going to need stitches to close that up."

"Yeahuh-huh."

The Coastie sniffed at the air. "Have you been drinking?"

"Yeah. So what?" Horn was getting annoyed with this guy. Why couldn't he just leave and let him mourn his dead wife in peace?

"Sir, I'm going to have to place you under arrest for operating a boat while intoxicated."

Horn just stared at the Coastie. Some distant part of his mind told him he should be concerned about this. But between his grief and his drunkenness, he didn't care.

He let the Coastie help him to his feet. Horn struggled to maintain his balance. The Coastie grabbed hold of him twice to keep from falling.

Two more Coast Guardsman appeared and reached out to help Horn aboard their vessel.

"Easy does it, Scott." The Coastie helped steady him. "You're doing fine. Just—"

A loud splash erupted behind them. Something crashed down on the speedboat. Horn felt himself fly through the air. He hit the water and went under. Panic seized him. He thrashed and kicked, trying to get to the surface.

A razor-sharp vice crushed his left leg. It yanked him deeper into the ocean. Horn opened his mouth to scream. Water rushed into his lungs. He stretched out his arms, the surface growing further and further away.

A cloud of red surrounded Scott Horn. He saw and felt nothing after that.

NINE

This is fun.

Rastun crawled deeper into the large muddy tunnel. He moved his Glock 17 back and forth, the beam from the flashlight under the barrel sweeping over the soggy earth. No sign of anything living.

He continued on, mud squishing beneath him. His shirt and pants were sodden. Rastun ignored the feeling. He'd been in much worse muck and filth than this.

He crept a few more feet, stopped and swept the flashlight around. Nothing. Rastun again slithered through the mud. How far had he come? Thirty feet? Forty? How far did the tunnel run? Would he find what he was looking for at the end? Part of him wanted to, but another part, the more sane part, hoped he didn't.

"You're the one who wanted to play tunnel rat, moron."

Rastun crawled another few feet, stopped and did another scan with his flashlight.

He tensed when the beam fell on a large, reptilian form. A pair of yellow eyes stared back at him.

His finger tightened around the Glock's trigger, then just as quickly eased off.

The creature's scaly neck extended forward. Its pointy mouth opened, as if challenging the intruder.

"Sorry," Rastun said to the snapping turtle. "Just passing through."

He backed out of the tunnel, his feet splashing into the creek when he emerged.

"Ew. I thought guys grew out of the playing in the mud phase when they were ten."

Rastun looked up to find Karen standing on the bank.

"I wouldn't exactly call this playing." He holstered his Glock and shook his arms, trying to fling away some of the mud.

"Did you find anything?" asked Karen.

"Yeah. One pissed off snapping turtle."

Rastun looked back at the tunnel. Dr. Ehrenberg had wanted to explore the theory that the Point Pleasant Monster might live on land but hunt in the water, like alligators and crocodiles. So the two of them, along with Karen and Dr. Malakov, had *Bold Fortune* drop them off at the Edwin B. Forsythe National Wildlife Refuge near Barnegat Bay. The rest of the FUBI group continued their search off Point Pleasant, in the area where the latest attack occurred.

After an hour of hiking along the shoreline, this was the largest tunnel they'd found big enough for something like the Point Pleasant Monster.

Rastun wondered if Ehrenberg and Malakov, who patrolled further north, had better luck.

Worry crept through him. He hadn't wanted to separate, but Ehrenberg insisted, saying they could cover more ground. If anything happened to the two doctors, he wouldn't be there to help them.

We need more field security specialists on these expeditions.

Karen climbed down the bank and headed toward the tunnel.

"What are you doing?" asked Rastun.

"Going in there to get a picture of the snapping turtle."

"That's not as exciting as a sea monster."

"It's either this or I start posting on the photo gallery, 'Sorry, no monster today. Try again tomorrow.'"

"Just be careful. That thing looks fully grown. It's gotta be at least a hundred-fifty pounds."

Karen gave him a perturbed look. "Please. I've photographed lions, sharks and grizzly bears. I think I can handle a snapping turtle."

"Sorry. Just trying to do my job."

With a parting grin, Karen crawled into the tunnel. She didn't hesitate for a second. Just put her head down and she was gone. He couldn't imagine his former fiancée, Marie, doing that. She didn't even like doing yard work.

Rastun liked this adventurous side of Karen. He liked it a lot.

He scooped up handfuls of water from the creek and cleaned off his muddy arms best he could. Then he stripped off his filthy Woodland BDU coat and undershirt and pulled out a fresh set from his pack. He'd just started to unfold his undershirt when Karen reappeared.

"Okay, I got a nice close-up of...oh!" Her wide eyes fixed on Rastun's bare torso. Her cheeks flushed red.

"Sorry." Rastun put on his undershirt. "Just wanted to put on some clean clothes."

"Um, yeah. I don't blame you." Karen took a deep breath and regained her composure. She then looked down at her own mud-stained clothes. "I should probably do the same. Times like these I'm glad I put extra clothes in my pack."

"Always helps to be prepared." Rastun donned a fresh BDU jacket.

Karen gazed around the marsh before pointing to a clump of trees thirty yards away. "I'll be over there. No peeking."

"No peeking." He held up his arm and raised two fingers. "Scout's honor."

Karen chuckled and headed off to the trees.

While Rastun promised not to peek, he didn't say anything about imagining Karen undressing behind the trees. Or undressing in his cabin back on *Bold Fortune*.

"Okay," Karen called out. "You can turn around now."

Rastun did as told. Karen walked toward him in fresh khakis.

"Wow, you didn't peek," she said. "I'm impressed."

"I'm a man of my word. Now just give me a minute."

He went behind the trees, removed his muddy BDU trousers and put on fresh ones.

The pair set off down the shoreline. Forty minutes later they found another tunnel, a bit larger than the first, in a cove. As with the last one, they found no sign of the Point Pleasant Monster.

They continued through the refuge for another fifteen minutes before Rastun turned to Karen and asked, "You need a break?"

"Are you kidding? I've run full marathons, twenty-plus miles, without a break. This is nothing. Unless you need a break." She gave him a wry grin.

"Me? I had to complete a twelve-mile march, in full gear, in under three hours when I was in Ranger School. This is a pleasant afternoon stroll for me."

"Then keep strolling... General."

He snickered at what seemed to have become Karen's favorite nickname for him.

They hiked for another half-hour before Rastun called for a halt.

"You're not tired, are you?" Karen asked playfully.

"No, I'm starving. Even tough guys need to eat."

"So do tough girls. C'mon, let's see what's on the menu."

They sat under a weeping willow and pulled out MREs from their packs.

"Mm, cheese tortellini." Karen held her packet in front of her. "My favorite."

"You actually have a favorite MRE?"

"You don't?"

"Do you know how many of these things I ate when I was in the Army? There's a reason they're called Meals Rejected by the Enemy."

Karen chuckled. "I don't know. I always get some when I have to go out in the field. Most of them aren't bad."

Rastun sliced open his chicken with dumplings MRE with his Tanto tactical knife, reached in and pulled out a tiny plastic bottle. "This is the one thing that makes most of this food edible."

"Oh, the Tabasco sauce. Yeah, that does help spice up the food."

"It can also help keep you awake."

Karen was about to put her main course into the ration heater when she gave him a puzzled look. "How?"

"You put a few drops in your eyes."

"Seriously? You've done that?"

"Hey, a lot of times at Ranger School, you're operating on two or three hours of sleep a day, if you're lucky. You gotta do something drastic to stay awake."

Rastun started heating up his meal when Karen asked, "What made you want to become a Ranger?"

"I had an uncle who served in the Rangers in World War Two. When I was growing up, he used to tell me stories about all the battles he was in over in Europe. At first I thought he was telling me that stuff because it was cool.

When I got older, I realized that he knew his generation was dying out, and he was passing along his stories so people wouldn't forget when he and all the other World War Two vets were gone."

"Is your uncle...gone?" asked Karen.

"He died when I was fifteen."

"I'm sorry."

"Thanks." Rastun stared at his ration heater for a few quiet seconds. "When he died, I felt like I had to honor him, to do what he did and serve this country. So I read everything I could on the military, exercised like crazy, took Tae Kwon Do, did whatever I thought would help me become an Army Ranger. One time when I was eighteen, I went to this little airport outside Philly and went skydiving."

"Wow, and your parents were cool with that?"

"Are you kidding? I didn't tell them."

"What?"

"I was eighteen," said Rastun. "I was an adult. I didn't need my parents' permission."

"Well you were the little rebel back then, weren't you?" Karen grinned.

"It wasn't about rebelling. You have to be airborne qualified to be a Ranger. I figured it was better to find out whether or not I could jump out of a perfectly good aircraft before I went into the Army."

"Sounds like you were really committed," said Karen. "So why did you leave the Army?"

Rastun's lips tightened. He didn't want to lie to Karen, but much of what happened in Western Sahara remained hush-hush.

"Victim of the budget axe. One administration builds up the military, the next one tears it down."

He checked his ration pack to make sure his chicken and dumplings were fully cooked, then turned back to Karen. "So what about you? What made you want to become a wildlife photographer?"

"When I was nine, my parents took me to this park near our house for a picnic. We'd just started to eat when my mom started screaming and pointing at the lake. An alligator crawled out of it. I thought it was the coolest thing in the world. My parents, however, didn't. They grabbed me and took off running for our car."

"Did it chase after you?"

"No. It just turned around and went back in the lake. But I was thinking, if there were alligators near our house, what else was out there? And if I did see something, I wanted other people to know what I saw. So I saved up my money and bought a camera. Took it with me everywhere I went."

"And the rest is history."

"Yeah." Karen removed her tortellini from the ration heater. Instead of digging in, she stared at her food.

"You okay?" asked Rastun.

"Yeah. Just thinking. It's gonna feel weird living in Virginia. The only connection I have with that state is a great-aunt I've seen maybe twice in my life. I love Florida. Beaches, boating, jet-skiing, the biodiversity."

"Spring training."

Karen laughed. "Oh my God. You are such a sports fan."

"Not just any sports fan, a Philadelphia sports fan. The most obnoxious kind in the world."

Karen laughed harder. "Well, like I said, it'll take some adjusting, but working for the FUBI is too great an opportunity to pass up. I know I can make it work, for me and Emily."

"I can only imagine how hard it has to be, to have a job like yours and try to raise a daughter."

"It is hard. Sometimes really, really hard. But my aunt and uncle help, and sometimes I can bring Emily with me when I'm on assignment."

Rastun nodded and shifted his eyes to the ground, wondering if his next question might be inappropriate.

"So between a globetrotting job and raising a daughter, how do you manage having a personal life?"

"You mean dating? I manage, on occasion. Finding the right guy, however, that hasn't happened yet."

"So you're not seeing anyone right now?"

Karen tilted her head. "You interested?"

"Yes, I am."

Karen looked off in the distance, then turned back to him. She slid closer, her beautiful face barely a foot away from his.

"Do me a favor, Jack."

"What?"

"I want you to be honest with me when I ask you this next question."

"You have my word as an officer."

"You are not married, about to get married or involved with another woman, are you?"

Rastun processed the question. It sounded like Karen had been down this road before. Could it have been with Dr. Pilka? He wanted to dismiss it. The marine biologist had to be 20 years Karen's senior.

So? Karen wouldn't be the first woman to be involved with a much older man. It would also explain the latent hostility that existed between them.

If there had been anything between them, it was obviously over.

Rastun looked her in the eyes. "I am not married, engaged or seeing anyone right now."

Karen smiled. "I'm glad to hear that."

Rastun placed his hand over Karen's. He leaned forward and kissed her.

***

Looks like I've got some competition.

Piet observed Jack Rastun and Karen Thatcher through his binoculars, his green, leaf-covered ghillie suit blending in with the surrounding marsh. He had been stalking them for hours. His FUBI contact informed him that some of the expedition members would search this wildlife refuge to see if the Point Pleasant Monster lived on land and hunted in the water. Piet hoped that would be the case. It would make it easier for him and his men to secure the beastie for Mr. Gunderson.

They hadn't found the monster, but Piet's surveillance wasn't a complete waste of time. He now knew that Rastun had a thing for that delicious-looking photographer. That could come in handy later on. He could take Thatcher hostage and get Rastun to do whatever he wanted to spare the life of his lady love.

Piet smiled as he watched the pair continue to go at it. He knew Rastun's weakness. He could exploit it, beat him, then Thatcher would be his to fuck in every way he could imagine.

And if he was feeling generous, he'd let Rastun watch.

TEN

The sun began to set when *Bold Fortune* pulled into a slip at the Point Pleasant Marina. Rastun, standing on the starboard side, looked over his shoulder at the vast Atlantic Ocean.

Where are you?

They'd been searching for a week with nothing to show for their efforts except false sonar contacts and a long list of bogus eyewitness reports. He'd seen a few news stories that questioned the competency of the FUBI. That didn't surprise him. If a situation did not get resolved instantly, the people handling it were incompetent. An easy judgment to make for well-dressed assholes sitting in a comfortable TV studio instead of searching hundreds of square miles of ocean for one particular creature.

At least the death of Scott Horn two days ago had, finally, gotten the public to take the danger the Point Pleasant Monster posed seriously. Very few boaters and jet skiers went out into the ocean. That would certainly hurt the businesses that rented watercraft, but better to lose money than any more lives. Five was five too many.

And if it runs out of people to eat here, will it move somewhere else? If it did that, they might never catch the monster. The press would have a field day with that.

Fuck 'em. He couldn't afford to worry about reporters. The same with local officials and business owners upset about all the summer tourism dollars the monster cost them. He and the rest of the expedition had to focus on their jobs, period. After a night's rest, they'd take on more fuel and supplies and head back out to sea.

Meantime, Rastun had an idea how to spend his downtime.

After Hernandez secured *Bold Fortune* to the dock, Rastun went belowdecks to the sleeping quarters. He approached Karen's cabin when he heard her talking.

"Hopefully we'll find this monster soon and I'll be home... Of course I'll be careful. I always am."

It sounded like she was talking to her daughter, Emily. Rastun stood a few feet from the doorway and waited.

"Just keep looking at the FUBI website and you'll see everything I'm doing... Good. You keep being a good girl for Aunt Melanie and Uncle Troy and I'll talk to you tomorrow... I love you too, sweetie. Night-night."

Rastun went up to Karen's cabin and knocked on the doorframe. "Hey there."

She smiled when she saw him. "Hey, Jack."

"Are you doing anything now?"

"I was just saying good-night to my daughter." Karen put her cell phone back in the holder attached to her belt. "You have something in mind?"

"Yeah. Dinner. This time at an actual restaurant."

"Sounds like you're asking me out on a date."

"Well, I didn't think having MREs under a tree was all that romantic."

"No, but I enjoyed the company." Karen beamed at him. "And yes, I'd love to go to dinner with you. Just give me a few minutes to change."

"You got it." Rastun leaned forward and gave her a kiss before she closed the door.

He went to his room and stripped off his t-shirt, BDU pants and boots. He looked through his luggage for decent date clothing. There wasn't much to choose from. It wasn't like he expected to take a woman to dinner while searching for a killer sea monster. The best he could come up with was sneakers, blue jeans and a gray ARMY t-shirt.

Five minutes after Rastun changed, Karen came out of her cabin in flip flops, jeans and a cream-colored top. Her brown hair was pulled back in a ponytail.

She looked gorgeous.

They drove a few miles to a two-story white and blue colonial-style house near the boardwalk. A red neon sign over the entrance read Vargo's Restaurant and Bar. The hostess seated them at a table near the corner of the first floor. The large window to their left looked out on the Atlantic, the sky above it a canvass of orange and dark blue.

A waiter soon appeared and asked what they wanted anything to drink.

"You know," Karen said. "I am in the mood for a margarita."

The waiter turned to Rastun.

"A Sprite for me."

The waiter wrote down their orders and left. Karen looked at Rastun. "Wow, a Sprite. You wildman. C'mon, live a little. We're off the clock."

"Honestly, I'm not much of a drinker."

"Seriously? I thought all you military guys loved to pound down beers."

"I found out in college that I'm a lightweight. Three beers and I'm plastered."

"Three beers? You wuss."

Rastun grinned. He thoroughly enjoyed Karen's playful needling, something he never had with Marie. Then again, looking back on it, she never had much of a sense of humor.

It made him wonder why he'd been with her in the first place, never mind proposing to her.

Karen thoroughly enjoyed her margarita. Their meals were just as good, with Rastun having the crusted grouper and Karen the red snapper in wine sauce. They talked about a variety of things, none of which had to do with the Point Pleasant Monster. Growing up in Philadelphia and Tampa, their cross country experiences, which Karen had done much better at, since she finished fourth at state her senior year and earned a scholarship to Florida Atlantic University. Rastun also listened with great interest about Karen's photo shoots in places like Alaska, Costa Rica and Madagascar.

"Maybe I should stop," she said at one point.

"What for?"

"'Cause here I am talking about all these cool places I've been to, and all the Army did was drop you into one war zone after another."

"Not true. There were other places I went to besides Iraq and Afghanistan. I've been to Norway for arctic warfare training with the Jägers, their special ops force. I was in Britain for counter-terror training with the SAS, Thailand for jungle warfare training with their paratroopers."

"Did you do anything else in those countries besides learn how to blow stuff up?" Karen asked as she cut into her snapper.

"Well, it wasn't like the Army sent me over there on vacation, but I still got to see some interesting places, without lugging around an eighty-pound pack and a rifle."

Once they finished eating, Rastun paid for their meals and walked Karen out the door. Instead of going toward the parking lot, he took her by the hand and guided her along the walkway next to Vargo's.

"Isn't your car that way?" Karen pointed to the parking lot.

"We're not going to my car. At least, not yet."

"Then where are we going?"

"I thought you might enjoy a nighttime stroll on the beach."

Karen's face brightened. "How romantic. Lead the way."

Once they reached the sand, they took off their shoes and headed down to the surf. White frothy water washed over their feet. The bright lights of the boardwalk glowed about a mile away.

"By the way, thank you." Karen kissed his cheek.

"For what?"

"For this. It's been a while since I've been on an honest-to-goodness date."

Rastun squeezed her hand. "You're welcome. Actually, it's been a while for me, too."

His lips tightened as he stared straight ahead.

"Ooh, I sense there's a story behind this."

Rastun drew a slow breath. "I was engaged, back when I was in the Rangers. Marie was her name. We...broke it off."

"How long were you together?"

"Three years."

Karen looked down at the water around her feet. "What happened, if you don't mind me asking?"

"Let's just say I learned the hard way she was a different person from the one I fell in love with, or thought I fell in love with. But better I found that out when I did instead of after we walked down the aisle."

Several seconds passed with the only sound the rolling surf around them. Finally, Karen spoke. "It sounds like we're both in the same boat."

"You had someone do you dirt, too?"

"Oh yeah. Big time. I was engaged, too, when I was younger. I thought he was the most incredible man in the world, but like your fiancée, he turned out to be something completely different." Karen let out a sigh. "It ripped my heart to shreds when it happened, and it was a long time before I let myself trust another man."

"What made you move past it?"

"I just said to myself there are millions of men out there, and some of them have to be decent. I shouldn't deny myself a chance to be happy with someone because of one asshole."

"Well, hopefully you have a decent guy walking right next to you on this beach."

Karen turned to Rastun, grinning. "I do."

He quickly turned in front of Karen. She yelped in surprise and delight as she bumped into his chest. He wrapped his arms around her waist and gave her a long kiss. His lips moved to her cheek, then behind her ear, then down her slender neck. Karen ran her hands up and down Rastun's back.

He pulled her down to the sand. Karen giggled as she lay on top of him. "Are you trying to re-enact *From Here to Eternity?*"

"Is there a problem with that?"

"No, there isn't."

Karen leaned down, kissing him first on the lips, then on the neck. Rastun ran his hands along her sides.

Something rose from the water.

Rastun pushed himself up to a sitting position.

"What's wrong?" Karen untangled herself from him, a surprised look on her face.

"There's something in the water."

Karen knelt next to him, staring out at the darkened ocean. Rastun got to one knee, his hand hovering near his inside-the-pants holster. A large dark shape lumbered through the waves. He could make out something long extending from the shoulders. A neck. A neck that ended in a crocodilian snout.

Rastun was staring at the Point Pleasant Monster.

ELEVEN

Rastun sprang to his feet and pulled out his Glock.

"Oh my God, I don't believe it." Karen also stood, reaching into her large fanny pack.

"Back up, slowly."

Rastun brought up his pistol, putting the sights right on the creature's center of mass. It continued forward, now twenty yards away. It lifted its snout, as if sniffing the air.

He had no doubt it could smell them.

A white flash caught his attention. Rastun glanced at Karen, who had a camera up to her face. She snapped another picture.

The Point Pleasant Monster swung its neck toward them. Another flash came from Karen's camera. The beast stood still for a moment, then continued forward.

Rastun lowered his Glock and aimed to the monster's left. He fired three shots. Little spouts of water kicked up near its leg.

It kept coming.

"So much for scaring it off." Rastun aimed for the monster's torso and fired. Four 9mm rounds spat from the Glock.

The monster didn't slow down.

Another flash came from Karen's camera.

"You think you got enough pictures?" he asked.

"Considering how close it's getting, I'm gonna say yes."

"Good. Run!"

They raced across the sand. Rastun checked over his shoulder. The Point Pleasant Monster lowered its head and charged.

He wheeled around and fired two shots. No effect.

Rastun kept running. He eyed a wooden staircase leading up to the boardwalk. Lots of lights, lots of noise, lots of people. Maybe it would be too overwhelming for the monster. Maybe it would get scared and run back to the ocean.

"Boardwalk! Boardwalk!" he shouted at Karen. "Go! Go!"

Rastun ran for all he was worth. He checked on Karen. She ran a few paces ahead of him without any hint of fatigue. He thanked God for her cross country and marathon background.

Rastun looked over his shoulder. A stab of fear went through his chest. The monster couldn't be more than 15 yards behind them, and closing.

"Go! Go! Go!"

The world slowed down. The steps didn't seem to get closer. Panic grew inside him. He clamped down on it and fought past the adrenalin overload. He just kept his legs pumping and made sure Karen stayed with him.

Suddenly his bare feet thumped on wood.

Rastun and Karen bolted up the stairs. They ran past benches and lampposts toward the row of stalls and shops, all blazing with neon lights and churning out carnival-like music and sound effects. Dozens of people lined the wooden railing along the boardwalk, staring out at the beach. Some pointed. Some gasped. Others held up cameras and cell phones.

Rastun looked back to the beach. He tensed.

The Point Pleasant Monster loped toward the stairs.

"Get outta here!" he shouted at the crowd. "Get outta here!"

A few people ran off. Others stared at him with expressions of shock or curiosity.

"He's got a gun!" one woman shrieked.

"Don't shoot us, man!" a teenage boy held up his hands.

"Dammit, get the hell outta—"

The snap of wood sounded behind Rastun. He swung around.

The monster shattered part of the railing as it stomped onto the boardwalk. Rastun fired three shots.

Screams went up from the crowd. Men, women and children stampeded down the boardwalk.

"Go!" Rastun nudged Karen forward and fired two more shots at the monster. He turned and ran after her. The boardwalk trembled from the pounding feet of the crowd.

And the feet of the Point Pleasant Monster.

People jumped over the railing and onto the beach. Others dashed inside shops, pushing and shoving to get through the door.

Rastun again checked over his shoulder.

The monster gained on them. Twenty yards and closing.

"Jack!"

He looked to Karen, who pointed to a nearby bench.

A little girl with short brown hair and a pink dress sat beside the bench, crying. She couldn't have been more than four. Where the hell were the parents?

Probably caught up in the mob, unable to reach her. Probably freaking the hell out, terrified their daughter would be eaten.

Not on my watch.

"Karen! Get her!"

He swung around to face the Point Pleasant Monster. It tramped right underneath a lamppost. Bathed in the white glow, Rastun finally had a good look at the beast.

It looked like a 12-foot-tall velociraptor on steroids. The monster's tail swung over the ground. Muscular hind legs supported its grayish body. A dark green shell ran down its back. Not like a turtle's shell. More like an armor-plated dinosaur such as ankylosaurus. The plating went up its snake-like neck and ended at its skull. The monster's long arms ended in webbed hands with sharp claws.

Rastun aimed for the head and emptied his Glock. The monster flinched and paused. Had he hit something vital?

The Point Pleasant Monster opened its mouth and hissed. It lowered its head and charged.

Rastun looked around. He spotted an abandoned popcorn cart to his left. It was a desperate plan, but right now it was the only one he had.

Rastun grabbed the cart by its handle. The monster bore down on him and opened its jaws. He could count every single razor-sharp tooth.

Rastun pushed the cart over and leapt away. He landed on the wooden surface and rolled.

The monster's right foot crushed one of the wheels, but got caught up on the other. It hissed and pitched forward. A shudder went through the boardwalk. Wooden boards cracked and buckled underneath its bulk.

"Jack!" Karen called out. She was carrying the little girl, who cried louder than before.

The monster pushed itself up. Rastun jumped to his feet. He spotted an open stall filled with colorful stuffed animals.

"This way!" He led Karen to the stall. She whispered, "It's gonna be okay, sweetie," to the little girl over and over.

Rastun ejected the spent magazine from his Glock and inserted a fresh one. Karen climbed up and over the counter with the girl. Rastun turned around.

The Point Pleasant Monster was up, its dark eyes aimed right at him.

He fired three shots and jumped over the counter. Karen found a rear exit and tried the door.

"It's locked!"

A horrific crash went up behind Rastun. He dove to the floor. The little girl shrieked.

He rolled over and sat up. The counter had been pushed in by the monster.

Rastun put three rounds into its neck. It didn't even notice.

He spotted something gray out the corner of his eye. A small metal bucket had tipped over. Its contents, rubber balls of various colors, spilled across the floor.

The monster slammed into the counter again. It opened its mouth and leaned forward.

"Jack!"

Rastun barely registered Karen's cry. He grabbed the bucket and swung. It cracked against the monster's crocodilian head. It drew back.

Rastun rammed the bucket over the monster's snout. It hissed in rage. Rastun hurried to the door. He only had a couple seconds at best.

"Turn away!"

Karen obeyed, clutching the crying girl tight.

Rastun aimed for the lock and fired three times. Something metal clattered behind him. He turned.

The Point Pleasant Monster had shaken loose the bucket.

Rastun twisted to the side and launched his left foot into the door. It flew open with a bang.

"Go!" He shoved Karen and the girl inside. Rastun turned back to the monster. It stomped over the mangled counter.

He fired two shots and rushed through the door. Jaws snapped behind him. He felt a quick shiver go through him.

That was way too close.

Rastun hurried through a corridor with Karen and the little girl. There were small offices on either side, probably for the various boardwalk businesses. The girl kept crying as Rastun searched for an exit.

A door opened ahead of them. A squat man with tan skin and a thick mustache emerged, pulling something. A trolley with three racks filled with spray bottles, paper towels, a dustpan, a bucket and a mop.

The man had to be a janitor. Rastun wondered what he was still doing here. Surely he'd heard the commotion outside.

Then he noticed the earbuds the janitor wore.

He turned his cart and stopped in shock when he saw them.

"Hey! No one's supposed to be back here." His eyes widened when he noticed Rastun's pistol.

Rastun held up his hand. "Sir, you need to—"

A groaning, cracking sound cut him off. Both Rastun and Karen turned around.

The Point Pleasant Monster smashed through the door. The corridor was just wide enough for it to fit through.

The janitor screamed something in Spanish and took off running. He turned right into another corridor and vanished.

An exit maybe?

"Follow him!" Rastun fired three rounds at the monster. It didn't move as fast in the confined space.

He turned to follow Karen, then paused by the janitor's cart. He stared at the bucket of soapy water.

The monster hissed, stomping closer to him.

Rastun picked up the bucket and threw it on the floor. A mass of water and white foam spread before him.

He ran, catching a glimpse of Karen turning the corner. Just as he reached the intersection, he heard a loud thump behind him. The monster had slipped and fallen. It hissed as it struggled to rise from the slick, damp floor.

Rastun dashed around the corner. Karen reached the exit and pushed open the door with her shoulder. He followed her out a few seconds later.

"Are you okay?" Karen shouted over the wails of the girl.

"Yeah. You?"

She nodded.

Rastun spotted the janitor running across the street. He was tempted to follow, but felt the terrain too exposed. The Point Pleasant Monster would recover from its fall soon, and for whatever reason, the damn thing was determined to get them. They needed a place to hole up, close by.

"C'mon."

He led Karen along the rear of the boardwalk.

"I want my mommy," the little girl said through her sobs.

"We'll find your mommy, sweetie." Karen tried to sooth her. "I promise."

Rastun came to the back door of some business. Locked. So was the next one.

The third door was unlocked.

"Inside!"

Karen hurried through the door with the little girl. Rastun followed and slammed it shut. He secured the deadbolt and checked over the door. It was made of solid metal. No way was the monster getting through that.

"What the fuck's goin' on?" someone said in a thick Jersey/Italian accent.

Rastun spun around and saw a man with dark hair, a huge belly and an apron. His hands quickly shot up.

"Yo, take it easy with the gun, man."

"Calm down, we're not here to hurt you." Rastun pointed his Glock to the floor. He noticed the smell in the air. Tomato sauce, melted cheese, pepperoni and sausage.

They were in a pizza parlor.

"My name is Jack Rastun." He shoved a hand into his pocket, his fingers brushing against his keys and lighter before pulling out his wallet. "I'm with the FUBI." He showed him his ID.

"That's that group that looks for monsters, right?" asked the cook.

"Yeah, and we found one. The Point Pleasant Monster. The damn thing chased us through the boardwalk."

"No shit."

"Yes shit."

"So that's why everyone was goin' nuts out there?"

"Yeah. Just tell everyone here to stay put. We should be all right." Rastun holstered his gun and drew deep breaths, replenishing his lungs. Karen also took deep breaths as she lowered the girl to the floor and knelt in front of her.

"What's your name?"

"Ashlee."

"My name's Karen, and that's Jack, and we're not gonna let that big scary monster get you, okay?"

Ashlee nodded. "I want my mommy."

"As soon as it's safe, we'll find her. Here, let me dry your face, okay?"

Karen got some paper towels and wiped Ashlee's tear-stained face. It looked like she was finally calming the little girl. Then again, Karen had a daughter of her own. She was more used to dealing with kids than him.

Rastun pulled out his cell phone and was about to dial 911, but stopped. They must already be flooded with calls about a monster rampaging on the boardwalk. The cops had to be on their way, hopefully with more firepower than his useless Glock.

He instead dialed Dr. Ehrenberg's cell.

"Jack, what's up?"

"I'm with Karen at the Point Pleasant Boardwalk."

"A-ha! I had a feeling there was something going on between you two. You enjoying yourselves?"

"We were until the Point Pleasant Monster started chasing us."

"What?" Ehrenberg's tone became more serious. "Are you all right?"

"Yeah. We're both fine. We're holed up in a pizza parlor with a little girl we rescued. You better get hold of the police. We're going to have to coordinate—"

Glass shattered. Ashlee screamed.

"Holy shit!" the cook yelled.

Rastun looked up at the window near the corner of the kitchen. The Point Pleasant Monster's snout poked through it.

TWELVE

Rastun brought up his Glock. The monster's snout twitched left to right. He held his fire, fearful of a ricochet.

The monster withdrew its snout.

"Jack? Jack!" Ehrenberg shouted. "What's going on?"

"It's here." He spoke loud to be heard over Ashlee's crying. Karen held the girl tight. "The monster's outside the restaurant."

"All right, I'm headed to the weapons locker now to get some tranq rifles. We'll be over there as soon as possible."

A loud thump came from the door. The cook jumped back. Ashlee cried louder.

Rastun pointed his Glock at the door. "Better move your ass, Randy."

"It's moving. Stay safe."

Ehrenberg hung up.

The monster thumped the door again. It held up against the assault.

Rastun looked around the kitchen, trying to find anything he could use as an improvised weapon. His gaze halted on a nearby table with containers of shredded cheese, sauces and sliced pepperoni. Beyond that was the stove with a couple of chicken breasts cooking on it.

He grimaced, regretting his decision to hide in here. He'd seen photographs of cars, RVs and homes trashed by bears who'd entered them searching for food. Would the Point Pleasant Monster do the same?

No more thumps came from the door. Rastun saw no other way into the kitchen from the outside. Maybe—

Screams erupted from the dining area.

"Shit!" He dashed through the kitchen and pushed open a green swinging door. A crowd of people stood in the middle of the dining area, many looking terrified. Others scrambled out of booths that lined the side of the restaurant, dominated by a row of huge windows.

Through those windows Rastun saw the Point Pleasant Monster.

"Get back!" he shouted at the customers. "Get back, now!"

Many of them backed up against the far wall. Some still screamed.

"Shoot it!" yelled one hysterical woman. "Shoot it!"

I have been shooting it. It doesn't do any good.

The monster put its head down and charged. The sound of screaming merged with the sound of breaking glass. Rastun brought up his Glock, but held his fire. He didn't know if any civilians were outside the restaurant in the line of fire.

Several people rushed out the front doors. Others stood against the wall, frozen in fear. The Point Pleasant Monster looked to the ones running.

Rastun put his pistol down on a nearby table. He picked up a chair and hurled it. It struck the monster just below the neck.

It swung toward him. Rastun grabbed another chair.

Someone dashed out of the kitchen. It was Karen, holding a fire extinguisher. White spray blasted the monster. It hissed and trashed about, knocking over chairs and tables.

Rastun hurried across the dining area to the four people pressed against the wall, eyes wide with terror.

"Get outta here!" He grabbed a woman by the arm and pulled her away from the wall. "Go! Go! Go!"

The woman ran for the door. The other three followed. Karen sprayed the Point Pleasant Monster again. Its tail whipped around and knocked over a table and three chairs.

Rastun snatched up his Glock and ran back to Karen, giving the enraged monster a wide berth.

"Time to go." He clutched her shoulder and yanked her toward the kitchen. They sprinted through the swinging door. Ashlee stood next to the cook.

"Dining area's clear." Rastun ran to the metal door and threw back the deadbolt. "Karen bought us some time with the fire extinguisher. Let's get out of here."

He flung the door open. Karen, carrying Ashlee, went through first. The cook followed.

A thud went through the kitchen. Rastun turned.

The monster tried to force its way through the kitchen door. The walls around it buckled.

"This thing just doesn't quit." Rastun went through the back door and slammed it shut. He spotted a large plastic garbage can next to him, filled to the rim. He tipped it over in front of the door and took off running.

"Jack!"

Rastun saw Karen standing on the sidewalk with Ashlee.

"What do we do now?" she asked.

"Keep moving."

They ran across the street. Sirens wailed in the night. Lots of sirens, growing louder by the second. It sounded like the entire Point Pleasant Police Department was headed for the boardwalk.

They turned a corner and stopped near the front yard of a two-story white and blue wooden house. Rastun took deep breaths, thinking. Should they wait for the cops to arrive? Should they try for his car? It was well over a mile away. Could they make it? For some reason, the monster had a hard on for them.

Why us? They hadn't made the pursuit easy. Most predators would have given up by now. What made them special? Did they give off a scent it really liked? Their suntan lotion? Residual smells from their dinner?

It didn't matter. The ugly bastard wanted to eat them. Rastun was determined not to let that happen.

So how do you do it, smart guy? His Glock was useless. He sure as hell wasn't going to go one-on-one with it with his little tactical knife.

Rastun looked around and spotted a mailbox attached to a wooden post along the curb. A small motorhome was parked in the driveway.

Now he had an idea.

He ran to the mailbox and tried pulling it out of the ground. It wouldn't budge. He took out his Glock and fired two rounds. They tore through the wooden post. Rastun gave it a shove. It fell over.

"What are you doing?" asked Karen.

"You'll see." He lifted the post over his head and slammed it against the sidewalk once, twice. The mailbox snapped off. He took off his t-shirt and tied it around the top of the post. Rastun dashed across the sand-covered front yard to the motorhome and crawled under it. He took out his lighter and flicked it on. The fuel tank was just to his left. He snapped off the lighter, got his tactical knife and rammed it into the tank. Gasoline spilled onto the driveway.

Rastun crawled out from beneath the motorhome and grabbed the wooden post. He shoved it under the punctured fuel tank, soaking the t-shirt with gasoline.

Karen screamed.

Rastun spun around.

The Point Pleasant Monster rounded the corner of the house. It lowered its head and charged.

"Karen!"

Rastun jumped up and shoved Karen and Ashlee out of the way. All three toppled onto the sand. Ashlee shrieked. The monster rushed by. It slammed into the motorhome. The boxy vehicle went up on two wheels and tipped over.

Rastun rolled off Karen and Ashlee and got to one knee. He held the lighter next to the gasoline-soaked t-shirt and flicked it.

Nothing.

"Oh c'mon. Not now!"

The Point Pleasant Monster moved toward him.

He flicked the lighter again.

Whoosh! The t-shirt went up in flames.

Rastun stood and thrust out his makeshift torch. The monster hissed and backed off.

He thrust the torch at the beast again. It backed up further, then cut to the right.

Toward Karen and Ashlee.

Rastun leapt into the monster's path. He rammed the torch into its mouth.

The monster stumbled backwards. It hissed and spun in a circle. Its tail swung toward Rastun. He jumped out of the way and rolled across the sand. He got back to his feet, torch held out.

The Point Pleasant Monster stomped around the house, still hissing.

"Stay here," he told Karen and took off after it.

He ran around the house. The monster loped back toward the boardwalk as Rastun dug out his cell phone and called Ehrenberg.

"Jack, are you and Karen all right?"

"We're fine. I've got eyes on the monster. It's retreating to the boardwalk."

"Retreating?"

"It came after me and Karen again," Rastun told him. "I shoved a torch in its mouth."

"Where did you get a torch?"

"I'll explain later. How far out are you?"

There was a pause before Ehrenberg answered. "According to the GPS, we're about a mile-and-a-half from the boardwalk."

Rastun watched the monster scramble up the boardwalk. It smashed through the wooden railing on the other side and jumped onto the beach.

He kept after it. The sirens grew louder. The police couldn't be more than a block away.

Rastun went up on the boardwalk and stopped by the shattered railing. He watched the darkened silhouette of the Point Pleasant Monster enter the surf swim out to sea.

"Randy, you might as well back off the gas. The monster's gone back into the ocean.

"Dammit." A pause. "All right. You and Karen get back to *Bold Fortune.* I'll have Captain Keller scrounge as much fuel as he can and we'll try to track it down."

"We're on our way. See you soon."

Rastun put the cell phone back in his pocket and turned around.

"Freeze!"

Four Point Pleasant cops stood on the other side of the boardwalk, guns pointed at him.

"I'm Jack Rastun! I'm with the FUBI!"

"Drop the torch! Get on the ground now!"

He was about to identify himself again, but stopped. To the cops, he was a shoeless, shirtless stranger carrying a torch.

Rastun threw the torch onto the sand and got on his knees. Two cops hustled over to him, while the other two kept their pistols trained on him.

"What the hell do you think you're doing?" asked one officer as he handcuffed Rastun.

"Oh, just taking a beautiful woman for a stroll on the beach and getting chased by a sea monster. You know, typical date night stuff."

THIRTEEN

The cops took Rastun's Glock, knife, lighter, cell phone, keys and wallet before they handcuffed him. One cop, a sergeant named Graffanino, asked him, "Where are your shoes, sir?"

"Back on the beach."

"Where's your shirt?"

"That's on the beach, too. But it's probably a pile of ash by now."

Graffanino furrowed his brow. "And why were you carrying a gun and a torch?"

"I was fighting the Point Pleasant Monster. The gun wasn't working, so I made a torch. That worked."

Graffanino drew his head back, an expression of disbelief on his face.

"Yeah, sounds crazy, I know."

Graffanino stared at him in silence for several seconds before checking Rastun's wallet.

"You're really with the FUBI?"

"That's right."

"Is there anyone who can verify it?"

"Call the FUBI operations center. They can connect you with Colonel Salvatore Lipeli. He's my immediate supervisor."

Rastun gave Graffanino the number. More police arrived, along with a couple of ambulances and news vans, as the sergeant spoke on his phone. Rastun watched two paramedics rush into a shop just across from him. He remembered how dozens of people made a mad dash to get indoors. There had to be injuries. He hoped none of them were serious.

Ten minutes later, Graffanino uncuffed him.

"Your info checks out, Mister Rastun." He gave him back his things. "Sorry for the misunderstanding."

"You don't have to apologize, Sergeant. If I saw a half-naked guy with a torch on the boardwalk, I wouldn't take any chances, either."

"So what happened? Nine-one-one got slammed with calls about a monster trashing the boardwalk."

"That's about the size of it." Rastun gave Graffanino a brief rundown of their flight from the Point Pleasant Monster and how he chased it off with his improvised torch. The sergeant looked like he couldn't make up his mind whether to be impressed or skeptical.

"You'd better stick around," Graffanino told him. "We're going to need an official statement from you. Our chief's on the way here, too. I'm sure he'll want to hear this."

Rastun nodded, thinking about how *Bold Fortune* was about to go after the monster without him. He called Ehrenberg.

"Jack! I was just about to call you. Where are you and Karen? We're almost ready to go."

"We're still at the boardwalk. The cops want to talk to me about what happened."

"How long do you think it'll take?"

"I doubt it'll be quick."

Several seconds of silence passed before Ehrenberg responded. "The Point Pleasant Monster couldn't have gotten too far. We have to move on this, now. I'm sorry, Jack, but I can't afford to wait for you."

Rastun let out a frustrated breath. He'd seen first-hand how dangerous the monster was. He needed to be on *Bold Fortune* to protect Ehrenberg and the others should it attack them.

But the cryptozoologist was right. The monster couldn't be that far from shore. Their mission was to capture it, and if they had a shot at doing that, they had to take it.

"Understood." Even though he didn't like being left behind, he had to admit Ehrenberg made the right call. Rastun's respect for him as a leader went up.

"Just be careful," he added. "I put two full clips from my Glock into that thing and it barely noticed."

"It must have a thickened hide, probably to withstand the pressure and cold in the deeper parts of the ocean. That would make it practically bulletproof."

"Which means our tranq darts might be the only thing we have that can take it down."

"Gotcha. We won't take any unnecessary chances."

Rastun had another thought. "Is the Coast Guard sending any cutters after the monster?"

"I don't know. I'm sure they are. I can check."

"Do it, and get one of them to shadow you. Most cutters carry heavy machine guns and twenty-five millimeter cannons. I doubt the monster can survive that kind of firepower if the tranquilizers don't work."

"Will do, Jack."

Ten minutes later, the police chief arrived. Rastun gave him his statement.

"You are one very lucky man, Mister Rastun," the chief said when he finished.

"I won't argue with you there. By the way, any word on how many people were injured?"

"Last I heard, there were twenty injuries, mainly cuts, bruises and sprains. Nothing life-threatening."

"Thank God for that."

"Yeah, it could have been a lot worse," said the chief. "Thank you for what you did, Mister Rastun. You probably saved a lot of lives tonight."

"Just doing my job."

The cops cut him loose. He walked away from the boardwalk and found Karen across the street talking to another officer, probably giving her statement, too. When she finished, Rastun headed over to her.

"Jack." She hugged him. "Are you okay?"

"I'm fine. You?"

She looked up at him and nodded. Rastun felt a slight shiver go through her. With the danger past, she was likely dwelling on how close she came to dying.

That thought made him hug her tighter.

"Where's Ashlee?"

"She's with the police. They're trying to find her parents."

"Good." Rastun told her that the rest of the FUBI expedition had already set out to try and find the Point Pleasant Monster.

"So what are we supposed to do in the meantime?" asked Karen.

Before Rastun could answer, his cell phone rang. It was Colonel Lipeli.

"Doctor Ehrenberg called and told us what happened. Are you and Miss Thatcher all right?"

"We're fine, sir. Not so much as a scratch."

"Good to hear. I'm with Director Lynch right now. We also have Roland Parker and Nathan Hipper with us."

Rastun knew about Roland Parker, the billionaire philanthropist who played a huge part in setting up the FUBI. As for the other man...

"Who's Nathan Hipper?"

"Our liaison with the Department of Agriculture."

Rastun stifled a groan. The FUBI also received funding from the Department of Agriculture. Since that was federal money, it came with strings attached. One of those strings had to be Hipper.

Lynch asked for a report on the Point Pleasant Monster attack. Rastun put the phone on speaker so Karen could participate as well. They were explaining how they found and rescued Ashlee when Hipper interrupted.

"You actually took that kid with you? What if her parents file kidnapping charges? What if they sue the FUBI for endangering their daughter?"

"What were we supposed to do?" Karen blurted. "Leave her there to get eaten?"

When Hipper didn't respond, they continued, running down their flight through the amusement stall and the monster's attack on the pizza parlor.

"My God, we could be talking tens, maybe hundreds of thousands of dollars in damage." Hipper's voice went up an octave. "The owners of those businesses could blame us for it. We have to be mindful of lawsuits."

Rastun clenched his jaw, pushing down his rising anger for this damn bureaucrat. "I was trying to be mindful of staying alive."

When Rastun told them about his makeshift torch and the motorhome getting wrecked, Hipper completely lost it.

"Now you're actually vandalizing someone's property! Oh my God, we are going to get sued over this. Couldn't you have just waited for the cops to show up instead of playing action hero?"

"Yeah, we could have just sat and waited for the cops. But you know what would have happened if we had done that?"

"What?"

"You'd have two less people on the payroll, jackass!"

"No need for insults, Jack," said Lipeli.

Actually, Rastun felt there was a need to insult Hipper. The man was a typical bureaucrat. No imagination, no initiative, afraid to make a tough decision because he might get in trouble if it went wrong.

The kind of guy whose sole purpose in life was to be a pain in the ass to people in the field.

Rastun kept those thoughts to himself and answered Lipeli with a, "Yes, sir."

"It sounds like you and Miss Thatcher were very lucky tonight," said Parker.

"Sometimes it pays to be lucky rather than good."

"True, but if you run into that monster again, I wouldn't count on your luck holding out."

"I agree, sir."

"Colonel," Parker said to Lipeli. "Do we have better weapons that can kill the Point Pleasant Monster if that becomes our only option?"

"The FUBI doesn't, but I do know someone who does."

"Then get in touch with him tonight," ordered Lynch. "I don't care if you have to wake him up. The sooner we get those weapons to our people, the better I'll feel, and I think the better they'll feel."

"I'll get right on that," replied Lipeli. "Just sit tight, Captain. Help's on the way."

"Much appreciated, sir."

When the call ended, Rastun and Karen headed back to the beach to retrieve their shoes.

"So what now?" asked Karen as they walked toward Vargo's parking lot. "*Bold Fortune's* out to sea. Who knows when they'll be back?"

"Not much we can do. We might as well find a hotel and crash for the night."

"We should also stop somewhere and get some fresh clothes." Karen stared at his bare torso. "Um, I guess you could use a new shirt." She sounded uncertain, like she'd rather have him walk around shirtless.

As they neared Rastun's car, a female voice called out, "Excuse me. Excuse me."

Rastun saw a short woman with curled brown hair hurrying up to them. His eyes widened when he noticed Ashlee beside her, hand-in-hand.

"Are you Jack Rastun and Karen Thatcher?"

"We are," he answered. "I take it you're Ashlee's mother."

"I am. We got separated when everyone started running from that monster. I tried to go back for her, but I couldn't get through the crowd. The police told me what you did and I... I had to find you, and..." Ashlee's mother threw herself at Rastun and gave him a crushing hug. "Thank you." Her voice cracked. "Thank you so much. You saved my baby's life."

"You're welcome."

She then hugged Karen. "There's no way I can repay you for this."

"You don't have to. We just did what we had to do."

Karen bent down to hug Ashlee before she and her mother left.

"I wish that Hipper guy could have seen this," said Karen. "That doesn't look like a mother who's going to press charges against us."

Rastun snorted. "Hipper doesn't know shit."

***

They drove to a Wal-Mart a few miles away. When they entered, one of the employees, a pudgy, middle-aged woman with brown hair, walked up to Rastun.

"I'm sorry, sir, but you have to wear a shirt to enter the store."

"Ma'am, I'm well aware of the rule and respect it, but I'm asking you to cut me some slack. We had our first date tonight and it almost ended with us being eaten by the Point Pleasant Monster."

The woman gave him an unsure look. "Um…uh, I think I should call my manager."

She walked away. Rastun and Karen had to wait a few minutes before she returned.

"My manager said a monster really did attack the boardwalk. He saw it on the news. He said you can come in, so long as the first thing you buy is a shirt."

"That's my plan."

Rastun and Karen went their separate ways, with him heading for the men's department. He passed a couple of teenage girls who gave him admiring looks. A white-haired woman who had to be in her seventies gave him a big smile.

Even one guy gave him a big smile.

He snatched a plain green polo shirt from the rack and went to the nearest checkout counter to pay for it. He quickly put it on and continued shopping, picking up socks, underwear, a pair of pants, another shirt and some toiletries. Karen met up with him and they paid for their things and left.

A mile down the road they found a Super 8 motel. Rastun got a room on the second floor. Karen's room was two doors down from him. First thing he did was strip off his clothes and take a nice, long shower. Once he dried himself off, he turned on the TV. The local stations, FOX News and CNN all ran live coverage of the Point Pleasant Monster attack. Were his parents watching the news? Did any of the broadcasts mention his and Karen's involvement?

I guess I should call them.

Rastun did. All he said was that he and Karen had been chased by the monster and they got away. He saw no reason to mention all their close calls and his hand-to-claw combat. That would just make Mom freak out.

She freaked out anyway.

"Is it possible you could find a job where you're not likely to get killed?"

"People might have died if I wasn't here." *Karen might have died.* A stab of fear went through him at that thought.

"Then will you please be careful. I spent too much time worrying about you when you were in Iraq and Afghanistan. I shouldn't have to worry about you eighty miles from our house."

Mom did calm down, a little, by the time they said their good-byes. Rastun just hit the END button when he realized his mother hadn't asked him a single question about Karen. He figured she would want to know about a new woman in his life, especially considering how bad things ended between him and Marie.

She was probably more concerned about me getting eaten than my love life.

He stood in the middle of the room, thinking about the monster charging Karen. One minute they were lying on the sand, kissing. The next she could have been...

What if...

Rastun did not want to finish that thought.

He pocketed his cell phone, left his room and walked the short distance to Karen's room. He knocked.

Karen opened the door, wearing a t-shirt and shorts. She carried a towel in one hand and her hair was damp. She probably just finished taking a shower herself.

"Hey, Jack." Karen stepped aside to invite him in.

"Hey."

"What's up?"

"I just wanted to see how you're doing."

"I'm fine." She looked away from him and rubbed the towel over her wet hair.

"You sure?"

"Yes, I'm fine," Karen snapped, then crossed the room. She stopped in front of the mirror over the bathroom sink, clutching her towel. She shivered.

Rastun had seen this from soldiers in Iraq and Afghanistan. He'd even gone through it himself. During firefights, they dodged bullets and RPGs. There was no time to be scared. Training kicked in. They reacted to the threat and neutralized it. Hours later, when all was quiet, it sank in just how close they came to dying. If they had waited a second longer to duck, a bullet would have taken off their head. If they hadn't moved from one piece of cover to another, a mortar round would have landed right on top of them. It was a sobering and scary experience for him and many other soldiers.

Rastun put a hand on her shoulder. "There's no shame in being scared."

Karen spun around. Her face scrunched in anger, as though she'd been offended by his words. She then bit her lip and looked down.

"You don't think I was scared back there?" he said. "You don't think I was scared when I was in Iraq and Afghanistan? Anyone who says they're not scared in situations like that is lying or they're a fool. You're not a liar or a fool."

Karen moved away from him. She stopped at the foot of the bed and wiped her cheek with the towel.

Rastun walked up behind her, placing both hands on her shoulders.

"When that monster was coming at me," said Karen. "I thought about Emily. She's only ten. Her father...her father's useless. The thought of not watching her grow up, of never being there for her again..." A sob escaped her throat.

"Well, you are going to be there for her. You made it out alive. That's what matters."

She turned to face him, again using the towel to wipe her eyes. "I wouldn't have if it wasn't for you. I never had anyone risk their life to save mine."

"You saved my ass, too, when you came out with that fire extinguisher. A lot of people would have frozen up. You didn't. You kept your head and you kept that little girl safe. You did good back there."

"Thank you." Karen dropped her towel, wrapped her arms around Rastun and kissed him. She put a hand on his cheek. "You really are one of the good guys."

"I try to be."

They kissed again, more intense. Karen grabbed the back of Rastun's shirt and pulled it up and over his head. He yanked off her t-shirt. They fell onto the bed.

FOURTEEN

"GEDDOWN!"

A monstrous roar swept over the street as dozens of rifles and machines guns opened up. Bullets cracked through the air.

Captain Jack Rastun looked toward the Humvees. Some of the hostages were already in the boxy vehicles, others crouched next to them. Many of them screamed.

Flame burst from the window of a nearby building. Rastun glanced at the Humvee behind him. Sergeant First Class Wendell Hewitt knelt by the hood, smoke coming from the grenade launcher under his M-4 carbine.

"Everyone mount up!" Rastun radioed the others and climbed onboard the Light Strike Vehicle. "Time to get the hell out of Dodge."

He got into the cage of the dune buggy-like vehicle and grabbed the handles of the .50 caliber. A man in olive drab fatigues appeared in the doorway of a nearby building, clutching an AK-47. Rastun mashed the fire button. The huge machine gun chugged. Chunks of wood exploded around the doorframe. The gunman spun and fell. The LSV's driver, Branch, raked another window with his M240 light machine gun.

A bright orange contrail streaked toward them.

"RPG!" Rastun yelled.

A sharp fluttering sound passed by him. Seconds later, an explosion tore open the building where they'd just freed the State Department delegation.

"Everyone okay?"

A chorus of "yeahs" came through his headset. Rastun leaned forward. "Branch, gun—"

Something moved to his right. An overweight woman ran by, screaming frantically.

"Ma'am! Get back here!"

Rastun slid out of the LSV's cage. A muscular black man in desert fatigues raced by him.

"Ma'am!" shouted Sergeant Jim Tate. "Come back!"

Rastun's feet hit the ground when the woman went into spasms. Moments later she stumbled and fell. Tate spun into the wall and collapsed.

"Tate!"

His eyes swept the rooftop. He spotted a machine gunner on a rampart. Rastun ran toward Tate and the woman, firing his M-4. The gunner tumbled off the roof.

"Tate! Tate!" Rastun dropped next to the unmoving Ranger. His stomach clenched when he saw blood pouring out of Tate's throat and head.

He crawled to the woman, who lay face down. He grabbed her shoulder, turned her over…

…and stared into the face of Karen Thatcher.

Blaring music drowned out the roar of gunfire.

***

Rastun's eyes snapped open. He was tangled in twisted and sweat-soaked sheets.

Just a dream.

He shut his eyes, trying to push the images of Western Sahara from his mind. How many times had he suffered through that nightmare? And Karen? Why had she been part of that dream?

The music continued. It was "The Trooper" by Iron Maiden.

Rastun reached down to the floor and pulled the cell phone from his pants pocket. He checked the display as Karen groaned and pushed herself up on her elbows.

It read RANDY E.

"Mornin', Doc."

"Jack, how are you?"

"Fine. You guys have any luck out there?"

"The only luck we had was no luck. We searched all night and couldn't find a trace of the monster."

"Damn," Rastun muttered as Karen curled up beside him.

"Damn is right. We're on our way back to the marina. I have a meeting with the mayor and police chief at nine. They're having a teleconference with the mayors of the surrounding towns and the Coast Guard. Looks like they're going to recommend closing the beaches."

"After what happened last night I don't see where they have any choice. You need me there?"

"Nah, I can handle it," said Ehrenberg. "Captain Keller and his crew will be refueling and restocking *Bold Fortune* while I'm gone. I want us back out to sea around noon."

Rastun glanced down at Karen, who rested her hand on his chest and rubbed her leg against his.

Fine by me.

"All right, Doc. Karen and I will see you then."

Rastun plopped his cell phone on the nightstand and ran his fingers down Karen's back. She grinned and kissed his chin.

"Good morning," she said.

"Mornin'." He kissed Karen.

"So was that Randy?" she asked.

"Yup."

"Sounds like they didn't find the monster."

Rastun told her about his conversation with Ehrenberg, including how *Bold Fortune* wasn't scheduled to get underway until noon.

Karen looked at the alarm clock on the nightstand. "It's almost seven. Looks like we've got a few hours to ourselves. That is, if you're not too worn out."

"Worn out? I'll have you know endurance was a big part of being an Army Ranger. We're conditioned to keep going even past the point of exhaustion."

A huge grin formed on Karen's face. "Lucky me."

Rastun rolled her on her back. Their kissing grew fiercer. His lips moved along her shoulder, her neck, then to her breasts. Karen moaned in delight.

His cell phone rang again.

"Don't answer it," Karen pleaded.

"Sorry. It might be important."

Karen let out a frustrated groan. "Damn soldiers and your 'duty calls' bullshit."

Rastun kissed her cheek and picked up the phone. A jolt of surprise went through him when he saw the name on the display.

WENDELL H.

"What the hell?" He glanced at Karen, who traced a finger along his chest, then looked back at the phone.

This better be good.

He put the phone to his ear. "Geek?"

"A cheery good morning to you, Cap'n," said Wendell "Geek" Hewitt.

"What the hell are you doing calling at seven in the morning?"

"What, no, 'Good to hear from you, Sergeant?' No, 'Geek, what a pleasant surprise?' No, 'I'm glad you're coming here to help us with the Point Pleasant Monster?'"

"What?" Rastun sat up straighter in bed.

"Colonel Lipeli called my boss at Aster Technologies last night, asked if we had any equipment that can take down a big, nasty, pissed-off sea monster. And, of course, we do. So they sent me up here with some pretty kick ass stuff."

"Nice to know you still have my back."

"I always will, Cap'n."

"So where are you at now?"

"The Point Pleasant Marina," Geek answered. "Just pulled in about five minutes ago. I had to do an all-nighter to pack and drive up here. So when can you get down here?"

Karen slid on top of him. She pressed her breasts against his chest and kissed his shoulder.

"In a little while."

***

After another go-around in bed, Rastun and Karen showered, changed and headed to the lobby to check out.

"So who exactly is this Geek?" asked Karen.

"He was my senior NCO in the Rangers. Damn good man to have around when the you-know-what hits the fan."

"Why do you call him Geek?"

Rastun gave her a sly grin. "You'll see."

After checking out, they got in Rastun's car and drove to the marina. He saw a black Escalade SUV parked at the far corner of the parking lot. Next to it stood large, muscular man with close-cropped dark hair and black horn-rimmed glasses.

"That's the Geek?" Karen leaned forward, mouth open in surprise.

"Yup."

"I didn't expect him to be so big."

"Yeah, he's got some size on him."

"'Some size?'" Karen turned to him with an incredulous look. "He's built like a tank."

Rastun parked next to the Escalade and got out. Geek stared at him, grinning, his large arms folded across his chest, arms that made Rastun's look like spaghetti strands.

"Great to see you again, Geek."

"Likewise, Cap'n." They clasped hands and slapped one another on the back, Geek's blow nearly knocking the wind out of Rastun.

"Look at you." Geek shook his head. "You're a civilian now and you still find ways to almost get yourself killed."

"It wasn't intentional, believe me. And this still beats being a rent-a-cop at a zoo."

"Ha! If you really were just a rent-a-cop, you'd be getting crapped out a sea monster's ass right now."

"I could be getting crapped out a sea monster's ass right now regardless of what I am," said Rastun. "That was a damn close call we had last night."

"Well, don't worry. I brought some stuff to even the odds." Geek looked to Karen. "New friend?"

"This is our expedition's photographer, Karen Thatcher. Karen, this is former Sergeant First Class Wendell Hewitt, better known as the Geek."

"Nice to meet you," she said.

"Likewise, ma'am." Geek shook her hand.

"Please, just Karen."

"You got it."

"So, what do you have for us?" asked Rastun.

"Let me show you."

They gathered at the rear of the Escalade.

"Sweet ride, by the way," said Rastun.

"Thanks, but it's not mine, unfortunately. It belongs to Aster Technologies. It's got some pretty cool bells and whistles. Nav system, real-time weather report, Bluetooth connection, GPS tracker, Kevlar lining in the doors, bullet-resistant glass."

"Those last couple of things sound excessive," said Karen.

"Not when you consider the kind of equipment Aster has."

"What exactly does your company do?"

"Aster Technologies produces weapons and gear for soldiers and law enforcement personnel," answered Geek. "I went to work for them as a field tester when I left the Army."

He opened the rear hatch. Several dark cases filled the cargo hold. Geek pulled one out, set it on the ground and opened it.

"Whoa." Rastun's eyes widened.

"Oh my God." Karen gaped at the weapon in the case. "What the hell is that?"

"A USAS-12 semi-automatic shotgun." Geek pointed his hand at the weapon, which resembled a bulked up M-16 rifle with a bigger barrel and longer clip. "One of the most kick-ass shotguns in the world."

"You are the man." Rastun slapped Geek on the back.

"Colonel Lipeli said you needed more firepower. I'd say this qualifies, especially with the ammo I brought. Aster gave me a ton of their sabot rounds."

"Sabot?" Karen gave Geek a puzzled look.

"It's a special round that fires an armor-piercing dart. I've fired those things through brick walls. Trust me, they'll put down your sea monster."

"If we have to," said Rastun. "Remember, our main goal is to capture the Point Pleasant Monster alive."

"I know, and I came prepared for that. I brought a bunch of flash-bang grenades to distract it or stun it, and we've got this."

Geek retrieved another case and opened it.

"Behold. The Aster Model Seven dart launcher."

Rastun examined the weapon. It had a suppressor on its thin barrel with a foregrip and a four-round cylinder. "Nice."

"We designed it as a silent kill system for the special ops boys to take out enemy sentries. It's got a built-in laser sight, too. Let me show you the darts."

Geek removed a small metal box from the cargo area and opened it. It contained small glass cases with ten needles each. Eight had blue feathery tails. The other two had red tails.

"What's the deal with the colors?"

"Very important you pay attention here." Geek held out one of the cases. "The ones with blue tails are your standard tranq darts. The red ones you want to be very, *very* careful with. That silent kill system I was telling you about, this is what puts the 'kill' in it. Each dart is full of a toxin derived from a Golden Poison Frog."

"Oh my God." Karen's jaw dropped. "Are you serious?"

"Holy shit, Geek. They're one of deadliest animals on the planet. One drop of their toxin can kill a man like that." Rastun snapped his fingers.

"Believe me, I know. I got lectured out the wazoo on these darts."

"You did bring the antidote with you?" asked Karen.

"You bet. Standard procedure. But unless you have someone standing next to you with the injector right over your arm, you're pretty much fu—" Geek paused and stared at Karen. "Screwed. But we had to have something that works instantly. The special ops boys can't afford to have a sentry linger long."

Rastun stared at the dart. "I'd say we're much better prepared for round two with the Point Pleasant Monster." He turned to Geek. "Thanks, Geek. You stickin' around?"

"Oh yeah. Aster considers this a field test, and they need a representative on hand to monitor it, so I'm here for the duration."

"Well then, welcome to the wonderful world of monster hunting."

FIFTEEN

"I think this is exactly what we're looking for," Piet said as he looked at the stubby boat bobbing in the water. He turned to the portly, balding man next to him on the pier. "You said you restored this yourself?"

"Yes I did," replied Alan Murphy, a retired real estate broker and boat enthusiast. "It pretty much got trashed during Hurricane Sandy. It was due to be retired anyway, so the government put it up for auction. I got it for a bargain."

Piet nodded and jumped onto the boat. He walked around the compact island, then to the stern. "How are the engines?" he asked, making a conscious effort to hide his accent.

"Brand new. They're even better than the originals. I can get a max speed of twenty-eight knots."

Piet stared from stern to bow. "This boat looks to be in good shape. But I'd like to take it out for a test before I make my final decision."

"No problem," said Murphy. "Let's go."

Murphy stepped onboard, as did a tall blond man with a firm body. Olef, a member of Piet's mercenary team.

Not that Murphy had any idea they were mercenaries.

Murphy untied the boat from the pier and started the engine. He piloted it out to the middle of Long Island's Great South Bay before letting Piet take the wheel. The boat plowed through the waves at a steady speed. Piet cut the wheel left and right, testing the maneuverability.

He steered the boat back to the pier. Murphy tied it up and turned back to him. "Handles well, doesn't she?"

"She does."

"Then I think you found a boat for your movie. So how about we talk price? I'm thinking an even hundred thousand."

"That might be a little much for my producer. How about seventy thousand?"

Piet and Murphy haggled for another minute or so until they settled on a price of $88,000. After they shook on it, Piet took out his smart phone and began an electronic deposit from one of Gunderson's shell companies into Murphy's account.

"So what's this movie about again?" asked Murphy.

"It's about a group of treasure hunters."

"Anyone famous in it?"

"We're still in the middle of casting. We haven't hired anyone yet." Piet looked up from his phone. "All right. The money should be in your account now."

Murphy took out his phone, tapped the screen a few times and nodded. "Eighty-eight thousand, all there." He gave Piet the keys. "All yours. Pleasure doing business with you. Good luck with your movie."

"The pleasure was mine, Mister Murphy. Thank you."

With a parting smile, Murphy walked back to his house.

"We should kill him," said Olef.

"That is unnecessary," Piet told him.

"When did you become squeamish about killing?"

"It has nothing to do with being squeamish. Killing Murphy would not be practical."

"Since when did you become practical about killing?"

Piet grinned. "Alan Murphy has friends and family. If we kill him and dump his body, they will call the police, who will investigate. We risk exposure if that happens. But if he is alive, he enjoys his money, thinks he really did sell this boat to some Hollywood people and no one is suspicious of us."

He slapped Olef on the shoulder. "Don't worry. When the time comes, we'll do our fair share of killing."

"I certainly hope so."

Olef went back to the car while Piet got into the boat. He started it up and headed south toward New Jersey.

It was late afternoon when he reached the docks in Barnegat Township. Heinrich and Doern, the other two mercenaries in his team, waited for him on one of the ramps with a pick-up truck and boat trailer. Once the boat was secured to the trailer, Heinrich slowly walked around it.

"This is the boat you wanted, isn't it?" Piet asked the Austrian.

"What? Oh yes." Heinrich gazed at it with an appraising eye. "Yes, this is indeed a forty-one foot utility boat."

"You doubted I'd be able to get it?"

"*Nein.* I didn't doubt you, just the seller's website. You know as well as I do you can't trust everything on the internet."

"Too true," said Piet.

"He painted it gray, though. No matter. We have plenty of white and orange paint to turn it back into a Coast Guard vessel."

"And the uniforms?"

"The first two sets should arrive at our P.O. box tomorrow," Heinrich answered. "They're the older blue working uniforms, not the current ones."

"No matter. To most civilians, one Coast Guard uniform is the same as another. They won't be able to tell the difference."

"A real American Coast Guardsman would."

"If they stop us," said Piet. "Which I doubt they will. That's the reason you wanted this particular boat, isn't it? Authenticity?"

After his research on the U.S. Coast Guard, Heinrich had been insistent they get this boat from Alan Murphy. The 41-foot utility boat was being phased out, but enough remained in service that it wouldn't raise suspicion from any actual Coast Guard crews they encountered.

Most importantly, it would allow Piet and his men to get close to the FUBI expedition should they capture the Point Pleasant Monster. Then that four million dollar bonus from Gunderson would be his.

And so would that photographer bitch.

SIXTEEN

Rastun knew he should have changed the channel before he sat down to lunch.

"Is the FUBI out of its element in the ocean?" the dark-haired male anchor asked. "That's what some along the Jersey Shore are asking after nearly two weeks of fruitless searching for the Point Pleasant Monster. Here's CNN's Monica Lopez with more."

"This is gonna be good," Rastun muttered. He stared at the TV in *Bold Fortune's* salon/conference room. Just a couple of days ago the press hailed him and Karen as heroes for driving off the monster. He doubted this story would be as glowing.

"Over the past year, the FUBI's success at finding cryptids has been confined to land," a female voice spoke over footage of a Bigfoot lumbering through the woods. "Field expeditions have discovered several Bigfoot colonies in California and the Pacific Northwest. But the fledgling organization may have met its match when it comes to creatures that live in the water. The FUBI has conducted unsuccessful searches for alleged monsters in Lake Champlain and Chesapeake Bay. Now they are engaged in their most important search ever, to find the Point Pleasant Monster. Five deaths have been attributed to this creature, including that of Temple University football star Glenn Flynn."

Security camera footage of the monster on the boardwalk played while Lopez talked. "Despite the Point Pleasant Monster's recent rampage along a Jersey Shore boardwalk, the FUBI expedition led by noted cryptozoologist Doctor Randy Ehrenberg has failed to capture the beast."

A portly, balding man with glasses appeared on screen. The graphic identified him as Point Pleasant Borough Councilman Sean McKinney.

"It makes me wonder if the FUBI knew what it was doing assigning a guy who's spent most of his time looking for Bigfoot to lead an expedition to find a sea monster," McKinney said. "There have to be cryptozoologists that are more qualified than Doctor Ehrenberg. Maybe if they got one of them, they would have found this monster and we wouldn't have tourists and residents leaving the town in droves."

The screen showed a line of vehicles creeping across the bridge spanning the Manasquan River, heading out of Point Pleasant. The next image was of a deserted boardwalk.

"While initial reports of the Point Pleasant Monster had people flocking to the Jersey Shore, the boardwalk attack is now driving them off. Officials with the Point Pleasant Chamber of Commerce estimate the number of tourists has dropped by more than sixty-five percent in the last week. That's causing concern among boardwalk merchants who make most of their money this time of year."

A skinny man with glasses and black ponytail appeared. Dave Ward, owner of Dave's Best Boardwalk Dogs and Fries.

"That monster was actually good for business when it just stayed in the water," he said. "But ever since it came on land, I'm lucky if I get ten customers during lunchtime. If this keeps up, how am I gonna put food on the table for my family? How am I gonna pay my bills? Why can't the FUBI find something that big?"

A lithe woman with a heart-shaped face and long black hair appeared, holding a microphone. Monica Lopez in the flesh, Rastun presumed.

"FUBI Director Edward Lynch has told CNN that Doctor Ehrenberg has conducted searches for aquatic cryptids in the past. He also wants to remind everyone that the search area encompasses hundreds of square miles, which means the Point Pleasant Monster has plenty of places to hide. Still, that might not be much consolation to the numerous business owners whose livelihoods depend on the tourists the monster is now chasing away."

Rastun glared at the TV, crushing his half-eaten roast beef and cheese sandwich between his fingers.

"Well, at least they did throw us a bone at the end," said Geek, who sat to Rastun's right.

"Not much of one. Typical stupid reporting, just like when we were over in Iraq. Making it look like we're screwing up every single thing, but God forbid they offer any kind of solution."

"I don't know about that," Hernandez chimed in. "It seemed like their solution was for us to leave."

"That's not a solution," said Rastun. "That's quitting."

Karen looked at the TV, then to Rastun. "Well, I'm sure they'll change their tune when we find the monster."

"No, they're more likely to bitch about why it took us so long to find it."

"C'mon, Jack. Don't let them get to you like that." Karen patted his hand.

He turned to her and grinned.

That's when Raleigh Pilka entered the salon. The marine biologist slowed his pace as he neared the table.

"Doctor Pilka." Geek nodded to him.

Pilka didn't respond. His face muscles tightened as he stared at Karen's hand on top of Rastun's. She met his harsh gaze with one of her own.

Rastun felt Karen squeeze his hand tighter.

Pilka stormed past the table and exited the salon.

"He's in a cheery mood today," Geek commented.

Rastun turned to Karen. Her eyes shifted from the door Pilka had exited to him, then to the table.

What the hell is going on between those two? He certainly couldn't ask Karen now, with Geek and Hernandez around. He'd have to wait till later. Part of him wondered if he should even bring it up. Things were great between him and Karen. Why rock the boat?

No. Something major had happened between her and Pilka. So far it hadn't interfered with their mission, but could it interfere with their relationship?

He would have to confront Karen about this. She needed to be forthcoming with him.

Like you've been forthcoming about why you and Marie broke up?

After lunch, Rastun retrieved his Aster 7 from the weapons locker. He tried to force his concerns about Karen and Pilka to the back of his mind. Time to focus on the mission.

He paced up and down the deck of *Bold Fortune,* scanning the Atlantic with his binoculars every few minutes. He saw nothing but waves.

As Rastun made his way aft, he saw Geek looking out his binoculars. "This is some gig, Cap'n. Putter around the ocean in a nice boat and just soak up the sun."

"You sound disappointed."

"Hey, I came here expecting to see an actual sea monster."

"Then go online," said Rastun. "There are videos of the boardwalk attack all over the internet."

"I mean I want to see it with my own eyes."

"I have. Trust me, the experience is overrated."

"Maybe you should go back to being a zoo security guard," said Geek. "A lot less dangerous."

"And a lot more boring," replied Rastun. "Nah. Even after getting chased all over Point Pleasant by a sea monster, this is the right job for me."

"That's good to hear. Angela's been worried about you adjusting to civilian life."

"Your wife has enough on her plate with you and three kids. She doesn't need to waste any worry on me."

"Angela's worry well will never run dry. Especially with you. You were her favorite officer."

A smile spread across Rastun's face. He'd always had a soft spot in his heart for Geek's wife. Angela was so down to earth, a welcome change from the wives of some of his fellow officers who based their social status on their husband's rank. Angela Hewitt just wanted to be a good wife, a good mother and treated the men in Rastun's unit like extended family. He'd always pictured Marie becoming just like Geek's wife.

Of course, that'll never happen.

"Smile, guys."

Rastun and Geek turned. Karen stood by the railing, camera up. She snapped a picture of them.

"Don't you get bored taking pictures of us?" asked Rastun.

"I never get bored taking pictures of you." Karen gave him a playful smile.

"And suddenly I feel like a third wheel," said Geek.

Before Rastun could say anything, the door to the bridge slid open. Pilka stepped out. The marine biologist didn't glare at Karen like usual. In fact, he barely paid any attention to her.

"Montebello just got a hit on sonar. He thinks it might be the Point Pleasant Monster."

"Where?" Rastun unslung his Aster 7.

"Twenty-five hundred meters east of us."

Rastun headed to the bow, Geek and Karen behind him. He scanned the ocean with his binoculars.

"I got nothing. What about you guys?"

"Negative," replied Geek, who also looked through binoculars.

"I don't see anything, either," said Karen.

Rastun heard more footsteps behind him. Ehrenberg, Malakov and Hernandez hurried out onto the deck.

Montebello's voice burst from Rastun's walkie-talkie. "Um, hey, everyone. It's Charlie. Can you hear me?"

"Rastun here. I read you five-by-five."

"Huh?"

"That means I can hear you fine."

"Oh. Okay."

The others also confirmed they could hear Montebello over their walkies.

"The contact's two thousand meters east of us," Montebello reported.

"Copy that," said Ehrenberg. "Captain, put us on a direct course with the contact."

"Aye aye, Doctor," Keller answered.

Rastun brought up his Aster 7 and turned to Geek, who had his USAS-12 shotgun. "You know the drill. If the tranqs don't put it down, you take it out."

"Hu-ah." Geek used the Ranger slang for, "Heard, Understood, Acknowledged."

"Don't you dare kill this creature!" Malakov hollered at them.

"Uh-huh," they both muttered.

"I mean it. If you kill this creature, you will both regret it."

"Uh-huh." Rastun and Geek kept their weapons trained on the water.

"Fifteen hundred meters and closing," Montebello announced.

Rastun's eyes swept over the waves, looking for any dark shape, anything out of the ordinary.

He only saw water and whitecaps.

C'mon, show yourself.

"Does anyone see it?" Pilka demanded.

Everyone answered, "No."

"One thousand meters and closing."

Rastun held his breath. The damn thing was still underwater. Would it try to attack *Bold Fortune?* Dr. Malakov had said the Point Pleasant Monster might associate boats with food.

There was a lot of food on this boat.

"Hey, guys!" Montebello blurted. "There's another large contact. Two thousand meters to the south."

"What?" Surprise blazed across Ehrenberg's bearded face.

Pilka headed toward the stern, staring southward.

"I have another contact," Montebello reported. "Another."

"What the hell is this?" Geek's head swept left to right. "A full-scale assault?"

"This can't be." Ehrenberg shook his head.

Rastun's eyes darted from one section of the ocean to another. His finger wrapped around the trigger.

"Um, hey, guys," Montebello said in a subdued tone. "I've got a positive ID on our contacts. It's a pod of pilot whales."

Rastun lowered his Aster 7 and groaned. "Another false alarm."

"Unless pilot whales eat people." Geek tacked on a half-smile.

"Pilot whales eat squid, you dolt," snapped Malakov.

"Jeez, lady, get a sense of humor," Geek muttered under his breath.

Rastun saw a stocky form with a bulbous forehead break the surface. Farther away, another pilot whale poked its head out of the water.

Karen snapped a picture of the first whale, looked to him and shrugged.

"At least it's something."

***

They spent two more days at sea without success. Night had long since fallen by the time *Bold Fortune* docked at the Point Pleasant Marina. Once Hernandez secured the boat to the pier, Rastun and Geek headed down to the storeroom. They sat cross-legged on the floor, with Rastun opening the black plastic case that contained his gun cleaning kit. The pair stripped and cleaned their handguns, the Aster 7 and the USAS-12. They started putting their weapons back together when Dr. Malakov entered the storeroom, followed by Hernandez.

"Must you do that in here?" Malakov sneered, her eyes fixed on Geek's big shotgun.

Geek looked around the room. "Why not? This is such a nice storeroom."

Rastun barely suppressed a laugh.

"Do it somewhere else! I hate guns. They're evil."

"A gun is an inanimate object, Doctor," said Rastun. "It has no feelings, no consciousness. It takes a person to decide whether to use it for good or evil."

"But don't worry," Geek beamed at Malakov. "We'll use it for good, because, well, we're the good guys."

"If I were in charge of this expedition, there wouldn't be one damn gun on this boat."

"If you were in charge of this expedition, Doctor," Rastun reconnected the barrel to the Aster 7, "I'd ask for a transfer."

Malakov stomped the short distance across the room to Rastun. He barely looked up at her.

"Maybe I'll find a way to transfer you out of here. Maybe I'll find a way to get you out of the FUBI period! This is a group dedicated to finding and studying cryptids, not killing them. You and your pet ogre have no place here."

"Uh-huh." Rastun ran a cloth over his Aster 7. "Well, you're certainly entitled to your opinion, whether it's right or wrong."

Malakov's entire body shook in fury. She spun around and stalked off. "Just get those damn guns out of my sight."

"If you don't like guns so much, you can wait outside until we're done," suggested Geek.

"I have to check on our supplies. Randy wants us to do another land search for the Point Pleasant Monster. I have to see what we need to get while we're docked and I need to do it now."

Malakov went through cabinets, drawers and boxes, barking out items they needed to Hernandez. He inputted them into an iPad.

When Geek finished putting together his shotgun, Rastun went to the weapons locker. It had a keypad with a six-digit code that he knew it by heart thanks to one of his favorite memorization tricks. He always used the uniform numbers of Philadelphia athletes. For this code, he went with former Flyers. 28 for Kjell Samuelsson. 15 for Bill Clement. 37 for Eric Desjardins. Rastun and Geek stowed their weapons inside the locker and shut it. Rastun then closed the gun cleaning kit and put it next to the locker.

When he returned to his cabin, he stripped out of his clothes and showered off the day's accumulated sweat and suntan lotion. He put on a t-shirt and shorts and went into the corridor.

Karen's door was halfway open. He peeked inside to find her sitting cross-legged on her bunk, typing on her laptop.

"Hey there."

"Hey." Karen looked up, smiling.

Rastun sat next to her. "Loading up the photo gallery again?"

"Yup."

He put his hands on Karen's shoulders and massaged them. "So how long before you're done?"

"Soon."

"How soon?"

"Soon," she giggled.

"Well, are we talking five minutes? Ten? Twenty?"

"Oh my God, were you born without any patience?"

"Not when it comes to beautiful photographers." Rastun kissed Karen on the cheek, then on her neck.

"You're making it hard to concentrate."

"That's sort of the idea." He gently kissed her neck again.

"Okay. Five minutes."

"What?"

"Give me five minutes," said Karen. "Updating the photo gallery is part of my job description. You wouldn't want me to be in, what is it you soldiers say, um, dereliction of duty."

Rastun let out an exaggerated sigh. "All right. Five minutes. But not one minute more."

He kissed and left her cabin.

Someone stood in the corridor to his right. He turned to find Raleigh Pilka staring at him.

"Doctor." He nodded to him.

Pilka said nothing. His gaze shifted between Rastun and Karen's cabin.

Rastun stepped into his cabin, giving Pilka a parting glance. He slid his door closed.

What is up with those two? This tension between Pilka and Karen started to bother him more than he'd like to admit. Maybe it was time he –

"What do you want?" He heard Karen's muffled voice through the door.

"Are you enjoying yourself?" Pilka asked in a demanding tone.

"What are you talking about?"

"Rubbing your soldier boy in my face."

"Are you kidding me? You really think this is about you?"

"It's what I'd expect from you."

"Newsflash, Raleigh," said Karen. "The world doesn't revolve around you. Sure as hell my world doesn't."

"Do you think I'm stupid?" Pilka's voice rose. "Do you expect me to believe you—"

Rastun slid his door open. Pilka turned around.

"Is there a problem?" Rastun gave the marine biologist a withering glare.

Pilka took a step back, avoiding eye contact with him. "No," he muttered, then ambled toward the salon.

When Pilka disappeared, Rastun looked to Karen. "What was that all about?"

She stared at him in silence, then switched her gaze to her computer. "Nothing."

"Bullcrap."

Karen let out an annoyed sigh. "It's just...don't worry about it."

"Not an option anymore. There's been tension between you and Doctor Pilka from day one. I didn't say anything because it didn't become a detriment to this mission. But after this display, that's changed."

"For God's sake." Karen sprang off her bunk. "Do you have to act like a soldier every damn minute?"

"I have a responsibility to make sure personal problems do not jeopardize this crew's ability to carry out its duty. Now, are you going to tell me what the problem is between you and Doctor Pilka?"

"You really want to know?"

"Yes, I do."

"It's none of your damn business!"

Karen slammed the door in his face.

SEVENTEEN

At the next morning's briefing, Karen seated herself at the other end of the table from Rastun. He fought to keep his concentration on Ehrenberg as he talked about how the Point Pleasant Monster looked similar to the alleged sea monster carcass picked up by a Japanese trawler in 1977. But every once in a while, Rastun's gaze shifted to an unsmiling Karen. Their argument the night before played through his mind.

He glanced at Pilka, who seemed determined not to look at Karen or him.

For reasons both professional and personal, he had to get to the bottom of this.

"These next three days might be our last chance to catch the monster." Ehrenberg's words brought Rastun back to the present.

"What do you mean?" Pilka leaned forward, a stunned look on his face.

"I talked with Director Lynch a little while ago. There've been no sightings of the monster since the boardwalk attack. Lynch, the Coast Guard, and many local government officials believe it's moved on. If we can't find it over the next few days, we'll be recalled."

"No!" Malakov slammed both hands on the table. "You have to convince Lynch we need more time."

"I tried, but they can't keep us out here indefinitely. Plus, the longer the beaches are closed, the more money the towns along the Jersey Shore lose."

"Greedy bastards," Malakov muttered.

"Sorry, Lauren." Ehrenberg frowned. "We just have to do the best we can and hope we find the monster."

He typed on the laptop in front of him. The plasma screen showed a map of The Shore. "We're going to do another expedition on land, in the area around Manahawkin Bay. Lauren, Geek and I will check out the swamps and creeks inland."

Malakov scowled while Geek shot her a friendly smile.

Ehrenberg continued. "Jack and Karen will take a Zodiac and explore some of the islands in the bay. The rest of you will stay with *Bold Fortune* and continue searching open water."

Rastun looked over at Karen. She avoided eye contact.

This is going to be a fun day.

***

Rastun went down to the storeroom to get his Aster 7 and flash/bang grenades from the weapons locker.

"Good morning, sir," Hernandez greeted him while sweeping the deck.

"Hernandez, how are you?"

"Fine, sir. You?"

I've been better. "Same." He punched in the code, then glanced at the deck. The gun-cleaning kit had been moved away from the weapons locker, probably by Hernandez while he was cleaning.

Rastun got his gear and headed up to the deck.

Bold Fortune sailed through the inlet separating Barnegat Light State Park and Island Beach State Park, then turned south toward Manahawkin Bay. After going a few miles, Hernandez and Tamburro helped lower the Zodiacs into the water. Geek, Ehrenberg and Malakov piloted one to the shoreline, while Rastun and Karen headed toward the small islands that dotted the bay.

"We'll check out Sloop Sedge first." Rastun looked at the map on his iPad. "Then Sandy Island, then Marsh Elder Island."

"Fine," Karen replied.

Rastun groaned to himself. *So that's how it's going to be today.*

There wasn't much to Sloop Sedge. The little island was barely 500 feet long and 200 feet wide with lots of trees and three ponds. Rastun and Karen spent nearly an hour on the island, checking for footprints, broken branches, disturbed grass, even scat.

They found nothing.

They kept their conversations to a minimum. Strictly professional. None of the joking and flirting Rastun had become used to.

Next they headed to Sandy Island, much bigger than Sloop Sedge at more than 2,000 feet long and 1,500 feet wide. With the exception of a dock and a couple of buildings, the island consisted only of marshes and ponds. They slogged through the interior, again finding no sign of the Point Pleasant Monster.

Rastun decided to take a lunch break before returning to the Zodiac. He and Karen sat under a tree and pulled MREs from their packs.

"So, can we talk about what happened last night?"

Karen had her MRE opened halfway, then stopped. She looked up at him.

"You want me to say I'm sorry?" Rastun continued. "Fine. I'm sorry. I should have handled things better. But whatever is going on between you and Pilka is out there. So what is it?"

Karen put down her MRE and pulled her legs against her chest. "When I was in college, I took a summer job at the marine institute in Palm Beach."

"That's where Pilka worked."

Karen nodded. "Maybe it was because I was young, but I thought he was so smart, so confident, and he was in great shape back then. The more we worked together, the more...well, you can imagine."

Rastun clenched his jaw. He really didn't want to imagine Karen and Pilka doing ...that.

"So what happened?" he asked.

"We broke up."

"And?"

Karen stared at him, biting her lip.

"C'mon, Karen. I had a couple of bad break-ups when I was in college, but eventually I got over them. Why can't Pilka do the same?"

An uncomfortable silence hung between them. Karen drew a slow breath. "Raleigh was married when we were together."

"Did you know he was married?"

"Yes."

Rastun's face tightened. Dammit! His first relationship since Marie and now...

"Jack, please don't look like that. I know it was stupid, okay? Yes, I was young, but I should have known better. Raleigh's marriage ended because of what we did. That's why he's so hostile around me. I swore I'd never do anything like that again."

Rastun stared hard at the ground. He'd always had a dim view of adultery, maybe more than others. Duty, honor and loyalty had been hammered into him by the Army. Not just as an officer, but as a man. To commit adultery, to cheat on a person you supposedly loved, was a violation of all three values. That might make him old fashioned, but so what? In this day and age, duty, honor and loyalty were more important than ever.

He turned back to Karen, saw the pleading look in her eyes, the regret on her face.

Like she said, she was young.

I was young, too, and I never cheated on my girlfriends.

Not everyone is like you.

Karen had made a mistake, a big mistake. Then again, he'd made a big mistake, too, one that forced him to leave the Army.

"Let he who is without sin cast the first stone."

"That's why you asked me that question, back at the wildlife refuge. About whether I was involved with someone."

Karen again nodded. "Like I said, I'm not going to make that sort of mistake again."

Rastun stared off in thought. His gaze returned to Karen. "Is Raleigh Pilka Emily's father?"

"Yes."

"That guy you said you were engaged to, that was Pilka, right?"

"Yes. We were supposed to get married after he got divorced. Luckily I wised up before saying, 'I do.'"

Karen slid over to him. "I'm sorry, Jack. I'm sorry I didn't tell you this." Tears glistened in her eyes. "It's just...this is my first assignment for the FUBI, and it's a big one. I was afraid if anyone found out about me and Raleigh, I might be taken off this expedition. And... And I didn't want you to think differently about me."

She took hold of his hand. "You're a great guy, Jack. I like being around you. I'm sorry."

Rastun reached out with his free hand and gently grasped Karen's shoulder. "You made a mistake. Who hasn't? The main thing is learning from that mistake. And I believe you when you say you're not going to get involved with a married man."

"Thank you."

Karen kissed him. "You're not going to tell anyone about me and Raleigh, are you?"

"No. But I am going to have to do something about it."

***

Bold Fortune returned to Manahawkin Bay at sunset. Rastun and Karen returned to the boat first, with nothing to show for their efforts. As they sailed toward the shoreline, Rastun found Pilka along the starboard railing.

"Doctor. A word, please?"

Pilka's harsh gaze went to Karen first, then him. He groaned. "All right."

Rastun led them to the storeroom and shut the door. Karen stood on one side of the room, Pilka opposite her, and Rastun in the middle.

"First off," he looked at Pilka. "Karen told me what happened between you two when she was in college."

Pilka's eyes widened, fixed on Karen. "You what? What were you—?"

"Quiet!" Rastun ordered.

Pilka shut his mouth. His face stiffened, as though holding back a torrent of anger.

"I overlooked all the tension between you two because you were able to keep it from boiling over, until last night. I've seen what happens when soldiers can't separate their personal and professional lives. Not only do they become ineffective in the field, but they become a liability to the entire unit. That's not going to happen on my watch."

Rastun looked from Pilka to Karen. "I know you two will never like one another. Whatever. I am not here to mend fences or resolve your issues or have you hug it out. When I was in the Army, I had to work with other officers I didn't like. But I sucked it up and did my job, because whether or not we liked one another was irrelevant. We were on the same team and we had the same goal. That's how it's going to be with you two. No more arguments, no more glaring at one another. From here on out, you will conduct yourselves with the utmost professionalism. Any conversations you have between one another will deal strictly with the search for the Point Pleasant Monster. Is that understood?"

"Yes," said Karen.

Pilka just nodded.

"Doctor. I said is that understood?"

"I understand."

"Good. And another thing, Doctor. Karen and I are involved. You may not like it, but that's the way it is, so deal with it. Understood?"

"I understand."

"Good. Now, what was said in this room stays between the three of us. So long as you two can work together, I see no need to bring it up to our superiors. But if there is another incident like what happened last night, I'll have no choice but to report it to Doctor Ehrenberg, then whatever happens is out of my hands. Understood?"

Both Karen and Pilka answered, "Yes."

"Good. Dismissed."

Pilka left the storeroom without a word.

Karen started toward the door, then stopped in front of him.

"Thank you, Jack."

"You're welcome. Just don't let me down, Karen."

"I won't. That's a promise."

***

Rastun's eyes snapped open when the alarm on his cell phone blared Led Zeppelin's "Black Dog." He lay spooned against Karen, about the only way they could sleep together in his small bunk.

He freed his arm from her and rolled out of bed. Karen, for her part, moaned and pulled the blankets tighter around her.

Rastun shut off the alarm, put on a pair of red and white Philadelphia Phillies boxer shorts and padded into the bathroom. He relieved himself and splashed water on his face before heading back out, ready for his morning regimen of push-ups and sit-ups.

Karen was still in bed.

"You plan on getting up any time soon?" he asked.

Karen muttered something into the pillow that sounded like, "Five more minutes."

Rastun cracked a half-smile and stepped over to the bunk. "Rise and shine, Thatcher!"

He ripped the blanket off her.

"What the hell?" Karen looked at him, a shocked expression on her face.

"The alarm goes off, that means you get out of bed, now." Rastun's smile grew.

Karen flipped him the bird. "This is why I never wanted to join the Army. Jackasses like you waking me up from a sound sleep."

Rastun continued to grin, running his eyes over Karen's naked, slender body. He was tempted to jump back into the bunk for a little more quality time with the sexiest wildlife photographer in the world.

Before he could act on his desires, Karen got up and put on a t-shirt. She went to the bathroom, mumbling something under her breath.

"You're not much of a morning person, are you?"

Karen answered with a groan, then slid the bathroom door closed, hard.

Rastun chuckled, then started doing push-ups. They'd survived their first argument and things were good between them again. Better than good.

Actually, life in general was pretty damn good. He had a challenging job. He had an incredible girlfriend.

For the first time since leaving the Army, he didn't find civilian life all that bad.

Someone knocked on the door.

"Coming." He put on a t-shirt before sliding the cabin door open. Geek stood before him.

"What's up?" asked Rastun.

"We just got word from the Coast Guard. They found a sailboat covered in blood near Surf City. Looks like our monster is back."

EIGHTEEN

Rastun walked along *Bold Fortune's* port side, scanning the ocean. Karen did the same on the starboard side, while Geek and Pilka were positioned on the bow and stern respectively.

The Coast Guard learned the sailboat belonged to a middle-aged couple from Beach Haven and assumed both had been on board when the monster attacked. That brought the death toll to seven. Seven too many as far as Rastun was concerned.

He passed the yacht's curved bridge and saw Karen on the opposite side, shaking a tube of sunscreen. When she opened it, some of the beige substance spat out and over the side. She squeezed more into her hand, rubbed it on the back of her neck, then dabbed some on her ears.

Probably a good idea. He had been in such a rush to change he'd only slathered some lotion on his arms. It wouldn't be long before the sun was high enough to start burning his neck and ears.

He reached into his tactical vest for the sunscreen.

"Heads up, everyone," Ehrenberg radioed. "We may have a sonar hit on our monster. It's three thousand meters south and closing."

"Roger that." Rastun unslung his Aster 7 dart launcher and checked the four-chamber cylinder. He had it set up to fire the toxin dart last. Next he looked over the four flash/bang grenades on his vest.

"Geek." Rastun waved over the big ex-sergeant.

"On the way, Cap'n." USAS-12 in hand, Geek headed over to him. The pair hustled toward the stern. Karen was already there, scanning with her camera while Pilka looked through binoculars. Ehrenberg and Malakov emerged from the bridge, followed by Hernandez.

Rastun pressed the binoculars to his eyes with one hand, looking for any large, dark shape in the water.

"Contact is two thousand meters south of us," Montebello radioed. "Still closing on us."

"Great," said Geek. "If this thing sees boats as a source of food, it's got a whole damn buffet here."

"Contact one thousand meters south and closing," reported Montebello.

"Anyone have eyes on this thing?" asked Rastun.

Everyone answered in the negative.

Except Karen.

"I see it." Her camera clicked a couple of times before she pointed. "There! See that wake?"

Rastun looked, as did everyone else gathered on the stern. Karen continued to take pictures.

He saw a dark hump poking through the waves, then a serpentine neck ending in a crocodilian snout.

No doubt about it. That was the Point Pleasant Monster.

Ehrenberg turned to Hernandez. "Manny. Get the lift net ready."

"You got it, Doc." Hernandez ran to the lift net along the port side and jumped into the control seat. He pulled the levers and switches on the console. The net moved left to right, then up and down.

"The lift net's working fine."

"Contact five hundred meters south and closing." Montebello's voice quivered.

Rastun brought up his Aster 7 and activated the laser sight under the barrel. "Geek?"

"I got your back, Cap'n." He stood next to him, shotgun at the ready.

"Don't you—"

"Yeah, yeah, yeah," Geek cut off Malakov. "Don't kill it. I heard you the other hundred times you said it."

Rastun tuned it all out. His universe focused on the monster. It made a beeline for the *Bold Fortune.*

Four hundred meters. Three hundred meters.

Just a little closer. Their hunt was going to end right here, right now. He'd make damn sure of that.

Two hundred meters. One hundred-fifty meters.

"What are you waiting for?" asked Pilka. "Shoot."

Rastun ignored him. He put the red dot from the laser sight on the monster's neck, then switched to its back. It was a much bigger target.

One hundred-twenty meters. One hundred-ten. One hundred. Ninety.

A soft pop of air came from the Aster 7. A blue feathery tail jutted out the monster's back.

"Got 'im!"

"Good job, Jack." Ehrenberg nodded to him, then looked to Hernandez. "Stand by to fish it out."

"I'm ready."

The Point Pleasant Monster didn't slow down. Eighty yards. Sixty. Forty.

"Everyone back up!"

The group obeyed, except for Karen. She continued snapping pictures.

"That means now."

Rastun grabbed the back of her t-shirt and pulled her away from the stern. The monster drew closer. Rastun willed the tranquilizer to start working. Contrary to Hollywood bullshit, tranquilizer darts didn't normally take effect instantly.

Even worse, Rastun could no longer see the dart sticking out of the monster's back.

Water exploded near *Bold Fortune's* stern. The Point Pleasant Monster leapt out of the ocean and crashed onto the deck.

NINETEEN

Water sloshed over the deck. The bow rose from the monster's weight. Rastun tried to keep his balance and aim. The heel of his boot hit a patch of water. He slipped and fell. His finger squeezed the trigger. The tranq dart struck the gunwales.

"Shit!" Rastun scrambled to his feet.

The Point Pleasant Monster rose and stared at them.

"Inside!" yelled Ehrenberg. "Everyone inside!"

He herded Malakov, Pilka and Hernandez toward the bridge.

"Don't let them kill it!" Malakov hollered at Ehrenberg.

The monster started after them.

Rastun couldn't afford to wait for a tranq to work.

"Geek! Take it out!"

Geek raised his USAS-12. The big shotgun boomed twice.

"No!" Malakov screamed before Ehrenberg pulled her into the bridge.

Rastun expected to see bloody holes in the monster.

The sabot rounds failed to penetrate it.

"You gotta be fucking kidding me!" Geek fired three more shots.

The monster remained unaffected. It lowered its head and charged.

"Move!" Rastun leapt to the right. He hit the deck, rolled and sprang up on one knee. He saw Karen snap a picture before hurrying through the bridge door. She slammed it shut.

The monster smashed into it.

"No!"

Rastun jumped to his feet. Shattered pieces of glass littered the deck. The bridge's fiberglass hull crumpled as the monster tried to push its way inside. Captain Keller pressed himself against the helm, eyes wide with terror.

There was no sign of Karen.

Rastun hurried to the other side of the bridge. Geek came up behind the monster and fired three rounds. The shotgun still had no effect.

Panic swelled within Rastun as he stared through the darkened windows on the front of the bridge. He still couldn't see—

There! Karen was huddled against the right side of the helm. The monster extended its neck and snapped its jaws, missing her by a few feet.

Rastun pulled out his Glock and fired two rounds into the window. The glass exploded.

"Karen!"

She looked up at him and scrambled over the helm. The Point Pleasant Monster snapped at her again. Rastun holstered his pistol and pulled Karen through the window.

"Captain, c'mon!"

Keller just gaped at the monster, the color drained from his face. The hull of the bridge groaned as the monster pushed harder.

"Captain! Move your ass!"

Keller remained frozen.

"Dammit!" Rastun picked up the Aster 7. There was no way he could miss from this range. His finger wrapped around the trigger.

The monster smashed through the bridge. Keller screamed as it slammed into the helm.

The impact threw Rastun from the pilothouse just as he fired. He struck the deck. Pain hammered his back.

The monster threw itself against the helm again. What glass remained shattered. The front of the bridge cracked and bent.

"Jack! Are you okay?" Karen knelt beside him.

"Yeah, I'm fine."

The monster poked its head out the window. Rastun swore it looked right at Karen. It hissed and crashed against the helm.

"Get to the stern," Rastun ordered. "Now."

"What about—"

"Go!"

Karen bit her lip, worry in her eyes. She got to her feet and ran.

Rastun got to one knee and brought up his Aster 7. The only dart left was the toxin one.

The Point Pleasant Monster rammed into the helm. The bridge exploded in a shower of white fiberglass.

Rastun fired. He glimpsed the red feather of the toxin dart sticking out of the monster's stomach. It pitched forward. Rastun rolled out of the way just as it crashed onto the deck.

He got to one knee, brought up the Aster 7, then lowered it. The gun was empty. Given the way the monster looked he doubted he'd—

It raised its snout.

Rastun's eyes widened. There'd been enough Golden Poison Frog toxin in that dart to kill a dozen men. How the hell could the monster still be alive?

The beast turned toward him. Rastun glanced at his Aster 7. No time to reload it. He flipped it around and held it by the barrel like a club. If he was going down, he was going down fighting.

The monster twisted around. Its tail whipped toward Rastun. He threw himself to the deck. The tail struck the dart gun. It tumbled out of his grip and clattered along the deck. He scrambled after it.

The dart gun slid under the railing and fell over the side.

"Dammit!"

Rastun got to his feet. His chest clenched when he spotted Karen, along with Geek, by the boat's stern, the monster bearing down on them. He drew his Glock and fired. Maybe he could distract it.

The monster kept after Karen and Geek.

Geek fired another useless blast from his shotgun. He then grabbed a hatch on the deck and threw it open. Karen slid through it, followed by Geek.

"Geek! Look out!"

The Point Pleasant Monster lunged at him.

Geek dropped through the hatch just as the monster's jaws snapped closed, missing his head by inches. The monster shoved its snout through the opening, its hands banged and scratched the deck.

Rastun balled his fists. He had no dart gun, his Glock was useless. How the hell was he going to stop this thing?

Dumbass! He looked down at his tactical vest, where the flash/bang grenades hung.

Rastun grabbed one and maneuvered around the remains of the bridge. He pulled the pin on the black, cylindrical device. The grenade was better suited for use in a confined space, not outdoors.

But right now it was all he had.

Parts of the deck around the hatch caved in. The Point Pleasant Monster continued to pound and tear its way into the engine room where Karen and Geek had fled.

Rastun threw the grenade. It bounced across the deck. He turned away, closed his eyes and covered his ears.

The grenade detonated with a snare drum *crack*. Tremors went through the deck. Rastun opened his eyes and turned. The monster hissed and stomped around.

Another flash/bang flew out of the hatch. That had to be from Geek. Again Rastun turned away.

The grenade exploded. The monster spun furiously, no doubt blinded by the one million candela flash and deaf from the concussive blast. It tumbled over the stern and hit the water with a huge splash.

Rastun rushed to the stern. He saw a wake moving away from *Bold Fortune*. Within seconds, it dissipated.

He slid through the hatch into the engine room. Karen and Geek stood at the other end of the short corridor. She hurried over and threw her arms around him. Rastun hugged her tight and kissed the top of her head.

"You two all right?" he asked.

Geek replied, "After this, I'd feel a lot better with a few beers in me."

"I'm okay," Karen said, then let out a small gasp. "Jack, you're bleeding."

Rastun examined his arms. Blood trickled from several small cuts. He ran his right hand over his face. It came away with a couple smears of blood.

"Flying glass. I'll be fine. C'mon, let's check on the others."

He led them out of the engine room and up to the salon. Ehrenberg, Malakov, Pilka, Montebello, Tamburro and Hernandez were all present.

"Where's Captain Keller?" asked Rastun.

Tamburro hung his head. He swore the big, hairy man looked like he was about to cry.

Ehrenberg's shoulders sagged. "I'm sorry, Jack." He turned to the small stairway leading to the bridge.

Rastun went up the steps and looked into the wreckage of the bridge. His jaw tightened when he saw Keller. His body had been crushed to a pulp. Both arms were twisted at unnatural angles. His head had been split apart. Blood covered what remained of the helm.

Rastun went back down to the salon and walked up to Tamburro. "Can you shut down the engines?"

"What?" The engineer was in a daze, probably thinking of Keller's gruesome death.

"Mister Tamburro! Focus. The helm is destroyed. We have no way to steer. If anything's in our way, we can't avoid it. Now can you shut down the engines?"

"Um, yeah. Yeah, I can."

Tamburro plodded out of the salon. Ehrenberg watched him go, then took out his satellite phone. "I'll contact the Coast Guard and have them come get us."

Geek scowled at his shotgun. "This is bullshit! These rounds shoulda blown holes in that thing the size of the Holland Tunnel."

"The toxin dart worked for shit, too," said Rastun.

A minute later, the engines fell silent. *Bold Fortune* slowed, then drifted along the waves.

"Geek." Rastun looked to him. "You and me, back up on deck. We need to keep an eye out for the monster in case it comes back."

Rastun took up position along the port side, scanning the ocean, a grenade in his hand. He couldn't believe the monster was immune to sabot rounds and frog toxin. Either one should have killed it.

So why didn't they?

Something else bothered him. Rastun had only been a few feet from the Point Pleasant Monster when he shot it with his last dart. He had been close, he had been defenseless. He would have made an easy meal.

So why didn't the monster eat him?

TWENTY

Ever since his time in the Army, Rastun had mastered the art of falling asleep soon after he closed his eyes. Such a skill had been necessary. You could be operating in the field for 18, 20, even 24 hours a day, for days and weeks at a time. Every minute of sleep you could steal became precious.

He expected sleep to come easy after such a long day. The Coast Guard had sent a cutter to tow *Bold Fortune* to USCG Station Barnegat Light. As soon as they docked, they were swarmed by reporters. Thankfully, Ehrenberg dealt with their questions. Next came a lengthy debriefing with the FUBI brass via conference call. When they finished, they had a quick meal at the station's mess hall and checked into a hotel.

Rastun turned to the clock radio on the nightstand. It was a little after midnight. He groaned and went back to staring at the darkened ceiling. No matter how hard he tried, sleep would not come. He couldn't stop thinking about the Point Pleasant Monster's attack.

Geek had hit it with at least ten sabot rounds. Rastun nailed it with a toxin dart. So why hadn't the monster died? Could it have some sort of resistance to toxins, like mongooses or hedgehogs? Even if it did, he doubted any animal on earth had a hide thick enough to stop an armor-piercing sabot round.

Defective rounds? Rastun didn't think so. He'd heard of Aster Technologies long before Geek worked for them. The company had an excellent reputation in military and law enforcement circles.

So what then? Why couldn't they kill it?

Why couldn't he save Captain Keller?

He recalled Keller's crushed and bloodied body. It wasn't the first time he'd lost men. It never got easier.

Rastun thought about the tranquilizer darts he'd fired at the monster. He hit it with his first shot. Looking back on it, he figured the needle didn't penetrate the armor plating that ran down its back. He would have hit it with his other shot had the monster not crashed through the bridge just before he fired.

Who's to say the tranq would have worked quickly?

Who's to say it wouldn't have?

One dead, but eight saved. He had to take consolation in that fact.

It could have been two dead if...

He turned to Karen. She lay next to him, her shoulders rising and falling with slow, steady breaths as she slept. How close had she come to ending up like Keller?

A jolt of fear went through him. Fear of what could have happened to her, of what might happen to her if they encountered the Point Pleasant Monster again.

And if something happened to her, if I let something happen to her...

Rastun ran two fingers along Karen's shoulder. She moaned and shifted under the blankets.

His cell phone rang.

Rastun looked at the screen. It was Geek.

"What is it?" he asked as Karen rolled over, her eyes cracking open.

"I need to see you, Cap'n. Now."

Rastun noted the serious tone in the former sergeant's voice. "What for?"

"Meet me in my room. I'll tell you when you get here."

"I'm on my way."

He hit the end button and got out of bed.

"Jack? Where are you going?" Karen mumbled.

"Geek wants to see me."

Karen looked at the clock radio. "Now? Why?"

"I don't know, but it sounded important."

Rastun got dressed, kissed Karen on the cheek and left. He strode down the second floor walkway to Geek's room and knocked on the door. Geek opened it, his face a tight, serious mask.

"That is not a good look from you, Sergeant."

Geek nodded. "Come in."

Rastun heard "White Room" coming from the clock radio. He turned to Geek as he shut the door.

"I didn't know you were a Cream fan."

"Just being careful in case we've got bug problems, if you catch my drift."

Rastun furrowed his brow. "All right, I give. What's with the cloak and dagger stuff?"

Geek went over to a table where five shotgun shells laid. Two had been taken apart. He picked up one of the intact ones. "See this?"

"Yeah. It's a shell from your shotgun."

"That's what I thought, until I took some of them apart." Geek put down the shell and grabbed a sliver dart, the actual sabot round removed from its casing.

"Give this a feel." Geek threw him the dart. Rastun looked it over and closed his palm around it.

"What the hell? It's rubber."

"Yeah. I checked out ten different shells. They're all like that."

"No wonder you couldn't kill the monster." Rastun looked at the fake sabot dart, then back to Geek. "How the hell could we have gotten blanks? Did someone at Aster screw up?"

"No way. I checked the ammo myself before I left. It was good. The only thing I can think of is somebody switched it *after* I got here."

"You know what you're implying?"

"Yeah. I do."

Rastun stared at the dart, barely able to believe it.

Someone in the group intentionally sabotaged their weapons.

TWENTY-ONE

Despite the late hour, Rastun didn't hesitate in calling Colonel Lipeli. Both had been rousted out of bed for alerts and drills plenty of times during their Ranger days. Given what he and Geek just discovered, he knew his former CO wouldn't mind being awakened.

"Geek, you're sure you didn't take blanks with you by accident when you left Aster?" asked Lipeli.

"Absolutely not," Geek replied into Rastun's cell phone, which lay on the hotel room's table on speaker mode. "We clearly mark our live ammo and our blanks."

"I didn't think you'd make a mistake like that. So, where did they come from and how did they get into your magazine?"

Rastun answered, "I don't know about the how part. Whenever Geek's not carrying the shotgun, it's secured in the weapons locker. Only four people had the code for it. Me, Geek, Doctor Ehrenberg and Captain Keller, and he's dead."

"It's not like you can buy these sort of blanks at a gun store or online," Geek explained. "Someone had to actually make 'em."

"Is anyone on the expedition capable of doing that?" asked Lipeli.

Rastun shook his head. "The only people on this expedition with any military experience, besides us, are Nick Tamburro and Captain Keller. Well, who *were* on this expedition in Keller's case. Still, both were ex-Navy and spent most of their time on ships. I'd be surprised if either one of them has fired a weapon since basic."

"And I doubt any of our scientists or our photographer have experience when it comes to making ammo," said Lipeli. "That can only mean one thing. Whoever replaced your ammo is getting help from the outside."

Rastun let out a slow breath. This had gone from an act of sabotage to a damn conspiracy. His gaze shifted to the window and the drawn down blinds. He wondered if someone could be observing them right now. Had someone been spying on them from day one?

We're going to have to be a lot more careful from now on. That might sound paranoid, but as he learned in Iraq and Afghanistan, a healthy dose of paranoia helped keep you alive.

"Any idea who could be behind this?" he asked Lipeli.

"We've gotten phone calls, emails, tweets and Facebook posts from more than a dozen animal rights and environmental groups demanding we not kill the monster. It could be one of them. It could be a group we don't even know about."

"So how the hell did they smuggle the blanks onboard *Bold Fortune?*" asked Geek.

There was a noticeable pause before Lipeli answered, "The only thing I can think of is the switch had to take place when you were docked overnight."

Rastun felt his anger building. He was responsible for the security of this expedition, and someone had slipped onto the boat and replaced the shotgun shells right under his damn nose!

"So I guess now we have to ask who's the most likely candidate to be our mole." Geek looked at Rastun. "And why would they switch my shells with blanks?"

"The why is easy. The Point Pleasant Monster has to be one of the rarest animals on the planet. A lot of animal rights groups would go to any length to keep it alive. As for the who, you want to take a guess which person is at the top of my list?"

"Good ol' Doctor Malakov."

Lipeli sighed. "I knew it was a mistake to put her on the team. She was much too radical for my tastes. But Doctor Ehrenberg has been friends with her for years, and she has some impressive credentials."

"She's just not a real team player," said Rastun.

"No argument here." Lipeli paused. "Still, our personal feelings don't count for anything. We need proof."

"How do we get it?" asked Rastun. "Call the cops?"

"A police investigation is bound to leak to the press. We're already getting hammered by them for our inability to catch the Point Pleasant Monster. No, we need to do this covertly. That means bringing in someone the three of us can trust and who has the skills to conduct this kind of investigation."

Rastun stared up at the ceiling. Who would fit that bill? Someone he, Geek and Colonel Lipeli knew and trusted. It had to be a fellow Ranger, one that went into law enforcement after leaving the Army.

One man came to mind.

Rastun looked to Geek, who shot him a knowing smile.

"Looks like you just read my mind, Sergeant."

***

"So what did Geek want?" Karen asked when Rastun returned to their room.

"He had some ideas about how to deal with the monster if we run into again. Aster might have some more equipment that can help us."

The answer seemed to satisfy Karen. Much as he wanted to tell her the truth, Colonel Lipeli made it clear that everything about the FUBI mole and the blanks was to be compartmentalized between the former Rangers. Rastun wasn't about to blab about it to anyone else. Rangers took operational security very seriously.

The next morning, Rastun and Karen lounged in bed for a while before getting up to do their exercises and go on a run. With *Bold Fortune* out of commission, there was no reason for them to rise early.

They put in five miles before returning to the hotel, showering and eating breakfast. Karen got on her laptop and updated the photo gallery on the

FUBI's Facebook page. Rastun cleaned his Glock and his knives. He was always mindful of the time. His appointment with Colonel Lipeli's special investigator was set for 1130.

When 1030 rolled around, Rastun got up and said to Karen, "I'm going to get Geek and go on a supply run."

"A supply run? What for? We're stuck here."

"Not indefinitely. Hopefully we'll be back out to sea soon. Might as well get ready. You want me to get you anything while I'm out?"

"I'll take a raspberry iced tea and a couple of protein bars."

Rastun nodded. "You got it. I'll be back soon."

He kissed Karen and headed out the door.

After getting Geek, the two started out for the local grocery store, two-and-a-half miles from their hotel. Just a brisk walk to a pair of Rangers.

A salty scent hung in the air as they passed several suburban neighborhoods with some small businesses sprinkled among them. Side streets ended at the beachfront to the west and Manahawkin Bay to the east. Several times Rastun led Geek up and down those streets. He took furtive glances over his shoulder, checked car windows and side mirrors, and looked into storefront windows. Given what he learned last night, he wanted to make sure no one was following them.

Again, a little paranoia could help keep you alive.

Rastun didn't spot anyone suspicious. Luckily, it was late morning on a weekday. The sidewalks weren't very crowded. Most people would be at work, and the Point Pleasant Monster kept most tourists away. If anyone was tailing them, he should have been able to spot them.

The grocery store was part of a small block of businesses. Unlike the large chain stores in their utilitarian rectangular buildings, this store, with its white wood siding and green trim, had a quaint, small town feel to it. The sort of place locals came to shop, dine and converse.

Rastun took one final look around. Again, he saw no one suspicious. He turned back to the store, where several white plastic tables shaded by umbrellas were set up along the side. He smiled when he saw a tall black man with a solid build sitting at one table. The man held up a glass of iced tea and nodded to them.

"Great to see you again, Sherlock," said Rastun.

"Likewise, sir," replied Arthur "Sherlock" Dunmore.

Rastun felt ten times better with the former staff sergeant on hand. Sherlock had been with the 16th Military Police Airborne Brigade for three years before joining the Rangers. Upon leaving the Army two years ago, he joined the U.S. Marshals Service. Like his fictional namesake, Sherlock was intelligent, observant and meticulous.

The perfect man to get to the bottom of this conspiracy.

"Marshal Dunmore." Geek slapped Sherlock on the arm. "So where's your cowboy hat and tin star?"

"Does this look like the Old West to you?"

Geek just grinned as he sat down.

Rastun also took a seat. "How did Colonel Lipeli pull you out of the Marshals Service to help us out?"

"It wasn't so much the Colonel as it was your benefactor, Roland Parker. Apparently he's good friends with the Marshals Service Director. They belong to the same health club. Mister Parker put a call in to the director, and here I am."

Sherlock leaned forward. "Quite the job you have now, sir, chasing monsters."

"Heh! Lately, it's the monster that's been chasing us." Rastun picked up a menu. "And now we have a mole to deal with."

"So Colonel Lipeli tells me."

An overweight, middle-aged waitress came out of the store. Once she took their orders and went back inside, they resumed their conversation.

"So you're sure your shotgun shells were replaced with blanks after you got here?" Sherlock asked Geek.

"Absolutely."

"And I have a feeling that's not the only thing they replaced." Rastun ran a hand over his sweaty brow. The late morning air was already hot and muggy. "They must have done something with the toxin dart, too."

"Are you sure about that?"

"That thing was filled with Golden Poison Frog toxin."

"How potent is it?"

"One milligram can kill an elephant."

Sherlock's eyes went wide. "That's pretty damn potent."

Rastun nodded. "We should be dragging that monster's ass back to Virginia right now. There's no way it should have survived."

Sherlock looked to Geek. "Can you get me some of those shotgun shells and toxin darts? I can have the Marshal's Service lab in DC analyze them."

"No problem."

"Can you trust the guys in the lab?" asked Rastun.

"There are a couple I get along with well. They can keep this confidential."

The waitress returned with their drinks. Rastun downed most of his water, relishing the ice cold feel as it flowed down his throat.

"So what about the crew?" asked Sherlock. "Have either of you noticed suspicious behavior from any of them?"

"Doctor Malakov's a raging, lefty psycho bitch." Geek sipped his Diet Coke. "But I think that's more a personality defect than suspicious behavior. Still, she's my bet for the mole."

"Let's not jump to any conclusions until we get more facts."

Geek shrugged. "Hey. People bet on who's gonna win the Super Bowl before the season starts. I can say who the mole's gonna be before you make any arrests."

Sherlock shook his head. A slight grin traced his lips.

"I know Doctor Ehrenberg can be a little eccentric," said Rastun. "But nothing that sets off any alarm bells. Tamburro and Hernandez seem like okay guys, and our tech guy, Montebello, usually keeps to himself."

"You know what they say about the quiet ones." Geek wagged a finger. "Everyone thinks they're shy and don't bother anyone, until the cops find the remains of an entire Brownie troop stuffed in their freezer."

Sherlock looked to Rastun. "What about Karen Thatcher and Raleigh Pilka?"

He hesitated. He had sworn to keep their issues between the three of them. But given the threat posed by this mole...

"Karen dated Pilka when she was in college."

"What?" Geek stared at him, mouth agape. "Karen and Doctor Pilka? Are you shittin' me?"

"No. Not only did they date, Pilka's the father of Karen's daughter."

"Holy shit. We've got a damn soap opera happening on our boat."

Sherlock's eyes shifted from Geek to Rastun. "I take it this isn't common knowledge among the crew?"

"No."

"Did their relationship end badly?"

"Very."

"Any lingering issues between them?"

"Yeah." Rastun nodded. "It started out as a glaring contest between the two, but it escalated into a pretty heated argument. I laid down the law, told them to put their differences aside or I'd bring it up to Doctor Ehrenberg. So far they're both behaving."

Sherlock took another gulp of his iced tea. "There was nothing in their personnel files to indicate they were ex-lovers?"

Rastun cringed, not wanting to think about Karen and Pilka doing the sort of things lovers do. "To be honest, the personnel files were pretty bare bones. Looks to me like we've got some lazy or incompetent people in our HR department."

"Well, I've got the resources to conduct more thorough background checks. Hopefully I'll find some clues as to who our mole is working for. Meanwhile, Geek, when can you get me those shells and darts?"

"I'll give you a call as soon as we get back to the hotel. We can arrange a place to meet up."

"Good. Meantime, if you see anything out of the ordinary from anyone on the expedition, let me know ASAP."

"*Hu-ah,*" both Rastun and Geek replied.

The waitress returned with their lunches and to refill their drinks. When they finished eating, Sherlock bid them farewell and went to his car. Rastun thought about asking him for a lift back to the hotel, but decided against it. He didn't want to risk someone from the expedition seeing him and Geek with Sherlock.

Rastun and Geek went inside the store and bought duct tape, batteries, first aid supplies, plastic bags, notebooks and pens. Some of those items they probably wouldn't need, but he'd told Karen they were going on a supply run. If he wanted to maintain that cover story, it wouldn't do to return empty handed.

Rastun took three steps outside, then stopped.

"Aw, dammit."

"What?" asked Geek.

"I forgot to get Karen her iced tea and protein bars. I'll be right back."

He headed back inside when Geek started laughing.

"What's so funny?"

"You and Karen have barely been together two weeks and she's already got you whipped." Geek kept laughing.

Rastun glowered at him. "Shut up."

TWENTY-TWO

Rastun tried to beat down his worry as the HH-65 Dolphin lifted off from the flight deck of the Coast Guard cutter *Vigorous*. He didn't like leaving the rest of the FUBI expedition, not with a mole among them.

Geek's still onboard, along with over seventy Coasties. That sort of security presence ought to deter the mole from doing anything to harm the expedition members.

Still, it didn't stop Rastun from worrying.

The helicopter, which to him resembled a large orange dolphin with a black nose, swung away from the *Vigorous* and flew south. Rastun knelt beside the open door and scanned the ocean with his binoculars. Since coming aboard the cutter two days ago, they'd had no joy finding the Point Pleasant Monster. But if he did find it, he was more than ready to deal with the beast. Colonel Lipeli had personally delivered new sabot rounds and toxin darts to him and Geek before they went to sea. Plus the helicopter carried an M240 light machine gun and a Barrett .50 caliber rifle.

The Dolphin flew from Point Pleasant down to Cape May and back again. Just like the previous patrols, they came up empty.

When the helicopter returned to *Vigorous,* Karen, Geek and Ehrenberg were waiting for him.

"Let me guess." Ehrenberg had to shout over the roar of the rotor blades. "No sign of the monster."

Rastun shook his head as they walked toward the cutter's island. "Did you really expect anything different?"

Ehrenberg shrugged. "I'm the eternal optimist."

Rastun grinned. That grin faded when suspicion scratched the back of his mind.

Could Dr. Ehrenberg be the mole?

He hoped not. Actually, he seriously doubted it. Ehrenberg was a good guy. Friendly, easy going and hardly ever got angry.

The perfect guy no one would suspect.

The cutter bobbed up and down in the choppy water, forcing Rastun to mind his steps. The weather forecast showed a storm moving along the coast of Delaware. It was due over *Vigorous'* patrol area in a few hours.

He wasn't looking forward to that.

"Well, now that you're back," Ehrenberg slapped Rastun on the shoulder, "you can join us for one of the most fun parts of this expedition."

"Lunch?"

"Nope. Another briefing."

"You could have held it while I was up there." He jerked his head toward the cloudy sky.

"And deprive you of the enjoyment of a bunch of people sitting around blathering on and on and not getting anything accomplished? I couldn't live with myself if I did that."

"You're all heart, Doc."

"Besides," said Ehrenberg, "the folks down at Alexandria came up with a *great* plan to catch the Point Pleasant Monster."

Rastun chuckled. "Well, that wasn't the least bit sarcastic. So what do they want us to do?"

"You'll see."

Five minutes later, the expedition gathered at a table in the chief petty officer's mess. Rastun's eyes flickered from one person to another. The same question went through his mind.

Which one of you is the mole?

"Okay, gang." Ehrenberg seated himself at the head of the table. "I talked with Director Lynch about an hour ago. The FUBI is sending some rafts up here. The *Vigorous* will dock at Cape May tomorrow to pick them up, then we'll fill them with raw meat and try and bait the monster."

Malakov gasped in disbelief. "You can't be serious."

"I may not be, but Director Lynch is."

"How will we know if the Point Pleasant Monster goes after one of those rafts?" asked Pilka.

"Each raft will have a camera," Ehrenberg answered. "Plus radio trackers will be embedded in the meat. If the monster swallows it, we should be able to follow it."

"That's the most asinine thing I've ever heard of!" Malakov threw up her hands. "We're more likely to attract sharks and seagulls than a sea monster."

"I have to agree with Doctor Malakov." *Much as it pains me*, Rastun wanted to add out loud, but didn't. "This kind of plan smacks of desperation."

Ehrenberg nodded. "I know. I've seen these kinds of baited traps used on Sasquatch hunts. Usually they just attract bears, mountain lions and other known animals. But the press is hammering us every day for not finding the Point Pleasant Monster. I guess Director Lynch and everyone else back at FUBI Headquarters feel they need to try everything possible, no matter how desperate it may be."

Malakov snorted. "Well, if we have to do this idiotic plan, we should put some of those rafts farther south."

"Why's that?" asked Pilka.

"The first time *he* tried to kill it," she shot Rastun a brief scowl, which he ignored, "the monster fled south. It may have felt its territory was being challenged, and it lost that challenge. A few days ago *he* tried to kill it again. That's another territorial battle it lost. It may have retreated farther south. Not only that, but with all the watercraft restrictions put in place by the Coast Guard, its food supply is drying up. It might travel south to find more prey."

"You could be right," said Ehrenberg. "Jack, you'd better warn the authorities along the Delaware coast the monster could be on its way there."

"You got it, Doc."

Ehrenberg turned to Montebello. "Charlie, be sure to get in touch with headquarters and get the frequencies for those radio trackers, then pass them along to the Coast Guard."

"Okay."

Ehrenberg looked around at the expedition members. "So that's the skinny, people. We may be grasping at straws with this plan, but you never know. It might actually work."

"Well," said Geek, "if you have any lucky shirts or lucky underwear, better put 'em on."

A few of the expedition members chuckled. Malakov scrunched her face in disgust.

When the meeting broke up, Rastun went to the crew's study, which consisted of some chairs, a couch and a couple of tables and internet stations. No one else was around. He used his satellite phone to contact USCG 5th District Headquarters and the Delaware Emergency Management Agency to alert them of the potential threat posed by the Point Pleasant Monster. Next, he logged into one of the computers to check his e-mail.

Four messages downloaded. Two were from his mother and his cousin Olivia, wanting to make sure he was all right – meaning not eaten by a sea monster. The third was his monthly e-newsletter from the 75th Ranger Regiment.

The last was from Sherlock.

Rastun pulled out his cell phone and texted Geek.

Meet me in the crew's study NOW.

Geek strode in three minutes later. "Something important, Cap'n?"

"I just got an e-mail from Sherlock."

"About time. Let's see what our favorite marshal's got to say."

Geek stood over Rastun's shoulder as he clicked on the e-mail.

Captain,

Sorry for taking so long, but that's the nature of running background checks.

I started out with a search of criminal records. Both Charlie Montebello and Manny Hernandez are clean. Sam Keller and Nick Tamburro both had a couple of disciplinary write-ups while in the Navy for drunk and disorderly. Dr. Ehrenberg was arrested for marijuana possession back in college. Karen Thatcher was cited for exposing her breasts during a spring break trip to Fort Lauderdale her sophomore year in college.

Rastun shifted in his seat. That was information he could have done without.

He continued reading.

Dr. Pilka was involved in a domestic dispute about 11 years ago. It was verbal with a few items around the house broken. No physical violence. Both Pilka and his wife were cited for disturbing the peace.

Eleven years ago. That would put it around the same time as Karen's affair with Pilka.

Three guesses as to what that dispute was about, Rastun thought, *and the first two don't count.*

After reading that Pilka had also been busted for DUI, he got to the part involving Malakov.

Dr. Malakov's record set off some alarm bells for me. She's been arrested at protests on three occasions, including the 1999 WTO demonstrations in Seattle.

Rastun remembered seeing footage from the "Battle for Seattle" when he was younger. The shattered storefronts, damaged vehicles and clashes between cops and protesters.

Yeah, Malakov would have definitely fit in with the type of groups that took part in that.

Also, when she was in college, Malakov and two of her friends were arrested for dumping red paint throughout a clothing store that sold fur.

"Sherlock's making my point," said Geek. "The crazy lady's gotta be our mole."

Rastun just nodded and kept reading.

Next I dug a little deeper, looking at past associations and financial issues. Once again, Hernandez and Montebello came up clean. Both Keller and Tamburro have, or in Keller's case had, an ex-wife and a couple of children. I can't look into their bank records without a warrant, but it's not difficult to imagine how alimony and child support can turn into a financial burden for them. It would certainly make either one a desirable recruit for a mole.

Prior to joining the FUBI, Dr. Ehrenberg had two of his cryptid expeditions funded by The Kobel Trust. It's named after Chris Kobel. He was one of the dot com millionaires from the 1990s. Died in a car crash at age 31. Some of his friends established the trust after his death. Kobel had a big interest in cryptozoology. He talked about creating a zoo featuring cryptids. Maybe someone involved in the trust feels the same way.

Rastun scowled. He didn't like the thought of Ehrenberg being the mole.

Malakov is a member of several environmental and animal rights groups, some legitimate, others radical. One of her college classmates, Tara Rodriguez, is the head of a group called the North American Animal Liberation Army.

"NAALA." Rastun looked up at Geek. "Yeah, I know all about them. They've vandalized labs that experiment on animals, released animals from pet stores, farms and zoos. One member even burned down a farmer's house in North Dakota a few years ago. Killed the entire family."

"Basically, the kind of group that would do anything to keep the Point Pleasant Monster alive."

Rastun nodded and turned back to the screen.

I'm still trying to get more information about Pilka. I ran into a wall when I tried to find out his reason for leaving the marine institute in Palm Beach. I

109

have a feeling it was something pretty serious if he goes from a top position there to teaching at junior colleges.

One thing did stick out when I checked into Karen Thatcher's past.

Rastun felt his muscles tense.

Two years ago, she was hired by Exotic Animals Magazine to investigate reports of Sumatran Rhinos in Thailand.

Rastun's brow furrowed. Sumatran Rhinos were among the most endangered animals on the planet. Less than 300 remained in a handful of parks and reserves between Borneo and the Malay Peninsula. He didn't think there were any left in Thailand.

They actually found a couple of them. A year after the story was published, the World Wildlife Fund sent some people to Thailand. They found the body of a rhino with its horn cut off.

"What's up with cutting off the horn?" asked Geek.

"Rhino horns are very valuable. They're ground into powder and used in different medicines throughout Asia. One pound of rhinoceros horn powder can be worth about forty-five thousand dollars."

Geek's eyes bulged. "No shit."

Rastun stared at the screen.

The interesting thing about Exotic Animals Magazine is it's part of a publishing company founded by a former big-game hunter from Germany named Holger Mertesacker. A few articles I saw about his company indicate it's been losing money for quite some time. The expedition Karen was on may have been a recon team in disguise. When they confirmed the existence of the rhinos, Mertesacker could have sent poachers in to kill them and profit from the horns. He may have similar designs on the Point Pleasant Monster, with Karen helping him again.

Rastun didn't want to believe it. He couldn't believe it. But there it was, staring him in the face, a theory put forth by one of the smartest men he knew.

A theory that Karen might be the FUBI mole.

TWENTY-THREE

Ensign Frank Gale clenched his teeth, trying to push the rising bile back into his stomach. Sheets of rain pounded the stubby 47-foot motor lifeboat. The vessel pitched up and down. He kept checking through his binoculars for any sign of the Point Pleasant Monster.

It could be ten feet off the bow and I wouldn't see it. Visibility was shit in this squall.

Still Gale kept scanning the roiling ocean, if for no other reason than to keep his mind off the nausea burning his stomach.

It did no good.

He clenched his teeth. He couldn't puke on his own bridge, not with Chief Boatswain's Mate Morehead at the helm. The man was an 18-year USCG veteran. Gale was just two months removed from the Coast Guard Academy in New London. What kind of officer threw up at sea? Not one the enlisted personnel and chiefs would respect.

He held it in, then straightened out the blue GORE-TEX foul weather parka that covered his thin frame. He looked out the windows of the small, curved bridge at Seaman Peterson, who stood on the bow staring through binoculars. Boatswain's Mate Third Class Krantz did the same on the stern.

After five minutes of seeing nothing but rain and swells, Gale turned to the thickly built Morehead. "Let's head closer to shore. Maybe we'll have better luck there." He tried to sound confident.

Morehead just nodded. "Yes, sir."

The chief turned the wheel. The boat pushed through the waves. Huge sprays of water cascaded over the bow, soaking Peterson, who fought to stay on his feet.

Gale, meanwhile, fought to keep from throwing up.

Just think of finding the monster. Think of what it'll mean for your career.

He imagined commendations and a promotion to lieutenant, junior grade. Maybe a sweet assignment in Florida, where it never snowed and he could make a name for himself chasing down drug dealers.

He just had to play it smart. He'd already radioed in three sightings of the monster, all of which turned out to be false alarms. The CO of the motor lifeboat squadron back at Barnegat Light had already ripped him a new one for it. Next time, he'd make damn sure what he saw was the Point Pleasant Monster before calling it in. He also had Krantz carry a waterproof camcorder to document it.

The MLB pitched up and down as it plowed west. A couple of times, Gale grabbed the console to keep from falling. The pain in his stomach grew sharper. He started to doubt he could get through this storm without barfing.

Gale raised his binoculars. He saw rain and rough seas. Same as every other time he –

A dark hump appeared off the port side.

Gale stepped closer to the window. He kept the binoculars trained on that spot.

He thought he saw the hump again. It was hard to tell through all the rain.

Dammit, c'mon. Gale waited for the hump to reappear. Roughly a minute passed without seeing it.

He couldn't call Barnegat Light with this. His CO would make him scrape barnacles off every MLB for the next month.

"Chief. Left standard rudder, twenty degrees."

"Left standard rudder, twenty degrees, aye."

Gale unslung his Remington 870 shotgun and headed for the exit hatch.

"Trouble, sir?" asked Morehead.

"I'm not sure yet."

Morehead responded with a slight nod. Gale figured the chief thought he was overreacting again.

He opened the hatch. Rain pelted him. Wind lashed his body. He squinted and made his way toward the port railing.

"Krantz!" he shouted to the short, stocky woman. "Stand by with that camera!"

"Aye, sir."

Gripping the shotgun behind the pump handle with one hand, Gale held up the binoculars with the other. The MLB's bow was pointed right at the area where he'd seen the hump. His heart beat faster as he scanned the ocean.

Still no sign of it.

Gale lowered his binoculars. Maybe it was a seal or a shark. Maybe he mistook a wave for a monster's hump.

He lowered his head. Once again, he looked like an overzealous idiot.

Gale headed back to the bridge, determined not to make eye contact with Chief Morehead.

A dull thud went through the boat.

"What the hell?" Gale looked around. A groaning noise came from rear. The engine sputtered and fell silent. The MLB bobbed among the waves.

Gale threw open the hatch to the bridge. "Chief. What's going on?"

"We hit something." Morehead tried to restart the engine. There was a sick, mechanical cough, then nothing. "Dammit. Whatever it was took out our propeller."

"Better contact Barnegat Light." Gale frowned. Wonderful. Here he was, a Coast Guard officer, having to call the Coast Guard to be rescued. He'd be a laughing stock back at base.

Gale went back outside. The boat swayed from side-to-side. He took careful steps toward the stern, where Krantz leaned over the railing.

"You see what hit us, Krantz?"

She turned to face him. "Negative, sir. You'd think there'd be a—"

A huge, reptilian form burst from the water. Gale watched wide-eyed as crocodilian jaws snapped down on Krantz's head and shoulders and yanked her overboard.

***

Rastun braced himself against the bulkhead. The *Vigorous* lurched to the right, then straightened out.

But only for a second. Then it was back to up and down and side to side. It felt like riding a bull in slow motion.

This storm's getting worse.

He continued through the passageway, grateful his stomach wasn't rebelling against all the rocking and swaying. He'd heard Montebello puking in one of the heads ten minutes ago. Doctor Ehrenberg didn't look so good the last time he saw him. Even a handful of Coasties appeared ready to lose their lunch.

Too bad Captain Keller isn't here to see this. He recalled the wager they'd made on whether or not Rastun would get sick at the first sign of rough seas.

But instead of giving him his twenty, Keller was smeared over what remained of *Bold Fortune's* bridge. What's worse, his death could have been prevented if Geek's shotgun hadn't been loaded with blanks.

Of course, Keller might have been a victim of his own sabotage. Being dead did not eliminate him as a candidate for the mole. One of six candidates.

A one in six chance Karen could be the mole.

I can't believe that.

No, you don't want to believe it.

A voice blared from the speakers of *Vigorous's* 1MC system.

"This is the captain. All FUBI personnel report to the bridge immediately."

Rastun picked up his pace. He just reached the ladder leading to the bridge when Karen hurried out of the passageway to his left.

"What's going on?" she asked.

"We'll find out soon."

Rastun clambered up the steps, Karen right behind him. He entered the bridge to find Ehrenberg and Pilka already there.

"Dammit, Ensign! Calm down!" a pear-shaped man with glasses shouted into the radio. It was Captain DiPino, *Vigorous's* CO. "State your position again."

The panicked voice at the other end rattled off a string of numbers and letters. DiPino turned to the helmsman. "Helm. Did you get that?"

"Coordinates entered into NAVPLOT. They're about thirty-five miles northeast of us."

"Plot a course to that position, full speed."

The helmsman acknowledged the order and spun the wheel left.

DiPino turned back to the radio. "MLB Forty-Two, this is *Vigorous.* We are headed to your position now."

"Roger, *Vigorous,*" the ensign replied as Malakov and Geek entered the bridge. "It just happened so fast. I was just talking to her and…"

The pause lasted five seconds, ten seconds.

"Oh my God!" A few people jerked in surprise at the ensign's scream. "It's back! It's back!"

Crackles came over the radio. Not from static. From gunfire.

Rastun looked to Ehrenberg. "Point Pleasant Monster?"

The cryptozoologist nodded. "It attacked one of the Coast Guard's boats a few minutes ago. It's already killed one person and the boat's engine was damaged."

Rastun turned back to the radio. He heard more gunfire. Frustration and helplessness grew within him. More than anything he wanted to be out there helping those Coasties.

"Peterson!" the ensign hollered. "It got Peterson. Our guns aren't even hurting it."

"Hang on, Ensign," said DiPino. "We're coming for you."

"Captain." A lean, dark-haired man stepped toward DiPino. It was Lieutenant Olivas, the Dolphin's pilot. "The chopper will get to them a lot sooner."

"In this storm?" Ehrenberg stared out the bridge windows. Rain pounded the thick glass.

Olivas didn't show a trace of concern. "I've flown in worse conditions than this."

He looked back to Captain DiPino, who nodded. "Go."

"Permission to join Lieutenant Olivas, Captain," said Rastun.

"Me too," Karen chimed in.

Rastun turned to her, then glanced out the windows. Did she know what she was getting into?

"You two are civilians," replied DiPino. "I can't allow you to fly in this kind of weather."

"I've been in hairier situations than this," Rastun told him. "Besides, the Point Pleasant Monster is an FUBI responsibility. You need someone from our group on that chopper."

"As expedition photographer, it's my job to document everything having to do with the monster," Karen added. "Besides, it's not like I've led a sheltered life, either."

DiPino's eyes flickered between the two. He let out a slow breath. "Permission granted. Go to the storeroom and have the quartermaster draw your gear."

"Yes, sir." Rastun almost brought up his hand for a salute. He had to remind himself he didn't need to do that. Like DiPino said, he was a civilian.

"Thank you, Captain," said Karen.

Olivas strode out of the bridge. Rastun and Karen followed.

"Don't take long." The pilot glanced over his shoulder at Rastun and Karen. "I plan on being wheels up in five minutes."

"We'll be ready in four," Rastun promised.

While Olivas headed to the flight deck, Rastun and Karen went to the storeroom. The quartermaster, a thin woman with dark hair, gave them flight helmets with radios, goggles, waterproof gloves and orange survival vests, each one with a strobe light, whistle, personal locator beacon and an MK-79 illumination signal kit.

"Either of you have experience with the MK-79?" asked the quartermaster.

"I've used flares before, but not that particular type," Rastun answered.

"I know how to use a flare gun," said Karen.

"Well, the MK-79 is a lot different than a flare gun." The quartermaster pulled out a three-foot-long black tube and a small plastic bandolier with seven gold cartridges. "This is the launcher." She held up the black tube, then plucked a cartridge off the bandolier. "Move the trigger screw to the bottom of the slot and to the right to cock it, then screw in one of the cartridges. Hold it arm's length away from your body and move the trigger screw to the left to fire it. Got it?"

"Yeah," Rastun and Karen both replied.

They quickly put on their gear and hurried to the flight deck. Rain and wind battered them. *Vigorous* rolled in the churning ocean. Rastun and Karen ran toward the helicopter, fighting to stay on their feet. The rotor blades spun with a deafening roar and created a mini-hurricane around the aircraft. Rastun clenched his teeth as a combination of natural and artificial wind buffeted him.

He climbed through the Dolphin's open side door, then helped Karen aboard. Two others were in the cargo hold. Bailes, the athletic-looking rescue swimmer, and Yeager, the stocky flight mechanic. Rastun attached a gunner's belt around his chest, a necessary piece of equipment to keep from falling out of the helicopter. Even more necessary when flying in weather like this. Once his belt was secure, he helped Karen put hers on.

Olivas did a comms check. The helmet radios worked fine. Rastun watched the deckhands remove the tie downs from the Dolphin. It lifted off the flight deck...

And slewed to the right.

Rastun tensed. *Please don't crash.*

The Dolphin straightened out and rose into the stormy sky.

Rastun let out a relieved breath. He turned to Karen. Her eyes bulged and her breathing quickened.

"You good?" He put a hand on her shoulder.

She looked him in the eyes, swallowed and nodded. "I'm fine."

The Dolphin pointed its blunt nose to the northeast and sped away from the *Vigorous*. Rain and wind hammered the helicopter.

Rastun turned to Karen. Her head was down, both hands clutching her camera in a death grip. It seemed like she had second thoughts about flying in this storm.

Rastun stared outside at the dark sheets of rain. He, too, wished Karen remained on the *Vigorous*.

He couldn't say if it was out of concern for her safety, or because he wasn't 100 percent sure he could trust her.

TWENTY-FOUR

Piet leaned out the opening to the bridge and threw up. After his final heave, he slammed a hand against the doorframe. Olef had puked. So had Heinrich and Doern. Piet had been determined not to follow suit.

He'd failed.

"Shit," he grumbled. He'd done operations on boats before, but never in weather like this. What the hell possessed him to come out in weather like this?

That four million dollar bonus for the Point Pleasant Monster did. If the FUBI and the American Coast Guard captured it, he needed to be in a position to intercept them.

Piet groaned and stared out at the rain and swells. The Coast Guard presented a big problem for him and his men. In addition to small arms, USCG cutters also carried heavy caliber machine guns and automatic cannons. There was no way they could take on that sort of firepower with submachine guns and pistols.

But now they could, thanks to more of Norman Gunderson's money and one of Piet's arms dealing contacts in The States. His team now had an arsenal of M-14 rifles with sniper scopes, AK-74 automatic rifles, M79 grenade launchers, an M-60 machine gun, even a couple of RPG-7s. They were more than ready to deal with the Coast Guard.

Or the Point Pleasant Monster. Piet heard the news stories about its attack on the boardwalk. The FUBI's theory was the monster had so much blubber it made it immune to small arms fire. His boat did carry tranquilizer guns, nets and catchpoles to secure the monster. If they couldn't, Piet had peace of mind that they had enough ordnance to blow it to bits. It would mean losing the four million dollar bonus, but you can't spend money when you're dead.

"Hey, Piet," Doern called out from his radio console. "I just picked up a message from the cutter *Vigorous*. They dispatched their helicopter to help a motor lifeboat that was attacked by the Point Pleasant Monster."

Piet straightened up. He forgot about the hot, stale taste of vomit in his mouth. "Do you have a position on the lifeboat?"

"I do." Doern read off the GPS coordinates.

"Do they think the beastie is still there?"

"It sounds like it."

Piet grinned at his fellow countryman. "Then let's go catch ourselves a sea monster."

***

Another jolt went through the Dolphin. Rastun didn't even flinch. He'd been through his share of bumpy helicopter and plane rides.

Karen tensed, her goggles failing to hide the fearful look in her eyes. Rastun reached out and took her hand. He mouthed, "We'll be fine," so the Coasties couldn't hear.

Karen nodded, trying to rid her face of fright. She squeezed his hand back.

"Vigorous! Vigorous!" The ensign's voice burst through the headphones in Rastun's helmet. "It's back again! Oh my God, it's on board!"

The chatter of automatic weapons fire came over the radio.

"Chief, look out! Oh my God! It's -"

Rastun heard a rumble in his headphones. He held his breath, waiting for the ensign to say something, or to hear automatic weapons fire, or any other sound.

There was nothing but silence.

"MLB Forty-Two, this is *Vigorous.*" Rastun heard Captain DiPino back on the cutter. "Do you read?"

Nothing.

"MLB Forty-Two, respond. Ensign, are you there?"

Nothing.

"MLB Forty-Two, this is Dolphin Five," Olivas said from the cockpit. "We are about two minutes from your pos." He used the slang for position. "Do you read?"

No response.

Rastun's shoulders sagged. He had a bad feeling they were too late.

The Dolphin plowed through the rain. Rastun took a few glimpses out the door, trying to spot the MLB. He couldn't see shit in this storm.

A very long minute passed before he heard the co-pilot, Lieutenant, Junior Grade Jernigan. "I got a visual on the MLB. Ten degrees off starboard. One hundred-fifty yards."

Rastun leaned out the door. Through the curtains of rain he could make out the stubby white and orange vessel.

The Dolphin slowed and descended. Rastun unslung his Aster 7. Karen brought up her camera. Bailes, the rescue swimmer, stared through his binoculars.

"Anyone see any survivors?" asked Olivas.

Everyone replied in the negative.

"All right, I'm taking us in closer."

Rastun looked over Bailes' shoulder, hoping to see any signs of life from the MLB. Karen knelt behind him, taking pictures.

Despair took hold as the Dolphin neared the MLB. The boat bobbed in the water, its mast and pilothouse wrecked.

Rastun raised his Aster 7. He saw no sign of the Point Pleasant Monster. Of course, with the rain and roiling ocean, it could be skirting the surface and he wouldn't know it.

"I see someone!" Bailes hollered. "I've got movement next to the pilothouse."

Rastun focused around the ruins of the pilothouse. He spotted a person on the starboard side slowly rolling on his back. Relief shot through him. At least someone had survived.

"Bailes, I'm going to put us right over the boat," said Olivas. "Get down there and bring that guy back ASAP. That monster could still be hanging around."

"Yes, Sir." Bailes turned to Yeager. "Time to go outside."

The flight engineer nodded. "Watch your ass, buddy."

"How about you cover my ass with that machine gun so I don't get eaten?"

"Deal."

The two Coasties bumped fists.

Rastun continued checking around the MLB, and Karen kept taking pictures, while Bailes sat in the doorway and attached the hoist hook to his vest. Yeager looked over the rescue swimmer, then tapped him on the chest. Bailes released his gunner's belt, checked his gear, then gave Yeager a thumbs up. The flight mechanic played out an orange trail line until it reached the bobbing MLB. All the while, Olivas kept the Dolphin in a hover directly over the boat.

Hurry up, guys. Rastun's eyes swept over the waves. Visions of the monster breaking through the surface and snatching the survivor spooled through his mind.

Yeager lowered Bailes toward the MLB. The rescue swimmer used the trail line to stabilize himself as he neared the boat, which continued to pitch and roll. Olivas did his best to keep the helicopter steady.

Bailes landed on the deck, slipped and went down on one knee. He quickly recovered and raised his right arm, the signal for, "I am all right."

Bailes unhooked himself from the hoist and started forward.

A geyser of water erupted next to the MLB.

"Shit!" Rastun took quick aim and fired.

Bailes turned around. The Point Pleasant Monster's jaws clamped down on his shoulder. Karen screamed as the beast yanked Bailes off the boat.

"It's got Bailes!" Yeager shouted. "It's got Bailes!"

Yeager took aim with the machine gun, but didn't fire, probably for fear of hitting his friend. Rastun also sighted up the monster. He fired another tranquilizer dart.

Both the monster and Bailes disappeared beneath the waves. Rastun had no idea if he had even hit the beast.

"Oh my God." Yeager stared down at the MLB, mouth agape.

"Yeager? Yeager, what's going on?" Olivas demanded. "Bailes, do you read me?"

"Bailes is dead." Rastun slid over to Yeager and slapped him on the shoulder. "Hey! There's nothing we can do for him, but we still have one man we gotta get out of there. Lower me down."

Yeager blinked in surprise. "But-But you're a civilian."

"I've rappelled out of helicopters before in the Rangers. Now get me down there."

Yeager just stared at him, like he was mulling over the idea.

"Let him do it, Yeager," said Olivas. "It's not like Mister Rastun is a virgin at this."

"Yes, Sir."

Yeager brought up the hoist and gave Rastun a crash course in what to do. It was certainly different from rappelling, where all he did was slide down a nylon rope to the ground. Nice, flat ground that didn't move, unlike the MLB below him.

Rastun slung the Aster 7 over his shoulder and attached the hoist hook to his vest.

"Be careful," Karen said, her face taut with worry.

He gave her a quick smile. "I'll be fine."

Yeager lowered the hoist. Rastun gripped the trail line. Rain pelted him. The wind tried to push him to the left. He fought through it, using the trail line to maintain a steady descent to the MLB. The shattered vessel dipped and rolled.

Fifteen feet to go. Rastun looked left to right, rivulets of water snaking down his goggles. No sign of the Point Pleasant Monster. It was probably still feasting on poor Bailes. Hopefully that would give him a few minutes to get the survivor back to the chopper.

Rastun hit the deck and detached himself from the line. The boat rocked to the right. He stumbled and fell to his knees. Rastun got back to his feet, turned to the helicopter and raised his right arm. He unslung his Aster 7 and moved the cylinder so the toxin dart would fire. If the monster appeared again, he wasn't going to mess around. He was going to put the ugly bastard down, permanently.

Rastun hurried across the deck. Some debris covered the survivor's legs and waist. Rastun lifted it off him. The man's pants were torn. Blood stained his right leg. He also had a red gash down his right cheek. Rastun noticed a fabric rank device on the collar of his parka. A gold ensign's bar. The nametag on the parka's left breast read GALE.

"Ensign Gale? Can you hear me?"

Gale looked at him, his eyes slightly glazed, his face pale.

The guy was clearly in shock.

"It got them all," Gale mumbled. "It got them all. I couldn't do anything."

"Ensign, can you stand?"

Gale acted like he hadn't heard him. "It got them. Got them all."

"Ensign!" He grabbed Gale by the collar and pulled him up so their eyes met. "Pull it together! Can you stand up?"

Gale blinked a couple of times. "I ...I think so."

"Then get your ass up if you want to live."

Rastun helped him up. Gale tried to stand straight, then slumped to his right.

"My knee." His face twisted in agony.

"I got you." Rastun slung the Aster 7 over his shoulder and put an arm around Gale's back. He half carried the ensign back to the hoist. Again he checked around the MLB for any sign of the monster. He found none.

Rastun reached the hoist and secured a rescue sling around Gale. Once they were both secured, Rastun gave a thumbs up. He felt his feet leave the rolling deck.

Something moved to his left.

The Point Pleasant Monster leapt out of the water and crashed onto the stern. It lifted its head, dark eyes aimed at him and Gale.

An icy shiver went up Rastun's spine. With one hand on the rescue sling and the other on the trail line, he had no way to defend himself or Gale.

The monster lunged forward.

Something bright red shot through the air. A little flaming ball zipped by Rastun. He turned away, but not before several multi-colored dots formed before his eyes. He blinked a few times and turned back to the monster. It looked away from him and Gale and eyed the flare.

Another red glow caught Rastun's attention. He looked up at the helicopter.

Karen leaned out the door, clutching the flare launcher. She disappeared back inside the helicopter. Seconds later she reappeared and fired another flare.

Rastun looked down. The monster tracked the third flare as it fell into the water. It jumped out of the MLB and plunged into the ocean.

When Rastun and Gale reached the Dolphin, Yeager disconnected them from the hoist.

"Rastun and survivor aboard," Yeager reported to Olivas. "The survivor has a pretty bad leg injury. It looks like he also might be in shock."

"Roger that. The closest hospital is AtlantiCare Regional Medical Center in Atlantic City. We'll take him there."

The Dolphin headed west. Rastun laid the injured ensign on the deck while Yeager got the first aid kit. They bandaged Gale's leg and covered him with a thermal blanket.

"You're gonna be all right, Ensign." Rastun patted Gale on the shoulder. He then looked over to Karen. She pushed her goggles atop her helmet and just stared at him.

Rastun lifted his goggles and slid over to her. He said nothing, just took in her beautiful face, dampened by the rain.

"You saved my ass back there."

Karen opened her mouth, but said nothing. Instead she flung herself at him and gave him a crushing hug. They held each other for what had to be a good minute. Just as Karen released Rastun, he gave her a long kiss. He then stared into her eyes, eyes that held worry, relief, joy ...and something else.

It was in that moment Jack Rastun knew with absolute certainty that Karen could not possibly be the mole.

TWENTY-FIVE

Piet saw the orange form of the Coast Guard helicopter fly away from the bobbing motor lifeboat. He scanned the vessel through his binoculars. The pilothouse was wrecked. He couldn't find anyone aboard. Any survivors were probably on that helicopter.

"I just picked up a transmission from the helicopter to the cutter *Vigorous*," Doern reported. "They picked up one survivor from the motor lifeboat and are flying him to a hospital in Atlantic City."

"What about the monster?" asked Piet.

"It sounds like they used flares to distract it. It dove back into the ocean."

Piet nodded and looked back at the abandoned MLB. There was a chance the Point Pleasant Monster could still be around, which meant they wouldn't have to wait for the FUBI or Coast Guard to capture it. They could do it themselves and get the four million dollar bonus.

"Heinrich. Make for the motor lifeboat. Doern, get the tranquilizer gun. I'll man the M-60 and Olef can use the RPG."

Piet led Doern out into the wind and rain. They opened a cargo container and pulled out their weapons, along with the nets and catch poles.

Hefting the long-barreled M-60 machine gun, Piet headed toward the bow. The constant rocking and bouncing of the 41-foot utility boat made it difficult for him to keep his balance. Somehow, he managed.

They closed with the MLB. Piet swept his head to and fro, scanning the ocean.

"You fellows see anything?"

Both Doern and Olef replied, "No."

Piet kept looking, his finger coiled around the M-60's trigger. If that bloody thing tried to hop aboard this boat, it'd be in for a nasty surprise, like a face full of 7.62mm rounds.

"Over there!" Doern pointed to something off the starboard bow.

Piet squinted against the rain and wind. Something in dark blue clothing floated in the water. A body, face down and missing its left arm.

"Looks like the beastie didn't finish its supper," said Piet.

"It might come back for it," suggested Doern.

"It just might. Be ready with that tranquilizer gun."

Doern nodded.

Piet ordered Heinrich to cut the engines about 20 feet from the corpse. The boat bobbed among the waves as the mercenaries waited.

They didn't wait long.

"There!" Doern pointed.

Piet saw a long, reptilian neck emerge from the roiling water. The monster stared at the floating body, then lifted its head. Its gaze was aimed right at the utility boat.

"Doern. Send it to dreamland."

Doern nodded. He got on one knee and balanced the tranq rifle on the railing. The boat continued to pitch up and down. The monster's attention shifted from the boat to the corpse.

"Dammit," Doern cursed. "I can't aim for shit with this boat bouncing up and down."

The monster surged forward through the waves.

Doern fired.

The monster brought down its head. It clamped its jaws around the corpse and pushed it underwater.

"Did you hit it?" asked Olef.

Doern shook his head. "I don't think so. I doubt it. Who the fuck can aim properly on this damn thing?"

Piet scowled. Would the monster surface again? Was there something they could do to lure it back to the surface?

"Hey!" Heinrich called from the pilothouse. "There's an American Coast Guard cutter approaching to port."

The mercenaries turned. A white ship with an orange stripe down each side plowed through the rain and waves, headed for the wrecked MLB.

"What do we do?" asked Olef.

Piet stared at the approaching vessel. "If we stick around, we run the risk of being made. One call to a Coast Guard base and they'll find out we're imposters. Plus we don't have the Point Pleasant Monster. Better if we leave."

The other mercenaries nodded.

"Doern. Keep monitoring the radio. If that ship actually finds the monster, we'll have to come back and take it from them."

"All right." Doern headed back into the pilothouse, with Piet and Olef following.

Heinrich spun the wheel. The utility boat turned a full 180 degrees and sped off. Piet checked over his shoulder a few times. The cutter continued straight for the MLB. Maybe the Coasties hadn't seen them, or maybe they thought they were just another USCG vessel, nothing to be suspicious about.

It wasn't long before the cutter was out of sight. Doern monitored the Coast Guard vessel's radio frequency, provided to them by their mole inside the FUBI. It lingered in the area for an hour without seeing the monster, then sailed away.

"What now?" asked Heinrich.

Piet stared out the windows. "I don't know about the rest of you, but I've had enough of this shit weather. Let's head home."

The trip back to the Manasquan River seemed to take longer than normal. Piet threw up again and wondered why any fool would want to join the Navy. When they returned to the abandoned boathouse in the woods, Piet was the first off the utility boat. The ground was soggy, but at least it didn't move. Once inside the boathouse, he used his smart phone to check the weather forecast. The storm was expected to move out of the area by late tonight. Tomorrow should be a much calmer day on the ocean.

Piet peeled off his sopping wet clothes and put on fresh ones. He thought back to the encounter with the monster. They'd been so bloody close. Had it not been for this damn storm, Doern would have easily put a tranq dart in that thing. Then they could have delivered it to Gunderson's "research ship" and collected their bonus.

Now he had to hope for another opportunity to nab the Point Pleasant Monster.

TWENTY-SIX

"We have the resources to capture it. Just let us do our job, dammit!"

Rastun winced at Malakov's shrill tone. The animal behaviorist had come halfway out of her chair, staring daggers at the tall, white-haired man in a white service dress uniform sitting at the head of the conference table.

"Unfortunately, Doctor Malakov," said Admiral Gerad Timmins, commander of the 5th U.S. Coast Guard District, "you no longer have a proper research vessel at your disposal, and Director Lynch informs me its replacement developed engine trouble and won't be here for two more days. I'm not going to wait that long for it to arrive."

"We'll give you all the tranquilizer darts you need. Just drug it and bring it back to us."

Timmins shook his head. "After what happened yesterday, I refuse to risk the lives of any more of my people to capture that thing."

Rastun noted the admiral's tight face and the narrowed eyes. He saw similar expressions when he and Karen returned to the *Vigorous*. A combination of anger, sorrow and fear. The Coast Guard had lost four of their own to a monster that had already killed seven others. He didn't think they'd be inclined to capture it.

"Mister Lynch, Mister Parker, please." Lauren stared at the speakerphone in the middle of the table. "Will you make this man see reason?"

"Lauren," Lynch replied. "I understand your concern. But without a proper research vessel, there's no way to safely secure the monster."

"You said the replacement ship should be here in two days. There's no guarantee the Coast Guard will find the creature before then. We still have a chance to capture it alive."

"I don't think it's worth the risk anymore," said Rastun.

"Nobody asked you," Malakov snapped.

"It's time to face reality, Doctor," Rastun fired back. "We have gone above and beyond trying to capture the Point Pleasant Monster. You know when a wild animal attacks a human it has to be put down. This creature has killed eleven people. It has absolutely no fear of humans, and right now it's sitting on top of the food chain."

"I don't even think it's solely about food anymore," said Ehrenberg.

Timmins tilted his head. "Explain, Doctor."

"The way it attacked your boat yesterday, killing one person after another. It couldn't have eaten them so fast. I talked with both Lauren and Raleigh. There's a possibility the monster was defending its territory more than looking for a meal."

"All the more reason to take it out," said Rastun.

"No, it isn't."

"Doctor Malakov." Timmins gave her a harsh stare. "Are you even bothered by the fact this thing has killed almost a dozen people? Where are your priorities?"

"My priority is to keep animals like this alive. You can't hold the Point Pleasant Monster responsible for what it does. It's acting on instinct, not hatred or vengeance like men do."

Timmins looked around the table. "So does anyone else feel the same as Doctor Malakov?"

"I have to side with her," said Pilka. "We can't take the chance that we might kill the last of this species. We have an obligation to science to capture it alive."

Ehrenberg cleared his throat. "I'd love nothing more than to agree with you, Raleigh. But, given the number of people killed, I guess…" He sighed and stared at the table. "Damn. I can't believe I'm about to say this. I guess we have no choice but to kill it."

"Randy!" Malakov gaped at him. "How could you?"

"I'm sorry, Lauren, but people have to come first."

"Mister Parker and I also agree with Doctor Ehrenberg and Mister Rastun," said Lynch. "Admiral Timmins, you will have the full support of the FUBI in hunting down and destroying the Point Pleasant Monster. Doctor Ehrenberg, your team will deploy on *Epic Venture* as soon as it arrives. If you spot the monster, you will contact the Coast Guard immediately. Understood?"

"Yeah."

"Good. Again, I wish we could have handled this differently. Good luck and be careful."

A click came from the speakerphone as Lynch hung up.

"Well, now that that's settled…" Timmins stood and straightened his uniform. "I'm going to start redeploying our cutters and helicopters to search for the monster."

"I guess we'll stay on the *Vigorous* until our new boat gets here," said Ehrenberg.

"Negative, Doctor. Since this is no longer a capture operation, the presence of your team on our cutters is no longer necessary."

Ehrenberg looked stunned. "Admiral, my team has valuable knowledge that can help you find the Point Pleasant Monster."

"If we need your advice, you're just a phone call away. Besides, you saw for yourself that our cutters aren't big enough to accommodate many guests."

Rastun mulled over Timmins' explanation. Was he telling the truth, or was it an excuse to not have the scientists on board in case they tried to prevent the Coast Guard from killing the monster?

Rastun got out of his chair and stood at attention as Timmins walked by. He then forced himself to relax, reminding himself he was a civilian.

Old habits die hard.

"So what are we supposed to do now?" asked Geek as everyone filed out of the conference room.

Ehrenberg put his hands on his hips and stared at the floor, thinking. "Maybe we can do some more searches on land. Who knows, we might get lucky."

"Well, it beats sitting in a hotel room doing nothing for the next two days," said Karen.

"But no splitting up," Rastun told everyone. "Wherever we go, we all go together. Also, Geek, we load the Aster Sevens with toxin darts only."

"You got it, Cap'n."

"You people disgust me!" Malakov stomped down the hallway of the administration building of Coast Guard Station Barnegat Light.

"Hopefully she'll keep walking right into the ocean," Geek muttered under his breath, just loud enough for Rastun to hear.

"Give her some space," Ehrenberg suggested. "She'll calm down soon."

Rastun stifled a grunt. *Yeah, and tomorrow I'll wake up a Dallas Cowboys fan.*

"Meantime," Ehrenberg continued. "Let's get some hotel rooms, look at some maps and figure out where we should search."

"It'd help if we had some wheels," Geek pointed out. "But my car and the Cap'n's car are still back at Point Pleasant."

"I'm sure we can get the Coasties to give us a ride up there," said Rastun.

"Hey, you saved one of their guys," Geek noted. "They might even buy us lunch on the way."

Ehrenberg nodded. "You two get on it. We'll get set up at the hotel."

Rastun and Geek headed back down the corridor to the base commander's office while the others made for the exit. As they turned toward a stairwell, Rastun's cell went off. He checked the screen.

"It's Sherlock."

"With good news, I hope," said Geek.

Rastun put the phone to his ear. "Go, Sherlock."

"The lab just finished examining the blanks from Geek's shotgun and the darts from your gun."

"What did you find?" Rastun walked back to the conference room, Geek following.

"Some partial prints that belong to you and Geek."

"Just us, huh?"

"Just you two."

"Damn." Rastun put his cell phone on speaker and placed in on the table.

"No prints on the shells or the darts except ours," Rastun told Geek as he closed the door. "What about the dart? They had to replace the toxin with something."

"They did," Sherlock replied. "It was a simple intravenous solution. Amino acids, vitamins, that sort of thing. I also checked the footage from the security cameras where *Bold Fortune* was docked."

"And?"

"Nothing. Someone put covers over them for about fifteen minutes, then removed them. When the cameras were uncovered, they made sure to stay in their blind spots."

"Sounds like we're dealing with pros," said Geek.

"What about our mole?" asked Rastun. "Are you any closer to finding out who it is?"

"Sorry, sir. I'm still digging."

"All right. Well, for now we're stuck on land."

"Why's that?"

"The Coast Guard won't let us back on the *Vigorous*," Rastun answered. "The mission parameters have changed. We're not trying to capture the monster any more. If we find it, we kill it. I think the district CO was afraid someone from the expedition might do something to sabotage them. Probably a good thing, considering we still don't know who the mole is."

"We'll find him, sir," said Sherlock. "Or her."

Rastun nodded. That her could only be Malakov.

"There's one other thing," Sherlock added.

"What's that?"

"I read over your after-action reports from the attacks on the boardwalk and *Bold Fortune*. Something piqued my curiosity."

"And that would be...?"

"On the boardwalk, the monster smashed through the window of a pizza parlor to get at you and Karen. Then on *Bold Fortune*, you said it was only a few feet away from you, but instead went after Karen on the other side of the boat. "

"That's right."

"You're the animal expert," said Sherlock. "Are animals always that determined in catching their prey?"

"Hell yeah. Out in the wild it's a matter of life or death." Rastun's brow furrowed. "Still ..."

"What is it?"

"Predators usually go for the easy kill. The youngest, the slowest or the weakest. Chasing down an animal burns a lot of energy. They can't afford to do it for long. Plus if you have an animal that can fight back, like a sable antelope when it's confronted by a lion, the predator can be injured, even killed. It usually won't risk a fight. Wounded predators don't survive very long."

"But you put up two serious fights with the Point Pleasant Monster," Sherlock pointed out.

"Yeah, I did, and the more I look back on it, the more it should've retreated earlier."

"But it didn't. Can you think of anything that would make an animal go after someone for so long?"

"Blood, for one, but neither me nor Karen had any open wounds. Some animals are attracted to bright colors or shiny objects. Maybe it smelled the meal Karen ate, or something in her shampoo or deodorant or sunscreen. Even so, to hone in on her to that extent, I don't know."

"Then what would make an animal go after someone to that extent?"

"There's only one thing I can think of, but I don't think it's likely."

"Why?"

Rastun explained his reason.

Sherlock paused. "Do me a favor, Captain. Get some samples of Karen's toiletries. Everything she uses. Put them in plastic freezer bags and label them. Call me when you're ready and I'll pick them up."

"All right. I still think it's pretty far-fetched."

"Maybe it is, but we should still look into it, just in case."

Rastun nodded. "Okay. I'll get your samples ASAP."

"Thank you, sir. Meanwhile, I'm going to check out *Bold Fortune.*"

"There's not much to check out," said Geek. "The monster pretty much wrecked it."

"Topside, yes. Not below deck. The storeroom is still intact. Maybe I can lift some prints off the weapons locked."

"All right. I'll be in touch as soon as I have the samples."

With that, Sherlock hung up.

Rastun picked up his cell phone and exited the conference room, his lips pressed together in a thin line. They were still no closer to learning the identity of the mole. He also didn't expect anything to come of Sherlock's examination of Karen's toiletries. How could it?

But if it does... Rastun slowed his pace. If it actually did pan out, the implications would be staggering.

He pushed open the glass door and stepped outside. Less than twenty feet away, Malakov stood near a flagpole, cell phone to her ear.

She turned to Rastun. He continued walking, but didn't take his eyes off her. He fully expected her to break from her conversation and say something derogatory to him and Geek.

Instead, Malakov grinned at him. A decidedly wicked grin.

What the hell is that about?

TWENTY-SEVEN

Despite their short time together, Rastun already knew one thing about Karen.

She was a sound sleeper.

It was just before 1130, when he knew for certain she was asleep, that he slipped out of bed and stepped softly across the floor of their hotel room. Karen didn't stir at all.

Rastun went into his duffle bag and pulled out a handful of plastic freezer bags, a roll of masking tape and a black Sharpie he got on the return drive from Point Pleasant. He started with Karen's bathroom kit, pulling out a plastic bottle of hairspray. Rastun unscrewed the cap, poured some of the contents into a bag and sealed it. He put the cap back on the bottle, returned it to the kit and put a piece of masking tape on the bag. He wrote on it, *Hair spray. Karen Thatcher.* The process continued with deodorant, sunscreen, mouthwash, nail polish, shampoo. Before long, he had well over a dozen bags of toiletry samples.

Rastun got dressed and tread lightly to the door. He opened it slowly and looked back at Karen. She looked so peaceful, so beautiful, just sleeping in their bed.

He smiled and closed the door. They'd known each other for barely three weeks, but so much had happened in those three weeks. Rastun had saved Karen's life twice, and she had done the same for him. He knew first-hand from his time in Iraq and Afghanistan when one person saves the life of another, a deep, special bond forms between them.

How deep and special was that bond when the person who saved you was the woman you...

Is it too soon to think that way?

He shook off the thought and pulled out his cell phone. It took three rings before Sherlock picked up.

"I got the samples," Rastun told him.

"Good," Sherlock replied in a groggy voice. Rastun figured the call had woke him up. "Where can we meet?"

"There's a little office complex a block north of my hotel."

"All right. I'll be there in ten."

Rastun strode across the parking lot, checking around. Nearly all the windows of the two-story hotel were dark. Either folks had already gone to bed or the rooms were unoccupied. Definitely more of the latter, given the parking lot was only a quarter full.

Man-eating sea monsters tended to be bad for business.

It took a few minutes to reach the office complex, which contained five business spaces, two of them vacant. Rastun picked out a shadowy spot between a lawyer's office and chiropractor's place and pressed his back against the wall. Not only did he have a clear view of the parking lot, he also couldn't be taken from behind. Rastun wondered if he was being overly paranoid.

A little paranoia can keep you alive.

There was a mole in their expedition, working for some unknown person or group. He had every right to feel paranoid.

A car pulled into the parking lot. Rastun's hand hovered by his holster, then relaxed when he realized the car belonged to Sherlock.

The deputy marshal pulled alongside the walkway. Rastun went up to the open passenger side window.

"Here you go." He handed Sherlock the bags.

"Thanks. I'll do a midnight run to Washington and get this checked out."

"Good. Did you get anything from *Bold Fortune?*"

"I found some prints on the weapons locker. I still have to run them through the system."

"How did you get onboard?" asked Rastun. "The boat's still tied up at the Coast Guard station."

"You can thank Colonel Lipeli for that. He set me up with credentials so it looked like I was an insurance adjuster for the FUBI."

"Good ol' Lip." Rastun patted the roof of the car. "Let me know if you turn up anything."

"You'll be the first. Good night, sir."

Sherlock drove off. If there was anything to be found in those toiletries, Rastun wouldn't just be surprised.

He'd be floored.

***

Karen was still asleep when Rastun returned to their room, and remained that way when he crawled into bed. He closed his eyes and was asleep in less than a minute.

Music blared in his ears. Something from the Motown era. "Ain't No Mountain High Enough" by Marvin Gaye and Tammi Terrell. Rastun looked at the radio alarm clock. 5:15. He reached over, silenced the alarm and sprang out of bed.

Karen, as usual, shifted under the covers and mumbled something incoherent.

When she finally got out of bed, they did their calisthenics, went on a run and came back to the hotel to shower. While waiting for Karen to finish in the bathroom, Rastun turned on the TV to FOX News. They were midway through a story about more controversy surrounding a bill in Congress regarding immigration reform. The next story dealt with the arrest of an Oklahoma man who kidnapped and murdered two teenage sisters.

There's a guy who needs killing.

The third story started by showing a group of protestors. Rastun's eyes widened when he saw the location.

Barnegat Light, NJ.

"Three dozen people gathered outside the Coast Guard station in Barnegat Light, New Jersey this morning to protest the Coast Guard's decision to kill the Point Pleasant Monster," said the female anchor off-screen. "Admiral Gerad Timmins, commander of the Coast Guard's Fifth District, said the creature represents a grave danger to people both in the water and on shore, adding, quote, 'We have no choice but to destroy this animal in order to prevent further loss of life,' end quote. Many animal rights activists say the Point Pleasant Monster is a unique animal that must be protected at all costs."

Rastun groaned. He hoped those crazies didn't give the expedition any trouble. He had enough shit to deal with.

After breakfast, the group piled into Rastun's car and Geek's Escalade, both retrieved from Point Pleasant yesterday. Montebello stayed behind to monitor the Coast Guard frequencies in case they sighted the monster.

Traffic was pretty thick. Typical for the weekday morning commute in the Mid-Atlantic States. Rastun checked his mirrors more than usual. Dozens of vehicles flowed around him. None looked suspicious. Not that he'd be able to tell. The Rangers taught him a long list of skills. Being able to spot a tail in traffic wasn't one of them. Not much use for it on the battlefield.

He remembered a term from some Cold War spy documentary he saw years ago. "Dry cleaning." Driving a circuitous route to determine whether or not you were being followed. It seemed like a good idea. But how would he explain it to the rest of the expedition, including the mole, without making them suspicious?

Rastun stuck with the route programmed into the GPS. Route 72 to Route 9, then south to the salt marshes around Little Egg Harbor. He and Geek parked near a creekside boat dock. As they broke out their gear, Rastun looked around at the thick grass, shrubs, trees and small ponds. A brief smile traced his lips. This was the sort of environment he'd trained in as a Ranger.

If someone tailed them here, he'd know it.

TWENTY-EIGHT

Too easy.

Piet stared through his binoculars at Rastun and the rest of the FUBI group as they hiked through the marsh. He and Doern had followed them all the way from Barnegat Light without any problem. Rastun and his friend from Aster Technologies did no "dry cleaning." They just took the most direct route, no unexpected turns, no circling back. Nothing.

Even here in this marsh, Rastun hadn't spotted him or Doern. Their green, grass-covered ghillie suits blended in perfectly with the terrain.

"I wonder if this is just a waste of time," Doern whispered. "That beastie's got to be in the ocean, not here."

"Our contact says the FUBI still thinks it's possible the monster lives on land and hunts in the water, like a croc or an alligator. They're the experts, it makes sense to shadow them."

Still, Piet couldn't help but wonder if Doern was right. With the exception of the boardwalk, all the monster attacks occurred at sea. But after the Coast Guard announced their intent to kill the Point Pleasant Monster, Gunderson had been adamant that Piet and his men do everything possible to secure it, alive.

He had no choice but to split his already small force. He and Doern followed the FUBI, while Olef and Heinrich plied the Atlantic in their fake Coast Guard boat, which so far had raised no suspicions from any real USCG crews they had encountered.

Piet's binoculars settled on the FUBI photographer. His gaze lingered on her slender legs, then crept up to her breasts. They weren't that big, unfortunately, but he would still enjoy sucking on her nipples, before slicing them off.

***

"We're being followed," Rastun whispered to Geek.

"Where?" Geek asked as the two walked through the tall grass behind the rest of the expedition.

"About two hundred yards behind us."

Geek twisted around, making like he was retrieving something from his waistband. Rastun knew the former sergeant, in reality, was checking their six.

"I don't see anything," said Geek.

"Trust me, they're there. I saw a head pop up and duck back into the grass. Sometimes the grass is moving when there's no breeze."

"You think they might be connected to our mole?"

133

"Maybe." Rastun glanced over his shoulder. In the distance, he saw a section of grass drop forward and spring back up, like someone was crawling through it.

"We have to tell the others."

"It could work to our advantage," said Geek. "Our mole might get nervous and tip his hand, or hers if it's Malakov."

Rastun nodded and headed over to Ehrenberg.

"Randy. We've got one, maybe two people following us."

Ehrenberg turned to him, his face a mix of surprise and disbelief. "You sure?"

"Positive."

"Do you know who they are?"

"Negative. But right now we have to consider them a threat."

Ehrenberg's face tightened, burying the earlier expression of surprise. "So what should we do?"

"Go there." Rastun jerked his head to the right, toward a coppice of trees 150 yards away. "Once we're under cover, Geek and I will set up an ambush."

"Ambush? You mean like shooting?"

"If we're lucky, it won't come to that."

Ehrenberg looked around at the tall grass around him as he continued to walk. Again Rastun observed the man's expression. The fear and worry were obvious. Eventually, they gave way to acceptance, even some resolve. The process took way too long for Rastun, but Ehrenberg was a civilian. They didn't have that switch that put them into instant action mode.

"Okay. Let's do it."

Ehrenberg veered right. The rest of the expedition followed. Rastun glanced over his shoulder every so often. A couple of times he saw grass rustling despite the lack of a breeze.

When they reached the trees, Ehrenberg called for a break. The others sat down, taking draws from their CamelBaks.

"Everyone listen up," Ehrenberg spoke in a rare, serious tone. "Jack says we're being followed. We don't know by who, and we don't know what they want."

"Are you sure?" asked Pilka.

Malakov snorted. "What kind of bullshit is this?"

"It's not bullshit," said Rastun. "They're out there, and if they're trying not to be seen, I doubt they're up to any good."

"So what do we do?" asked Karen.

"We neutralize them."

Rastun scanned the faces of the expedition members. Karen looked concerned. Malakov looked annoyed. Ehrenberg still wore that determined leader face.

Pilka appeared worried. Very worried. Though it seemed like the typical worry a civilian would have in this type of situation.

"Neutralize?" blurted Malakov. "You mean you're going to murder them."

"We will defend ourselves, and killing will be a last resort."

Malakov looked liked she didn't believe him. Rastun wondered if she might know the people following them.

If she does, they'll tell us. I'll make damn sure of that.

Rastun directed everyone to get behind a thicket of trees. He then pointed Geek to a tree on the right. The ex-sergeant hurried behind it. Rastun took cover behind another tree. He slung the Aster 7 over his shoulder and drew his Glock. Rastun crouched and did what he'd done plenty of times in the Rangers.

He waited.

The wait, it turned out, wasn't very long.

Barely ten minutes after they'd taken cover, two figures rose from the tall grass, about 50 yards from the trees. Both looked male, wore camouflage and had their faces covered by balaclavas.

They also carried submachine guns.

Rastun's grip on his pistol tightened. He peered as far around the tree as he dared.

The two looked to one another, then marched forward, submachine guns up.

Rastun eased himself around the tree, remaining unseen as the two passed by. He peeked from behind the trunk. Both men had their backs to him.

Now!

He sprang to his feet and leaned around the tree, pistol up.

"Drop your weapons!"

Both men jumped and spun around.

Geek emerged from behind his tree, his USAS-12 shotgun aimed at the pair.

"Drop your weapons!"

The two gunmen whipped their heads from Rastun to Geek, eyes wide with fear.

They still held their submachine guns.

"Drop your weapons or you're dead!" Rastun aimed his Glock at the head of the gunman on the left.

"Holy shit, don't shoot!"

"Chill, dude! Chill!"

The pair dropped their weapons.

Rastun rushed forward. "Hands on your head! Get on your knees!"

The two did as ordered.

Rastun kicked the submachine guns across the ground. He then yanked the balaclava off one man's head.

"Don't kill me, dude!"

The guy looked to be in his late teens or early twenties, with a scruffy brown beard and a piercing on his lip.

Rastun's brow furrowed. He removed the balaclava from the other man. He was about the same age, but with no beard and blond hair instead.

"Who are you?" Rastun demanded, while Geek covered them with his shotgun.

"Dude, dude," the bearded guy stammered. "I'm-I'm Mike, and that's Dave. P-Please don't kill us."

"Why were you following us?"

"We-We wanted to make sure you didn't kill the Point Pleasant Monster."

"Who sent you?"

"Lexi. Lexi Campbell."

"Who's that?" asked Rastun.

"She's our President," Mike answered.

"President of what?"

"Freedom for Animals."

"Never heard of it."

"I'm not lying, dude!" The blood drained from Mike's face. "We're not a big group, okay? Maybe, like, twenty people. We just wanted to make a name for ourselves."

"By shooting all of us?" said Geek.

"Yeah... No, I mean, not with bullets."

"Then what's in the guns?" asked Rastun.

"Red food dye. They're not real guns, they're just water pistols."

Rastun backed away, angling himself toward one of the submachine guns. Glock still trained on Mike and Dave, he bent down and grabbed the weapon. It looked like an Uzi, with one big difference.

It was made of plastic, not metal.

He pointed it at the ground and squeezed the trigger. A stream of red liquid shot out of it.

"You stupid shits!" Rastun slammed the fake Uzi on the ground. "We could have killed you!"

"W-Well you shouldn't be killing animals," Dave muttered.

Rastun glared at him. Dave swallowed and lowered his gaze.

"How did you know we were coming here?" asked Geek.

"We followed you from your hotel," Mike answered. "Lexi saw some of you guys there the other day, so we, like, staked it out."

"How did you know we were with the FUBI?" asked Rastun.

"From your web page. The photo gallery's loaded with pics of you guys."

Rastun groaned. Whoever put a mole in their expedition, sabotaged their weapons and covered their tracks had to be smart and organized. They'd never hire these two dipshits.

Rastun lowered his Glock and motioned for Geek to do the same. He went over to one of the water pistols and brought his boot down on it. It shattered.

"You can't do that," said Dave. "Those are ours."

Rastun swung around and glared at him.

Dave shrank back. "Um, never mind."

Rastun stomped on the other Uzi and walked back to Mike and Dave. "Get up."

They obeyed.

"You two go back to your little clubhouse and tell your pals I don't want to see any of you in the same zip code as us, otherwise I'll go to the police and file harassment charges. Got it?"

"Yeah. Yeah, dude."

"Get out of here."

The two hurried out of the little knot of trees. Ehrenberg and the others had already emerged from hiding. They all looked relieved. Except Malakov. As usual, she looked pissed. She probably thought he'd been too harsh on those poor, wayward miscreants.

I could have been a hell of a lot harsher.

"Well," Geek sidled up next to him. "At least we had some excitement today."

That proved to be the only exciting thing that happened. The rest of the day passed without any sign of the Point Pleasant Monster. They had similar success the next day when they explored other salt marshes north of Atlantic City. When they returned to their hotel in Barnegat that evening, they checked in with Montebello.

"Anything from the Coast Guard?" asked Ehrenberg.

"They thought they saw the monster a couple hours ago and shot at it. It turned out to be a shark."

"Stupid bastards!" Malakov barked. "How many more animals are they going to kill by mistake?"

Rastun hated to admit it, but Malakov had a valid point. After the attack on the motor lifeboat, there would be a lot of jumpy Coast Guard personnel with shotguns, automatic rifles and machine guns. Any of them who saw a hump in the water might be quicker on the trigger than normal. There could be a lot of dead sharks, whales and seals all along the Jersey Shore.

Oh yeah, and the press would rake them over the coals for it.

Can't just one thing go our way?

When they got back to their room, Karen showered while Rastun turned on the TV to the channel that usually carried Phillies games. It was well after seven. They ought to be playing by now.

In the top of the second, the Phillies trailed the Cubs 3-0.

Absolutely nothing was going his way.

Karen stepped out of the bathroom in a fresh t-shirt and shorts, toweling her wet hair. Rastun then showered, staying under the warm water longer than usual, letting it relax him.

When he finished, he exited the bathroom to find Karen at the table with her laptop, most likely updating the photo gallery.

"Oh, Jack. Your phone rang while you were in the shower."

"Thanks."

Rastun went over to the nightstand, picked up his cell and checked the last call.

It had come from Sherlock.

"It's from Geek," he lied. "Eh, he's just a few doors down. Might as well go see what he wants."

He gave Karen a quick kiss on the cheek and left. When he got to Geek's room, he held up the phone. "Sherlock called."

"Please let it be good news."

"We'll find out soon enough." Rastun stepped inside and pressed the button for Sherlock's number. Geek had just closed the door when the deputy marshal answered.

"Tell us you've got something." Rastun laid the phone on the dresser.

"I do. You know that theory you said was the most unlikely?"

"Animal pheromones in the toiletries? Yeah." Rastun tensed. "You're not serious."

"My man at the lab confirmed it. Karen's sunscreen was laced with pheromones, pheromones that aren't a match to any known species."

Rastun stared at the phone for several, silent seconds. He drew a breath before speaking. "Remember what I told you about pheromones?"

"Yeah. They'll only attract animals of the same species. My lab tech told me the same thing."

"Then you know what that means," said Rastun. "Someone out there has another Point Pleasant Monster."

TWENTY-NINE

"Are you shittin' me?" Geek turned to Rastun with an incredulous look. "You really think someone got their hands on another Point Pleasant Monster?"

"It's the only thing that makes sense."

"Well, I guess now we know why that thing chased you and Karen all over Point Pleasant, and why it tried to burrow through *Bold Fortune's* deck to get at her. She must have been covered with those pheromones."

"Which means someone wants her dead." Anger lines creased Rastun's face. He thought of Karen, their date at Vargo's, the first night they made love, the way he felt when he was around her.

If anything happened to her, if he *let* anything happen to her...

"So if Malakov's our mole," said Geek, "and that's who I've got my money on, why would she want Karen dead?"

"There's also Raleigh Pilka," Rastun pointed out. "He and Karen had an affair that ended his marriage. This might be his chance for revenge."

"I don't know," said Sherlock. "There are easier ways to kill people. Someone could have just hit her on the head and thrown her overboard, then write it off as an accident."

"Then why put those pheromones in her sunscreen?" asked Rastun.

"I think it's obvious. They wanted to lure out the monster. Whoever's responsible might have just picked Karen's sunscreen at random."

"I don't care if it was random or not, she could've been killed." Just saying that last word caused Rastun to shiver.

"All right," said Geek. "So our mole put pheromones in Karen's suntan lotion to lure out the Point Pleasant Monster. Then what happens? We capture it. So what good does it do 'im? They can't make off with it by themselves."

"No, they can't. But they can call for back-up and hijack your boat," Sherlock explained.

"And they'd still have to get past all the Coast Guard cutters and helicopters out there." Geek shook his head. "What does it even matter how they plan to do it? We're no longer trying to capture the monster. We're trying to kill."

"They may try to capture it themselves," said Rastun.

"Sounds a little too risky on their part."

"They might think it worth the risk. Exotic animal smuggling nets anywhere between ten to twenty billion dollars a year."

"Billion?" blurted Geek. "Like with a 'b'?"

Rastun nodded. "I once heard that the hide of a Siberian Tiger can go for twenty thousand dollars on the black market. They're one of the rarest animals on the planet. Imagine what the price would be for a live Point Pleasant Monster."

"I bet it's a hell of a lot more than twenty grand."

"Try seven figures. Even eight wouldn't surprise me."

"That kind of money would make a lot of people take big risks," said Sherlock.

Geek sighed. "We can stand here all night making SWAGs." He used the slang for Scientific Wild Ass Guesses. "It won't bring us any closer to finding out who our mole is or who sent 'im here."

"We may be on the right track. Remember, someone out there has another Point Pleasant Monster." Sherlock paused. "Captain, you're the animal expert. What would you need to take care of a sea monster?"

"A pool or an aquarium tank for starters."

"A pretty damn big tank," Geek chimed in.

"You got that right. But you also have to have special equipment. Filters and pumps to clean and circulate the water, heaters and chillers to maintain water temperature, water monitoring equipment."

"Are there a lot of companies that sell those kinds of things?" asked Sherlock.

"I couldn't tell you how many companies there are," Rastun replied. "My experience is with zoos, not aquariums. We only had a handful of aquatic animals at the Philadelphia Zoo."

"Well, it shouldn't be too hard to find out. Unless they avoided dealing with legitimate companies." Sherlock paused. "Captain, how difficult would it be to transport a sea creature, a large one, overland?"

"Again, you're going to need all sorts of special equipment and a good-sized trailer to haul it, or a plane."

"A plane?" blurted Geek. "Shit, that means, the other monster could be anywhere in the country."

"I don't think they'd use a plane," said Sherlock. "It'd be too hard to fly a large airplane over the U.S. without the FAA or Homeland Security knowing about it. They'd probably use a tractor trailer, and probably not go very far inland. The longer you stay on the road, the greater the risk for detection."

"Well, that narrows it down to most of the East Coast," said Rastun.

"Yeah, hundreds of miles of coastline." Geek put on a sardonic smile. "That's really narrowing it down."

"Captain, anything else you'd need to take care of a large sea creature?" asked Sherlock.

"Yeah. Food. A lot of it."

"Define a lot."

"An example, one of the tigers at the Philadelphia Zoo eats, on average, thirteen pounds of meat a day. I'll bet you the Point Pleasant Monster eats even more."

"Thirteen times three hundred sixty-five." Sherlock paused for a moment. "That's a little over forty-seven hundred pounds of meat a year."

Geek whistled in surprise. "That'll put a dent in someone's wallet."

"Which confirms we're dealing with a person or group that has a lot of resources," said Sherlock. "Where do zoos normally get food for their animals?"

"A lot of it's prepared in-house. Each animal has different nutritional needs. There are also companies that specifically prepare food for carnivores. Most animal smugglers, however, don't give a damn about proper feeding."

"Which means they might go to a local supermarket to get the monster's food."

"And how many supermarkets are there along the East Coast?" asked Geek. "We're talking a needle in a haystack."

"Geek's right," said Sherlock. "I may have to bring in some more people from the Marshals Service to help."

Concern flared within Rastun. "I don't know, Sherlock. Colonel Lipeli wanted us to keep this investigation compartmentalized. Just like when we were in the Army, the more people who know about an operation, the harder it is to keep it a secret."

"I know, sir, but if we want to find out who has the other monster, and who our mole is, we may not have a choice. I'll run it by Colonel Lipeli and see what he thinks."

"What about the weapons locker on *Bold Fortune?*" asked Rastun. "You said you found some fingerprints on it."

"Yeah, yours and Geek's. No one else's."

"Damn," Rastun muttered.

"I even dusted around the area of the weapons locker. The floors, walls, some boxes stacked nearby, on the off-chance the mole touched something inadvertently. Nothing."

Rastun pressed his palms on the dresser, his eyes narrowing. They were still no closer to finding the mole, the SOB who had put Karen's life in danger.

One damn slip up. Was that so much to ask for? Even the best can make mistakes. Why couldn't the mole have put a hand on the floor to balance himself or herself while kneeling, or rest a hand on the wall while getting to their feet? Little things people do without thinking.

Rastun's head snapped up. He closed his eyes when the realization hit him. "Dammit."

"What is it, Cap'n?" asked Geek.

"My gun cleaning kit."

"What about it?"

"The day I confronted Karen and Doctor Pilka about their affair, I remember someone moved it away from the weapons locker. I left it right in front of the locker the night before. I thought Hernandez might have moved it when he was cleaning, but what if it was our mole who did?"

"Do you still have your gun cleaning kit?" asked Sherlock.

"Yes, I do."

"Get it to me. I'll take it to the lab and see if any other prints are on it besides yours."

"Same drill as before," Rastun told him. "As soon as Karen's asleep, I'll sneak out and meet you at the office complex."

They said their goodbyes and Sherlock hung up.

"Well, I guess this counts as some sort of progress," said Geek. "I still can't believe there's another monster out there, and no one else knows about it."

"Let's just hope we have better luck with the gun kit than the weapons locker, because I want to find out who this mole is and strangle 'em with their own intestines."

Rastun snatched his cell phone off the dresser and went back to his room. Karen was still sitting at the table working on the FUBI photo gallery. She looked up at him and smiled.

He just stared at her. Images flashed through his mind of the Point Pleasant Monster's attacks on the boardwalk and *Bold Fortune*. Karen had literally been inches away from death. If he'd been a second slower to react...

"Are you okay?" Her face scrunched in concern.

Rastun didn't answer. He walked over to her and gave her a long kiss. When their lips separated, Karen's face radiated pleasant surprise.

He wanted to tell her about the mole, the attempt on her life. Didn't she deserve to know? He could trust her. How could he not after all they'd been through?

But his Army discipline kicked in. Colonel Lipeli had ordered him to keep this investigation secret. Operational security existed for a reason: To keep the enemy from finding out what you were up to, and to keep you and the men under you alive. Like he said to Sherlock, the more people who knew about something, the harder it was to keep it a secret.

So he said nothing.

A grin spread across Karen's face. "What was that for?"

Rastun grinned back and ran his fingers through Karen's hair. "Just because."

THIRTY

Rastun had become intimately familiar with Karen's body. He knew exactly where to kiss or touch her to arouse her. He knew instinctively when she wanted to go slow and easy and when she wanted it fast and hard.

Tonight was one of those fast and hard nights.

They went at it with reckless abandon. At times, Rastun half-expected the hotel manager to knock on the door and inform them about noise complaints from other guests.

When they finished, he had to resist the urge to fall asleep. Karen, however, didn't. She lay beside him, a blanket covering the lower half of her naked body. The room's air conditioner chilled the sweat that coated Rastun's body. He rubbed his eyes. He was spent, but there were still things he needed to do.

You've led men in combat bone-tired, so this is nothing.

Rastun eased himself out of bed and checked on Karen. She was sound asleep. He got dressed, picked up his gun cleaning kit and headed for the door. He extended his hand toward the knob and paused. That's when it hit him.

Karen still had her sunscreen.

He went to the sink counter, opened Karen's bathroom kit and pulled out the orange and beige tube.

No one was going to use her as sea monster bait any more.

Rastun held the tube in front of him, wondering if the mole's fingerprints could be on it.

Only one way to find out.

He put it in his pocket. With one final look at a sleeping Karen, he left the room.

Rastun stopped at the soda machine near the bottom of the stairwell and got a Mountain Dew. He drained it during the short walk across the parking lot. The jolt of sugar and caffeine should keep him going for a while.

He phoned Sherlock and made his way down the block to the office complex. Just like the other night, he constantly scanned the area to make sure no one followed him. No one did.

Rastun waited in the same spot he had the other night, between the law office and the chiropractor's office. Sherlock arrived a few minutes later.

"I brought you a bonus prize, Karen's sunscreen tube. I thought you might get some fingerprints off it, too."

"Good thinking." said Sherlock. "I recommend you find another tube to replace it so Karen doesn't get suspicious."

"Gotcha. It's a common enough brand. I can get another at a convenience store."

"I talked to Colonel Lipeli. He and Mister Parker are going to talk to my director tomorrow about adding more agents to this. Discreetly, of course."

"Mm-hmm." Rastun couldn't help but wonder how long the investigation would remain discreet if they brought in more people.

It might be worth the risk if we can catch the mole.

"All right. I'm off to Washington." Sherlock put both hands on the steering wheel. "Actually, first I'm off for coffee. It's been a long day."

"Same here."

Sherlock pulled out of the parking lot. Rastun walked north, further away from the hotel. He remembered there was a 24-hour drug store about a mile away. There had to be suntan lotion there.

Then again, it was the Jersey Shore and it was July. Every store had suntan lotion.

Most of the businesses along the way were closed. A few fast food restaurants had their drive through windows open. He also passed a couple bars. One had a sandwich board sign near the door with a rather artistic rendering of the Point Pleasant Monster holding a red glass.

Come try our newest drink. The Bloody Monster.

Rastun rolled his eyes and continued to the drug store. The section for sunscreen was in Aisle Two. He found the same brand Karen used, paid for it and left the store. Rastun slowed his pace, staring at the tube, the completely full tube.

Karen's had been half-full.

He stood over a trash can and squeezed half the lotion into it. Next, he bent and twisted the tube to give it a worn look. Hopefully it would look the same to Karen.

Rastun put the tube in his pocket and headed back to the hotel. He pondered what they would do if they couldn't find the mole's prints. So far nothing came to mind. He chalked it up to his tiredness and the fact he wasn't a cop.

But the Army had trained him to gather intelligence and assess enemy strengths and weaknesses. They showed him how America's enemies trained, organized and deployed their forces. They also taught him how to anticipate their future moves. Maybe he could put that into effect here.

First off, all operations needed personnel, both in the field and behind the lines for support. Whoever had the other monster would need drivers to transport it and security to guard it. They'd also need specialists, engineers and technicians to build and maintain its habitat. If they were smart, they'd hire some biologists or zoologists, even cryptozoologists, to make sure the monster was properly cared for. The thing was worth millions. You wouldn't want it to die before you could sell it.

Rastun estimated such an operation would involve a few dozen people. As he'd told Sherlock earlier, the more people who knew about something, the harder it was to keep it a secret.

A loud, angry voice burst from the entrance to the bar he passed earlier.

"This is fuckin' bullshit!" A large young man with black hair stepped halfway out. "This is a fuckin' bar, man, and I want another fuckin' drink!"

Rastun tried to ignore the scene and focus on the Point Pleasant Monster operation. A few dozen people would be involved at minimum. Whoever ran the show had to have lots of money.

Like that Kobel Trust Randy was associated with.

"Let me back in, you fuckers!" the big guy screamed. A slim blonde stood next to him, patting his arm and pleading with him. "Danny, c'mon. Danny, please!"

Danny backed further out of the bar. Two large bouncers appeared.

"You're done here, buddy," said one of them. "Now leave or we call the cops."

The bouncers went back inside. Rastun walked by just as Danny screamed, "Fucking pussies! Fuck you!"

Danny wheeled around, half-stumbling. His gaze landed on Rastun. "What the fuck are you looking at, faggot?"

Rastun ignored him and kept walking, and thinking. There were countless people out there who could drive a truck or stand around and look tough. Building a habitat and caring for a sea creature took special skill and experience. Maybe they could—

"Hey, asshole! I'm talking to you!"

Rastun looked over his shoulder. Danny started over to him.

"You got a fuckin' problem with me?"

"Danny, please." The blonde, his girlfriend, Rastun assumed, grabbed one of his enormous biceps. "Please stop."

"Shut up." Danny easily broke her grip. "I asked what's your fuckin' problem, man?"

"Actually, I'm dealing with a lot of problems right now," Rastun answered in an even voice. "But none of them involve you. Now I suggest you leave me alone."

"What if I don't? What are you gonna do about it, you little faggot?"

"Look, I don't have time for a pissing contest. Save yourself some pain and walk away."

"You wanna fight?" Danny staggered closer. Rastun smelled the beer on his breath. "I'll kick your little bitch ass."

Rastun sighed. He couldn't see a peaceful resolution to this.

He sized up his opponent. Danny had to be 6'3 and 210, maybe 215 pounds. Very little of it looked like fat. Another opponent bigger than him. Rastun had been down this road before, including his first day of Ranger School when the instructors had the trainees pair off in a sandpit for hand-to-hand combat. He was already a black belt in Tae Kwon Do. His opponent had been almost as big as Danny and a former high school wrestler.

Rastun got his ass kicked. But in the end, the wrestler washed out while he earned his Ranger tab.

Bigger didn't always mean tougher.

He'd soon learn how tough Danny was.

Danny stumbled to the right. He brought up his fist and cocked back his arm. He might as well have yelled, "I'm going to throw a punch now!"

Danny's fist shot out. Rastun dodged the blow. He grabbed Danny's wrist and twisted. Rastun pivoted and jammed his elbow into Danny's elbow joint. Danny doubled over and cried out in pain.

"Stop it! Stop it!" the girlfriend screamed.

Rastun kept the armlock on him, resisting his Ranger training to break Danny's arm. This was the civilian world, not a battlefield, and this guy was just an asshole, not a terrorist.

"Listen, and listen good. I have more important things to deal with than a drunk shithead like you. So whatever direction I'm walking in, you're going to walk the opposite way. Now answer me with a, 'Yes, sir,' or I snap your arm in half."

"Yes, sir. Yes, sir. I'm sorry, man."

Rastun let go. Danny held his arm, grimacing in pain.

Rastun looked over to the girlfriend. Her wide, shocked eyes shifted between him and Danny.

"I suggest you take your boyfriend home. Better yet, get yourself a new boyfriend."

He turned and headed back to the hotel.

Damn. I lost my train of thought. It took only a couple of seconds to remember where he'd left off.

Personnel. Maybe they could look for any animal experts or engineers with aquarium experience who were unemployed or had criminal records. That may take a while, but it wasn't like they'd go around bragging about smuggling a live sea monster.

Why not? Not everyone took security as seriously as he did. A sense of patriotism and the threat of massive fines and jail time hadn't stopped some soldiers and politicians from revealing sensitive information. They could have mentioned it to girlfriends or wives. They could have gotten drunk at a bar and let it slip.

The more people who knew about something, the harder it was to keep it a secret. Especially in this day and age. When someone saw or heard something, it was on Facebook or Twitter within seconds.

Rastun stopped. *Is it possible?*

He picked up his pace. When he got back to the hotel, he didn't go to his room. Instead, he knocked on Geek's door.

"Cap'n?" The former sergeant stood in the doorway, bleary-eyed and wearing an undershirt and boxers. "What are you doing here?"

"I need to use your laptop." Rastun strode into the room.

"It better not be for looking at Internet porn, not when you got a real woman a few doors down."

"Trust me, it's not for porn, but it's something I'd rather not do with Karen in the same room."

"Ah." Geek nodded as he closed the door. "Sounds like something to do with our off-the-books investigation. What'd you have in mind?"

"When we were in the Rangers, we reconned deserts, mountains and jungles. Now it's time we recon cyberspace."

THIRTY-ONE

"So what exactly are we looking for?" Geek asked as he powered up his laptop.

"Any sightings of the Point Pleasant Monster prior to its attack on Glenn Flynn and Sara Monaghan." Rastun sat at the bland, circular table near the window.

"What, you think whoever has the other one is trying to sell it on eBay?"

"No, but maybe some of the people involved blabbed to someone they shouldn't have. Heck, maybe someone outside this conspiracy saw something. Maybe they got a peek of it being loaded off a boat or when it was being transported. People post on Facebook when they burn a pie or if they're in a bad mood. You better believe they'd post about seeing a monster."

"And the rest of the world just ignores it?" Geek responded.

"Think back to over a year ago, before the Point Pleasant Monster, before those hunters found Bigfoot. If anyone posted about seeing a sea monster, what would your reaction be?"

"They're nuts."

Rastun nodded. "And that's how most people would've reacted."

Geek crossed his large arms. "Does the word long shot mean anything to you?"

"If you got a better idea, Sergeant, I'm all ears."

"Unfortunately, I don't. So I guess it's cyber recon time."

Geek grabbed his smartphone from the nightstand and sat next to Rastun, who said, "Let's try, 'Point Pleasant Monster past sightings.'"

Hundreds of thousands of links popped up for news stories, blogs, videos and posts about the monster. He and Geek went through a couple dozen results. Nearly all of them dealt with either the attacks on the boardwalk or the motor lifeboat.

"Here's one," said Geek. "'Son of Philadelphia Zoo Director Saves Man from Monster.' They even have a picture of you in your Ranger beret. Lookin' sharp, sir."

Rastun chuckled softly, then looked back at the screen and shook his head. "I don't think this is going to get us anywhere. Let's try a new search."

He had Geek type "Sea Monsters Found Dinosaur United States" into the search engine. Rastun, meanwhile, typed "Sea Serpent Long Neck Captured." They narrowed their search to the past five years.

Many of the websites Rastun clicked on yielded nothing useful. He thought the site "Sea Serpents of the World" might be promising. He found a couple of stories, one from Connecticut, the other from North Carolina, of eyewitnesses seeing a long-necked creature rising out of the water. Nothing to indicate they'd been captured.

He checked more sites, more blogs, more Facebook posts. They also contained nothing helpful.

"This looks interesting," said Geek.

"What is it?"

"It's from a year-and-a-half-ago. A Royal Bahamas navy patrol boat spotted a dinosaur-like creature off the coast of Andros Island, a hundred-forty miles from Miami. The thing had a long neck and a head like an alligator."

"Sounds like a good description of the Point Pleasant Monster," said Rastun. "So what happened?"

"The boat chased it for about a half-hour. They even shot at it. But they lost sight of it and never saw it again."

Rastun's shoulders sagged. "Moving on."

Website after website passed before Rastun's eyes. A few stories looked promising, but didn't pan out. His eyelids grew heavy. He forced them to stay open.

More time passed with no success. Rastun's eyes burned. A hazy sensation settled over his brain. All he wanted to do was sleep.

Instead, he checked more sites, blogs and posts. Still nothing.

You could do this for days, weeks even, and not find anything.

But that meant quitting. Rangers didn't quit until the mission was complete.

Rastun clicked on the site "The Unexplained Files." He did a double-take when he saw some of the headlines.

Sasquatch: Missing Link or Extra-terrestrial Colonists?

The Chupacabra: The Government's Failed Attempt to Create a Super Soldier?

"Are you fucking serious?" he muttered.

"What?" Geek turned to him.

"Nothing. Just more crazy shit."

Rastun was about to exit the site when another headline caught his eye.

Sea Serpent Captured, But Where Is It?

Rastun's finger hovered over the touchpad. Was this another dead end? Would he find some outlandish story of government conspiracies and genetic experiments?

He clicked on the story. It was dated from March of last year and just a few paragraphs long. When he finished reading it, he forgot about his tiredness.

"Geek. Check this out." He turned the laptop so Geek could see it, then read the story again.

A few months ago, the boat I was on caught an amazing creature. It looked like a dinosaur, not a really big one. Some of the crew members tried to beat it to death with poles but that didn't work. Actually, the monster got really pissed and started snapping at them.

Our captain decided to take it back home. He also took away our phones and computers so we couldn't contact anyone, which I thought was bullshit. I mean, this was one of the most incredible discoveries ever.

But everything went to hell before we docked. A friend of mine got too close to the monster and got his leg bit off. Then when we docked, there were all these tough-looking guys I'd never seen before. They took the monster and told us to shut up about it.

Well, I've kept quiet long enough. Me writing this may not convince you this creature exists, but one day I'll have proof. I'm close. I'm going to blow this whole thing open.

The author went by the name MonsterMaster491.

"Is this guy for real?" asked Geek.

Rastun drummed his fingers on the table. This MonsterMaster491 hadn't given a location, the name of the vessel or the date when this occurred. Considering the other stories on this site, it was likely another crazy-ass conspiracy theory with no basis in reality.

That's what he would think if there wasn't another Point Pleasant Monster out there.

"Geek. Let's search for any stories about boating accidents where someone lost a leg going back two years."

"Way ahead of you, Cap'n. Check this one out."

Geek showed him the site for a newspaper called *The Daily Advance* from Elizabeth, North Carolina. It featured an article titled, "Fisherman Survives Shark Attack." The story identified the victim as 52-year-old Gabe Monroe, who'd been trying to untangle some nets on a boat called the *Bountiful Betty* when the shark appeared and bit off part of his leg. There were quotes from Monroe about the suddenness of the attack and the pain and shock of losing his leg.

It sounded like a legitimate story.

Unless someone forced him to lie.

"Are there any other boating accidents where someone lost a leg?" asked Rastun.

Geek checked his smartphone and found quite a few. Many, though, occurred on lakes or rivers known for recreational opportunities. There would have been plenty of witnesses around. It would be impossible to cover up a monster attack.

Rastun told Geek to go back to the article about Gabe Monroe and check the date. It was three months prior to MonsterMaster491's story.

Rastun pulled out his cell phone.

"Sherlock. We may have something for you."

THIRTY-TWO

Sherlock took another slug of coffee from his travel mug as he drove down a rural road lined with shade trees, weeds and old wooden houses, some in dire need of repair. Despite the caffeine, the heavy feeling of fatigue clung to his eyes.

He didn't get back to Washington until after 0330. He managed about two hours of sleep before dropping off the gun kit and sunscreen tube at the USMS lab. Next, he did some research on the information Rastun gave him. Sherlock had to give the former captain credit for turning up this lead. Rastun had the tools to be a good cop. Not that he thought he could convince him to join the Marshals Service or any other agency. Knowing Rastun like he did, the man probably found his true calling with the FUBI.

Locating Gabe Monroe was easy. The ex-fisherman lived in an apartment in Buxton Landing, a small town on Hatteras Island in North Carolina. Sherlock traced Monroe's former boat, the *Bountiful Betty,* to the Kearny/Ryan Fishing Company in Manns Harbor. The place had been in business since 1946. A few years ago, it was on the verge of bankruptcy when a corporation called Coast to Coast Fish, Inc. bought them.

The only issue Sherlock found with Kearny/Ryan was an OSHA violation from ten years ago concerning one of their storage freezers. That violation had been promptly fixed. Coast to Coast Fish, meanwhile, owned several fishing companies and fish farms throughout the country and looked legitimate.

But looks could be deceiving.

Sherlock went to the forensic accounting office to have them dig deeper into Kearny/Ryan, Coast to Coast Fish and the Kobel Trust. While they did that, he headed to Buxton Landing.

"You have reached your destination," announced the GPS's monotone, female voice.

Sherlock pulled along the curb, which was dirt and grass. No sidewalk. He scanned the neighborhood. All the houses were wooden, one story and looked like they might have been built in the 1930s. Most were in desperate need of a new paint job.

A couple were in desperate need of a wrecking ball.

He stepped out into the muggy summer air. An elderly couple sitting on the porch of one house turned to him. He spotted a woman peeking out the window of another house.

All three were white.

He stuck out like a sore thumb here.

Then again, in his collared white shirt, tie and dark pants, and driving a two-year-old Chrysler 200, he'd stick out here whether he was black or white.

Sherlock looked across the street at a narrow brown house converted to small apartment units. A man with a scruffy brown-gray beard, hairy arms and an enormous gut sat in a lawn chair. He had his left pant leg rolled up, revealing a prosthetic leg. A six-pack, minus two cans, rested beside the chair. It wasn't even two in the afternoon yet.

Sherlock walked across the street, stepping around a couple of potholes. The man clutched his beer and eyed him with suspicion. He probably hadn't seen many well-dressed black men in this neighborhood before.

He probably hadn't seen many well-dressed men around here period.

"You lost, buddy?" the man asked.

"No. Are you Gabe Monroe?"

"Yeah."

Sherlock pulled out his badge. "Good afternoon, sir. I'm Deputy U.S. Marshal Arthur Dunmore."

"U.S. Marshal?" Monroe took a closer look at the badge. "What'd you want with me? I didn't do nothin'."

"You can relax, sir. I'm not here about you. It's your former employer I'm interested in."

"The fishing company?"

"Yes, sir. Do you mind if we go inside and talk?"

Monroe's face crinkled, as though mulling it over.

"Sure." He grabbed his six-pack and stood. "You want one?" He held it up to Sherlock.

"No, thank you. I'm on duty."

"Suit yourself."

Monroe opened the front door and hobbled inside. Sherlock followed. The living room was small with plain furniture, all of it with tears and loose stuffing. Empty beer cans rested on a coffee table covered by dust. Garbage overflowed from the can by the kitchenette. More dust and empty beer cans sat on the counter. Monroe was definitely single. No wife or girlfriend would tolerate this mess.

"Have a seat." Monroe flopped down on his sofa and gulped his beer.

Sherlock sat in a sagging cushioned chair.

"So why are you interested in Kearny/Ryan?" Monroe took another gulp from his beer.

"It's part of a case I'm working on."

Monroe stared at him in silence, then muttered, "Uh-huh."

Sherlock noted the response. Most people would have reacted with some level of surprise, especially if they worked for a place as clean as Kearny/Ryan.

He pulled out a notebook and pen. "How long did you work for Kearny/Ryan?"

"Just over thirty years. Started right when I got outta high school."

"In that time, did you notice any suspicious activity or behavior there?"

"Um, no." Monroe shifted to the right and drank his beer.

"Did you ever see any people at the company who you felt didn't belong there?"

"No." Monroe lowered his gaze and took another swig from his beer.

"Did you enjoy working for Kearny/Ryan?"

Monroe shrugged. "Don't know about enjoy. It was work, you know? Work is work. But the bosses were all right, even when the company got sold. They paid for my new leg here." He raised his prosthetic.

"How did that happen, if you don't mind me asking?"

"Shark."

Sherlock nodded. He didn't say a word.

Monroe shifted on the couch again. The veins in his neck stuck out. "It came up in our net, with a bunch of Yellowfin we caught. Yellowfin, that's a tuna. Anyway, I got too close to the net. It started snapping and it got my leg. The rest of crew were pressing towels and shirts against my leg. The docs said that probably saved my life."

"What happened to the shark?"

Monroe's eyes darted left, then right. "Um, uh, we killed it. Dumped it overboard."

Again, Sherlock just nodded. He took note of Monroe's nervous movements, his pauses and stutters, his discomfort during moments of silence, all the unnecessary information he put into his story.

Gabe Monroe was definitely lying.

"How far away were you from Manns Harbor when you were attacked?"

"Um, I don't know. A few miles, I guess."

"What kind of shark was it?"

Monroe didn't answer. His thumb rubbed the side of his beer can. "Um, uh... I don't know. It was a shark."

"There are all different kinds of sharks. So what kind was it?"

Monroe shifted on the sofa. "Um... uh..."

"Sorry," said Sherlock. "I just find it curious that you remember the kind of tuna you caught that day, but not the kind of shark that cost you your leg."

"Um...it was a...a Tiger Shark. Yeah, a Tiger Shark. What does this have to do with your investigation, anyway?"

"Sorry. I guess I got sidetracked. Actually, my investigation concerns a former crewmate of yours, a person by the online name of MonsterMaster491."

Monroe took a loud breath. He looked away, then pushed himself off the sofa.

"Mister Monroe?" Sherlock stood.

"I think you better leave."

"Why?"

"I just... I can't talk about it."

Sherlock stepped closer to Monroe. "Did this MonsterMaster491 threaten you?"

"He didn't. But..."

"Mister Monroe, all I need to know is the identity of MonsterMaster491. After that, I'll be out of your hair. If you could just give me his name."

"I can't! They'll..." Monroe's mouth hung open for a few moments, then closed.

"Who are they?"

Monroe looked left, then right. The fear on his face was evident. "They told me to shut up about what happened. The company, they paid for my leg, they still pay for my therapy. If I tell anyone what happened, they said they'd take back my artificial leg, cut off my other leg and dump me in a swamp."

"No one has to know. Just tell me who this MonsterMaster491 is. I won't mention your name to anyone."

"I... I..."

"I can arrange protection if you're scared. These people from Kearny/Ryan have no right to threaten you. Help me and we can put them all in jail."

"I don't know, I don't know."

"Just tell me his name. He's the one I really want to talk to."

"You can't."

"Mister Monroe, please. I need to—"

"He's dead! They killed him."

"Who are they?"

Monroe's mouth hung open wordlessly. He turned and retreated into the kitchenette.

Sherlock walked up behind him and put a hand on his shoulder. "I saw MonsterMaster491's story on The Unexplained Files. I know it wasn't a shark that bit off your leg. It was a sea monster. In fact, I think it was similar to the Point Pleasant Monster. Someone from your company took it. They killed MonsterMaster491, your crewmate... your friend."

Monroe pressed his hands against the counter. His head and shoulders slumped.

"Who was he? Who was MonsterMaster491?"

Monroe didn't answer.

"Did he have a family? Parents? Wife? Girlfriend? Kids? He had to have people who miss him. People who'd want whoever killed him brought to justice."

Monroe's body trembled. "Leo. Leo Fallon was his name."

Sherlock nodded. "What can you tell me about him?"

"He was nice kid."

"How old was he?"

"Twenty-one. He was only twenty-one. He was a hard worker, wasn't cocky like a lot of kids his age. Smart, too. Talked about going to college. He was only working the sea to make enough money for school. But..."

"But what?"

"He believed in all these crazy conspiracy theories. Thought the moon landings were fake, that the government kept crashed UFOs, that they used some big antenna to control the weather. Then when this happened..."

"What exactly happened?"

"It wasn't a shark that did this." Monroe pointed to his leg. "It was a sea monster, just like the one in New Jersey. I remember when we caught it, we were all excited. Thought this would make us rich and famous. Then..."

"Then what?" asked Sherlock.

"That's when things got weird. After the captain radioed our bosses about it, he ordered all of us to hand over our phones, cameras, computers. When we asked why, he said it was company policy. Leo started arguing with him, accused him of suppressing a big-time discovery. I mean, they were really going at it. The captain even threatened to fire Leo if he didn't shut up. But he kept going, I had to pull the kid away before he got himself in any more trouble."

"Did Leo cause any more trouble on your ship?"

"No. He grumbled a lot, said he was going to expose it, but he didn't raise another stink until we got back to Manns Harbor."

"What happened then?"

"We were just a couple miles from shore when that thing bit me. The crew carried me off the boat. I thought there'd be an ambulance there for me, but there wasn't. There were a couple corporate guys in suits and some other guys. Big guys. Real gorillas, you know? One of 'em told me to say a shark bit my leg, otherwise no one would call an ambulance." Monroe bit his lip. "So I did. Shit, my leg was gone and I was bleedin' all over the place, and I was scared, man. What else could I do?"

"I understand."

"Anyway, the corporate guys made everyone sign non-disclosure forms, said anyone who broke them would be fired and sued. I also heard from a couple buddies of mine that they sent the gorillas around to the rest of the crew. They threatened them, threatened their families, if they talked."

"I assume one of these gorillas visited you."

Monroe nodded. "Yeah, he did."

"What did he look like?" asked Sherlock.

"Big. Not tall, but big, muscular. The guy was a tank."

"Can you take a guess as to his height and weight?"

Monroe looked to the ceiling in thought. "Maybe just under six foot. Maybe two hundred pounds."

Sherlock jotted it down in his notebook. "What else? Age? Race? Distinguishing marks?"

"Maybe mid-thirties, looked Hispanic. I don't remember any marks. I just remember he came off as a guy who'd kill you without a second thought."

"Did he give his name?"

"Nope."

"When did he visit you?"

"The day after it happened. I was still in the hospital."

Sherlock again wrote in his notebook. "What about Leo Fallon? I take it they visited him."

"Oh yeah. Actually, he visited me in the hospital a few days later. He had a black eye and a swollen lip. He mouthed off to the guy they sent and he messed him up."

"But I take it that beating didn't deter him."

"No." Monroe's gaze fell to the floor. "He'd call or swing by every so often, told me he was looking into what happened with the monster. I told him to drop it, that it wasn't worth it. But he didn't listen."

"Did Leo find anything?" asked Sherlock.

"I think so. Leo came by one night and told me he wrote a thing about the attack on this website. I told him he was nuts, that he was asking for serious trouble. I told him to stop, but he said he had an idea where they took the monster. Then about three days later, Leo came by again. This time he looked scared. Really scared. Said he found out where they were keeping the monster, but thought someone spotted him. He gave me his iPad, said he had all sorts of information on it about the monster. Told me to put it all on the internet if anything happened to him."

"And did you?"

"No. I don't even own a computer."

"Mister Monroe, do you still have Leo's iPad?"

"Hell no. I didn't want any part of it. I smashed it with a hammer and threw it in the garbage."

Sherlock tried to hide his disappointment. All that had happened well over a year ago. Whatever remained of Leo Fallon's iPad was likely scattered throughout some landfill.

"Sorry." A crest-fallen look formed on Monroe's face. "I guess I should've hung on to it. But these guys, they were fuckin' scary."

"I understand, Mister Monroe."

"I guess I screwed up your investigation, huh, Marshal?"

"Not necessarily. Did Leo mention where he thought they were keeping the sea monster?"

"He just said it was in some old house in Virginia," Monroe answered. "Just over the state line."

"Did he say exactly where?"

"Nope. Just that it was over the state line."

Sherlock stifled a grunt. There were a lot of old houses in Virginia, some dating back to before the American Revolution, and probably quite a few along the border with North Carolina. Needle in a haystack came to mind.

But at least it's a smaller haystack than before.

"How did Leo die?" he asked.

"They said it was a drug overdose. That's bullshit. Leo never messed with drugs."

Sherlock wrote in his notebook. "Thank you for your time, Mister Monroe. I think I've got what I need."

"I'm sorry I couldn't help you more. Really. Leo was a good kid. He didn't deserve that."

"I know."

Monroe finished his beer and put it on the kitchen counter with all the other empties. "You really think you can get those guys?"

"Yes I do. Whatever it takes, I'll see that whoever killed Leo Fallon pays for it, and that you no longer have to live in fear."

THIRTY-THREE

Rastun caught sight of their new boat when he got out of Geek's Escalade. Like *Bold Fortune,* it was another yacht converted into a research vessel. This one though, looked slightly larger with a sleeker bow.

"Pretty nice," said Karen as she stared at *Epic Venture*, which arrived at the Barnegat Light Marina an hour earlier.

"Yeah, it is. At least now we can actually do something instead of being cooped up at our hotel."

"Hey, being cooped up there wasn't all bad." Karen flashed him a wry grin.

Rastun grinned back.

Geek cleared his throat. "On that note…" He started across the parking lot toward *Epic Venture.*

Rastun and Karen followed. Once onboard, the boat's captain, a stout, gray-haired man named Bo Snider, greeted them and took them belowdecks.

When Snider pointed out Rastun's cabin, he noticed it was a clone of the one from *Bold Fortune.* It had a single bunk, a small bathroom and not much elbow room. He set his duffle bag by the foot of his bunk and went back to the Escalade with Geek to retrieve their weapons. Rastun grabbed a case containing an Aster 7 dart launcher, but didn't pull it out.

"Something wrong, Cap'n?"

"I don't want these weapons out of our sight. More importantly, I don't want the ammo out of our sight."

"You think our mole might try to switch out our ammo again?" asked Geek.

"I'm not giving him or her another chance to do it," said Rastun. "So we keep our weapons with us at all times."

"The famous Rastun paranoia at work again, huh?"

"And you're not paranoid?"

"No, but I am very, very, very concerned."

Rastun stared at him for a few moments, then shrugged. "Works for me."

They headed back to *Epic Venture.* Rastun just stepped onto the deck when Malakov emerged from the fly bridge. Her eyes darted to the gun cases he carried. Rastun readied himself for another anti-gun tirade.

To his surprise, she said nothing. Malakov just gave him a sideways glance and a smile that lacked any warmth.

The same kind of smile she had given him after the meeting with Admiral Timmins at Coast Guard Station Barnegat Light.

She's up to something. Rastun vowed to keep a close eye on her.

It was late afternoon by the time everyone's gear was stowed, all supplies loaded and the fuel tanks topped off. The group went to a restaurant a few blocks from the marina for dinner. Rastun knew he and Geek couldn't take their dart launchers or shotguns inside. Instead, they left them in Geek's Escalade. With all the security systems Aster Technologies had installed in the vehicle, no one would be able to break into it without them knowing.

When they finished eating, they returned to *Epic Venture* for a briefing. Ehrenberg suggested beginning their search 15 miles east of Little Egg Harbor, where the largest concentration of sightings had been reported by the Coast Guard.

"We'll probably be chasing ghosts," said Pilka. "I'll bet most, if not all, those sightings are shadows, sharks or whales."

"You might be right," Ehrenberg replied. "Still, it's as good a place as any to start."

When the briefing ended, Rastun and Geek went topside. Rastun stood near the bow, while Geek went to the stern. The sun hung low in the sky when *Epic Venture* left its slip and sailed north toward Barnegat Bay.

Rastun took a deep breath of salt air, staring out at the water and the small islands in the distance. Finally, they were back at sea. No more wasting time in a hotel room or searching wildlife refuges just to have something to do. Now they could do something productive to find the Point Pleasant Monster and eliminate it.

Epic Venture neared the inlet to the Atlantic Ocean when Ehrenberg's voice came over his radio. "I need everyone to gather in the conference room immediately."

I wonder what this is about. Rastun made his way to the salon. Malakov, Pilka and Montebello were already seated at the conference table when he arrived. Geek and Karen showed up a few seconds later, followed by Captain Snider and Tamburro.

Ehrenberg appeared, laptop tucked under his arm. Rastun noted the man's ever-present smile was absent. That usually meant bad news.

"I just received a call from Director Lynch." The cryptozoologist sat down and turned on his laptop. "A segment aired on ABC News a half-hour ago concerning this expedition. Or rather, one member of this expedition."

Ehrenberg tapped on the keyboard, then turned the laptop around so everyone could see the screen. It showed the ABC News website. A short commercial ran prior to the chosen segment. Rastun noticed Malakov sitting up straighter in her seat.

The theme for the newscast played. A voice off-screen introduced the dark-haired, middle-aged anchor.

"We begin tonight with information that has come to light concerning a member of the FUBI expedition searching for the Point Pleasant Monster along the Jersey Shore. Field Security Specialist Jack Rastun has gained notoriety over the past week for stopping the creature's rampage on the Point Pleasant boardwalk and his daring rescue of a Coast Guard officer whose boat was attacked by the creature. Prior to working for the FUBI, Rastun served with the U.S. Army Rangers and was a decorated veteran of the wars in Iraq and Afghanistan. But ABC has learned the reason for Rastun's controversial exit from the military. Here's correspondent Tori Newfield with an ABC News exclusive."

Rastun's face tightened, trying to suppress any sign of his rising concern.

A security camera image of Rastun shooting at the Point Pleasant Monster on the boardwalk ran as Tori Newfield began her commentary.

"A real-life action hero. That's how some have described FUBI security specialist Jack Rastun following his recent confrontations with the Point Pleasant Monster. Heroic acts are nothing new to this former Army officer. Military records show that Rastun has been awarded the Silver Star and the Distinguished Service Medal for gallantry in combat. His former commanding officers have praised him as an exemplary officer. Lieutenant Colonel Salvatore Lipeli, former commander of the First Ranger Battalion and current FUBI Director of Field Security, said in one report, quote, 'Captain Rastun is the embodiment of what a Ranger should be and will be a valuable asset to the United States Army for many years to come,' end quote. So why did such a highly regarded officer suddenly leave the Army?"

Rastun clenched his teeth. *They know.*

"A senior military official speaking on condition of anonymity told ABC News that Rastun was forced out of the Army for assaulting a superior officer shortly after last year's Western Sahara hostage rescue. Military records show that Rastun led the Army Ranger team that rescued nine of the ten State Department members held by the rebel Polisario Front for fifty-one days. Despite the deaths of one hostage and five servicemen, the Pentagon dubbed the mission a resounding success. The senior military official provided ABC News with an after-action report of the mission that details Rastun's behavior upon his arrival at Tan Tan Airport in Morocco."

A headshot of Rastun wearing his tan Ranger beret appeared on the screen, along with words from the report.

Newfield continued, "It reads, quote, 'Captain Rastun was despondent over the deaths of his men. He accused his superior officers of not providing enough support and of improper planning. Captain Rastun was ordered to stand down, but refused to comply. He then physically assaulted Colonel Osgood. While Colonel Osgood was on the ground, Captain Rastun drew his service pistol and pointed it at Colonel Osgood. Captain Rastun was disarmed and placed into custody before he could fire,' end quote. ABC News also contacted the officer in charge of the Royal Moroccan Air Force detachment at Tan Tan Airport, who confirmed there was, in his words, a violent confrontation between U.S. soldiers."

Rastun felt the eyes of everyone around the table on him as Newfield went on.

"As to why Rastun was not prosecuted for such a serious offense, that senior military official told ABC News the Army wanted to cover up the incident so as not to taint what had been a successful hostage rescue. As a result, Rastun and three other Rangers were forced to leave the Army. Pentagon officials have so far declined to comment on this matter."

Ehrenberg swung the computer around and turned off the sound.

Rastun gazed around the table. Many, including Karen, stared at him with shocked expressions. Geek looked pissed.

Malakov, no surprise, wore a smug smile.

"Is this true, Jack?" asked Ehrenberg. "Did you really pull a gun on another Army officer?"

Rastun exhaled slowly. Try as he might, he couldn't look Ehrenberg, or anyone else at the table, in the eyes.

"Yes."

THIRTY-FOUR

"I don't believe it." Karen stared at him with an incredulous look.

Rastun sat in silence. Anger, shock and concern all fought to dominate his emotions. He pressed his fists on the table, trying to settle himself.

That's when he saw Malakov out the corner of his eye. Her smile grew.

"You knew." Rastun's tone was low and ominous. "You knew this was coming down, didn't you?"

"Of course I did."

"What?" blurted Ehrenberg. "Lauren, what are you talking about?"

"I was interviewed by Tori Newfield five years ago on an article I wrote about climate change affecting the mating habits of various animals. It turned out she's just as passionate about protecting the environment as I am. We became friends, and I've helped her from time to time on environmental stories. I called in a favor, asked her to dig into your background." Malakov looked at Rastun. "You're an ex-soldier. You had to have committed some acts of brutality in Iraq and Afghanistan. I didn't expect something like this, but it ought to be good enough to get you thrown out of the FUBI."

"Lauren, you have crossed the line." Ehrenberg's eyes narrowed.

"Have I? You heard the report. Is this the type of man you want on an expedition? Maybe next time he has a meltdown he'll point a gun at you, and maybe he'll actually shoot you."

"You don't know shit, lady!" Geek came halfway out of his seat.

"Geek." Rastun held up his hand.

Geek aimed a harsh gaze at Malakov before sitting back down.

Rastun pushed himself to his feet and looked around the table. "I told you it's true. I did draw my pistol on a superior officer." His eyes settled on Malakov. "But like a lot of mainstream reporters, your friend Ms. Newfield conveniently left out a lot of facts, especially about the colonel in that report, Osgood."

"What about him?" asked Ehrenberg.

"Colonel Osgood was assigned to JSOC."

"JSOC?" asked Karen.

"Joint Special Operations Command. When that State Department delegation to Western Sahara was taken hostage, he managed to sell his pet project, economical warfare, to the Pentagon."

"Economical warfare?" Pilka's face scrunched in confusion. "What's that?"

"We all knew some big cuts to the defense budget were on the horizon," Rastun replied. "All the branches of the Armed Forces were doing their damnedest to lessen the impact of those cuts, so the brass was interested in any idea that let them do more with less. Osgood convinced them we could execute a hostage rescue mission with fewer personnel and assets than normal."

"Basically, hostage rescue on the cheap," said Geek.

Rastun nodded. "And since he served in the Rangers, he convinced the Pentagon we could pull off this mission. The problem with that is we Rangers specialize in light infantry tactics, recon and raids on insurgent bases. Delta Force and SEAL Team Six handle hostage rescue. But again, budget cuts were coming. Osgood thought if the Rangers added another specialty to our mission profile, those cuts wouldn't hit us as bad."

Rastun paused, memories of Western Sahara flooding his mind. "The whole mission was screwed up from the start. Osgood only allowed a dozen Rangers to be on the rescue team. He said we wouldn't need any more since the Polisarios had only ten men guarding the hostages. So much for a two-to-one or three-to-one advantage. He also allocated one Predator drone for recon and one V-22 Osprey for extraction." He shook his head, frustration boiling. "He even limited the amount of ammunition we could carry. Just enough to get the job done, he said."

"Good thing we scrounged more ammo behind Colonel Osgood's back," Geek said. "Otherwise we wouldn't be here right now."

"I tried to tell Osgood we needed more personnel and more assets, but he wouldn't hear it. He was determined to prove this economical warfare idea would work so he could get his star and a cushy office in the Pentagon."

"But it must have worked," said Karen. "You rescued those State Department people."

"All but one." Rastun clenched his jaw, remembering the woman gunned down near his vehicle.

Then Sergeant Tate falling just behind her.

"The rescue went fine. But when we started loading the hostages into our Humvees, the whole village lit up like a fireworks show. Gunfire was coming out of every window. Our one Predator was grounded due to engine trouble. We had no updated intel on our target area for fourteen hours, an eternity in my business. We had no idea the Polisarios had more people."

He noticed Karen giving him a sympathetic look as he went on. "We had to fight our way out of the village to the extraction point. That's when another of my men bought it, Leyva. Just when the Osprey was coming in, it took an RPG round and crashed. We managed to rescue the co-pilot and one of the flight engineers, but the pilot and other flight engineer were killed. Our back-up transport was a hundred-thirty miles away with a Marine Expeditionary Force off the coast. It took them over an hour to reach us. I lost another man, Harris, and had four others wounded. We were running low on ammo. Hell, I was about to order us to fix bayonets when the Marines showed up."

Rastun tried to push down the lump forming in his throat. His mind propelled him back to that night. He pictured the cargo hold of the Marine V-22. The stench of sweat and blood permeated the air. Hostages cried in relief. His Rangers cried out in pain. Thomas' left leg had been torn to shreds. Vazquez had his hands pressed over his eyes, yelling, "I'm blind! Shit, I'm blind."

And he couldn't do a damn thing to alleviate their suffering.

"When we got back to Morocco," Rastun continued, "Osgood was in my grill, saying I screwed up the mission. Then...then he tells me that with so many people dead and wounded, he'd be lucky if the Pentagon ever listened to another idea of his again. He said I probably cost him his star."

Rastun's anger felt as fresh now as it did that night in the desert a year ago. He didn't bother keeping it out of his voice.

"Three of my men were dead. Good men. Good friends. And four more were wounded. One of them went blind and two others lost limbs. But all that son-of-a-bitch Osgood cared about was whether or not he got to be a general. So yeah, I snapped. I decked Osgood."

"Then why did you point a gun at him?" asked Pilka.

"It's one of those facts Doctor Malakov's pal left out of her story, probably the biggest fact of all. Colonel Osgood went for his pistol first."

"You're lying," said Malakov.

"The hell he is," Geek barked. "I was with the Cap'n on that mission. I saw Osgood go for his gun. The Cap'n here was faster, had his Beretta out and aimed at Osgood's head before that prick could get his gun out of his holster. But Osgood brought a couple of special ops guys from JSOC as his bodyguards. In all my sixteen years in the Army, I've never seen a colonel with his own bodyguards. Goes to show how self-important Osgood thought he was."

"And those bodyguards didn't shoot him?" asked Captain Snider.

"Nope." Geek shook his head. "They were just taking their M4s off their shoulders when I jammed the barrel of my rifle into one guy's head. Another of our guys, Branch, did the same with the other bodyguard. Luckily, Colonel Lipeli was there, screaming at us to stand down. We did."

"I can't believe you didn't get in trouble after all that," said Ehrenberg.

"We did," Rastun responded. "Me, Geek and Branch were arrested. We were looking at assault charges, even attempted murder. But the Pentagon wanted this mission to be a success. It would be a black eye for them if word got out that members of the rescue team almost shot their fellow soldiers. So we were given a choice. Resign from the Army with an honorable discharge or be court-martialed."

"That doesn't sound like much of a choice," said Karen.

"No, it wasn't."

"Nice story," Malakov scoffed. "But it's your word against an official report."

"That 'official report' is bullshit," Geek told her. "That was Osgood's side of the story." He turned to Rastun. "How much you wanna bet he's that 'senior military official' they were talking about?"

"It wouldn't surprise me. I suppose Osgood does have an axe to grind with me."

"Did he have to leave the Army, too?" asked Ehrenberg.

"No," Rastun answered. "After all, he was the victim. But after an incident like that, they weren't keen on giving him a star and an office at Fort Fumble."

Most of the people at the table gave him perplexed looks.

"I mean, the Pentagon. So they made Osgood the CO of the Army Ammunition Plant in Iowa."

"Not exactly the plum assignment he was hoping for," Geek chimed in.

"So there's the story. The *real* story." Rastun glared briefly at Malakov. "And if Ms. Newfield really wanted to do her job, she could have also asked that senior military official for my after-action report, and Geek's, and Colonel Lipeli's, and the rest of our team's, because they'll confirm everything we said."

"It won't matter." Malakov maintained her smug expression. "The public won't believe you. It'll just look like damage control. I told you I'd find a way to get you off this expedition and out of the FUBI."

"That decision's not up to you, Lauren," Ehrenberg told her. "It's up to Director Lynch."

"What did he say about this?" asked Rastun.

"I guess you'll have to find out for yourself, Jack. Lynch wants to see you and Geek at FUBI Headquarters first thing tomorrow morning."

THIRTY-FIVE

Rastun stared out the window of Geek's Escalade, saying nothing as they drove down I-95. He barely registered the vehicles streaming around them, or the lights of nearby Newark, Delaware. All he could think of was his impending meeting with the FUBI brass.

There'd always been a worry hovering around the back of his mind that one day the Western Sahara op would come back to bite him in the ass. Thanks to that bitch Malakov, it did. Now a job he'd grown to love was in jeopardy. Worse still, if the FUBI fired him, would that affect his relationship with Karen?

They'd gone through so much during these past few weeks. They'd survived three attacks by the Point Pleasant Monster, they had saved each other's lives. They talked, they joked, they worked effectively as a team.

He didn't want to imagine life beyond this expedition without Karen.

Don't get ahead of yourself, he warned himself, thinking about the way things ended between him and Marie.

His mind drifted back a little over a year ago. He'd been sitting in a cell on the military side of Tan Tan Airport. He'd given his side of the story to a parade of investigators, ranging in rank from second lieutenant to brigadier general. They represented JSOC, the JAG Corps, CID – Criminal Investigation Division – the Department of the Army. Some were by the book, some were sympathetic. The general was irate for having to fly across an entire ocean to, "Clean up a cluster-fuck created by a captain who went nuts and tried to murder a superior officer!"

Rastun imagined spending the next 20 or 30 years in Leavenworth. He thought about how he had embarrassed the Army, embarrassed the Rangers.

Embarrassed the memory of his Uncle Roger.

The Army spared him any prison time, but at the cost of his commission. He flew back to Hunter Army Airfield in Georgia, home of the 1st Ranger Battalion, thinking of the men he'd lost and his career in ruins. He'd gone to Marie's apartment and told her what happened, expecting sympathy and understanding.

What he got instead was fury, not directed at the Army, but at him.

"I thought I was going to marry a man who'd make colonel or general one day. Now what are going to do? Manage a fucking Taco Bell?"

Rastun had been too shocked to respond. He had loved Marie. He wanted to spend the rest of his life with her. How could he have not realized she was so shallow?

In the days that followed, he looked back on their relationship. Signs emerged, signs he'd been blinded to when they were together, like all the times she encouraged him to attend formal dinners or parties.

"You need to rub shoulders with the higher-ups if you want to get ahead," she'd say, or, "Try to get a spot on some general's staff. You can show them how smart you are. They'll take that into account the next time you're up for promotion."

Rastun didn't get a staff appointment. He was no REMF – Rear Echelon Motherfucker. But he did go to those damn boring formals. He did rub shoulders with colonels and generals. He convinced himself it wasn't ass-kissing, just making his presence known. Score a couple of brownie points for advancement.

It was only after their break-up he realized Marie didn't make those suggestions to help him. It was all to help her. She had been enamored by the wives of senior officers, the respect they commanded from the wives of junior officers, even other base personnel. Marie wanted that for herself, like some high school girl desperately wanting to be popular. He was just the dumbass she hitched her wagon to.

He knew Karen was nothing like Marie. She had saved his life twice. She had risked her life to save little Ashlee. She was a caring mother to Emily. He couldn't imagine her being concerned about something as trivial as the social pecking order of Army wives.

What's going to happen to us now?

"This sucks," Geek blurted as they passed a road sign welcoming them to Maryland.

"Yeah, I got that after the fifteenth time you said that."

"Sorry, sir. This just isn't right what Malakov did to you."

"No shit."

Geek snorted. "Well, once we tell our side of the story, I'm sure your bosses'll understand."

"That would be nice." Rastun paused. "I'm sorry I dragged you into this."

"You didn't drag me into anything."

"You never would have put your weapon to that soldier's head if I'd just kept *my* head."

"What was I supposed to do? Stand there and let that dick pop you?"

"What if Aster fires you over this?" asked Rastun. "You've got a wife and three kids to support."

"Whatever happens, happens," Geek replied. "Me and Angela'll deal with it. And you'll deal with it, too, sir."

"Yeah." Rastun went back to staring out the window.

His cell phone rang. The call was from Sherlock.

"I've got good news, Captain. Gabe Monroe gave me the real story on what happened on the *Bountiful Betty.*"

"Was it just like the story on The Unexplained Files?"

"Yes, sir, but with a not-so-happy ending for the guy who wrote it. MonsterMaster491's real name was Leo Fallon. Monroe told me some people from the corporation that owns Kearney/Ryan threatened the fishing boat's crew to keep silent about the monster. Fallon didn't, so they silenced him permanently."

"How?" asked Rastun.

"A drug overdose is the official story. I checked the medical examiner's report on Fallon. He only found a single needle mark on his left arm. No tracks up and down the arms, no damage to the lining of the nose, no liver problems like you'd expect from drug or alcohol abuse. Fallon was pretty damn healthy when he died."

"And that didn't set off anyone's radar?"

"Fallon was found dead in his bed," replied Sherlock, "a needle on the floor and no sign of foul play. Whoever killed him probably did it while he slept."

"Sounds like we're dealing with some serious professionals."

"I agree."

"What about the company that owns Kearney/Ryan?" asked Rastun. "Did you find anything on them?"

"They're called Coast to Coast Fish, Incorporated. The forensic accountants back at headquarters are still checking on them." Sherlock paused. "By the way, sir, I saw the news, the story about you and Western Sahara."

"You have Doctor Malakov to thank for that. She got a reporter friend of hers to dig into my past for any skeletons. She found the biggest one."

"What do your bosses have to say about it?"

"Geek and I will find out tomorrow. We're driving down to Alexandria right now."

"I hope everything goes well for you," said Sherlock.

"I hope so, too. You find out anything else?"

"We may have a location on the second Point Pleasant Monster."

"Where?" Rastun straightened in his seat.

"According to Fallon, it might be in an old mansion along the Virginia/North Carolina border."

"That's still a lot of ground to cover."

"I know. I'm narrowing it down to counties near the coast, assuming the opposition didn't want to drive too far with a sea monster. I'll start checking county property records tomorrow."

"Sounds like you're going to need some help with that." Rastun bit down on his lower lip. What he was considering meant disobeying an order.

At this point, what do I have to lose?

"Where are you at now?"

"Home," replied Sherlock.

"All right. We should be there in another hour-and-a-half. We'll get some sleep and look at those county records tomorrow."

"Sir, you have a meeting with the FUBI tomorrow. I can get some other marshals to help me out."

"The last thing we need is a bunch of U.S. Marshals running all over Virginia and possibly tipping off the bad guys. Plus, if the monster is in some mansion, you're going to have to recon it, and no one does recon better than Army Rangers."

"What about your meeting with the FUBI?" asked Sherlock. "You know you're in for a world of trouble if you miss it."

"I'll get out of it somehow."

"If you say so, sir. I just hope you know what you're doing."

"I always do."

When Rastun hung up, Geek glanced over at him. "How are you gonna get us out of this meeting?"

"By calling in one big favor."

He punched up Colonel Lipeli's number.

"Sir, we just heard from Sherlock." Rastun ran down the information the deputy marshal had given him.

"Good," said Lipeli. "It sounds like we're getting closer to finding this other monster."

"I think so, too. That's why I need a favor."

"What kind of favor?"

"We're on our way to give Sherlock a hand with his investigation."

"Give him a hand? You do realize you're supposed to meet with Director Lynch and Mister Parker tomorrow."

"I know, sir," replied Rastun. "But who's more likely to find this house without spooking the bad guys? Three ex-Rangers or a bunch of marshals going around flashing their badges?"

"Captain, this is not the time to be playing action hero."

"Just give us twenty-four hours."

"How the hell am I supposed to do that?" demanded Lipeli. "That Western Sahara story has created a Category Three shitstorm. Director Lynch wants to see you and Sergeant Hewitt in his office tomorrow at oh-nine-hundred, and that is exactly where you two will be."

Rastun clenched the phone tighter. He racked his brain for a counter argument. Nothing came to mind.

His eyes came to rest on the dashboard. That's when the idea hit him.

"Hey, Geek. Did the check engine light just come on?"

Geek looked at his console, then turned to him and grinned. "Son-of-a-bitch, it did." He rapped on the dashboard. "Whoa, you hear that knocking sound? That can't be good."

"You really expect me to believe you guys are having car trouble?" said Lipeli.

Rastun pounded the dashboard. "It's getting louder. I don't think we'll be able to make it another mile, never mind Alexandria."

"We're gonna have to call for a tow." Geek's smile widened. "Too bad all the service stations around here are closed this time of night. We'll have to wait till morning for someone to look at it."

"And who knows how long it'll take to fix," Rastun added.

Lipeli blew out an exasperated breath. "All right. I'll sell your bullshit story to Lynch and Parker. But you two asshats better come back with something good, or don't bother coming back at all."

THIRTY-SIX

Rastun and Geek crashed at Sherlock's apartment, waking up at 0400. Divorced for five years, Sherlock lived like the typical single guy, meaning he didn't have much food in the fridge or cupboard. The trio went to a nearby convenience store for cereal bars, breakfast sandwiches, bagels, coffee and orange juice. They ate while they scanned the internet for 18th and 19th century mansions in Virginia. Specifically, the southeastern counties of the state, where the travel time from Manns Harbor was anywhere from an hour-and-a-half to two hours.

The less time spent on the road secretly transporting a sea monster, the better.

It turned out there were a lot of old mansions in that part of Virginia. They did their best to narrow down the list, first eliminating the ones in more developed areas. Whoever had the other Point Pleasant Monster would want it as far away from prying eyes as possible. They also eliminated the ones converted into museums, horse farms or bed and breakfasts.

That still left them with nearly 40 old mansions and houses stretching from Isle of Wright County along the Chesapeake Bay to Mecklenburg County some 90 miles inland. They tried to narrow it down even further, using satellite images from Google Maps to see which ones were in isolated areas.

The number dropped by half.

"Twenty possible targets," said Geek. "That's still a lot of ground to cover."

"We can narrow it down even more, but we need to go to Southern Virginia." Sherlock turned to Rastun. "You may want to consider changing, sir."

He looked down at his BDU pants and olive green t-shirt. "What for?"

"After that story last night, people might recognize you. Like you said, we don't want to risk tipping off any bad guys."

Rastun agreed and changed into jeans and the polo shirt he got from Wal-Mart after the boardwalk attack. Now he looked like an ordinary civilian. Sherlock also lent him a Washington Redskins ball cap to complete the ensemble.

"You seriously want me to wear this? I'm an Eagles fan."

"A ball cap and sunglasses makes for a nice, cheap disguise."

Rastun grimaced and donned the cap.

It could be worse. It could be a Dallas Cowboys cap.

The three piled into the Escalade. While Geek drove, Sherlock checked his smartphone for companies that specialized in building aquarium tanks.

"I found one. Jonnard's Aquariums. They're located in Newport News."

Rastun sat quietly in the back as Geek took I-95 south. With a two-and-a-half hour drive ahead of them, that left a lot of time for his mind to wander. He thought about his future with the FUBI, if he even had a future with them.

He worried about the FUBI expedition in New Jersey. With Geek having been recalled as well, he had to take the shotguns and dart launchers with him. They were property of Aster Technologies and they didn't want them used without one of their representatives on hand. All *Epic Venture* had now were standard tranq rifles, and hopefully a Coast Guard cutter nearby.

Most of the time, he thought about Karen.

They reached Newport News around noon. Jonnard's was located in a beige rectangular building along the Southwest Branch Back River. They walked across the parking lot toward the glass front doors. The blazing sun beat down on Rastun while suffocating humidity wrapped around him. He'd been in climates much hotter and more miserable than this. Still, he relished the cool air when he entered the building. A woman in her early thirties with glasses, pale skin and unnaturally bright red hair sat behind the reception desk.

"Good morning." She smiled. "How can I help you?"

Sherlock introduced himself and pulled out his badge. "Is your boss here? I'd like to speak with him."

"Um, no. Barry's out on a job. But his brother Greg is here. He's in charge when Barry's gone. I'll get him for you."

The receptionist, Crystal, according to the name plate on her desk, returned a couple of minutes later with a portly man with thinning black hair.

"Greg Powell. I'm the general manager here. What can I do for you?"

"We're working an animal smuggling case," Sherlock explained, "and think our suspects may have bought some equipment from your business."

"What?" Powell's eyes widened. "Hey, if anyone used our stuff for anything illegal, I didn't know about it. All our business is legitimate."

"Don't worry, Mister Powell, I'm not accusing you of anything. I just want to check your records and see if anyone purchased equipment for building a tank large enough to hold a dolphin or a shark."

"We've built large aquariums for all kinds of people. Can you be a little more specific?"

"It would have been sometime early last year."

Powell had Crystal call up the sales records on her computer. "Here's one." The date she gave was a day after Gabe Monroe's supposed shark attack.

"Actually, I remember this one." Crystal winced. "The guy who placed the order was kinda scary."

"Scary how?" asked Rastun.

"He was big. Not tall, just really buff. And his eyes. They were kind of cold, you know."

"Anything else you remember about him?" asked Sherlock. "Hair color? Race? Distinguishing marks?"

"He was white. I think he had dark hair."

It wasn't the guy Sherlock had told him about, Rastun thought, the one that paid the visit to Monroe after he lost his leg. But other than the ethnicity, the two could have been clones.

"What did he get?" asked Rastun.

Crystal ran down the list. Along with thick glass for the tank, the mystery man bought filters, pumps, overhead lights, temperature regulating equipment and water monitoring equipment.

"Do you sell accessories like stones or artificial reefs and plants?" asked Rastun.

"Yeah." Crystal nodded.

"And this guy didn't buy any of that?"

"Nope."

He took it as an indication they were on the right track. Most people bought stuff to decorate their aquariums. Animal smugglers, though, wouldn't give a damn about that.

"Can you give me a name and address on this man?" asked Sherlock.

Crystal looked at Powell, who nodded.

"Sure," she said. "I'll print it out for you."

A minute later Sherlock held a copy of the sales receipt. It was for a Jeff Mason, who lived at 117 Laskey Street in Gloucester, Virginia. There was also a phone number and credit card number.

Sherlock looked up from the receipt. "Did you build this aquarium for Mister Mason?"

"No," Crystal answered. "He said he had other people who'd build it for him."

"Is that normal?" asked Sherlock.

"We usually build the aquariums," answered Powell. "But sometimes the customers will do it themselves."

Rastun nodded. No way would animal smugglers let a legitimate company build a tank for something like the Point Pleasant Monster.

Sherlock shook hands with Crystal and Powell. "Thank you for your help. We appreciate it."

"You're welcome," they both said, with Powell adding, "Remember, we had no idea we sold to animal smugglers. Let your bosses know that."

"I will."

Rastun, Geek and Sherlock went back to the Escalade. Geek programmed Mason's address into the GPS and headed north to Gloucester.

Thirty-five minutes later, the GPS announced, "You have arrived at your destination."

Their destination turned out to be a square white building just off Main Street. Judging from the faded paint, graffiti and overgrown weeds, no one had been here for years.

"What a surprise," said Sherlock. "A bogus address."

"For a guy with a bogus name, I bet," added Rastun.

"And with a burn phone and credit card that's no longer active."

Geek groaned. "Great. We just wasted a bunch of time coming up here."

"It was a lead," said Sherlock. "We had to follow it up."

"Well, now let's check out our next leads." Rastun removed a piece of paper with a list of addresses from his pants pocket. He felt confident it would bring them closer to their objective.

After all, if you were keeping a sea monster worth millions, you had to feed it.

THIRTY-SEVEN

Rastun, Geek and Sherlock went to several supermarkets in Newport News, Norfolk and Portsmouth. Sherlock flashed his badge and asked if anyone had bought large amounts of meat or fish on a regular basis. Every employee and manager they asked said no. Sherlock also showed a photo of Leo Fallon and gave descriptions of the tough guys who threatened Gabe Monroe and showed up at Jonnard's. No one recognized them.

They drove to the next county over, Southampton, a small county made up of towns whose populations didn't come close to a thousand. It didn't take long to check out the handful of supermarkets within its borders. No one there knew of anyone buying large quantities of meat or fish. They also couldn't recall seeing Leo Fallon or the tough guys.

Next, it was onto Greensville County, which turned out to be even smaller than Southampton County. Only three towns showed on the map, Emporia, Jarratt and Skippers. They started in Emporia, since it was the biggest city. If a population of 6,000 could be considered big.

Their first stop was the Wal-Mart Supercenter, where again they had no luck finding anyone who saw Leo Fallon or the tough guys. Next they went to the Food Lion, a chain supermarket with stores throughout the Mid-Atlantic States. The store manager took them to the meat department. The person in charge of it, a pudgy man with gray hair and a thick mustache, greeted them.

"Ed Hutchinson." He shook their hands. "How can I help you gentlemen?"

"We're investigating an animal smuggling ring that may be operating in this area," Sherlock told him. "Has anyone come in over the last year buying large amounts of meat and fish on a regular basis?"

Hutchinson screwed up his face. "Not that I can recall."

Rastun stifled a groan. They were striking out more than Phillies slugger Ryan Howard.

Sherlock showed him the photo. "Have you ever seen this man in the store? His name is Leo Fallon."

"The face isn't familiar, but you said his name's Leo?"

"Yes."

"One of the girls here dated a fella named Leo. Hanna. Hanna Phillips. She should be working one of the checkout lanes right now."

Sherlock thanked him. The trio headed to the front of the store. Geek spotted a short, slim girl with long black hair and a nametag reading HANNA working the counter of aisle six. Rastun doubted she could have been older than 20.

"Hanna Phillips?" asked Sherlock.

"Yes?" She glanced at him while passing a can of soup over the scanner.

"Deputy U.S. Marshal Arthur Dunmore. May we have a word with you, please?"

Now Hanna turned her full attention to them. "M-Me? Why do you want to talk with me?"

Several other people in line also looked their way. Rastun figured it wasn't every day a real-life U.S. Marshal came into the Food Lion in little Emporia, Virginia. He also lowered his head, hoping no one recognized him from the news.

"It's about a man named Leo Fallon," explained Sherlock. "Did you know him?"

"Leo?" Another, bigger flash of surprise spread across her face. "Is he in trouble or something?"

"Why don't we talk about this somewhere else?"

Hanna called for another clerk to take over for her. She led them to a small break room that had a coffee maker, two small refrigerators and a few plastic couches and chairs that had seen better days. They all sat down.

"Is Leo okay?" asked Hanna.

"Why don't we start at the beginning?" Sherlock suggested. "How do you know Leo Fallon?"

"I met him last year. I just started working here and I walked past him in the soda aisle. He was kinda cute. We started talkin' and he asked me out, but we only went on a few dates."

"Were there problems between you two?"

"Kinda. I mean, get this. On our second date, he was telling me he was looking for this sea monster his bosses were hiding. This was, like, before anyone ever even heard of the Point Pleasant Monster."

"And you believed him?" asked Rastun.

"Well, not at first. But then he told me about this thing called the Mockting...no, Mucktun Monster?"

"Montauk Monster," Rastun corrected her.

"Yeah, that's it. Leo said it escaped from this secret lab in New York. He even showed me a picture of it on his phone. I mean, it really was a monster."

Rastun nodded. Ehrenberg had told him about the so-called Montauk Monster one night during dinner. He believed the creature to be a dead dog or raccoon and credited its monstrous appearance to a combination of decomposition and submergence in salt water.

"After seeing that picture, I figured Leo knew what he was talking about," Hannah continued. "He told me his company was keeping another monster, even bigger than that Montauk Monster. He found one of the guys involved in it and tracked his license plate to a rental car company in Norfolk. He told me if they had the monster he saw, they had to feed it. He thought maybe they were getting food for it from a supermarket."

"And you said this led to problems between you two?" asked Sherlock.

Hanna nodded. "He wanted me to keep an eye out for anyone who got lots of meat."

"And did you ever see any customers do that?"

"Nope, and that's what I told Leo, all the fucking time. I swear, he called, like, every day and asked me that. At first I thought it was cool, you know. Like something from a spy movie. But after a while it got annoying. He even asked me about it when we were making out. Can you fucking believe that? After that I dumped him."

Hanna paused, her eyes darting to all three of them. "Um, is Leo okay?"

Sherlock lowered his eyes. Geek shifted slightly in his seat. So did Rastun. He then sat up straighter. He was the officer in the room. This was his responsibility.

"Hanna. I'm sorry to tell you this, but Leo's dead."

"What?" Her hands went to her chest. "Really?"

Rastun nodded. "I'm sorry."

Hanna stared at the floor, mouth agape. "Oh my God. How did it happen?" Her eyes widened. "Was it something to do with this sea monster stuff? Was Leo telling the truth?"

"We're still trying to determine that," said Sherlock. "But thank you for your time, Hanna. You were very helpful."

"Sure. No prob." Hanna seemed to stare past Sherlock. Probably still trying to digest the fact a former boyfriend had died, Rastun thought.

The three ex-Rangers left the break room and headed back to the Escalade. They checked their list of supermarkets. The only one left in Emporia was an independently owned one called Greensville Food Market.

They drove there and met the owner, who introduced them to the head of the meat department, a skinny man with glasses named Dick Ortega.

"Has anyone been here over the last year buying large amounts of meat on a regular basis?" asked Sherlock.

"Yeah. A guy named Al. He comes in every week or so."

"What does Al look like?"

"The guy's built. Real stocky. Short hair."

"What color?" asked Sherlock

"He's got black hair," Ortega replied.

"Is he Caucasian?"

"Nope. Hispanic."

That sounded like the tough guy that threatened Gabe Monroe.

"Did he say why he needed all that meat?" Sherlock asked Ortega.

"Yeah. He works at this private animal sanctuary."

"When does he come in?"

"Thursdays, usually. That's our quality control day, when we get rid of stuff near the expiration date. Al gets it at a discount price. No sense letting all that food go to waste."

Rastun groaned to himself. Today was Tuesday. They didn't have time to stake out the place and wait for Al.

"Do you ever talk to Al when he's here?" asked Sherlock.

"A bit. He's not much into small talk."

"Did he ever mention where this animal sanctuary is located?"

Ortega shook his head. "Nope. He just said it's a ways from here."

That's nice and vague, Rastun thought. Al could be talking about someplace five miles away or 50.

They thanked Ortega and started to walk away.

"Hey!" Ortega blurted, his gaze on Rastun. "You know, you look like that FUBI guy they had on TV. The one who was in the Rangers."

Rastun cracked a small smile and shrugged. "I've been getting that a lot today."

He strode away from the meat counter before Ortega could say anything else.

"Some disguise you came up with." Rastun looked to Sherlock and pointed to his Redskins ball cap.

"Sorry, sir. It was the best I could do on short notice."

They checked their shortened list of suspect mansions. Three were located in Greensville County, none more than ten miles from Emporia.

The next part of their investigation required a place where they could work in private, have access to Wi-Fi and change their clothes. They picked a Holiday Inn Express just down the road. Rastun didn't think they'd be staying the night, but it would serve well as a temporary base of operations.

The trio stopped at a sub shop near the hotel. Rastun wolfed down a 12-inch roast beef and cheese hoagie, along with two bags of chips. He hadn't eaten since early this morning and was famished. So were Geek and Sherlock, judging by how quickly they ate.

After checking into their room, they sat at the table, turned on their laptops and went to the Greensville County government website to access property records. Geek checked the mansion to the east, Sherlock the one to the northwest and Rastun the one to the south.

His finger hovered over the touch pad as he read the document. The mansion in question was located at 50 Trotting Horse Way. Double-checking the satellite map, Rastun couldn't see another house near it for at least four miles. An isolated location in a county with a population under 13,000. Who would ever suspect someone had a sea monster hidden here?

He read on. The mansion had been built in 1854 as part of a plantation owned by one Thomas Ardner. Ardner, he noticed, died in 1863, maybe in the service of the Confederate Army. The mansion's ownership passed to Ardner's wife, Ellie, who sold it four years after the Civil War.

The property was owned by the Tannehill family until 1898 when it was bought by an Edward Holmes. That family retained ownership for the next several decades, transforming it from a plantation to a horse farm. The business closed in 1978, and the last Holmes on the list, Willa, lived in the mansion until her death in 1987. Ownership of the abandoned mansion and grounds transferred to something called the Briggs/McDaniel/Schaal Trust.

Rastun's eyes fell to the next few lines. It turned out the mansion had changed hands three years ago to . . .

He stared at the screen, unblinking. His entire body went numb.

"Cap'n?"

Rastun barely heard Geek. He just kept staring at the screen.

"Cap'n," Geek said louder.

Rastun slowly turned to him.

"You okay?"

"I found out who owns the mansion on Trotting Horse Way."

"Who?"

Rastun had to force the words out of his mouth. "Karen Thatcher."

THIRTY-EIGHT

It turned out Karen didn't currently own the mansion. She had sold it to an outfit called Old South Restoration. He felt a dark, invisible hand clench around his gut when he noticed the date of sale.

Three days after the attack on Gabe Monroe.

"Coincidence?" he muttered the word without much confidence.

"Do you really believe that, sir?" asked Sherlock.

Rastun shook his head. "It doesn't make sense. What about the suntan lotion? Why would Karen put it on herself and let the monster come after her?"

Sherlock stared at the floor in thought. "Would you say Miss Thatcher is someone not averse to taking risks?"

"Yeah."

"Then it might make sense for her to use that suntan lotion on herself. Whoever's running this op has to have a lot of money. I've seen people take crazy risks for money."

"Why doesn't she spike someone else's suntan lotion?"

"It's a good way to deflect suspicion. She makes herself look like a victim instead of the mole."

Rastun thought Sherlock might be reaching. But he'd always trusted the marshal's instincts.

No one is right one hundred percent of the time.

"Um, how about I check out this Old South Restoration?" Geek looked to Rastun.

He turned his head slightly to the former sergeant and nodded.

Geek tapped on his laptop. "Says here they specialize in refurbishing old homes and mansions and turning them into museums or bed and breakfasts."

Rastun and Sherlock leaned over to look at the screen. The home page showed two mansions side-by-side, one dilapidated, the other fully restored. The top of the screen had links for contacts and services. When Geek clicked on contacts, he got a general company email and a phone number. Sherlock called the number, then said, "Four rings, then voicemail."

"You think anyone would call back if you left a message?" asked Geek.

"I doubt it. This site has no physical address listed, no endorsements, no credentials, no photo gallery showing previous work like you'd expect from a business. It feels like someone just threw this together to give the company some sense of legitimacy."

Rastun looked back at the mansion's property records. He stared at Karen's name. It didn't make sense. Why would she own an abandoned mansion in Virginia?

He then remembered her saying she had some distant relatives in this state. Could they have been in charge of that trust? Could they have given the mansion to her?

It could be a completely different Karen Thatcher.

Rastun knew he was grasping at straws. The evidence kept mounting that Karen had to be the mole.

How the hell is this possible? She saved my life. Twice!

Maybe she had done that to gain his trust. Maybe that was also the reason she slept with him.

Another thought struck him. What if the people behind this had kidnapped Karen's daughter? What if they used Emily to force her to do their bidding?

Rastun thought about all the times Karen talked about Emily, trying to recall any signs of worry or fear. None came to mind. He doubted any woman would be able to completely hide those emotions when it came to their daughter.

Blindsided by a woman...again! How could this have happened after Marie? Was he a damn fool? Was he so easily taken in by a pretty face and some hot nights in the sack?

And he had actually felt...

"Cap'n."

Geek's voice snapped him back to the present. He turned to find the former sergeant and Sherlock staring at him.

"We need to come up with a plan to recon that mansion."

Rastun took a deep breath and nodded. "Yeah. Yeah, you're right."

He buried his feelings about Karen. Or at least, he tried to. Thoughts of her drifted around the periphery of his mind as they checked out satellite maps of the mansion. More than once he scolded himself.

You're not a lovesick teenager. You're an Army Ranger. Now act like it!

All his focus was locked on the screen. Trotting Horse Way went on for a little over a mile, ending at the mansion grounds. Trees lined the road and surrounded the property. Rastun's biggest concern was the grounds themselves. They had to cross between 70 to 100 yards of open space to reach the mansion's front door.

A perfect kill zone.

The same could be said for the rear of the property, and the flanks. None of them could make out any cover leading up to the mansion. No bushes, no ditches, nothing. Of course, civilian satellites didn't have the same sort of resolution as military ones. This one also didn't give them real-time intel on the target. He had no idea how many bad guys they faced, their security set-up or where they kept the monster.

The only way to find that out was to actually go there.

First, they needed some supplies.

The three drove to a local outdoors supply store. They picked up camouflage field caps, nightscopes, camo face paint and sports bottles. It would put a nice dent on all their credit cards, but Rastun knew they would need that gear.

The sun nearly touched the horizon by the time they returned to their hotel room. They took out their fatigues and boots from their luggage and changed. Rastun knew it would have saved time to change first, then head to the store. The problem was three men dressed in full camouflage walking around an outdoors retail store on a weekday evening might raise concern in some people.

They filled their sports bottles with water and checked their sidearms. Rastun holstered his Glock when Geek came up to him.

"You good, Cap'n?"

"I'm good."

"You sure?" A doubtful look crossed Geek's face.

Rastun felt a stab of irritation. What Geek was really asking was, "This whole thing with Karen isn't going to affect your judgment?"

"My head's in the game, Sergeant."

Several seconds passed before Geek said, "Yes, sir."

They waited until dark before setting out. It didn't take long for the small cityscape of Emporia to give way to forests. When they got within a quarter-mile of Trotting Horse Way, Geek pulled off the road. He maneuvered the SUV between two knots of trees. Rastun and Geek smeared black camouflage paint on their faces and donned night vision goggles. The night air felt warm and muggy. Rastun took a couple of pulls from his sports bottle. Geek and Sherlock did likewise.

Geek grabbed two USAS-12 shotguns, one for him, one for Sherlock. Rastun took an Aster 7. He put two tranq darts and two toxin darts in the chamber and stuffed two cases of extra darts in his assault vest.

"Let's go." Rastun led them into the forest.

They took their time, mindful of their footfalls, trying to make as little noise as possible. Rastun scanned for any sentries, booby traps or security cameras. He found none.

The trio reached the edge of the woods without incident. They squatted behind some trees and drank from their water bottles. Rastun pushed his goggles over his head and took out his night vision binoculars.

All the windows of the mansion were boarded up, with no light leaking through them. The wooden walls looked rotted. A chimney poked out of the eastern side of the mansion, much of it crumbled away.

"Looks like the restoration company that owns this place hasn't done much restoring," Geek commented as he, too, stared through his binocs.

Rastun zoomed out and examined the grounds around the mansion. They looked like they hadn't been maintained in years. The grass had grown waist high. That meant good concealment for them.

The three worked their way around the perimeter, staying among the trees. Every twenty yards they stopped and scanned the mansion and it grounds.

Rastun didn't see any sentries. He checked the mansion's roof and walls, and the trees near it, for any security cameras.

He did not see a single one.

They did find four sheds at the back of the mansion. Rastun guessed they had been used as stables when this place had been a horse ranch. He also saw no security cameras on them.

Then again, the stables looked so dilapidated they would collapse under the extra weight of a camera.

When they finished their recon, the only visible security they found was a barbed wire fence with a few NO TRESPASSING signs.

"I was expecting a little more than this," said Geek. "Actually, I was expecting a lot more."

"So was I," Rastun added. "A couple of drunken teenagers could breach this place."

"Sometimes the best security is no security," Sherlock stated.

Rastun looked at him. Sherlock had a point. If you posted sentries and put up security cameras and an electric fence, people would know something was going on.

But who would give a rundown mansion in the middle of nowhere a second glance?

"So what's the plan, Cap'n?" Geek turned to him.

"We infiltrate through the rear. I want to see if there's anything in those sheds first. The high grass should give us good cover, just keep an eye out for tripwires or motion sensors. There's also bound to be a good amount of wildlife in grass that tall."

"What kind of wildlife?" asked Geek.

"Rabbits, chipmunks, mice."

"That's not so bad."

"Skunks, rats, snakes."

Geek frowned. "That's not so good."

"We'll survive. Sherlock." Rastun looked to him. "Head back to the car. If things go south, we'll need you to extract us."

"Yes, sir."

Geek tossed him the keys. "Remember, it's a company ride. You scratch it, it comes out of my paycheck."

"I'll take good care of it."

Sherlock headed through the woods back to the Escalade.

"Ready to do this?" Geek asked Rastun.

He nodded. "Rangers lead the way."

THIRTY-NINE

Rastun crawled under the barbed wire fence with no difficulty. So did Geek. The barbed wire courses they'd gone through in basic and in Ranger School had been far more challenging.

They entered the tall grass. Rastun's eyes darted between the stables thirty yards ahead and the ground in front of him, mindful of tripwires or motion detectors. He found none.

Maybe there aren't any. Maybe Sherlock had it right, that the bad guys decided the best security was no security.

A voice whispered from the back of his mind, *As soon as you let your guard down, you go home in a body bag.*

He continued checking for tripwires and motion sensors. He still didn't find any.

The stables lay 15 yards away. He continued crawling, the grass brushing against his face.

A thin dark line appeared in front of him.

Rastun stopped. Every muscle in his body tensed.

The line moved toward him. A forked tongue flickered out of it.

Snake.

He remained statue still, studying it. Through the phosphorescent green of his night vision goggles, he couldn't determine the snake's color. He estimated its size at nearly three feet.

Eastern Cottonmouths reached three feet.

Rastun looked at the snake's head. It didn't have the triangular shape common to most venomous snakes. The head on this one was round. Maybe a King Snake. They were common to Virginia.

Whatever it was, it wasn't venomous.

The snake flicked out its tongue and slithered onto Rastun's arm. He didn't flinch. Growing up around zoo folk, he'd handled all sorts of snakes, from Garter Snakes to Anacondas.

This snake slid over his arm and continued on its way.

Rastun and Geek made it to the stables without further incident. They crept beside the rotted wooden wall. Rastun eyed the mansion. It remained dark and quiet.

He peered around the edge of the wall. One of the wooden double doors was missing. He peeked inside.

Empty.

They crawled across the ground to the second stable. It, too, was empty.

When they reached the third stable, Rastun opened the door a crack and checked inside.

An SUV sat inside.

Using hand signals, he told Geek there was a vehicle inside and to take up position across from him. Geek moved to other double door and crouched, clutching his shotgun. Holding his Aster 7 with one hand, Rastun held up his other hand and counted down.

3... 2... 1.

They opened the double doors and rushed inside, weapons up. Rastun swept the right side of the stables. He saw no one.

"Clear to the right," he stated.

"Clear to the left," said Geek.

They advanced on the SUV and checked inside. Empty. The vehicle was a newer model Ford Escape with Virginia plates.

"This confirms it," said Geek. "Someone's here."

"And probably up to no good if they're hiding a car like this in here."

Rastun committed the license plate to memory and headed back outside, Geek following.

The last stable also had an SUV inside it.

"So this puts the opposition at a minimum of two and a maximum of ten," Rastun explained. "I'd bet that number's closer to ten than two."

"So maybe ten bad guys against two ex-Rangers." Geek grinned. "The odds are still in our favor, Cap'n."

Rastun chuckled.

They exited the stable and crawled to the rear of the mansion. Rastun examined one of the windows. Boards covered it. He lifted his NVGs and peered through a crack between the boards. He saw nothing but blackness.

They crept along the wall to another boarded-up window. Again Rastun tried to peek through the cracks. Again he only saw pitch black.

He reached into his right boot and pulled out his tactical knife. He flicked open the blade and eased it through the crack. The tip poked a heavy fabric.

"Blackout curtain," Rastun whispered to Geek.

They continued along the wall. Rastun neared the corner when his brow furrowed. Something wasn't right. He tuned out his and Geek's soft footsteps, the gentle night breeze, the chirping of crickets.

His ears picked up another sound.

Rastun stopped, his left fist shooting up. He sensed Geek halt behind him.

"You hear that?" he whispered over his shoulder.

Geek scrunched his face and raised his head. "Sounds like a hum."

Rastun pressed his ear against the wall. The hum grew a bit louder. He quickly recognized the sound. He'd heard it plenty of times during raids on terrorist bases.

"Generator," he mouthed to Geek. "C'mon."

They made their way along the wall until they came to the rear door. The pair checked it for any sign of an alarm system. They found none.

Rastun gently turned the knob and gave the door a small push.

Locked.

Time for one of the little known skills the Army taught its elite forces.

Rastun shoved his tactical knife into the slit between the door and the doorjamb. He jiggled the knife back and forth until he heard the lock click.

Hand on the knob, Rastun stood alongside the doorframe. Geek was across from him, shotgun up. Rastun held his breath, hoping they didn't miss an alarm, wondering if someone waited on the other side with a gun.

He twisted the knob and pushed the door open. No alarms went off. No bullets flew at them.

Rastun took a quick look inside, then hurried through the door, Aster 7 up. Geek followed. They swept the room. Rastun saw cupboards, a pantry, a sink, a stove and a refrigerator. None of them looked like they had been used in years.

"Clear."

"Clear," Geek repeated. "Cap'n, look at this."

Rastun turned to find a plastic folding table with six folding chairs around it. A half-full garbage bag sat in the corner. He checked inside to find sandwich wrappers, Styrofoam containers, water bottles and soda cans. The trash couldn't have been here for more than a couple of days. Any longer and rats and other animals would have torn through the bag.

"Looks like they set up a little home away from home," said Geek.

Rastun looked down the hallway leading to the living room. Clear. He waved for Geek to follow.

The floorboards creaked under Rastun's feet. He winced, then took a much softer step. No creak. Three more steps and the floorboards creaked again.

He neared the end of the hallway and checked around the corner. He saw a large empty space that had probably been the living room at one time. A staircase was situated along the far end of the room, the top half blocked from view by a wall.

Rastun stepped into the living room. Another of the 150-plus year old floorboards creaked. Again he winced. He prayed that—

Thump.

Rastun's left fist shot up. He and Geek halted.

Thump. Thump. Thump.

Someone was coming down the stairs.

FORTY

Rastun and Geek retreated down the hallway and into the kitchen. They stood on either side of the entryway, backs pressed against the wall.

The footsteps got louder, then thumped on the ground floor. Rastun held his breath, concentrating on the footfalls. They got closer to the hallway.

He ran down his options. He didn't want to kill anyone, not until he knew for certain what was going on here. Rastun glanced at his Aster 7, but dismissed that idea. Unlike in the movies, tranquilizer darts didn't work instantly. They needed to find a way to take this person down quickly and quietly.

The footsteps echoed down the hallway.

Rastun waved to Geek, jerked his thumb toward the hallway, then tapped the butt of his dart launcher against his stomach. Geek nodded.

The footsteps got closer. Rastun pressed himself as flat as possible against the wall.

A man came into view. Burly, at least six foot tall with a military style buzzcut. He paused and started to turn toward Geek.

The ex-sergeant rammed the butt of his shotgun into the man's gut. He doubled over.

Rastun came in behind him. He slid his right arm under the other man's armpit and across his chest. Rastun yanked back and took him to the ground. Two quick punches to the face put the man out of commission.

Rastun slapped a piece of duct tape over the man's mouth. Geek used more tape to bind his hands behind his back. Rastun patted him down and found a stubby MP5K submachine gun in a shoulder rig.

"Definitely not standard issue for your average night watchman," said Geek.

"You got that right." Rastun continued his pat down and discovered a Browning Hi-Power Mark III pistol, along with extra mags for it and the MP5K. He gave the pistol to Geek and kept the submachine for himself.

"What'd we do with this dipshit?" Geek pointed to the semi-conscious guard.

Rastun looked around the kitchen. "Stick him in the pantry."

They dumped the guard inside. Rastun wrapped more duct tape around his ankles and shut the door. He looked over at the folding table. If the seating arrangement was any indication, they'd just cut down the opposition to five.

The pair headed into the living room. Rastun scanned left.

"Clear," he whispered, then heard muffled voices from upstairs. Not from actual people, but from a TV. He took a step toward the staircase when Geek tapped him on the shoulder. He pointed to what looked like the cellar door. Light came from the crack at the bottom.

Rastun went over to the door and put his ear on it. A steady hum came from behind it. The hum of a generator.

He opened the door slowly and checked inside. Wooden stairs led down to the basement. Sturdy-looking ones made of beige wood. Definitely a new addition.

Rastun opened the door all the way, wincing when it creaked. He pushed up his NVGs and took the stairs slowly, MP5K up. Geek followed, closing the door. A wall ran alongside them until they got halfway to the bottom. Rastun stopped and peered around the edge.

Bright fluorescent lights hung from the ceiling. A large refrigerator stood in the near corner. A portly, balding man with a black beard sat at a folding table typing on a laptop. Wires ran along the floor. At the far end of the basement a thin, brown-haired man checked over pumps, tubes and other equipment connected to a large aquarium.

Inside that aquarium was the other Point Pleasant Monster.

FORTY-ONE

Rastun charged down the stairs, Geek on his heels. He pointed the MP5K at the man at the laptop.

"On the floor!" he ordered in a forceful, though not loud, voice. "On the floor, now!"

The bearded man gaped at him, eyes wide with shock and terror.

Rastun marched up to the table and aimed between the man's eyes. "Get on the fucking floor or you're dead!"

The bearded man let out a small squeak of fear and practically fell on his stomach.

"Don't make a sound." Rastun covered the man's mouth with duct tape and tied his hands behind his back. He looked over at Geek. The ex-sergeant had the other man secured.

"Watch the door," Rastun ordered.

"Yes, sir." Geek hustled across the basement and up the stairs.

Rastun searched the bearded man. He had a wallet, keys, a few coins and a cell phone. No weapons. He checked the man's wallet. It contained seventy dollars cash, two credit cards and a Virginia driver's license for one Fred Bell.

He took out his cell phone and snapped a few pictures of the makeshift lab and the monster. He couldn't help stare at it for several seconds. Seeing it with his own eyes, he found it hard to believe a sea monster swam around a tank in a mansion in the middle of rural Virginia.

Rastun pocketed his phone and rolled Bell over on his back. The man took quick, terrified breaths. His eyes bulged. Rastun jammed the MP5K's barrel under his chin.

"You call out for help, I kill you. Got it?"

Bell nodded.

Rastun peeled back the tape from Bell's mouth. "Fred Bell? Is that your real name?"

"N-No." He shook his head. "It's... It's Steven Krueger."

"And what exactly do you do here, Mister Krueger?"

"P-Paleontologist."

Rastun looked from Krueger to the monster. He guessed it made sense. Paleontologists studied dinosaurs, and the Point Pleasant Monster sure as hell looked like something from prehistoric times.

"How many people are here?" Rastun demanded.

"Five. S-Six, including me."

"I assume your buddy over there is an engineer. What do the other four do?"

"Security."

Rastun nodded. That left three more guards to watch for.

"Who's running this operation?"

The veins in Krueger's neck stuck out. "I-I can't tell you."

Rastun pressed the MPK5 harder against Krueger's chin.

"Please. Please, I can't. He'll kill me."

"I kill you if you don't talk."

Krueger's jaw trembled. "If-If you shoot, they'll hear you." Rastun scowled. He drew back the submachine gun, put it on the floor and drew his tactical knife.

"Good thing knives don't make any noise."

Krueger whimpered as Rastun put the blade just behind his right ear.

"You answer my questions or you start losing body parts."

Krueger shivered. Tears spilled from his eyes.

"Who's running this operation?"

Krueger's mouth opened, but he didn't speak.

"Say good-bye to your ear."

"No, wait! Wait, please." Krueger closed his eyes, as though trying to keep from sobbing. "N-Norman Gunderson."

Rastun drew back his head in surprise. "*The* Norman Gunderson?"

Krueger nodded.

"Where did you find that monster?" Rastun nodded to the tank.

"Some fishermen caught it in North Carolina."

"And how did Gunderson get his hands on it?"

"He owns the fishing company."

"And this mansion?"

"He-He wanted a place to hide the Sea Raptor."

Sea Raptor? Rastun guessed that was their name for the Point Pleasant Monster.

"Gunderson bought this place through one of his dummy corporations right after we found the monster," Krueger explained.

Rastun's jaw tightened. His next question was on the tip of his tongue. Anger, betrayal and hurt threatened to overwhelm him. He fought it off. He had a job to do.

"What's Karen Thatcher's role in all this?"

"I don't know—"

Rastun heard the basement door open, then a voice.

"Hey, I'm just checking...what the hell?"

FORTY-TWO

Rastun heard the thud of metal on flesh, then the thump of a body hitting the floor.

"Geek!" He pocketed his knife and picked up his MP5K. He sprinted to the stairs and looked up.

Geek stood on the landing. Rastun peered around his legs to see a stocky man lying on his back, groaning.

"Another guard," said Geek. "I guess he got lonely without his buddy."

Rastun looked at the fallen guard. Blood streamed from a gash just under his eye, probably where Geek nailed him with the butt of his shotgun. He also noticed the guard was Hispanic. He'd bet anything this was the man who threatened Gabe Monroe and beat up Leo Fallon, maybe even killed him.

"Help!" Krueger screamed. "Help me! Help me!"

"Shit," Rastun cursed. "Time to go."

He and Geek ran toward the front door. Rastun pulled out his cell phone.

"Sherlock! Mission compromised! Immediate exfil! Immediate exfil!"

"I'm on the way!"

Rastun kicked open the front door. He waved Geek through, then turned to follow.

That's when he noticed movement from the staircase. Two silhouettes pounded down the steps. One of them carried something stubby.

An MP5K.

Rastun dove through the open door and landed flat on his stomach. A sharp chatter sounded behind him. Bullets tore through the wall and the doorframe.

"Cap'n!" Geek charged onto the front porch and dropped to a knee. He fired two blasts through the opening. He ducked out of view as more 9mm rounds punched through the wall.

Rastun rolled to his knees and returned fire. The silhouettes retreated up the stairs. He let loose two more quick bursts while Geek fired three times. Rastun glanced at the road. Where the hell was Sherlock?

Rounds chopped up the doorframe above him. Rastun lay on his stomach and fired. Again the bad guys retreated. Rastun fired until the 30-round magazine ran dry.

"Reloading!" he shouted.

Geek fired the remaining sabot rounds from his USAS-12 while Rastun changed out mags. Moments after Geek fired his last round, enemy bullets tore through the walls and doorframe. Wooden splinters rained down on Rastun. He ignored them and fired three bursts at the staircase.

An engine roared behind him. Rastun glanced over his shoulder. The Escalade smashed through the wooden gate and sped toward the mansion.

Rastun and Geek exchanged more shots with the guards until the Escalade jerked to a stop 15 feet away.

"Go!" Rastun shouted to Geek. "I'll cover you!"

He unleashed a stream of 9mm rounds at the guards as Geek dashed for the SUV. Rastun fired until he emptied the magazine, then leapt to his feet and sprinted off the porch. Geek was already in the front passenger's seat, and had left the rear door open for him.

Rastun threw himself inside.

"Go! Go!"

Sherlock stomped on the gas as Rastun twisted around in the backseat. He grabbed the door handle just as the two guards appeared on the porch. Rastun slammed the door shut as muzzle flashes sprouted from the MP5Ks. Bullets pounded the Escalade's side. A jagged crack formed in the window.

"Hey, Geek," he said. "Give my regards to Aster. The armor and bulletproof glass work great."

"Thanks. Now wish me luck when I explain how one of their rides got shot up."

The Escalade sped back to the road. The guards continued to fire. A few 9mm rounds struck the cargo hatch, but didn't penetrate it. Soon the mansion was out of sight.

"Please tell me this was all worth it," said Sherlock, who did not slow down.

"It was," replied Rastun. "The other Point Pleasant Monster's in there. I got pics of it and the name of the scientist taking care of it. Steven Krueger. He's a paleontologist."

"Good. I'll have the Marshals Service run his name and get the local cops out here."

"Well, here's another name for you, the guy behind this whole thing. Norman Gunderson."

Geek looked at him as Sherlock turned off Trotting Horse Way. "You say that like we oughta know who he is."

"People in the zoo business know him. He's a billionaire out of Texas. Made his money in oil and energy exploration. One of his side projects is buying failing zoos and supposedly turning them around."

"So what does he really do with them?" asked Sherlock.

"The zoos Gunderson owns have some of the highest animal mortality rates in the country. A lot of people think he buys them as part of an animal smuggling ring."

Sherlock looked at Rastun in the rearview mirror. "And he hasn't gotten nailed for it?"

"The word is witnesses are afraid to come forward. That, and when you're a billionaire, you can afford the best lawyers on the planet."

"And bribe anyone you have to," added Sherlock.

"Well, this time we should have enough to nail his ass. I better call the colonel." Rastun reached into his pocket for his cell phone.

"Sir," said Sherlock. "I think we're being followed."

Rastun looked out the rear window. A pair of headlights charged toward them.

He clenched his jaw. It had to be the guards from the mansion. He kicked himself for not thinking to puncture the tires on those SUVs in the stables.

An orange strobe winked from the SUV's right passenger window. Two cracks formed in the Escalade's rear window.

"I guess they really don't want anyone finding out about that sea monster," Geek quipped.

Rastun ripped out the MP5K's empty magazine and shoved in his last full one. He looked at the backseat windows, but decided against returning fire. The Escalade was armored like a Bradley Fighting Vehicle. He'd be safer hunkered inside it.

Unless the other SUV ran them off the road, or shot out a tire or two.

Two more rounds clanged off the Escalade's rear.

Enough of this shit. It was time to do what Rangers did best. Seize the initiative and go on the offensive.

Rastun leaned between the driver's and passenger's seats and studied the GPS screen.

"There!" He pointed. "About a quarter of a mile away, there's a side road to the right."

Geek checked the GPS. "It looks like it dead ends."

"That's okay. Sherlock, turn on that road, then pull to the side and stop."

"What then?" he asked.

"We give those assholes one hell of a surprise."

Sherlock nodded. So did Geek. Rastun was certain both men knew what he had in mind.

The guards in the other SUV kept firing. More rounds pinged off the Escalade. Rastun kept a tight grip on his MP5K, while Geek had his shotgun ready.

Sherlock cut the wheel right. The Escalade roared onto the side road. Sherlock pulled over and slammed on the brakes.

"Go! Go! Go!" shouted Rastun.

Doors flew open. The three ex-Rangers leapt out. Rastun took up position to the rear. Geek and Sherlock, who also had a shotgun, got behind the hood.

Tires squealed. The other SUV slid right, then barreled down the road. A man leaned out the backseat window, clutching a submachine gun.

"Open fire!" Rastun yelled.

His MP5K chattered. The shotguns boomed. Sparks jumped off the side of the SUV. Windows shattered. The man in the back flailed. His MP5K flew out of his hands.

The SUV sped by. Rastun fired his remaining rounds. The back window exploded into glass splinters. Geek and Sherlock blasted away with their shotguns. The driver jerked. His head dropped out of sight.

The SUV swerved and went down an embankment. The front end clipped a tree. The SUV spun in a cloud of dust and flipped over. It rolled three times and came to a stop, wheels up.

"Let's go." Rastun threw down his empty submachine gun and pulled out his Glock. He advanced on the SUV. Sherlock and Geek followed, shotguns up.

Rastun trained his pistol on an unmoving man lying on the road. The guy's chest had caved in. His arm lay under him, twisted in an unnatural manner. Blood and brains oozed from the head.

They continued past him to the SUV. Rastun motioned for Sherlock to cover the driver's side while he made for the passenger side. Pistol extended, he checked inside. One guard lay crumpled against the roof, blood pouring from his neck and shoulder. He felt for a pulse. As expected, there was none.

"Sherlock. What'd you have?"

"The driver's dead. Most of his head is gone."

Rastun holstered his Glock and took out his phone. He hit Lipeli's number. "Colonel, it's Rastun. We found it."

FORTY-THREE

Even though he had worked for the FUBI for three weeks, this was the first time Rastun had actually set foot in their headquarters. There wasn't much to it aesthetically. Until their permanent headquarters was built, the foundation worked out of an old industrial complex in Alexandria, Virginia with bland rectangular buildings.

The three ex-Rangers walked into the deserted lobby. Following the directions Lipeli gave them, they took the stairs to the third floor and went through the fourth door on their right. Inside was a room with a conference table and swivel chairs. The only touch of true decor came from a few framed photos on the wall. One was a still of Bigfoot from the famous 1967 Roger Patterson film. Another showed an underwater shot of an alleged flipper of the Loch Ness Monster.

Rastun's gaze lingered on a third photo. This showed the sagging carcass of a creature with a long neck hauled aboard the Japanese trawler *Zuiyo Maru* in 1977. Though badly decomposed, it did bear some resemblance to the Point Pleasant Monster.

"Gentlemen," said a lean, bald man in his early sixties. "Glad to see you're all safe."

"Thank you, sir," Rastun replied to Roland Parker, the billionaire philanthropist who helped establish the Foundation for Undocumented Biological Investigation.

"Have a seat."

Rastun sat and gazed at each man at the table. Besides Lipeli and Parker, a bronze-skinned man with a thick build and black ponytail and a pudgy man with glasses and receding dark hair also sat in on the meeting. FUBI Director Edward Lynch and Department of Agriculture liaison Nathan Hipper.

"So tell us what you were up to while waiting for your car to get 'fixed.'" Lynch gave them a half-grin. Rastun picked up the hidden meaning. The FUBI's director didn't believe their bullshit car trouble story, but was willing to look the other way given what they discovered.

The ex-Rangers told them how they located the mansion and the monster inside it. A few times they were interrupted by alarmed comments from Hipper.

"You did what... How bad did you hurt them...You actually killed people? Oh my God, the press will crucify us."

By some miracle, Rastun restrained himself from slamming Hipper's face into the table. *Typical bureaucrat.* The man had no clue what the real world was like beyond his cubicle.

"Do you have the photos of the monster?" asked Lynch.

"Right here, sir." Rastun slid his phone across the table to the director. Lynch's eyes widened when he looked at the pictures.

"I can't believe they were actually keeping this creature in a basement in the middle of Virginia." Lynch looked up from the phone. "We need to secure it as soon as possible. Do we know if the police have arrived there yet?"

Sherlock answered, "The last time I checked, the local cops were still trying to obtain a warrant. I assume they have it by now. It shouldn't be long before they arrive at the mansion."

"What if the monster's already been moved someplace else?" asked Hipper.

Rastun shook his head. "I don't see how they could. I've seen what it takes to transport an animal from Point A to Point B. It's not a simple job, especially when you're talking about an aquatic animal. They'll need several hours, at least, to get it ready to move."

"And you say that Norman Gunderson was behind this," said Parker.

"Affirmative."

"I can't say I'm surprised." Anger lines dug into Lynch's face. "I've heard the man loves exotic animals, and by love, I don't mean he tries to protect them. A friend of mine ran a little zoo in Brady, Texas that was bought out by Gunderson. One of their featured attractions was a Borneo Pygmy Elephant. It died three months after Gunderson bought the zoo."

"I take that it wasn't from old age," said Rastun.

"Those elephants can live up to sixty years. This one was only nine years old."

"It also explains why Gunderson would own that fishing company." Rastun pointed to the photo of the *Zuiyo Maru* carcass. "That trawler found a supposedly dead sea monster off New Zealand in 1977. And remember how the coelacanth was discovered? Everyone thought that fish died out along with the dinosaurs until a live one was found off South Africa in 1938 in a fisherman's net. Ninety-nine percent of the time when you throw a net in the water, you come up with sea life everyone knows. The other one percent, you get a surprise. Gunderson hit that one percent when *Bountiful Betty* snagged another Point Pleasant Monster, or Sea Raptor as they call it."

"But if Gunderson supposedly killed that elephant, and probably a lot of other endangered species, why is he keeping our other sea monster alive?" asked Parker.

"Unfortunately, I didn't get that far in my interrogation of Doctor Krueger."

"But you did find out who our mole is."

Rastun cast his eyes to the table, trying to summon the will to answer.

Sherlock beat him to the punch. "It's not one hundred percent confirmed, but all the evidence points to Karen Thatcher."

Rastun felt another sting to his heart, the same feeling he'd had every other time someone said Karen was the mole.

"The mole is just the tip of the iceberg." Lipeli looked from Lynch to Parker. "There has to be someone here in headquarters who put Karen on that expedition. We need to double-check, probably triple-check, every single FUBI employee and see who might be working for Gunderson."

"See to it, Colonel." Lynch then turned to Rastun, Geek and Sherlock. "Good work, all of you."

"Thank you, sir," the ex-Rangers replied.

"Now to get you back to *Epic Venture* so we can wrap up this mole business," said Lipeli.

Hipper raised his hand. "Um, I don't think that's a good idea, Colonel."

"Why not?"

"Well, we still have that news story to deal with. You know, what Mister Rastun did in Africa. There was concern from many scientists in the FUBI that the field security specialists would turn into some kind of para-military group, and after what they just did," Hipper nodded toward Rastun, Geek and Sherlock, "they have a point. Plus from the way that news story portrays Mister Rastun, people will think we have a maniac working for the FUBI."

Rastun gave Hipper a withering stare. The bureaucrat shrank back in his chair.

"Um, um, no offense."

Rastun continued glaring at him.

Hipper swallowed and turned away, looking instead at Parker and Lynch. "You have to admit, this doesn't look good for the FUBI. They're going to accuse us of covering this incident up."

"There was no cover up," stated Lipeli.

"You didn't mention what Mister Rastun did in Africa when you hired him."

"Because I couldn't. The Army made us all sign non-disclosure forms about the incident. Secrecy may not mean much to people like you in DC, but we Rangers take it very seriously. Some of us, anyway."

Rastun figured that was a backhanded jab at Colonel Osgood, whom he assumed was the "senior military official" the reporter referred to.

Lipeli continued. "The whole story will come out. It will show that Colonel Osgood went for his gun first and that Captain Rastun was prepared to defend himself. It will also show that his assault on Colonel Osgood, while not condoned, was understandable, given the fact we lost three of our men and had four more wounded."

Lynch folded his hands on the table. A thoughtful expression formed on his face.

This is it. Rastun knew the director was thinking it over. Within moments, he'd know if he still had a job with the FUBI, or if he'd be back working as a security guard at the Philadelphia Zoo.

Lynch looked up. "I think we can ride out whatever bad press this will generate. Like you said, Colonel, the truth of what happened over there will come out. We also can't overlook the fact that Jack's actions since joining the FUBI have saved many lives. This is a man we need to keep, not fire."

"Thank you, sir," Rastun said, relief flooding through him.

"You're welcome. Now, you three need to get back to *Epic Venture*. I don't want this mole on my ship one second longer than necessary. I'll try to arrange for the Coast Guard to fly you out there."

"While we're waiting for the chopper, we should try to get some sack time in." Rastun looked at the former sergeants.

"Sounds good to me," said Geek. "Firefights wear me out."

Everyone got out of their seats and filed to the door.

"Captain," Lipeli called out. "A word?"

"Yes, sir."

"Are you good to go?"

"Yes, sir."

"Are you sure?"

Rastun sensed his former CO's underlying message. His relationship with Karen wasn't exactly a secret.

"I can put aside my personal feelings and do my job."

"You weren't able to do that in Morocco."

"That was then. This is now."

Lipeli stared at him in silence. Rastun wondered if he'd bench him for the rest of this mission.

"Carry on, Captain. Don't let me down."

"I won't, sir."

Rastun exited the conference room, glancing back at Lipeli. He wondered if he really could put his personal feelings aside the next time he saw Karen.

FORTY-FOUR

Rastun slept in one of the chairs in the downstairs lounge for about three hours before Lipeli woke him up.

"The chopper's almost here."

"Thanks, sir." Rastun rubbed his eyes and stood, while Lipeli slapped Geek on the shoulder to waken him.

Sherlock was already up and talking on his cell phone. When he hung up, Rastun asked, "Anything new?"

"I just checked my messages." Sherlock told him what his lab techs and investigators from the Marshal's Service had found. The information gave them an ironclad case against their mole.

The ex-Rangers hit the bathroom before the helicopter, a Coast Guard HH-65 Dolphin, landed in the FUBI's near-deserted parking lot. They flew to the USCG air station in Atlantic City, refueled, then headed out to open ocean. The first rays of the sun crept over the horizon when they spotted *Epic Venture.*

"*Epic Venture, Epic Venture.* This is United States Coast Guard helicopter Dolphin Ten," radioed the pilot. "Prepare to receive three passengers."

"Dolphin Ten, this is *Epic Venture.*" That sounded like Hernandez. "What passengers?"

"Two of your field security specialists and a U.S. deputy marshal. We'll be winching them down to you. Request you bring your vessel to full stop."

"*Epic Venture* coming to full stop, aye."

The wake generated by the boat's engines soon vanished. The Coasties lowered Rastun first.

"Captain Rastun?" Hernandez looked at him in surprise. "I didn't think you'd be back."

"Well, I am. Now round up everyone. We're having a meeting in the conference room in five minutes."

Hernandez just stared at him, looking unsure. Technically, Rastun wasn't the captain of *Epic Venture* and probably didn't have the authority to order around the first mate.

Right now, he didn't care.

"Hop to it, Hernandez."

"Um, yes, sir."

Hernandez hurried back to the bridge as Geek set down, followed by Sherlock. The three headed to salon/conference room on the fly bridge. One by one, the expedition members filed in, with Ehrenberg first. He did a double-take when he saw them.

"Jack? Geek? Well, this is a pleasant surprise." He yawned and rubbed his eyes. "It would have been more pleasant a little later this morning."

"Sorry, Doc. This can't wait."

Ehrenberg gave Rastun a puzzled stare. "Is everything all right?"

"Not really."

Malakov came in next. Her jaw dropped when she saw them.

"What the hell are you doing here?" She turned to Ehrenberg. "Why are they here? We need to call FUBI Headquarters. They have no business being on this boat."

"For your information, Doctor, FUBI Headquarters sent us here."

"That's not...how could they after that story?"

"You'll find out soon enough."

Karen appeared next. "Jack." A huge smile formed on her face.

Rastun maintained a business-like expression.

Her smile faded. She eyed him with a mixture of confusion and concern. Before she could say anything, Pilka, Montebello, Captain Snider and Tamburro arrived, while Hernandez resumed his post on the bridge.

"So what's all this about, Jack? And who's this?" Ehrenberg pointed to Sherlock.

"This is Deputy U.S. Marshal Arthur Sherlock Dunmore. We served together in the Rangers."

"Why do we need the police here?" Malakov switched her harsh stare from Rastun to Sherlock.

"Because of what happened when the Point Pleasant Monster attacked *Bold Fortune,*" said Rastun.

"What do you mean?" asked Pilka.

"You all saw what happened when Geek and I fought the monster. Geek's shotgun didn't do a thing to it, even with armor-piercing rounds. The toxin dart I fired also did nothing. And now we know why. Someone on this expedition switched out our ammunition with blanks. We couldn't kill the monster, and because of that, Captain Keller is dead."

"That's when the FUBI brought me in," Sherlock began. "To find out who the mole is. Initially, you were at the top of my list, Doctor Malakov, given your extreme views on animal rights and environmentalism."

Malakov barked out a laugh. "Trust the police to treat someone who works to protect the planet as a criminal."

"You've also had associations with members of radical environmental groups that would use any means necessary to keep the Point Pleasant Monster alive. But you're not the only one with the motive and the contacts to do this. I also considered Doctor Ehrenberg a suspect."

"Me? You can't be serious."

"You've been on expeditions funded by the Kobel Trust. The man it was named after expressed a desire to start a zoo with various cryptids, should they ever be found."

"Chris Kobel has been dead for years."

"I know," Sherlock responded. "But I checked, and some of the people who run the trust still support that idea. A sea monster would be a big draw."

"I assure you, I have done nothing to sabotage this mission," declared Ehrenberg.

"I know you haven't. Neither you nor Doctor Malakov have done anything to jeopardize the success of this expedition or the lives of its members."

Sherlock turned to Karen. She furrowed her brow. "Why are you looking at me?"

"Miss Thatcher, are you familiar with a property on Fifty Trotting Horse Way in Greensville County, Virginia?"

"The old mansion? I sold it last year."

"To Old South Restoration, correct?"

"Yeah."

"Old South Restoration is a front. It only exists on paper. They created a fake company so they could buy that mansion and store another Point Pleasant Monster in it."

Gasps and shouts of surprise went up from the expedition members.

"What are you talking about?" Pilka blurted.

"There's another one out there?" Ehrenberg's eyes widened.

"This is ridiculous!" shouted Malakov.

"You think so?" Rastun pulled out his phone. "See for yourself."

He showed them the pictures of the monster. Everyone stared at it in amazement.

"I don't know anything about this." Karen jabbed a hand at Rastun's phone.

"So you don't know who Norman Gunderson is?" asked Sherlock.

"Sure I do. I mean, I know him by reputation, which isn't good when it comes to owning zoos." Karen paused. "Is he the one behind this?"

"Yes. The fishing boat that accidentally caught the other monster belongs to a company owned by Gunderson. He sent some of his people to threaten the crew to stay quiet. One of them didn't and was murdered. The people who were guarding this creature also tried to kill me, Captain Rastun and Sergeant Hewitt last night. I'm also willing to bet Gunderson is behind Old South Restoration."

"What?" Karen stared at Sherlock, mouth agape. "I don't know anything about this. Those people from Old South made me a good offer and I took it. All this other stuff ..." Karen turned to Rastun, a desperate look on her face. "Jack, you have to believe me. I had nothing to do with this."

Rastun said nothing.

But Sherlock did. "Technically, you did, when you sold that mansion to Old South Restoration. But I think that was arranged by the person who owned the mansion before you."

He turned to Pilka.

"M-Me?" The marine biologist leaned as far back from Sherlock as possible.

"I had some investigators look deeper into the mansion. They called before we came here. The mansion is administered by a trust, but it had been owned by the Holmes family, which included Gregory Holmes, your maternal grandfather."

Pilka swallowed.

"You let the trust handle everything with the property, since you were too busy trying to hold down jobs while drinking away your sorrows. Unfortunately, the real estate market hasn't been very good the past few years, especially with mansions a hundred and fifty years old and in poor condition. But before the trust could sell it and you could make some money off it, the court took it away from you and gave it to Miss Thatcher to help with the child support payments you never made."

"What?" Surprise flared across Ehrenberg's face...and Malakov's, and Montebello's and Tamburro's.

"You and Raleigh...?" Malakov couldn't finish the sentence. Her eyes just flickered between the two.

Karen's shoulders sagged. "We had an affair when I was in college. That's how Emily was born." She turned to Pilka. "The daughter you don't even want to admit exists. The daughter you've done shit to help since the day she was born!"

"Why should I help you or your brat? You cost me my marriage. You cost me my job at the institute."

"You cost yourself that job because you couldn't keep your dick in your pants. And here I was stupid enough to think I was special when you were screwing every intern and research assistant that walked through the door."

"I guess that explains why you couldn't get much info out of the marine institute," Geek said to Sherlock. "They probably hushed it all up. Don't want bad publicity."

"That's exactly what happened." Karen continued glaring at Pilka. "When I took this bastard to court for child support, they awarded me the mansion. I was going to put it up for a public auction when someone from Old South Restoration contacted me. They made me a good offer, so I took it. I took it to support my daughter. I had no idea they planned to hide a sea monster there."

"And that sale was made a few days after the fishing boat discovered the other monster," said Sherlock. "Were you the one who told Gunderson about the mansion, Doctor Pilka?"

"I-I-I had nothing to do with this. Obviously Karen's the one working for Gunderson."

"You lying piece of shit!" she yelled.

"I might still believe that if not for two pieces of evidence," said Sherlock. "One was a simple tube of sunscreen."

Pilka shuddered.

"I was suspicious when Captain Rastun told me how the Point Pleasant Monster seemed drawn to Miss Thatcher in the two attacks. So I had him obtain samples of her toiletries for analysis. The sunscreen came back tainted with pheromones from the other monster."

"What?" Karen blurted.

"That's how we learned there was another monster out there. But what really helped confirm Doctor Pilka as the mole was something he obviously overlooked when switching out Captain Rastun's and Sergeant Hewitt's ammunition. A gun cleaning kit."

"How did that help you?" asked Ehrenberg.

"Doctor Pilka somehow got the code for the weapons locker. That's how he managed to switch out the ammunition. I'm also sure you wiped the guns and the locker clean of prints. But Captain Rastun told me he'd left his gun cleaning kit near the locker, and the next day someone moved it. He assumed it might have been Mister Hernandez who'd done it while he was cleaning. But I took the kit to our lab, and they found your prints on it."

Pilka closed his eyes. His head lowered.

"An experienced thief would have wiped down the kit," said Sherlock. "But you did what most people do when something is in their way. Move it aside and forget about it."

Pilka covered his face with his hands. For a moment, Rastun wondered if the man would cry.

"You...You tried to kill me?" Karen stared in shock at Pilka.

The marine biologist lifted his face out of his hands. He met Karen's gaze, then averted his eyes.

"You fucking bastard!"

Karen launched herself across the table. The slap she gave Pilka sounded like a rifle shot. He nearly fell out of his seat.

Karen hit him again and again. Pilka tried to swat her hands away. Karen let out a primal cry and raked her fingers across Pilka's face. He howled in pain.

"That's enough. That's enough!" Rastun grabbed her around the waist and pulled her off of Pilka. Karen kicked and struggled trying to break free. When she couldn't, she spat at Pilka. A gob of saliva clung to the side of his nose. Rastun also noticed four red lines running down Pilka's left cheek. Some blood trickled from them. Lucky for him, Karen did not have very long nails, otherwise there'd be rivers of blood pouring down Pilka's face.

Rastun wouldn't have minded that at all.

"You son-of-a-bitch!" Malakov shouted. "You're a disgrace to your profession, a disgrace to this planet!"

"Doctor." Rastun turned to her. "For once, we're actually on the same page."

Pilka rubbed his cheek, trying to shrink away from Sherlock, who stood over him with his arms folded.

"You are in a lot of trouble, Doctor. For starters, you're involved in a criminal conspiracy that involves threats, intimidation and the murder of a twenty-one-year-old man. Spiking Miss Thatcher's sunscreen with pheromones counts as attempted murder, and Captain Keller's death qualifies as second degree murder. All this means you will be going to jail for a very, very long time. Maybe the rest of your life. You better start telling me everything you know about what Gunderson has planned with these monsters if you want a shot at spending the last few years of your life as a free man."

Pilka chewed on his lower lip. "You don't know what Gunderson is like. He'll kill me if I talk."

"We are going to take Gunderson down with or without your help, which means he won't be able to kill you or anyone else. Now, do you want to help and spend *some* time in prison, or keep quiet and spend a long time in prison?"

Pilka's head drooped. "What do you want to know?"

"How did Gunderson recruit you?" asked Sherlock.

"After I was forced out of the institute, he'd sometimes consult me on where he might find rare creatures like giant squid, leatherback turtles, fur seals. He then hired me to help study the Sea Raptor when it was caught."

"And the mansion?"

"We needed an isolated location to hold it. When I told Gunderson about the mansion the damn judge gave to her," Pilka looked briefly at Karen, "he liked the idea. If the Sea Raptor was ever discovered by the authorities, Gunderson had a paper trail created that would link it with Karen and one of her former employers."

"Who would that be?"

"Holger Mertesacker, the publisher of *Exotic Animals Magazine.*"

That made sense, Rastun thought. The guy was in debt, and a living sea monster would resolve his money issues and then some. He'd make a great prime suspect.

"What was Gunderson planning to do with the other monster?" asked Sherlock.

"He was hoping to find another one to mate with it."

"Then he has three creatures to sell instead of one," Malakov chimed in. "More money for a man who already has too much of it."

"How was Gunderson able to put you on this expedition?" Sherlock asked Pilka.

"He has people planted in the FUBI. One of them was in operations and recommended me. Her, too." Again he looked at Karen.

"Just to help add to her perceived guilt if your operation was ever exposed," said Sherlock.

"Yes."

"Who provided you with the fake ammunition?"

"A man named Andres Piet. He's a mercenary Gunderson's used in the past."

"Can you give us a description of this Piet?"

"Over six feet tall. Big, like him." Pilka nodded to Geek. "Maybe in his fifties, but still pretty tough looking. He also has an accent."

"What kind?"

"It wasn't British or Australian. I think it might be South African."

Sherlock pulled out a pair of plastic flexicuffs, grabbed Pilka's shoulder and lifted him out of the chair. "Raleigh Pilka, I am placing you under arrest."

While Sherlock read Pilka his rights, Rastun looked at Karen, who was still seething. He thought of the Point Pleasant Monster's attacks on the boardwalk and *Bold Fortune,* thought of Karen being inches away from the creature's snapping jaws.

"Pilka." He strode up to him.

The marine biologist made it a point not to look him in the eyes.

Rastun punched him in his large stomach. Pilka doubled over, nearly sagging to his knees. Sherlock pulled him back up.

"He assaulted me," Pilka wheezed.

"If the captain really assaulted you, you'd be unconscious right now."

"I'm gonna call the Coast Guard." Ehrenberg stood, angrier than Rastun had ever seen the man. "I want this…maggot off our boat."

"I'll lock him in his quarters until the Coast Guard gets here." Sherlock took Pilka out of the conference room and belowdecks.

After Ehrenberg called the Coast Guard, he collapsed in his chair, rubbing his forehead. "I don't believe this. I can't…my God, this whole time he was working against us."

"I know it's a lot to swallow, Doc," said Rastun. "But the situation is resolved. Pilka's no longer a threat. But we still have a sea monster out there we need to find."

"Yeah, you're right. Okay, let's go back to our quarters, get changed and go find this thing."

The expedition members rose from the table. Malakov looked first to Rastun, then Geek, then back to Rastun. She gave him a rather forced nod and walked away.

That's probably as close to an 'atta boy' as I'll get from her.

He turned to Geek. "Let's get out on deck and be ready if we spot the monster."

"Yes, sir."

As they headed for the hatch, Karen called out, "Jack?"

He looked at her, then back at Geek. "I'll catch up."

Geek nodded and went outside.

Rastun walked over to her. He didn't even try to keep the smile off his face. Karen wasn't the mole.

He reached around her waist and pulled her into a long kiss.

"It's good to be back," said Rastun.

That's when he noticed Karen wasn't smiling.

"What's wrong?"

"Your marshal friend sounded like he was convinced for a while I was Gunderson's spy."

"Yeah, he was."

"What about you?"

Rastun's eyebrows knitted together. "What'd you mean?"

"Did you actually think I was working for Gunderson?"

Rastun stared at her, trying to figure out how best to answer.

He remained silent, looking away from her.

"You did." Karen's jaw trembled. "Oh my God, you did."

"Karen, when we learned about the mansion, and that you owned it, I ... I..."

"How could you think that?" She backed away from him. "After everything we've been through. I saved your life on that Coast Guard boat, and you still thought I betrayed you and everyone on this expedition?"

"Karen, I'm sorry."

"Sorry?" Her voice rose in anger. A tear ran down her cheek. "I let you into my life, I gave you my body, I thought we trusted one another. This is how you repay me for that trust?"

"Karen..." Again, he struggled to find the right words.

Karen held up a hand. More tears escaped her eyes. "My God, Jack. I lo..."

She turned away, wiping her cheeks, and hurried toward the crew compartments.

He started to open his mouth. There were just three words he wanted to say to her. Three words he wished he'd said to her sooner. Three words that might bring her back to him.

Rastun kept those three words to himself.

FORTY-FIVE

This was the one thing Rastun hated about sentry duty. Ninety-nine percent of the time, nothing happened. When nothing happened, the mind wandered, even when that mind belonged to a highly trained soldier like an Army Ranger.

He could only stare at waves for so long before he thought of Karen, the outrage in her voice, the tears in her eyes.

It sickened him to know he'd been the cause of those tears.

He gripped the railing, wondering if he should give it some time before he sought out Karen to apologize. But would a simple "I'm sorry" be enough?

"Captain."

He turned to find Sherlock walking toward him. "What's up?"

"The Coast Guard's sending a motor lifeboat to pick up Pilka. ETA about thirty minutes. The FBI will have agents standing by at Coast Guard Station Atlantic City to take him into custody."

"Good."

"Meantime, I had my people back in Washington run a check on Andres Piet through INTERPOL."

"What did they find?" asked Rastun.

"The guy's a real piece of work. Fifty-four years old, but still has the physique of the body builder." Sherlock showed him a photo of Piet on his smartphone. The compact face that stared back at him had graying hair in a buzzcut and soulless eyes.

"He was born in Pretoria," Sherlock continued. "His father was a sergeant in the South African Defense Force who died when Piet was nine."

"How?"

"The African National Congress bombed an army barracks and killed seven soldiers, including Piet's father. After he died, Piet's mother suffered from depression. She also abused alcohol, drugs and Piet."

"Sounds like he had a great upbringing."

Sherlock gave him a sardonic smile. "The abuse stopped when Piet was fifteen. It sounds like a switch went off in his head and he figured why should I keep getting knocked around when I'm this big? He started beating his mother until he left home at age seventeen."

Rastun shook his head. He thought back to when he was that age, when he sometimes thought he had the worst parents in the world because they did not support his decision to join the Army. But his mother and father weren't in the same universe with some of the truly horrible parents in the world.

Like Piet's mother.

"So what happened with our golden boy?"

"He joined the army. When he was nineteen, Piet and some of his friends were going to a bar in Bloemfontein when they ran into a black couple. He thought the man gave him a nasty look. Piet bashed his head into the sidewalk, stomped in his chest, then used a broken beer bottle to carve out his eyes." Sherlock grimaced as he stared at his phone. "You don't want to know what he did to the girl."

"Sounds like this guy has some serious anger issues."

"Between a group of blacks blowing up his father and all the abuse from his mother, he has plenty of issues."

"So did his superiors do anything?"

"Yeah. They gave him a promotion."

Rastun's eyes widened in surprise, then he remembered. "Right. This was during Apartheid."

Sherlock nodded. "Piet was transferred to the national police force. He was part of a unit that specialized in raping the family members of anti-Apartheid activists in order to scare them into silence. By all accounts, he was very good at his job."

"So what happened when Apartheid ended?"

"It looks like Piet saw the writing on the wall beforehand. He fled South Africa in 1991, the year after Mandela was let out of prison. That's when he became a mercenary. He's wanted in more than a dozen countries for murder, weapons trafficking, rape and, well, it would take me an hour to list all his other charges. The TSA's been alerted to see if Piet flew into the country around the time of the first monster attack."

Rastun snorted. "The TSA. Let in a psycho mercenary, but make sure you do a body cavity search on a four-year-old girl with a lollipop."

"I also alerted the New Jersey State Police, as well as all the local PDs along the Jersey Shore. They'll contact me if they get a lead on Piet."

"Good."

Sherlock pocketed his phone, then pulled out a couple of vials of clear liquid. "I also found these in Pilka's cabin."

"What are they?"

"My guess is pheromone extract from the other sea monster. I'll have to have a lab test it to be sure."

"Mm." Rastun looked back out at the ocean. He folded his arms and stared at a patch of water in thought. "Your lab would only need one of those vials for testing, right?"

"Yes, sir."

"Good. Because as soon as the Coast Guard takes Pilka off our hands, I'm gonna run an idea past Ehrenberg."

Sherlock glanced at the vials in his palm, then back to Rastun. "You plan to use these pheromones to lure out the Point Pleasant Monster and kill it."

Rastun nodded. "You read my mind."

***

Piet stood on the bridge of their disguised motor lifeboat, staring at his satellite phone. There was an hour's difference between here and Texas. Still, Gunderson should already be up.

Even if he isn't, he needs to know this now.

He dialed the number. Gunderson answered on the second ring.

"Mister Piet. Good. I was just about to call you."

"You were?"

"We've had a significant problem come up. I'm sorry, but your services are no longer needed."

"What?" Piet's surprise gave way to anger. Four million dollars was at stake, and the old bastard was pulling the plug on him? "What for?"

"Let's just say the prize you were looking for, it had a twin. We were keeping it, but the wrong people found out about it."

Even though Gunderson used a secure phone, he was still careful with what he said. One never knew who could be listening in.

Especially in America these days.

So Gunderson had another monster stashed away. Then why offer so much money to catch this one? All Piet could think of was Gunderson hoped the two beasties would bugger each other and start popping out little beasties. He could make a lot of crown selling those things.

Not anymore.

"Understood," Piet told him. "Unfortunately, you have another problem. Our friend on the inside, the wrong people have him, too." Doern had been monitoring Coast Guard frequencies when they announced Pilka's arrest.

"Dammit!" Gunderson cursed. "Do you know what information they've gotten out of him?"

"No."

"Well, I need to know how much damage he might have caused me. I want you and your men to retrieve our friend."

"That could be risky," said Piet. "It would be better to just eliminate the problem."

"No. I need to know what he told the wrong people so I can deal with any fallout. Do you know where our friend is?"

"Yes." *Epic Venture* had radioed the Coast Guard that Pilka was still onboard and gave its GPS coordinates to the MLB sent to collect him.

"If you're worried about the risk, you can have your bonus, provided you successfully complete this job."

Piet stared at the overhead of the bridge in thought. Such an operation carried out on short notice stood a good chance of getting cocked up.

Four million dollars, however, made it a chance worth taking.

FORTY-SIX

Rastun turned when he heard the hatch to the bridge open. Karen stepped out, camera in hand. She turned to him, pausing when their eyes met. He took a step toward her.

She turned and walked to the stern.

Still mad at me. Not that he could blame her. He prayed she would eventually forgive him.

Unfortunately, they hadn't had an argument about some missed social engagement or a comment that offended a family member. He had thought, he had believed, Karen sold them out to a slimebag exotic animal collector and caused the death of Captain Keller.

How does one forgive something like that?

"Cap'n," Geek radioed. "There's a vessel approaching from the east. About four klicks off the stern, port side."

"Got an ID on it?"

"Looks like a Coast Guard motor lifeboat."

"Copy. Standby for confirmation." Rastun contacted Captain Snider. "There's a vessel approaching us from the east. Have they made contact with us?"

"That's affirmative. I was just about to let you know. U.S. Coast Guard Motor Lifeboat Twenty-Four coming to pick up Doctor Pilka. They're going to pull up along our port side."

"Roger. Geek, did you get that?"

"I did, sir."

"Let's give the Coasties whatever help they need, get this done and get back to our real job."

"Yes, sir."

The MLB soon pulled up next to *Epic Venture.* Hernandez caught the rope thrown to him by one of the Coasties and tied it to the railing. A skinny young man with fair skin jumped from the MLB onto the FUBI vessel.

"Ensign Capra, U.S. Coast Guard."

Both Rastun and Ehrenberg introduced themselves.

"Is the prisoner ready for transport?" asked Capra.

"He is." Rastun radioed Sherlock, who currently stood guard outside Pilka's cabin. "The Coast Guard's here. Bring up Pilka."

"We're on the way."

The two men appeared little over a minute later. Sherlock with a no-nonsense expression, looking every bit the cop, Pilka with his shoulders slumped, head hung low and hands cuffed behind his back, looking thoroughly defeated.

Rastun's hand hovered next to his holster. He seriously doubted Pilka would try anything stupid. But in case he did, he was ready. So was Geek, who clutched his USAS-12 shotgun. So was the stocky Coast Guard petty officer on the MLB who carried a Remington 870 shotgun.

Pilka would have to be really, *really* stupid to try anything.

"He's all yours," Sherlock said as he neared Capra.

"Thank you."

"You guys have back-up coming?" Ehrenberg leaned to his left, staring past Sherlock and Pilka.

"Sir?" Capra gave him a quizzical look.

Rastun turned, staring past *Epic Venture's* bow. Another USCG boat headed toward them. It looked similar to Capra's vessel, but with a square-shaped bridge instead of a rounded one.

Capra got on his radio. "MLB Twenty-Four to Coast Guard boat approaching my pos, do you copy? Over."

No response.

"Coast Guard boat approaching my pos, this is MLB Twenty-Four. Respond, please."

Again Capra was answered with silence.

Rastun looked from the ensign to the approaching boat. Why wouldn't they answer? Radio problems, perhaps?

His paranoia whispered in the back of his mind. His hand moved closer to his Glock.

"Coast Guard boat approaching my pos," Capra repeated in a more demanding voice. "Respond."

The boat sped past them. The roar of its engines decreased as it slowed.

What's it—

Someone stepped out of the bridge, balancing a slender tube with a conical tip. A stab of fear went through Rastun. He'd seen that weapon plenty of times in Iraq and Afghanistan.

"RPG! Down! Everyone down!"

Rastun, Geek and Sherlock all hit the deck. The civilians just looked at the other boat, confused. So did the Coasties. He doubted any of them had ever been under fire.

"Get down, dammit!"

The FUBI members and the Coasties dropped to their stomachs when Rastun heard the familiar crack of an RPG firing. Next came the sharp fluttering of the rocket-propelled grenade streaking through the air.

The blast shook *Epic Venture*. Shrapnel zipped over Rastun's head. Three people screamed in terror. Two female, one male. Karen and Malakov, and Pilka. Rastun looked across the deck at Karen. She laid flat, hands on top of her head. Her eyes were wide open and blazing with fear.

But he didn't see a trace of blood on her, thank God.

A light machine gun opened up. An M-60, judging by the distinct staccato chatter. A flurry of 7.62mm rounds punched through the bridge. Splinters of glass, wood and fiberglass showered the deck. Rastun drew his Glock and rolled behind a nearby storage locker. Three rounds ripped through it.

He peered around the locker. He grimaced when he saw Hernandez and Ensign Capra sprawled on the deck, blood pooling around them. The petty officer with the shotgun fired over the MLB's railing. Machine gun fire tore into the MLB. He ducked. Another RPG round raced over the water. Fire and smoke burst through the aft deck, right where the petty officer had taken cover.

The other MLB neared the twisted, smoking remains of *Epic Venture's* dive platform. Rastun gritted his teeth when he realized the bad guys had targeted the engines with that first RPG round.

Epic Venture was dead in the water.

Two men hurried out of the boat's bridge, each carrying AK-74s. Orange flashes spat from their barrels. Dozens of rounds ripped through *Epic Venture's* hull. What glass remained in the bridge windows exploded.

Rastun fired three rounds and ducked behind the locker. More high velocity rounds tore apart the top of it. He scowled at his Glock. What he needed was a Steyr AUG rifle. But all of them were in the weapons locker belowdecks.

"Captain Snider!" he radioed. "Send out a distress call! *Epic Venture* is under attack."

Nothing.

"Captain Snider!" He tensed as more rounds cracked above him. "Captain Snider, respond!"

Rastun looked at the bridge. All the windows had been shot out and the hull turned into Swiss Cheese. He feared Captain Snider wouldn't respond to anything ever again.

A shudder went through *Epic Venture.* The fake Coast Guard boat bumped into the mangled dive platform. The M-60 chattered again. Geek, now behind a vent box, blasted away with his shotgun. Rastun saw the machine gunner duck behind the gunwales. He grabbed a flash/bang grenade and looked at Ehrenberg, who lay flat on the deck a few feet away.

"Doc!" Rastun held up the grenade. "When this goes off, you get the women below."

Ehrenberg stared at him, his face the color of chalk, fear evident in his eyes. Still, he managed a slight nod.

"Cover fire!"

Geek reloaded his USAS-12 and opened up. Sherlock crawled over to Rastun and added his shotgun to the mini-barrage. Rastun pulled the pin and hurled the grenade. He threw another flash/bang for good measure. Brilliant flashes went off near the enemy boat. Thunderclaps followed.

"Get below!" Rastun blazed away with his Glock. Geek and Sherlock kept up their fire.

Karen, Ehrenberg and Malakov scrambled for the bridge on their hands and knees. Geek tossed another flash/bang and shoved a fresh magazine into his shotgun. The grenade exploded.

Five seconds passed without the enemy firing.

Rastun quickly ran down his options. They could try a direct assault on the boat. It meant having to cross about twenty-five feet of open space. That was just asking to be cut down.

"Geek. Get to the weapons locker. Get our Steyrs and all the ammo you can carry." Rastun got on the radio. "Doc. Call the Coast Guard and tell them—"

He heard a deep *thump*. Something clattered on top of the bridge.

"Grenade!"

The three ex-Rangers dropped to their stomachs and covered their heads. The fragmentation grenade went off with a *crump*. Shrapnel whizzed through the air.

Another grenade launcher thumped from the enemy boat. The projectile ricocheted off the rear of the bridge and bounced along the deck, away from Rastun and his men. The blast sent shrapnel in all directions. It pinged off the storage locker.

The machine gun opened up again. Rastun peeked around the locker. Two men leapt off the boat and fired their AKs. Rastun's eyes locked on one of them, the one with the compact face and graying hair.

It was Andres Piet.

FORTY-SEVEN

Rastun fired his Glock. Piet and his buddy dove behind the deck gate that led to the mangled dive platform. Geek's shotgun boomed twice. One of the bad guys fired at him, missing.

The man with the M-60 leaped onto *Epic Venture's* stern. He hefted the machine gun to his shoulder and sprayed Rastun and his men. Bullets cracked around them. Rastun heard two *thunks* as 7.62mm rounds tore through the storage locker. He leaned around it and sighted the machine gunner's torso. He fired his Glock three times.

The man stumbled briefly, but didn't go down.

"Shit! They got body armor."

"Big deal." Geek said as the machine gunner sent a stream of tracers at Rastun and Sherlock.

Piet and his friend fired a few bursts at Geek. He fired two rounds at them. They ducked behind the deck gate. Geek shifted the USAS-12 to the machine gunner. The man dashed toward a clamshell-shaped engine removal hatch. Geek fired once, twice. A huge, bloody hole exploded in the machine gunner's side. He dropped the M-60 and tumbled over the railing into the ocean.

Body armor wasn't much good against armor-piercing sabot rounds.

At least now the numbers were in their favor.

Another mercenary emerged from the bridge of the fake USCG boat and opened up with his AK-74.

Correction. We're even.

In terms of numbers, they were even at three-on-three. Piet's men still had the advantage in firepower.

The new merc let loose a sustained burst from the bow of the enemy boat. Rastun fired back. The bad guy ducked out of sight. Seconds later, he squeezed off three short bursts. Rastun returned fire until the Glock clicked empty. He scowled.

That had been his last magazine.

He holstered the pistol and unslung the Aster 7 from his shoulder. This was probably a worse weapon to have in a firefight than the Glock.

Still, any gun was better than no gun.

Rastun fired two toxin darts at the bad guy on the other boat. He responded with a volley of 5.45mm rounds that chopped through the storage locker. Rastun returned fire. Two shots. Two misses.

And the chamber was empty.

Rastun pulled out the plastic case containing the extra darts from his vest. He had to load each chamber by hand, scowling the whole time. A dart gun with a four-round cylinder versus an AK-74 automatic rifle with a 30-round magazine. Using the word "mismatch" would win him first place in the Understatement of the Year contest.

Rastun peered around the storage locker.

The merc on the other boat fired a grenade launcher.

"Grenade!" Rastun shouted.

The baseball-shaped projectile hit off the rear of the bridge and bounced near the vent box.

Right next to Geek.

The ex-sergeant snatched the grenade and threw it away. It barely disappeared over the side when it detonated.

Rastun glanced around the storage locker. Piet used the distraction of the grenade to break cover and throw open a deck hatch. Rastun fired a dart. It sailed over Piet's head as he slipped through the hatch.

"Shit! Piet's below!" he shouted to Geek and Sherlock. "Cover me. I'm going after him."

The ex-Rangers blasted away with their shotguns. Rastun crawled away from the storage locker. He snaked past Ensign Capra's body, his elbows and legs sliding over the pool of blood.

Rastun eyed the hatch leading to the shattered bridge. When he stared down at the deck, he realized something.

Raleigh Pilka was nowhere in sight.

***

Pilka could not stop shaking. His heart slammed against his chest.

They're gonna kill me.

Part of him couldn't believe he'd survived all that shooting and those explosions. Luckily, Rastun's marshal friend had been so concerned about not getting his head blown off that he didn't see him crawl away. Pilka managed to kick open the hatch and make his way below to the storeroom. He knocked a toolbox off a shelf, its contents spilling across the floor. Pilka looked over the mess until he spotted a utility knife. It wasn't easy, especially with his hands bound behind his back, but he eventually cut through the plastic handcuffs.

Now what? He rubbed his wrists and looked around the storeroom. Cracks, thumps and bangs filtered through the deck. Nausea burned his stomach and throat. Cold sweat drenched his large body. It was Piet. It had to be him. Pilka wanted to believe the South African was here to rescue him. He wanted to, but couldn't. Norman Gunderson struck him as a man who didn't give a damn about the people working for him.

Even worse, Piet struck him as a man who enjoyed killing people.

With the Sea Raptor in Virginia having been found, Pilka knew he was useless to Gunderson. He'd also ratted him out. There was no way he would forgive him for that.

What do I do?

He clenched his teeth, first fighting off the urge to throw up, then the urge to sob. He was on a boat in the middle of the ocean, a boat where two groups were shooting it out. One wanted to kill him, the other wanted to put him in jail for the rest of his life.

There had to be a way out of this.

Pilka's gaze settled on the weapons locker.

Back on *Bold Fortune,* he had to surreptitiously watch Rastun to learn the code for the weapons locker. Here on *Epic Venture,* Ehrenberg gave him the code after Rastun and Geek left so he could get a tranquilizer rifle in case they ran into the other Sea Raptor.

That Hawaiian shirt-wearing fool had given him a shot at his freedom.

He opened the locker and grabbed the other Aster 7. Next, he took out a plastic case of darts. There were eight, four with tranquilizer, four with Golden Poison Frog toxin. Pilka cradled the Aster 7 in his arms and tried to open the case.

The darts spilled onto the floor.

"Dammit!" He got on his knees, scooped up four darts and loaded them in the chamber. When he looked back down at the remaining ones, he noticed three had blue tails for tranqs, while the remaining one had red tail for toxin.

He couldn't afford to wait for one of Piet's men or Rastun's men to pass out if they got hit with the lone tranq dart. He needed to kill them instantly.

Pilka reached down for the last toxin dart.

He heard footsteps outside.

Pilka gasped and ran to a large gray refrigerator in the corner. A roll of tarp sat next to it. Pilka knelt behind it, clutching the dart gun.

The footsteps got louder.

Pilka's sweaty hands trembled. He tried to force himself to calm down. How could he shoot anyone like this? Did he even stand a chance against someone with a machine gun?

The footsteps were right outside the door.

"Oh my God."

It was a woman's voice.

The footsteps resumed, only this time they were running.

The woman screamed. Pilka recognized her.

It was Karen.

***

Rastun pushed open the hatch and crawled into the bridge. Ehrenberg and Malakov crouched near the shattered helm. Captain Snider lay between them, wailing in pain, his left arm and shoulder a bloody mess. Rastun felt a pang of sympathy. He'd seen wounds like that in Iraq and Afghanistan. The usual treatment was amputation.

He crawled over to the two scientists, who treated Snider with handfuls of gauze.

"You two okay?"

"We're fine," Ehrenberg answered. "But we have to get the captain some help."

"We all need help right now. Did you call the Coast Guard?"

Ehrenberg nodded. "They said they're sending every available ship and helicopter here, but it might be a while before they get here."

We might be dead in a while. "Where's Karen?"

"She went to the crew compartments to check on Charlie and Nick."

"Then that's where I'm going. Stay here, stay down and take care of him." He nodded to Captain Snider.

Rastun crawled to the ladder leading to the deck below. He slid down it and got to his feet, Aster 7 up and ready. He checked one cabin. Empty. So was the next cabin. He fought the urge to call out Karen's name. Piet was around somewhere. He didn't want to tip him off to his presence.

He also prayed Karen didn't run into the sick fuck.

Rastun checked another cabin. A chubby man crouched in the corner.

"Don't shoot me! Don't shoot me!" Charlie Montebello threw his arms over his face.

"Charlie, it's me. You okay?"

"Y-Yeah," he replied, breathing heavily.

"Where's Karen?"

"She-She was here, like, a minute ago maybe. I don't know now."

Rastun nodded. "Stay here."

"O-Okay."

Rastun continued on, trying to prevent his worry for Karen from overwhelming him. He also thought about Nick Tamburro. Hadn't he been in the engine room when Piet attacked? Had he survived the RPG strike?

He cleared the rest of the cabins and stood atop the ladder leading to the lowermost deck, the one containing the storeroom and whatever was left of the engine room.

His radio crackled.

"J-Jack?"

It was Karen. He held his breath. Something wasn't right about her voice.

"Jack, where are you?"

A chill went up his spine. Her voice was shaky, filled with fear.

Swallowing, he hit the reply button. "I'm here."

A pause. A very long pause. "I'm in the storeroom. You have to come to the storeroom."

"I'm coming."

He stopped himself from charging down the ladder. If he let emotion rule him, he'd get careless. Careless people got killed, and many times got others killed.

Rastun went down the ladder, scanning the corridor. He took one step forward, another. A haze of smoke hung in the air, probably from the wrecked engine room. It stung his eyes and seared his nostrils with the stench of scorched metal and fiberglass.

He ignored it and looked at the storeroom. The door was open.

Rastun halted when someone stepped out of the room. It was Karen. She said nothing. She didn't need to. Her expression told him all he needed to know.

She was terrified.

He saw the reason for that terror standing behind her, a muscular, middle-aged man with a graying buzzcut. The barrel of his SIG Sauer P226 pistol traced a slow line up and down Karen's brown hair.

"Greetings, Mister Rastun," said Andres Piet.

FORTY-EIGHT

"Let her go, damn you." Rastun raised his dart gun, looking for a clear shot. But Piet kept half his body inside the storeroom, and the other half shielded by Karen.

"She means a lot to you, doesn't she?" Pilka's left hand slid across Karen's stomach. She closed her eyes and grimaced. "I watched you that day you were at the nature reserve. You two were going at it like animals in heat. I can't blame you with prime pussy like this."

Piet's hand ran up to Karen's breast. He squeezed it hard. Her jaw tightened.

"You fucking bastard!" Rastun stared at Piet's hand. Could he put a dart in it? If he missed, Karen was dead.

He couldn't risk it.

"Put down your gun," Piet demanded.

"Put down yours."

Piet chuckled, running his thumb over Karen's breast. Rastun could barely hold back the tidal wave of rage. Never in his life had he wanted to kill someone so bad.

"You know, I don't have to kill her." Piet moved the barrel of his SIG behind Karen's ear. "But I can make her suffer. A bullet tearing through her ear, powder burns on her face. She wouldn't look pretty after that, would she?"

Karen visibly swallowed.

"Then I shoot her elbows, her hands, her knees, her breasts. I have fifteen rounds in this pistol. Fifteen body parts I can shoot. How long can you stand it, seeing the woman you love bleeding and screaming in pain?"

"Shut the fuck up, you sick shit!"

"I'm only here to get Raleigh Pilka," said Piet. "Just let me and my men have him. Then we'll be on our way, and you can go look for your sea beastie and bugger this leggy whore to your heart's content."

Rastun knew that was bullshit. Piet had no intention of leaving anyone on *Epic Venture* alive.

"Drop your gun." Piet pressed the barrel against Karen's ear, causing it to fold. Karen shut her eyes tight.

Rastun stared at Piet through narrowed, furious eyes. He forced himself to lower the Aster 7, then drop it to the floor.

"Kick it away," ordered Piet.

Rastun did so.

"Now the rest of your weapons."

He removed his Glock, the flash/bangs and his Night Stalker combat knife, dropped them on the floor and kicked them down the corridor. Rastun still had his Blue Tanto tactical knife in his right pocket, where he put it the night before when he and Geek fled the mansion. Not that the damn thing did him much good now. The moment he stuck his hand in his pocket, Piet would start putting bullets in Karen.

"Good boy," Piet snickered. "Isn't he a good boy?"

He squeezed Karen's breast. She grimaced in pain and revulsion.

"Now," Piet continued. "Get on your radio and tell your friends to stop shooting at my men and throw down their weapons."

Rastun took a deep, angry breath. He looked for any possible opening to take down Piet. None existed. Even if one did, what could he do with a switchblade in his pocket versus a gun to Karen's head?

His hand moved to his radio. "Geek. Sherlock."

Someone coughed at the other end corridor.

Rastun glanced past Karen and Piet. A bearded man with a paunch stumbled through the smoke coming from the engine room.

It was Nick Tamburro. Blood streamed down his arm and face. He walked with a limp.

"Wha...What's goin' on?"

"Tamburro! Get back!" yelled Rastun.

Piet's SIG came off Karen's ear. He twisted around and stood sideways, still shielded by Karen. He aimed his pistol at Tamburro.

Rastun took off running.

Three rapid cracks came from Piet's SIG. Patches of blood burst from Tamburro's chest. He fell backwards.

Piet turned back to Rastun.

I'm sorry, Karen.

Rastun lowered his shoulder and plowed into Karen.

FORTY-NINE

Karen and Piet tumbled to the ground. Rastun dropped on top of them. He glimpsed Piet's SIG fly out of his hand. It clattered down the corridor.

Karen, sandwiched between the two men, cried out in pain. Rastun feared he broke a couple of her ribs when he tackled her.

But it was the only way to save her life.

He rolled off her and pushed her away from Piet. She tumbled inside the storeroom.

"Shut the door! Stay—"

Piet sat up and punched Rastun in the jaw.

"Jack!" Karen screamed.

"Stay in there!"

Rastun shook off the pain as Piet started to rise. Rastun lay on his side and kicked the South African below the knee. He grimaced and sagged. Rastun launched himself off the deck and into Piet's gut. Both men hit the deck as Karen shut the hatch. Rastun got to one knee. He punched Piet's face.

The South African grabbed his wrist at the last moment and twisted it. Crushing pain shot up Rastun's arm. He bared his teeth, holding back a scream.

Piet used his free hand to punch Rastun twice below the armpit. He gasped for breath.

Piet let go of Rastun's wrist and gave him an upper cut to the chin. He just managed to stay upright.

Piet yanked the AK-74 off his shoulder. Rastun again jumped to his feet. He grabbed the barrel of the rifle, forcing it away from him. Piet pushed back. Rastun felt the pressure grow in his arms as he struggled with the bigger, stronger man.

He rammed his knee into Piet's gut once, twice. The South African lost his grip on the rifle. Rastun yanked it out of his hands.

Piet pivoted and delivered a sidekick. He struck the AK-74. It struck Rastun in the gut. He stumbled back.

Another kick from Piet nailed Rastun in the side. He dropped the rifle. Piet went for it.

Rastun jumped on his back. He snaked his right forearm around Piet's throat and squeezed. The South African grabbed Rastun's arm, trying to pull it away. Rastun had to fight to keep the pressure on Piet's throat.

He dragged Piet further down the corridor, away from the AK-74. The man's knees started to buckle. He gasped and hacked, trying to draw air into his lungs.

Then an arm reached around Rastun's head. Piet doubled over. Rastun flew over the mercenary's back. He slammed onto the deck.

Piet was on him. Two meaty, calloused hands wrapped around Rastun's throat.

Now he couldn't draw in any air.

Rastun gripped Piet's wrists, trying to pull his hands away. He failed. The pressure on his throat increased. His lungs burned.

He hooked his thumb and index finger under Piet's left thumb. Rastun wheezed for oxygen that would not come. He pulled back on Piet's thumb. Pulled...pulled . . .

SNAP!

Piet howled. His hands came off Rastun's throat. He doubled over, holding his thumb.

Rastun sat up and sucked in a lungful of air, then another one.

Don't let up.

Rastun sent three right jabs into Piet's stomach. Next came a palm strike to the mouth. Blood spilled from Piet's lips. Rastun went for the AK-74.

Piet grabbed his ankle. Rastun pitched forward onto the deck. He rolled on his back. Piet stomped toward him. Rastun kicked at his stomach. Piet blocked it. He lifted a booted foot and brought it down. Rastun rolled out of the way.

Something drenched his pants. He heard a sloshing sound. Other smells clung to the air beside smoke. Salt, diesel fuel and the coppery stench of blood.

Little waves of murky liquid flowed past Rastun. He had something else to worry about besides Piet.

Epic Venture was taking on water.

***

What are you waiting for?

Pilka remained behind the tarp, staring at Karen. She was doubled over on the floor, clutching her mid-section and crying. She had been hurt, hurt bad.

Good.

Pilka looked down at the Aster 7, then back at Karen. He should do it. The bitch had ruined his life. Bad enough he had an ex-wife trying to take away what little money he had, but that slut had also robbed him. That mansion had been his. The money it would have brought in when he sold it should have been all his.

But she took it from him, all because she'd been too damn stupid and too damn sentimental to abort that grubby little cunt of a daughter.

Do it!

The thumps and grunts continued outside. Piet and Rastun fighting. What if one of them came in here right when he stood up? Could he shoot them in time? Both men were trained killers. He was not.

Pilka looked at Karen again, his hatred for her trying to overcome his fear.

***

Rastun got to his feet. Piet threw a punch. Rastun blocked it. He rammed his knee into Piet's hip. The South African groaned and clenched his teeth. He punched Rastun in the gut, then went for the sheath on his belt. Out came an ominous-looking knife with little oval cutouts running down the middle blade. A Sultan's Warrior.

Rastun backed away just as Piet slashed. He felt the blade whip past his chest, missing him by inches.

Rastun tried to keep his distance. Not easy to do in the confined space of the corridor. He thought of the AK-74 and the SIG lying on the deck behind him. The last thing he wanted to do was turn his back on Piet. He still had his tactical knife in his pocket. But by the time he took it out, Piet would be on him.

They eyed one another, waiting for an opening. Water lapped over their boots.

Let him come to you. Charging an opponent with a knife while you had only your bare hands was a good way to get killed. Rastun would wait for him to make the first move, then counter it.

Piet didn't disappoint. He moved in and slashed. Rastun avoided it. Piet immediately followed with a thrust. Rastun moved to the right and clamped down on Piet's wrist with both hands. He tried to twist the knife out of his grasp.

Piet punched him in the side of his head. Rastun let up his hold on the South African for a moment.

A moment was all Piet needed.

The blade dug into Rastun's side.

FIFTY

Karen's head snapped up when she heard the agonized cry from outside.

"Jack," her voice cracked.

She stared at the door. Part of her wanted to open it, to see what was happening. Another part was too scared by what she might find.

Her heart pounded. The pain that seared her ribs was soon forgotten. Was Jack hurt? Was he dy...?

Tears spilled from her eyes. She didn't want to finish that thought, didn't want to think that the last words she said to him were words of anger. She recalled the hurt she felt that Jack believed she had betrayed him, betrayed the entire expedition. How could she ever forgive him for something like that?

Yet just beyond that door he was fighting that sick, perverted fuck, risking his life for her. How many other men would do that for her, for anyone? Karen saw the fear and anger on Jack's face. She could tell he wanted nothing more than to tear Piet apart, then hold her in his arms and never let go.

What if he dies? What if I never tell him...?

Karen stood, gritting her teeth against the burst of pain from her ribs. They were definitely broken. Broken by Jack! But what he'd done had saved her life. She could deal with broken ribs better than being shot.

She had to do something to help Jack. She looked around the storeroom and noticed some darts scattered on the floor. One of them had a red tail.

Golden Poison Frog toxin.

Karen bent down to get it when she noticed movement from the corner of the storeroom.

Raleigh Pilka stood up from behind a tarp, an Aster 7 dart gun in his hands. His face twisted in pure hatred.

"Hello, Karen."

***

Rastun let out a primal scream. He head-butted Piet in the nose. Bone and cartilage cracked and caved in. Piet howled and stumbled back. The knife came out of Rastun's flesh. He staggered against the wall and looked down. Blood stained his left side and ran down his pant leg. The pain grew into a white hot fire throughout his body. He pressed his left hand against the wound and clenched his teeth. The fight wasn't over. He had to keep going.

Rangers didn't quit.

He reached for his pocket and the tactical knife inside.

Piet charged. Rastun brought up his right forearm, aiming for his opponent's bloodied nose.

He hit Piet's chin instead.

Piet slammed him against the wall and kneed him in the wound. Rastun cried out and sagged to the deck.

Piet's boot slammed into his face.

*   *   *

"Raleigh, please." Karen held up her hands. "Don't do this. I'm begging you, think about Emily. She needs me."

"You think I care what happens to that little piece of trash? She's the reason my life went to hell!"

"Don't you dare call her—"

"Shut up!" Pilka jabbed the dart gun at her.

Karen shivered, staring at the barrel. Was there a toxin dart in there? Oh God, she didn't want to die. She didn't want to leave Emily alone.

"Everything was fine until you got pregnant. I would have paid for an abortion, but you wanted to have that thing. You thought it would make us a real family. Stupid, delusional whore! You cost me my real family! My job! Everything! And then you had the audacity to walk out on me!"

"Because you were groping every woman you worked with!"

Pilka trembled with anger. He moved closer to Karen. The gun was aimed at her chest.

Ice formed in the pit of her stomach. A clear image of Emily formed in her mind's eye.

Another image accompanied it. Jack.

"Raleigh, please don't. Please let me go. Please let me take care of our daughter."

"She's not my daughter! She's a fucking leech!"

Rage overshadowed Karen's fear. How could she have ever loved this man? Let him touch her? Have a child with him?

"You fucking bastard. How can you say that about your own child? At least Jack—"

"To hell with your precious Jack. The only reason you're sleeping with him is to piss me off."

"That's a lie."

"Then why would you?"

Karen drew a breath and squared her shoulders. "Because I love him, more than I ever loved you."

Pilka's eyes widened. Veins protruded from his neck. His look was beyond fury.

Karen tensed, expecting a toxin dart to hit her any second.

Pilka glanced at the dart gun. "Too quick."

He raised it over his head and swung. Karen brought up her right arm and blocked it.

She heard the crack of a bone breaking.

Karen screamed and clutched her arm.

Pilka clubbed her on the back. Karen crumpled to the deck.

Pilka kicked her in the stomach. It felt like her ribs exploded. She shrieked and rolled on her back. A fist struck her in the face. The coppery taste of blood filled her mouth before she blacked out.

FIFTY-ONE

Blood trickled from Rastun's mouth and chin as he tried to push himself up.

Piet kicked him in the face again.

"Pathetic." He looked down at him, slowly moving his knife back and forth. "I expected more of a challenge from an Army Ranger."

Rastun drew a wheezing breath. A vice crushed his ribs. Fangs of pain sank into his side. He swore he heard Karen screaming from the storeroom. Was she in trouble?

Once more, he tried to get up.

Piet kicked him in the stomach. Rastun rolled on his back. He felt something under his right buttock, something small and metal.

It was his tactical knife. It must have fallen out of his pocket.

He rolled on his side and curled up in a fetal position.

The South African laughed. "What, gonna have a cry now?"

Rastun moved his hands toward stomach, pretending to cover his side. Piet kicked him again. Rastun grunted in pain. He wedged his left hand under his side.

"You don't have to be scared, Ranger. I'm not going to kill you. Well, not right away."

Rastun moaned and rolled slightly from side-to-side, making a production out of the pain thrashing his body. His fingers slid through the water and under his damp pants. He felt the hilt of his tactical knife.

"I want you to see something before I finish you off," said Piet.

Rastun wrapped his hand around the knife.

"I want you to see your little photographer girlfriend screaming, as I'm peeling off her skin and fucking her up the ass."

Rastun looked up at him. "Fuck ...YOU!"

He pulled out his hand from under him. The blade popped out. Rastun roared and drove it into Piet's balls. A banshee-like shriek burst from his mouth. Rastun pushed the blade deeper into Piet's scrotum. He then gave it a twist. Blood poured over his hand. He pulled out the knife.

Piet wailed and collapsed on his knees. His Sultan's Warrior knife splashed on the deck.

Rastun pushed himself to his feet. He stared down at Piet's knife.

Pocketing his tactical knife, he picked up the Sultan's Warrior. Rastun grabbed Piet's head and yanked it back. The blade flashed across his throat. Blood cascaded into the water covering the deck. A gurgling noise came from Piet as he clamped his hands over his severed throat. He fell on his side. The gurgling noise tapered off. Soon Andres Piet made no more sounds.

A wave of dizziness swept through Rastun. He leaned against the wall and looked down at his bloody side. He needed to get a first aid kit. Hell, he needed to get to a fucking doctor.

That's when he remembered the scream coming from the storeroom.

Karen.

He moved around Piet's corpse and up the corridor. The blood-red water came up to his ankles.

"Karen!" Rastun nearly fell against the door as another dizzy spell hit him. He'd lost a lot of blood. It probably wouldn't be long before he went into shock.

But Karen's welfare came ahead of his.

"Karen." He twisted the knob and opened the hatch.

Dread surged through him when he saw Karen on the floor, moaning, blood trickling out of her mouth. Pilka stood near her, Aster 7 in his hands.

"Son-of-a-bitch!" Rastun staggered toward him.

Pilka raised the Aster 7. Rastun slashed with the Sultan's Warrior and struck the dart gun. It tumbled out of Pilka's hands.

Another dizzy spell hit Rastun. He tried to shake it off.

Pilka pushed him. Rastun lost his balance and fell. Pilka stomped on his wounded side. Rastun howled. The knife slipped from his hands. He clenched his teeth, pushing through the pain. He started to sit up.

"Don't."

Pilka had retrieved the Aster 7 and aimed it at Rastun.

FIFTY-TWO

Rastun glanced at the knife. It couldn't be more than a foot out of his reach.

And as soon as I reach for it, I'm dead. It didn't matter that Pilka was fat, middle-aged and never served in the military. From this distance, he couldn't miss.

"I've got you, and I've got the bitch." Pilka grinned as he kept the Aster 7 trained on him. "This is too good to be true."

"Pilka, you don't want to do this."

"Why not? That slut wasn't the only one to ruin my life. You did, too! Everything was going to turn around for me. We were going to make millions off those Sea Raptors. I'd have enough money to start a new life, someplace where Karen and my ex-wife couldn't get to me. But you had to play the crusading hero. You had to find that mansion. Why? Why?" he yelled. "All you had to do was march around with your gun and look tough, and everything would have been fine."

Pilka chuckled. "Well, you don't look so tough now."

"Think about it." Rastun hoped to keep him talking, to buy time for Geek and Sherlock to take care of Piet's men and get down here. Or maybe he could find some opening take down Pilka himself. "Right now you're facing a long stay in prison. But at least you'll be alive. You'll have a shot at parole, especially if you help us put Gunderson out of business. If you kill Karen and me, you can forget about that. You'll be looking at the death penalty."

Pilka stood in silence. Rastun studied the man's face and eyes. He could tell the marine biologist was thinking it over. Now if he'd just put down the dart gun, or look away. He could—

A wave of dizziness went through him. He slumped to one side.

Dammit, no! He couldn't afford to be weak now.

Rastun's head cleared. "You're not a killer, Raleigh. You're a scientist. You're trained to study evidence and come to a logical conclusion."

Pilka just stared at him.

"You're in the middle of the Atlantic Ocean. You have two former Rangers up top to deal with." Rastun prayed Geek and Sherlock were still alive. "Even if you somehow get past them, the Coast Guard has every boat and helicopter they can spare converging on our position. Do you really think you can escape?"

Pilka bit his lower lip. He still kept his eyes, and the dart gun, on Rastun.

Come on, look away.

A new look of resolve formed on Pilka's fleshy face. "You'd like that. Have me sit in some fucking cell, while you and that whore enjoy your lives, screw each other every chance you get, and laugh at how you both destroyed my life. I'll take my chances on death row."

Rastun saw Pilka's hands tighten around the Aster 7's pistol grip. He rolled to the left, hoping to avoid the dart, then come up and attack Pilka. It was a desperate plan, but desperate was all he had.

Rastun sprang to his feet. At least, he tried to. The pain in his side sliced through his body. Another dizzy spell took hold.

I'm dead.

His vision cleared. He remained on his feet.

Pilka was on the floor, face down in the water flowing from the corridor. A dart with a red tail stuck out of his back. Rastun blinked a couple of times, not really believing what he saw.

The dart containing the Golden Poison Frog toxin remained in Pilka's back.

"Jack?"

He turned his head. Karen stood over Pilka's body.

How...? Rastun checked around the room. He noticed a pile of darts on the floor a few feet from Karen. All of them had the blue tails of a tranquilizer dart. Karen must have grabbed the lone toxin dart.

His adrenaline began to wear off. His knees buckled. He half-sat, half-fell to the deck.

"Oh my God, Jack!"

Karen hurried over and knelt beside him. She clutched his shoulders, a distressed look on her face. "What happened?"

"Fight. Hell of a fight. But you should see the other guy." He tried to smile. Even doing that hurt.

Tears welled up in Karen's eyes as she gazed at his bloody side. "I'm gonna get a first aid kit. You lie down. Don't move too much."

"That sounds like a good idea."

Rastun laid back, water flowing around him. Only a couple of inches deep now. It would be more in a few minutes.

Karen ripped the first aid kit from its wall mounting and rushed back to Rastun. He noticed her right arm hanging by her side. Her teeth were bared in a pained expression. Dark bruises covered her face.

What the hell had Pilka done to her?

He looked at the marine biologist's body. Whatever he'd done, he'd paid for it.

Karen opened the kit. She used a pair of shears to cut away the part of his t-shirt around the wound. Next, she doused a handful of gauze with disinfectant and wiped it over the wound.

"I'm sorry, Karen. I'm so sorry."

"What?" She started bandaging the wound.

"I should've known you weren't the mole. I should've known you'd never work for someone like Norman Gunderson. I'm so sorry I didn't trust you."

He lifted his head. "I love you. I am so sorry if I hurt you."

"Stop talking like you're gonna die!" yelled Karen. "I finally met a great guy, so you can bet your ass there's no way I'm gonna lose you."

Rastun smiled and leaned his head back as Karen bandaged his wound.

Footsteps splashed in the corridor. Geek and Sherlock, he assumed.

Or maybe Piet's remaining two mercenaries.

"Gun." Rastun sat up. "Get the dart gun."

"Jack, you can't—"

"Gun!" he repeated through clenched teeth.

Karen gave him a worried look, but picked up the Aster 7 Pilka had used. She gave it to Rastun, who rolled on his stomach, grimacing as pain tore through his insides. He felt another dizzy spell coming on. He clenched his teeth and aimed at the open hatch.

The splashes drew closer.

Someone swung around the doorframe, holding a pistol. Much of the person's body was out of view, but whoever it was wore thick, horn-rimmed glasses.

"Don't shoot!" shouted Karen.

"I found the Cap'n and Karen," said Geek. He entered the room, Sherlock right behind him.

"Help him," Karen pleaded. "He's hurt."

"So are you." Sherlock bent down and examined her wounds.

Rastun set down the Aster 7 and rolled on his back. Geek knelt beside him.

"Good God, sir. What happened?"

"Got stabbed. Probably some broken ribs."

"At least you're better off than him." Geek nodded toward Piet's body.

"What happened to the other two bad guys?"

"A couple of flash/bangs, a couple of double-taps to the head, and it's another win for the good guys."

Rastun nodded. "Rangers lead the way."

"Rangers lead the way," Geek repeated.

"Doctor Ehrenberg says there's a Coast Guard helicopter fifteen minutes out," Sherlock reported. "We'll get you and Karen to a hospital in no time."

The marshal took off his field jacket, wrapped it around Karen's right arm and taped it to create a makeshift splint. He also gave her a cold pack from the first aid kit for the bruises on her face. Geek took the silver thermal blanket from the kit and gave it to Rastun.

"You lost a lot of blood, sir. We don't want you going into shock."

Rastun wrapped the blanket around him. Geek helped him into the corridor, where the water came up past their ankles. Sherlock and Karen followed. When they emerged topside, Rastun saw Ehrenberg, Malakov and Montebello near the stern. He felt the heat coming from the flames that engulfed the Coast Guard MLB. The mercenaries' boat, meanwhile, had drifted about thirty feet away from *Epic Venture*.

"Where's Captain Snider?" asked Rastun.

Ehrenberg lowered his head. "He lost too much blood. He's dead."

Rastun closed his eyes. *Damn.*

When he opened his eyes, he noticed a remorseful expression on Malakov's face.

"The Coast Guard'll be here soon," Ehrenberg told them. "You and Karen just rest until they get here."

"That might be hard to do, Doc," Rastun told him. "We're taking on water. I don't think this boat's gonna be floating for much longer."

"Terrific. Both our Zodiacs were damaged in that shootout, and the life raft there is shredded." Ehrenberg pointed at the casing along the superstructure. Inside was a torn up chunk of red and white plastic.

"There's another life raft on the other side," said Malakov. "It might be okay. I'll go check."

She headed over to the starboard side.

Rastun sat against the torn up storage locker. Karen slid down next to him and rested her head on his shoulder. He pressed his cheek against her hair and took a breath. Then another. Another. He felt like he was breathing quicker than normal. Rastun also felt a chill creep up his arms.

They were the signs of going into shock.

He thought back to his first aid courses in the Army. First thing to do was lie on his back and elevate his legs to get the blood to return to his heart.

Rastun lifted his head off Karen's and pushed himself away from the storage locker.

"Jack?" Concern tinged Karen's voice.

"Don't worry. I'm fine."

He lay on the deck, wrapping the blanket tighter around him. It would probably be another ten minutes before the helicopter arrived. He could hold out till then.

He didn't have much choice.

"The other raft's in good shape." Malakov called out. "If this boat starts to sink we can—"

A curtain of water erupted near *Epic Venture's* starboard side.

Malakov screamed as the Point Pleasant Monster slammed into her.

FIFTY-THREE

Karen screamed. Rastun threw off the blanket and got to his feet. The world spun before him. He stumbled until the dizzy spell passed.

Gunfire cracked next to him. Geek and Sherlock fired their pistols at the monster. Rastun knew they couldn't kill it, but maybe they could distract it.

The monster's jaws clamped down on Malakov's head.

"Lauren!" Ehrenberg shouted.

The Point Pleasant Monster's snout snapped up. That was followed by a wet, ripping sound.

Malakov's head was gone.

Ehrenberg gasped, his wide eyes focused on the headless body of his fellow scientist and friend. A river of blood spread across the deck. A deep *crunch* came from the monster's jaws.

"C'mon! C'mon!" Geek herded everyone around the superstructure, out of sight of the monster.

"So what now?" asked Sherlock. "That thing's between us and the life raft.

"C-Can't we just go around it?" Montebello trembled as he spoke.

Rastun shook his head. "It's still too close to the raft. There's no way we can get to it without that thing noticing."

He stared at the deck, trying to fight off the fog creeping around the edges of his mind. How else could they get off this boat? The Coast Guard MLB was only useful for holding a Viking funeral. They could use Piet's boat, but it had to be about 50 feet away. If they swam for it, the monster could easily pick them off.

Hell, it could pick us off even if we get to the boat.

If they had any hope of getting out of this alive, they'd have to kill the damn monster.

"Geek. Sherlock. Put some sabot rounds in that thing."

"Sorry, Cap'n." Geek shook his head. "We both ran out during the firefight."

Rastun scowled. They still had the Aster 7s. Both of which were belowdecks, now filling with water. What if they couldn't get to the dart guns before the monster finished devouring Malakov?

"Sherlock. You still have that vial you took from Pilka?"

"Yes, sir."

"Let me see it."

Sherlock gave him a puzzled look, but took the vial out of his pocket.

Rastun snatched it from his hand.

"What the hell?" Geek blurted.

Rastun unscrewed the cap and tipped the vial toward him.

"Jack! No!"

"Cap'n! Stop!"

Both Karen and Geek moved toward him.

The pheromone extract spilled all over Rastun's shirt.

"Jack!" Karen gaped at him in shock.

"What the fuck?" Geek threw out his large arms. "Are you nuts?"

"It's gonna follow me. I'll lead it below and take it out with a toxin dart. Geek, when the monster's clear of the deck, get everyone to the life raft and get outta here."

Rastun started to walk away.

"Dammit, I'm not gonna let you do this!" Karen grabbed his arm.

"Look at you, Cap'n," said Geek. "You don't stand a chance against that thing. You're not—"

"That's an order, Sergeant!" Rastun pulled out of Karen's grasp. "Get everyone off this boat!"

He strode around the superstructure before anyone else could protest. The Point Pleasant Monster had its snout buried in the pile of flesh and blood that had been Dr. Malakov. Rastun grimaced. He didn't like Malakov, but no way did he wish something like this to happen to her.

"Hey, you ugly son-of-a-bitch!" Rastun pulled out an energy bar he bought in Virginia and hurled it at the monster. It bounced off its shoulder. The monster lifted its snout and stared at him.

"Yeah. Come and get it." Rastun dove through one of the shot out bridge windows. He landed on his right side, the side without the stab wound.

Pain still slashed through his body.

Rastun gritted his teeth and pushed himself to his feet.

The monster rammed the superstructure. The hull cracked and buckled.

Rastun took the ladder down to the crew quarters. The world went out of focus. Thick cotton clogged his head. He stumbled and fell. Blazing pain spread through his body. His vision cleared, and he found himself lying on his back.

A crash echoed above him. The Point Pleasant Monster stomped across the bridge. He saw the crocodilian head above him.

"This was not one of my better ideas."

Rastun forced himself to rise. He tried to ignore the chill covering his body and hurried past the cabins. The corridor was lit by subdued red lights. The emergency lighting. The flooding must have knocked out the main generator.

He heard a loud hiss behind him. The Point Pleasant Monster crept down the steps on all fours.

Rastun went down the ladder to the next deck. The water was now waist deep. He felt *Epic Venture* list about twenty degrees to starboard. How long did he have before it sank?

He waded deeper into the corridor. Piet's body floated nearby. So did Tamburro's. Rastun drew a breath, a crushing pain squeezing his ribs, and went underwater.

Visibility was shit. He couldn't see the Aster 7. He couldn't see anything.

Rastun surfaced and drew a breath. He heard another hiss. The monster extended its neck toward him. He backed away. The jaws snapped, missing him by inches.

Rastun pushed his way through the water, now above his waist. He grabbed Piet's body and shoved it between him and the Point Pleasant Monster. Maybe it would consider having the dead mercenary for a meal. That would probably last a few seconds before its drive for the pheromones kicked back in.

A few seconds could mean the difference between life and death.

The monster slipped into the water. Rastun moved into the storeroom. He took out his waterproof mini LED flashlight, flicked it on and submerged. The beam only let him see a foot or two in front of him.

Rastun stepped forward, in the direction where Pilka dropped the Aster 7. He slid one foot, then the other, in a half-circle, hoping to make contact with the weapon.

He didn't.

A thump reverberated through the water. Rastun's head broke the surface. He took a breath and saw the monster trying to push its way into the storeroom. The walls around the door were caving in.

He went back under the water, searching for the Aster 7.

C'mon. C'mon.

Rastun swung his flashlight. He swept his feet around.

Another bout of dizziness gripped him. He shook it off.

Something groaned behind him. The walls were seconds away from collapsing.

His foot clipped something, a tubular-shaped object. He bent down and shined his light on it.

He'd found the Aster 7.

Rastun grabbed it and resurfaced. He let go of the flashlight, wrapped his hand around the trigger grip and turned.

The monster smashed into the storeroom. It lunged at Rastun.

He dodged to the right. The beast's head knifed through the water less than a foot from him. Rastun spun to face it.

He suffered another dizzy spell.

Rastun lost his footing and slipped. Water surrounded him. He planted his left palm on the floor and got his feet back under him. He clutched the Aster 7's foregrip.

The monster's snout plunged back into the water. A mouthful of sharp teeth rushed toward him. He shoved the dart gun's barrel into the monster's mouth jaws. Something ripped into his forearm. Rastun ignored the pain and pulled the trigger.

The dart punctured the roof of the Point Pleasant Monster's mouth. The toxin rushed through its bloodstream. The creature stiffened, then went limp in seconds. Rastun pushed himself away as the monster sank to the deck. He let go of the Aster 7, surfaced and gulped down a lungful of air.

The water came up to his chest. Rastun half-walked, half-swam out of the storeroom.

Epic Venture listed forty degrees.

Rastun crawled up the steps and onto the second deck. He used the doors and walls to support himself as he made his way down the corridor. Blood ran down his right arm. He must have cut it on the monster's teeth. His skin felt ice cold. He knew it had little to do with being sopping wet.

He was going into shock.

His muscles grew heavy. It became a struggle to keep his eyes open. More than anything Rastun wanted to lie on the deck and fall asleep.

And you'll die!

He kept going, every step an effort. His legs trembled. Rastun fell.

Don't quit! Rangers don't quit!

He crawled to the ladder. My God, he felt like someone stuffed him in a freezer naked. He could only keep his eyes open a crack. Why not just shut them? Why not rest?

No! He'd been through this before in Ranger School. He'd been beyond tired, his muscles had screamed in agony with every movement. Yet he'd persevered, he'd survived.

He could do it again.

Groaning, Rastun pushed himself to his feet. He climbed the ladder onto the bridge.

Epic Venture listed sixty degrees.

Rastun stumbled toward the starboard side. He more fell than climbed out of one of the shattered windows. He rolled along the deck and struck the railing. Pain hammered his mid-section.

He pushed himself to his knees, then dropped into the water. He kicked and stroked, trying to move away from the sinking research vessel.

Kick and stroke. Kick and stroke.

Rastun's arms and legs wouldn't move any more. His eyes shut. They cracked open for a split second, then closed again. He felt himself start to sink.

Suddenly he rose. Was God calling him to Heaven?

He managed to force his eyes open. He glimpsed Karen and Geek on either side of him, pulling him into the life raft.

"Jack?" Karen called out, her voice sounding distant. "Jack!"

Everything went black.

FIFTY-FOUR

The first thing Rastun saw when he opened his eyes was the color white. An antiseptic white. It then morphed into a ceiling.

Hadn't he just been in the ocean?

He slowly moved his head left to right, wincing. His whole body felt sore.

Rastun was lying in a bed, hooked up to some machines, one of which emitted a steady beep.

He was in a hospital.

It took a few seconds for him to locate the call button. He pressed it three times. A couple of minutes passed before a portly black woman entered the room.

"Mister Rastun," she smiled. "You're awake. How are you feeling?"

"Like hell."

"Well, that's understandable. You've been through a lot."

"Tell me about it," he said as the nurse checked the machines by his bed. Her nametag read LESLIE A.

"Where am I?" he asked.

"AtlantiCare Regional Medical Center in Atlantic City."

AtlantiCare. He remembered he'd been here before, after he had saved Ensign Gale when the Point Pleasant Monster attacked his MLB.

"Your vitals are looking stronger," Leslie said in a cheery voice.

"How long have I been out?"

"Two days. Not surprising, really. You needed a lot of time to recover. Luckily, the surgery went well. The damage from the stab wound wasn't too bad. We also had to give you a blood transfusion and pump you with antibiotics. But the doctors expect you to make a full recovery."

"Well, that's good news. What about the others?"

"All fine. Your friend, Karen, had successful surgery on her broken arm."

After Leslie finished, a doctor came in. He, too, checked Rastun's vitals and his chart, examined him and asked all sorts of questions. The doctor also told him he'd make a full recovery, though it might take a while.

A couple of hours later, Rastun got his first visitors, his parents.

"Hey, Mom. Hey, Dad." He tried to sound casual. Not an easy thing to do lying in a hospital bed.

His mother hugged and kissed him, tears spilling from her eyes. Dad also gave him a hug.

"How are you feeling?" asked Mom.

"About as well as I can be under the circumstances."

Mom wiped her eyes and grabbed his arm. Dad's face stiffened, like he was trying to keep from crying.

"You had us pretty worried, Jack," he said. "Thank God you're all right."

"Thanks."

His parents talked to him about the doctor's prognosis, his recuperation, all the calls and messages they'd received from other family members and friends praying for his recovery. Mom then fell silent, staring at the floor.

"Mom? You okay?"

She lifted her and swallowed. "Jack, maybe this isn't the time for it, but after what happened…The last time I was this scared for you was when you were in the Army. I mean, is being with the FUBI always going to be so dangerous? Maybe…"

"Mom." Rastun gently clutched her wrist. "I can't promise that something this dangerous won't ever happen again. But if I hadn't been on this expedition, a lot more people would have died. I helped rescue a rare sea creature from an animal smuggler, I took out one of the most wanted mercenaries in the world. I made a real difference. I know you probably wish I still worked at the zoo, but what I did on this expedition, this is what I'm good at. This is what I was meant to do."

Mom's shoulders slumped. More tears slid down her cheeks. This was definitely not the response she wanted. Still, she didn't argue. Maybe she would later, or maybe she'd actually accept his decision.

Only time would tell.

"Come on." Dad put a hand on Mom's shoulder. "We should let him get some rest. Besides, there's someone else who wants to see him."

Mom hugged and kissed Rastun again before following Dad to the door.

"Karen," Mom called out.

Rastun sat up straighter in his bed when Karen walked in. Her right arm was in a sling and bruises still marred her face. She walked up to his bed. Someone else was with her. A little girl with a round, pretty face and dark brown hair tied in a ponytail.

"Hey." Karen leaned down and gave him a long kiss on the lips. She then pressed her forehead against his. Rastun closed his eyes, relishing the feeling.

"You doing okay?" he asked.

"I am. I'm just so glad you're all right. There were some times…" Karen barely held back a sob. "I love you."

She kissed him again.

"I love you, too."

Karen smiled and turned to the girl. "Jack, I want you to meet my daughter, Emily. She flew up here with my aunt and uncle. Emily, this is Jack."

Rastun didn't know what to expect. He didn't have a lot of experience dealing with children. He thought she might be shy. Maybe she'd resent him, think of him as a stranger trying to take her mom away from her.

Emily went up to his bedside and gave him a hug. "Thank you for saving my mom."

Rastun patted her on the back. "You're welcome, kiddo. You've got yourself one heck of a mother." He looked up at Karen. "Thanks for saving me, again."

"It's getting to be a habit, isn't it? I save your life, you save my life."

"Well, here's hoping for a more quiet life from here on out."

"Not too quiet." Karen grinned.

Rastun grinned back. "So any news on the other Point Pleasant Monster, or Sea Raptor or whatever they're calling it?"

"It's at the Baltimore Aquarium. The FUBI's going to keep it there until they build a permanent facility for it."

"And Gunderson?"

"He was trying to leave the country. The Feds got him just before his plane took off. The scientist you found at the mansion promised to testify against him. I don't think Gunderson's high-priced lawyers are going to keep him out of jail this time."

"Good. About time that son-of ..." He glanced at Emily. "That guy gets what's coming to him."

"I couldn't agree more." Karen nodded. "So what about you? I mean, after what happened to you on *Epic Venture,* are you sure you want to stay with the FUBI?"

"Hey, I'm down, but I'm not out. As soon as I'm healed up, I'll be back on the job protecting everyone from poachers and monsters. You're not getting rid of me that easy."

Karen took hold of his hand. "The last thing in the world I want to do is get rid of you."

She bent down and kissed Rastun.

ABOUT THE AUTHOR

John J. Rust was born in Hamilton Township, NJ, where he graduated from Nottingham High School and Mercer County Community College. After receiving a communications degree from the College of Mt. St. Vincent in Riverdale, NY, he worked for New Jersey 101.5 FM before moving to Arizona to become a radio sports reporter and play-by-play announcer. Rust is the author of the military sci-fi book "Dark Wings" and the baseball-themed books "The Best Phillies Team Ever" and "Arizona's All-Time Baseball Team." He has also written several sci-fi short stories. Follow John J. Rust at www.facebook.com/johnjrustauthor and on Twitter at @JohnJRust.

CHECK OUT OTHER GREAT DEEP SEA THRILLERS

MEGA
by Jake Bible

There is something in the deep. Something large. Something hungry. Something prehistoric.
And Team Grendel must find it, fight it, and kill it.
Kinsey Thorne, the first female US Navy SEAL candidate has hit rock bottom. Having washed out of the Navy, she turned to every drink and drug she could get her hands on. Until her father and cousins, all ex-Navy SEALS themselves, offer her a way back into the life: as part of a private, elite combat Team being put together to find and hunt down an impossible monster in the Indian Ocean. Kinsey has a second chance, but can she live through it?

THE BLACK
by Paul E Cooley

Under 30,000 feet of water, the exploration rig Leaguer has discovered an oil field larger than Saudi Arabia, with oil so sweet and pure, nations would go to war for the rights to it. But as the team starts drilling exploration well after exploration well in their race to claim the sweet crude, a deep rumbling beneath the ocean floor shakes them all to their core. Something has been living in the oil and it's about to give birth to the greatest threat humanity has ever seen.

"The Black" is a techno/horror-thriller that puts the horror and action of movies such as Leviathan and The Thing right into readers' hands. Ocean exploration will never be the same."

CHECK OUT OTHER GREAT DEEP SEA THRILLERS

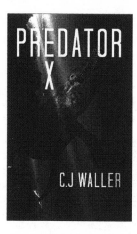

PREDATOR X
by C.J Waller

When deep level oil fracking uncovers a vast subterranean sea, a crack team of cavers and scientists are sent down to investigate. Upon their arrival, they disappear without a trace. A second team, including sedimentologist Dr Megan Stoker, are ordered to seek out Alpha Team and report back their findings. But Alpha team are nowhere to be found – instead, they are faced with something unexpected in the depths. Something ancient. Something huge. Something dangerous. Predator X

DEAD BAIT
by Tim Curran

A husband hell-bent on revenge hunts a Wereshark...A Russian mail order bride with a fishy secret...Crabs with a collective consciousness...A vampire who transforms into a Candiru...Zombie piranha...Bait that will have you crawling out of your skin and more. Drawing on horror, humor with a helping of dark fantasy and a touch of deviance, these 19 contemporary stories pay homage to the monsters that lurk in the murky waters of our imaginations. If you thought it was safe to go back in the water...Think Again!

CHECK OUT OTHER GREAT
DEEP SEA THRILLERS

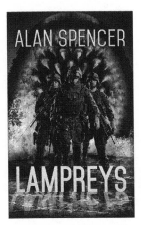

LAMPREYS
by Alan Spencer

A secret government tactical team is sent to perform a clean sweep of a private research installation. Horrible atrocities lurk within the abandoned corridors. Mutated sea creatures with insane killing abilities are waiting to suck the blood and meat from their prey.

Unemployed college professor Conrad Garfield is forced to assist and is soon separated from the team. Alone and afraid, Conrad must use his wits to battle mutated lampreys, infected scientists and go head-to-head with the biggest monstrosity of all.

Can Conrad survive, or will the deadly monsters suck the very life from his body?

DEEP DEVOTION
by M.C. Norris

Rising from the depths, a mind-bending monster unleashes a wave of terror across the American heartland. Kate Browning, a Kansas City EMT confronts her paralyzing fear of water when she traces the source of a deadly parasitic affliction to the Gulf of Mexico. Cooperating with a marine biologist, she travels to Florida in an effort to save the life of one very special patient, but the source of the epidemic happens to be the nest of a terrifying monster, one that last rose from the depths to annihilate the lost continent of Atlantis.

Leviathan, destroyer, devoted lifemate and parent, the abomination is not going to take the extermination of its brood well.